PENGUIN BOOKS

The Love Trainer

Julia Llewellyn lives in London. This is her first novel. As Julia Llewellyn Smith she is the author of *Travels Without My Aunt: In the Footsteps of Graham Greene*. She writes regularly for the *Sunday Telegraph*, the *Sunday Times* and many other publications.

The Love Trainer

JULIA LLEWELLYN

PENGUIN BOOKS

PENGUIN BOOKS

Published by the Penguin Group
Penguin Books Ltd, 80 Strand, London WC2R ORL, England
Penguin Group (USA) Inc., 375 Hudson Street, New York, New York 10014, USA
Penguin Books Australia Ltd, 250 Camberwell Road, Camberwell, Victoria 3124, Australia
Penguin Books Canada Ltd, 10 Alcorn Avenue, Toronto, Ontario, Canada M4V 3B2
Penguin Books India (P) Ltd, 11 Community Centre, Panchsheel Park, New Delhi – 110 017, India
Penguin Books (NZ) Ltd, Cnr Rosedale and Airborne Roads, Albany, Auckland, New Zealand
Penguin Books (South Africa) (Pty) Ltd, 24 Sturdee Avenue, Rosebank 2196, South Africa

Penguin Books Ltd, Registered Offices: 80 Strand, London WC2R ORL, England

www.penguin.com

Published in Penguin Books 2004

5

Copyright © Julia Llewellyn, 2004
All rights reserved

The moral right of the author has been asserted

Printed in England by Clays Ltd, St Ives plc

To my mum and dad

Katie Wallace was nervous as she entered the stripped-beech lobby of the Greenhall and Graham agency but the teenage receptionist was too immersed in her magazine article about the best body scrubs to notice.

'Name?' she sighed, without looking up.

'Katie Wallace.' Katie's voice wobbled slightly. This was a big day for her.

'Here to see?'

'Rebecca Greenhall.'

The girl shut her magazine and looked Katie up and down in disbelief.

'Rebecca? You mean Tara?'

'Tara?'

'Rebecca's assistant.'

Katie pulled herself up to her full five feet five inches and smiled in what she hoped was a winning fashion.

'No. I'm here to see Rebecca herself.'

A sceptical stare, then the girl punched out a number with a magenta fingernail. 'Tara. There's a girl in reception *says* she's here for Rebecca . . . Oh. OK. I'll send her up.

'Third floor,' she said out of the corner of her mouth, her eyes now back on celebrity hairdo blunders. 'Lift's over there.'

The lift arrived with a computerized ping. Katie had been hoping to check her reflection in its mirrors, but it was upholstered in burgundy leather, like a lunatic's cell after a visit from the *Changing Rooms* team. She peeked into the chrome control panel but all she could see was a cloud of dark, curly hair and a slightly too round, pale face.

With the help of her cousin and flatmate, Jess, Katie had spent most of the day dressing for the interview, rejecting T-shirts, trousers, boots and trainers in favour of camel ankle boots, a pastel striped shirt and a long denim skirt. The look was meant to say businesslike yet funky. 'You've got to impress Rebecca,' Jess commanded.

Neither Jess nor Katie had ever met Rebecca, but they knew all about her from their friend Miranda, who long ago had worked with her at Gadney's literary and talent agency, before Rebecca left to set up her own, rival company. Miranda showed them some shots of Rebecca in the party section of one of Jess's old copies of *Hello!* She was laughing with Salman Rushdie and Moby, wearing a cream Bianca Jagger trouser suit. She looked skinny and pretty and brown.

'She was probably trying to persuade them to sign up with her,' Miranda informed them. Miranda, who had left Gadney's to become a primary school teacher, didn't know Rebecca all that well, but you would never have guessed to hear her talk. 'She's brilliant at hooking in the big names. She was the person who got Bill Briggs his chat show and she talked Julie Malone into writing her diet book.'

'Oh,' they said, impressed. Julie Malone was a formerly chubby pop star, who had lost about four stone in the past two years. The book had been a huge bestseller. Jess had a well-thumbed copy and swore by it.

'So is it just Rebecca?' Jess asked. Jess was a not very

successful actress and the idea of a new, dynamic agent was very appealing. Katie *had* to get this job.

'No, there's her partner, Ben. Rebecca tends to represent most of the authors – you know, trying to create TV shows for them and things. Ben does more the actors and musicians. They're quite a team.'

Katie was trying to keep her cool, but inside her stomach was somersaulting. Life really could be very wonderful sometimes. Only a week ago she had been convinced she would never work again, after her unjust sacking from Delman and Prout, the estate agents where she had been a secretary for four months. But what was it they said about doors closing and windows opening? She was going to get a new job. Rebecca would be her mentor. She would teach her everything. The two of them – plus Jess – would be more like friends than colleagues.

'When you go to parties Rebecca'll say: "Katie, do you want to borrow my Dolce and Gabbana dress?"' Jess agreed in her best Crocodile Dundee accent. Miranda had told them Rebecca was Australian. 'And when you leave her, to . . .'

'Set up my own kick-ass business.'

' . . . Or whatever. Rebecca's going to say: "You bitch. I can't bear to let you go."'

The lift doors opened and Katie stepped out into a large open-plan room, furnished with wide desks, and with a couple of glassed-off offices at the far end. The walls were lined with pictures of cheesily smiling TV presenters. There was a transparent fridge stocked with cans of Red Bull and a miniature stereo playing Eminem. March rain lashed against the window panes.

A woman in linen combats and with badly bleached hair got up and approached Katie, smiling.

'Katie? I'm Tara, Rebecca's PA. I'll take you in.'

She opened the door of the glass box. Rebecca herself was on the phone. Her angular face was animated as she waved one long hand in the air.

'So I said: "Why don't we slip away for the weekend?" but he said he had a deadline.'

She had shoulder-length, auburn hair, blue eyes and a mouth like a melon slice. Not beautiful perhaps, but very attractive. Katie knew she was in her mid-thirties, but she looked at least five years younger. A tight strawberry-coloured T-shirt displayed two perfect breasts to best advantage. *Real?* Katie wondered, and decided probably not.

Rebecca looked up, nodded curtly and carried on talking. 'Yeah, yeah, so I said . . . Oh sorry, darling, Tara's buzzing me. Hang on . . . What is it, Tara? . . . Oh, Mark Wells.' She sounded disappointed. 'Tell him to hold . . . Suze, I'll have to call you back . . . OK . . . *Mark! Darling.* How *are* you? Did you have time to read it?'

The conversation with Mark was largely unintelligible, something to do with manuscripts being couriered and embargoes broken. Standing in the doorway, Katie glanced over her shoulder at Tara. She grinned cheerily and rolled her eyes. She seemed sweet. Why was she leaving? Probably for some amazing new job.

Eventually Rebecca hung up. There was a pause while she examined Katie as if she were one of the more boring animals at the zoo: a donkey in the children's area rather than a caged cheetah.

4

'Hello,' Rebecca said. 'Miranda's . . . er . . . friend. Sorry, what was your name again?'

'Katie.' Katie held out her hand. Rebecca hesitated briefly before shaking it limply.

'Yeah, Katie. Well, listen, Katie, I'm sure you're OK because Miranda vouched for you. And quite honestly there doesn't seem much point grilling you about your experience and all that because any idiot — no offence — could do this job.'

Thrown, Katie just nodded and grinned.

'So look, I was thinking. It's a bit pointless having this chat here. We ought really to be at my place. So you can see what it's all about. I was thinking of knocking off a bit early tonight anyway, to get ready for my boyfriend.'

'Oh?' said Katie. Personal stuff. Clearly, Rebecca was warming to her.

'Yeah. He's called Tim. He's a writer. He won the Trevor Costello prize for best first novella two years ago.' She gave Katie a patronizing look. 'Do you have a boyfriend?'

'Yes.'

Rebecca looked faintly put out. 'Really? Serious? Wedding bells?'

After three years with Crispin, people asked Katie this often enough, but the idea still seemed ridiculous. 'Oh. No.' She giggled, embarrassed. 'Not for now, anyway.'

Rebecca was distracted, looking beyond Katie out through the glass box. Her pretty face broke into a huge grin. 'God, that's so sweet,' she gasped. She jumped up and rushed to the door. Katie swivelled round. Tara had just taken delivery of an enormous bunch of yellow roses. The other women in the office oohed and aahed.

'Aren't they gorgeous?' Rebecca gasped. 'Quick. Find a vase.'

'Thanks,' Tara said.

'Well,' snapped Rebecca, 'what does the card say?' She reached for the envelope.

Tara took a step back. 'Actually, Rebecca, if you don't mind, it's . . . personal.'

'Oh.' Rebecca's features wobbled, then re-formed in a fixed smile, like an Oscar-night loser. Clearly, she had thought the flowers were for her. 'Sorry. Just being nosy. I mean . . . I take it they're from Andrew? What a sweet-heart.'

Tara grinned. 'They're to celebrate our nineteen-month anniversary,' she confessed shyly.

'Nineteen months! Has it really been that long? Time flies, doesn't it?' Rebecca had gone pink. 'Well, lucky old you, Tara.' She turned back into the office, shut the door and looked at Katie with momentary confusion, obviously trying to remember what this girl was doing there.

'Right,' she said, suddenly brisk. 'Sorry about that. Anyway. It's nearly six so let's shoot. We'll jump in a cab and I'll give you a quick tour of the flat.'

This was more serious than Katie had thought. Working from Rebecca's home. Being her right-hand woman. Of course, with someone like Rebecca you needed two PAs: one at home and one in the office. 'Wait until I tell Jess,' she thought as Rebecca shut down her computer and put on a fabulously expensive-looking red coat.

Outside, the rain was falling steadily. Rebecca, who was wearing combat trousers and four-inch sandals, stepped straight into a puddle.

'Bugger!' she squawked. She glanced ruefully at Katie. 'I've never learned to listen to the weather forecast in the morning.'

Dodging more puddles, she hailed a taxi and they climbed in. It was probably only a twenty-minute walk from Rebecca's office just off Bond Street to her home in Bayswater and in the rainy, rush-hour traffic the cab took just as long. Rather than make conversation with her new employee, Rebecca spent the entire ride punching text messages into a tiny silver Motorola and giggling at the replies.

Katie watched her in fascination. She wondered about Rebecca's background. All she knew about Australia came from the *Holiday* programme. She couldn't quite understand why anyone would have wanted to leave sparkling seas and powder sands for rainy London, but zillions of Aussies did it every year. And Rebecca had obviously made something of her life.

'So who were you working for before?' Rebecca asked, wiping the misty window with her sleeve to peek through at the boutiques.

Katie felt embarrassed. An estate agent. It wasn't exactly cool. And she did not want to tell Rebecca about the ignominious way she had lost her job. Telling a client over the phone that the only thing in her price range was a one-bedroom flat in Richmond, but that frankly she wouldn't touch it herself because it was rat infested and, judging by the number of warts on her chin, the current owner was a witch who had probably left a curse on the place. How was she to know she was speaking to the owner/witch who had rung up impersonating a buyer, in an effort to find out why she was having no joy? No. Better gloss over all that.

'Um, they were based in Putney.'

'Putney?' Rebecca raised an eyebrow. 'Some nice houses round there.'

Miranda must have told her about her old job. 'Yes, I was pretty busy.'

'Don't worry,' Rebecca said, smirking. 'I'll find plenty for you to do.'

The taxi pulled up in front of a vast Sixties mansion block behind the Bayswater Road. From the outside it looked like a hospital. Inside, it was more a five-star hotel. The lobby was carpeted in red and furnished with leather sofas. Soft muzak played. A young, dreadlocked porter sat in front of a bank of television screens.

'Hi, Johnny,' said Rebecca, pressing the button for the lift. He waved absently, then returned to his copy of the *Sun*.

The lift carried them to the twelfth floor. Rebecca was studying her mobile like Sherlock Holmes presented with the vital clue. 'Sorry,' she said with a sudden grin. 'I know it looks insane but I'm expecting an important call. And I always lose my signal in the lift.'

They turned left into a carpeted corridor. At the end was a red door. Rebecca unlocked it and they stepped straight into her living room, miles of pale wood flooring, flowers everywhere and wall-to-ceiling windows that looked straight over the black expanse that was Hyde Park. In the distance, there was the floodlit dome of the Albert Hall and the towers of Knightsbridge, glittering in the rain like Elizabeth Taylor's cleavage.

But the flat itself was a tip. The floors, at second glance, were dusty. The flowers were dead or dying and the water in their Swedish crystal vases had turned black. On the russet velvet sofa, two chewed biros nestled beside a pair of tights and an open paperback. The Bang & Olufsen stereo was surrounded by CDs out of their cases.

'So here we are,' Rebecca said cheerfully, dumping her coat on a leather armchair. 'Fancy a drink while I show you round?'

Katie followed her into the kitchen. A huge Smeg fridge, a steel gas cooker, some dirty glasses in the sink. One surface was covered with smeared bottles of Amaretto and Bailey's. Rebecca rifled through them.

'It's my duty-free collection,' she laughed. 'I can never resist adding to it, whenever there's a delay at the airport.' She studied the bottles. 'Gin and tonic? Oh no. I'm out of tonic. Let's see what mixers we have.' She opened the fridge. Over her shoulder, Katie could see a packet of wheatgrass powder and several perfume bottles. 'Well, that's not much good. Except . . . oh!' She turned around brandishing a bottle of champagne. 'Moët, sweetie? We might as well. After all, I want you to think well of me.'

From the back of a cupboard she produced two flutes, then gently popped the cork. 'So how do you know Miranda?' she asked, more polite than curious, as she poured the drinks.

'Through my cousin, Jess,' Katie replied, trying surreptitiously to wipe the grubby glass on her shirt. 'They're old mates.'

Good old Miranda. Katie owed her big time for this. As soon as she had heard that Katie had been sacked she was on the phone. 'Look,' she had said, after half an hour of commiseration, 'don't count on it. But I think Rebecca's looking for someone to work for her. I'll put a word in.'

'Hmm,' said Rebecca. 'Miranda knows Tim. In fact she helped us get together. He saw me at a party. I didn't even notice him. The next day he got my number from Miranda and sent me the biggest bunch of flowers you've ever seen.'

'How lovely,' Katie said enthusiastically. She always loved how-we-met stories. 'And is he one of your clients now?'

Rebecca looked put out. 'Of course not. He has a very good agent of his own. No need for my help.' Abruptly, she put her glass down. 'Right. So here we are anyway. And look, I don't want you to think I'm using this champagne as a bribe or anything, but if you could do just a little work for me tonight I'd be really grateful.'

'Of course. What would you like me to do?'

Rebecca looked around vaguely. 'Well, you know. Sort things out a bit.'

Katie didn't know. Was she supposed to file all Rebecca's party invitations?

'I'll just feel so much better if when Tim and I get back tonight everything's under control,' Rebecca continued.

Suddenly Katie got it. Emails. They'd be coming in all night from her American clients. Phone calls too. Of course Rebecca needed someone to handle them.

'So is there a home office?'

Rebecca laughed. 'Oh God, no. That would be totally sad. I mean, I have a laptop here, obviously, but I like to keep home and work separate.'

'So what equipment shall I use?'

This time, Rebecca looked at her slightly strangely. 'Well, I'm not exactly sure what I've got. But it should be in this cupboard under the sink.'

'Under the *sink*?'

'Well, yes. Or there's probably some stuff in the bathroom as well. To be honest I wouldn't have a clue. My last cleaner just bought whatever she needed and presented me with the bill. You do the same.'

Katie wasn't sure she'd heard correctly. 'Cleaner?'

'Yes. She was brilliant, but in the end she had to go. Didn't Miranda tell you? She was caught shagging in my bed. Can you believe it? My cousin Kim was staying with me and she came home midmorning from the shops and there was Alicia going for it hammer and tongs with some bloke. Kimbo called me at the office in a terrible state. She was saying, "What shall I do?" and you know for a moment I wasn't absolutely sure.' Rebecca giggled. 'Because I didn't know if I'd ever be able to replace her. I mean, a good cleaner is like discovering the perfect foundation. It changes your life.

'But then I realized I was being stupid. Alicia had to go. Anyway, she and the boyfriend came out of the bedroom, smoothing down their clothes, and Kim asked for the keys back. Tim thought it was hilarious.'

Katie nodded and smiled weakly.

'Well, look,' said Rebecca. 'Just break the back of things tonight. Do the washing up. Clean the bathroom. Tidy the bedroom. Hoover maybe.' She looked pensive. 'Where *is* the Hoover? Three hours, say? Call it twenty-five pounds.'

'Twenty-five pounds?'

'Yes. Alicia was on twenty pounds for three. Anyway,

let's say three times a week at twenty-five pounds a time. I'll dig out a spare set of keys. Monday, Wednesday, Friday afternoons. How does that sound?'

Katie opened her mouth but nothing came out. Cleaning. 'I thought I was going to be a glamorous PA on thirty grand,' she wanted to scream. Seventy-five pounds a week. How was she supposed to live on that? Even in her crappy last job she'd been earning four times as much.

She opened her mouth to say no, but something stopped her. No point making a fuss. Rebecca clearly had no idea there had been a mix-up. She was only talking nine hours a week here, plenty of time for other stuff. Katie's adored grandmother had died a couple of years ago and left her a few thousand pounds, so for now she could live off that, while she was looking for a new job. Something would come up. Something better. It was what Katie always told herself.

In the meantime, she'd get to have a good snoop around Rebecca Greenhall's fabulous (if dirty) home. 'I could take photos of the mess to show Jess,' she thought. 'I can check out her wardrobe. I can try on her makeup.' A little thought hovered. 'I can use the washing machine.' Katie's rented flat had no washing machine and she was heartily tired of having to take all her clothes over to Crispin's place, or use the launderette.

The phone on the wall rang. Rebecca snatched it up. 'Hello? . . . Oh. Jenny. Hi.' She sounded disappointed. At the other end of the line a voice yabbered away.

Putting one hand over the receiver, Rebecca gestured to Katie, who was still standing dumbfounded by the sink. 'Go on then,' she mouthed.

For a few more moments Katie didn't move. Then she opened the cupboard and began searching for the Marigolds.

2

The following night, in Katie's home on the other side of London, her flatmate Ronan laughed and laughed and laughed.

'You're going to be a cleaner,' he hooted. 'A cleaner!'

Katie tried to laugh too, but she'd already heard all the jokes from Jess last night, when she finally got back from Rebecca's at nearly midnight. Ronan had been in bed. He needed his ten hours, he always said, just like the supermodels.

'But why didn't you tell her?' Ronan asked. 'Why didn't you say: "There's been some horrible mistake"?'

'I should have. But I was too embarrassed. I just didn't know what to do. I have to talk to Miranda. Find out what she told Rebecca. But she's in Brazil for a fortnight. Anyway, in the end I thought, sod it. It's only going to be for a couple of weeks until I find a proper job. And it's cash in hand. At least it'll cover my rent for next month.'

'But Katie, you are the *worst* cleaner in the world. You think washing up means piling dishes into the sink and leaving them. You think cleaning the bath means pouring in a capful of bubbles. Your bras are all grey and your tights have holes in them. You're a disgrace to womankind.'

'I'd be tidier if I was ever here,' Katie protested. 'Remember, the last few months I've been busy selling overpriced shoe-boxes to grumpy-looking couples.'

'Bollocks,' Ronan grinned. 'You were always crap. What about all those years of temping? Home by the dot of six every night, but you still never lifted a finger. Oh no. Straight on with the telly or out to the pub.'

'But you did everything for me,' Katie argued. 'And with Rebecca it's different. She pays me for a start. It makes a difference, you know. It's not as if you need a PhD to be a cleaner. Anyway, I told you. It's only temporary. Until I find another *real* job.'

Ronan turned back to the stove to stir his squid-ink risotto. 'You're a funny one, Katie. So sorted in some ways and so hopeless in others.'

'It's because I'm Libra with Aries rising,' said Katie. She had no idea what this meant, but it sounded good.

'So what would you like that real job to be?'

There was a long pause. Katie was twenty-nine years old. All of her adult life she had been an 'Oh, right'. At least, that was how people responded to her, when she told them she was a secretary, or a runner with a film company, or a data-inputter for a television listings maga- zine. Then their eyes would glaze over and they would start looking over her shoulder for someone more interesting to talk to.

Occasionally, she had been a 'Really?' – for example, during her time as a shop assistant at Joseph, or, ironically – given how boring the job was – at Delman and Prout, which had everyone falling over themselves to tell Katie· how shocking house prices were these days and how could nurses or social workers afford to work in London any more?

In truth, it was all getting a bit embarrassing. Katie had always thought she was ambitious. She had gone to university because her school had said, 'You don't want to end up typing for a living,' got her degree and now here she was, years on, typing for a living.

The problem was that Katie had no real idea about which direction her ambition lay in. Once she had wanted to work in TV and, had her time at *Channel Update* not been so painful, perhaps she would have made it. But her experiences there had been so unpleasant that she had left for the safety of a job as PA to a sportsclothes manufacturer.

Since then she had drifted, earning enough money to survive, having fun and pouring scorn on such concepts as careers and mortgages and husbands. 'Where's the freedom?' she would cry when she was a bit pissed. 'Where's the fun? I could just take off round the world tomorrow.'

The problem was she never did.

'Well, if I were you, I'd take your time before you decide what to do next,' Ronan said, chucking a handful of salt into the pot. 'After all, Crispin's got plenty of cash. He can bail you out.'

'But I don't want to sponge off Crispin.'

'It wouldn't be sponging. Crispin is your boyfriend. He wants to look after you. If you're worried about the rent, move in with him.'

'And what about you?' countered Katie, filching a Silk Cut from his packet.

'I'd be fine. I'd still have Jessica. We'd survive here on our own. Don't worry about us.'

Katie chuckled. 'Look, I know you hate me. Just don't be so subtle about it, OK?'

'Oh, Katie. You know we love you. But we just want you to be happy.'

Katie looked down at her vodka and tonic. 'But I *am* happy living with you.'

Katie, Ronan and Jess had already celebrated more than two years of domestic bliss. It was amazing how quickly the time had passed. Every time Katie's birthday or New Year came round Ronan and Jess expected her to announce she was moving in with Crispin. But Katie seemed happy with the status quo. 'Why would I want to live with Crispin?' she would ask. 'He doesn't have a huge wardrobe like Jess and he can't cook like Ronan.'

She watched fondly as Ronan poured a glass of wine, sniffed it, then chucked it into the pot where it sizzled briefly. Ronan was six feet four and so handsome he was almost boring to look at. Thanks to his lantern jaw and floppy dark hair, his passion for cooking and the fact that he was an actor, women invariably thought he was gay. On learning he wasn't, few people could believe he had never slept with either of his flatmates. On Jess's side, it wasn't for want of trying. She'd met Ronan on their first day together at drama school and instantly felt her legs grow weak with lust. Ronan, however, was in love with Jeanette in the year above who treated him like dirt. For three years Jess followed him around, pretending to be his mate. She listened patiently to his monologues about how Jeanette was the spit of Béatrice Dalle (in fact, she looked more like a constipated duck) and his misery when she ignored him all evening in the pub.

Other men were appreciative of Jess's low-cut tops and carefully applied lip gloss. Ronan never even noticed. When she got off with someone else, he would say, 'Nice one,' then return to analysing Jeanette's cruelty. Eventually, Jeanette did the decent thing and got pregnant by an ex-student who was now a regular in *The Bill*. Ronan was up for grabs, but to her relief, Jess discovered that the idea of sex with him disturbed her. They really were just friends and now, five years later, Jess was sure he had no idea how she had once felt about him.

As for Katie, she had initially disliked Ronan, on the principle that all handsome men were bastards. And Ronan was a particularly stupid bastard, having picked hideous Jeanette over Jess. But then they had found the flat above the King Kebab 'restaurant' in Elephant and Castle and needed a person to occupy the third bedroom. Ronan was looking for somewhere to live. Jess told Katie that if she didn't get over her prejudices, she'd report her to the Equal Opportunities Commission for discrimination against unfeasibly good-looking men.

Still, for a few months Katie barely spoke to Ronan, despite his constant cleaning and cooking. She finally thawed one Saturday night when Jess was out clubbing and she and Ronan were staying in, enjoying a marathon of *Blind Date*, *Stars in their Eyes* and a nostalgia show called *I Luv the Eighties*. They slumped next to each other on the sofa, curry-smeared plates at their feet. Every now and then Katie would glance at Ronan as he chortled at the cheesy hits and ludicrous hairdos of his not-too-distant youth.

'Why haven't you gone out?' she asked eventually.

Ronan noted her hostile tone. 'Why haven't *you*?' he retorted.

'Because I feel like staying in and vegging out.'

'And so do I,' Ronan said.

Katie couldn't explain why she felt so irritated. She tried. 'But someone like you should be out there. Picking up girls. Breaking their hearts.'

'Well, so should you. Boys' hearts, I mean.'

'But I'm not a heartbreaker.' She gave him a sideways look. 'Unlike you.'

He swivelled round and stared at her, astonished. 'Where did you get that idea from, Katie? You know I have no luck with women.'

It was true. Ronan never brought anyone home.

'Well, maybe you should go out more?' she parried.

'Maybe. But not to clubs. They're so loud and everyone's off their tits on drugs. How can you get to know someone in that environment? I wish you and Jess would introduce me to some of your friends.'

Katie's friends were longing to meet Ronan, but she had warned them off. Now she felt guilty. She remembered how cruelly Jeanette had used him. By way of apology, a few weeks later Katie introduced Ronan to her friend Tiffany. She dumped him after a couple of weeks because he was 'too nice', leaving him more vulnerable than ever. It was official, Ronan was a kindred spirit. Katie could never resist another love casualty. She melted completely and from then on their friendship flourished, although despite her best efforts she had never been able to stop him sabotaging all his relationships through over-keenness.

Sometimes she felt guilty that she and Crispin had the relationship Ronan had always wanted. If Ronan had been with someone as long as she'd been with Crispin he would be married by now and his wife pregnant with at least the second baby. He would happily stay at home and look after it and say goodbye to humiliating auditions for ever. Despite his beauty, Ronan's career had never really taken off – probably because he had very little acting talent – and he was getting tired of the constant rejections. He couldn't understand how his flatmates seemed in no hurry to settle down – in either work or their love lives.

At this rate, Ronan would say, the three of them were going to end up like the *Sex and the City* girls but without the SoHo lofts and the designer wardrobes. In their late thirties but still acting like teenagers. No spouses, no children. They didn't even own a washing machine, for Christ's sake, let alone a decent set of kitchenware. Ronan was sick of living in a flat where pride of place went to the dralon sofa rescued from the skip and covered with an Indian blanket.

Katie found it comforting to dry herself in her mother's old towels and sleep under a duvet cover she had had since she was eleven. To Ronan, it was frustrating. He loved wandering up Tottenham Court Road, gasping at the window displays in Heal's and Habitat, fantasizing about his dream kitchen and bathroom. But what was the point of buying furniture if you didn't have a home of your own to put it in? The occasional TV advert kept Ronan in rent and beer, but was nothing like enough to propel him on to even the lowest rung of the London property ladder. Ronan told Katie he was convinced that this was the reason for his lack of success with the ladies. Who wanted a man with no mortgage prospects?

She replied he was talking nonsense and women were perfectly capable of buying their own homes these days. He hadn't believed her. Sometimes Ronan felt like the youngest son in a Jane Austen novel, the one reserved for boss-eyed, pimply spinsters.

The front door slammed. 'Honey!' screamed a raucous Ulster voice. 'I'm ho – ome.'

Jess had bobbed brown hair, round eyes, a snub nose and a huge mouth. She strolled into the kitchen, dumped her bag on the table and peered hungrily over Ronan's shoulder.

'What's *that*? I'm starving.' She snatched a prawn from the pot. 'Ow! It's hot! And why's it black?'

Ronan slapped her hand. 'It's squid risotto. The black comes from its ink. It'll be ready in ten minutes. Pour yourself a drink while you wait.'

Katie grinned. 'So how was your audition, dear?' Jess had been up for a yoghurt advert.

'A waste of time,' said Jess cheerily, removing a can of Stella from the fridge. 'I have to run a bubble bath, light candles and then lie there expectantly. A gorgeous guy arrives and drops his towel but I'm only interested in the pot of Yoggle in his left hand. It's *scheisse*. Not that I'll get it anyway.'

'What about the gorgeous guy?'

'Gay,' Jess said instantly. 'Good fun though. He knows a great ketamine dealer. Said he'd text me his number.'

Jess and Katie. 'We are fam- i- lee,' as Jess liked to sing after a few, although Katie grew up in the suburbs of

Birmingham and Jess in Belfast. Until their early twenties they had met only three times – at Jess's parents' silver wedding, their great-aunt's funeral and their grandfather's ninetieth birthday.

They got to know each other when they were twenty-two and had both just arrived in London: Katie to temp; Jess for another three years of student life at drama school. Both needed somewhere to live and someone to live with. That was seven years ago, since when they had progressed from a one-bedroom flat in Battersea with no central heating (Jess liked to titillate boyfriends with tales of how they shared the same bed all winter), to a maisonette with cockroaches in Hackney, to their current three-bedroom home, with its leaky roof and grumpy neighbours.

'So, Katie,' said Jess, grabbing one of Ronan's Silk Cuts. 'Did you find a job today?'

'Well, I bought the *Guardian*,' said her cousin. 'But I couldn't see anything that was right for me.'

'Well, never mind,' Jess said. 'For now you get to give us the low down and dirty on Rebecca G.'

'Dirty being the right word.'

Ronan rolled his eyes as he began dishing out dinner. 'As the pot said to the kettle.'

'So what's she like?' Jess urged.

Katie thought. 'Well, on the surface she's scary. Barks out orders. Gives you looks that say "No messing". But at the same time, there's something quite sweet about her. She steps in puddles and she goes on and on about her boyfriend, who sounds like an arse, and she lives like a pig. A stylish pig, but a pig.'

Jess pulled a chair up to the table. 'I still don't think it's fair you got the job of cleaning up after her. What about me and Ronan? We're permanently unemployed.'

'We're *resting*,' Ronan corrected. Jess swatted him on the head.

'Speak for yourself, loser.'

They ate their supper. 'God, you're a good cook, Ronan,' Katie said. 'That's what you should be – Rebecca Greenhall's private chef. All the stars have one of those.'

'Yes, but she'd want me to cook nothing but egg-white omelettes,' said Ronan. 'Green salads, no dressing. No carbs, ever. What's the fun in that?'

'So, Katie,' said Jess, her mouth still full, 'even if you won't actually introduce us to Rebecca, when are you going to give us a tour of her flat?'

'I'm not going to do that!' Katie exclaimed. 'She'd sack me. I told you how the last cleaner got the boot.'

'Oh, Katie. Don't be so boring. We won't get caught. And even if we are, who cares? You said it was only temporary.'

Katie smiled serenely.

'C'mon, Kate. It's not as if we're going to nick anything. We just want to have a look. Don't we, Ronan?'

'Not particularly,' said Ronan primly, loading his plate with seconds. 'I don't want to get Katie into trouble.'

'God. You two,' Jess sighed. She turned around in her chair, picked up the remote and began channel surfing. '*Holiday Swaps*? *Food and Drink*? Some boring documentary. What's it to be?'

'Oh, turn it off, Jess,' said Ronan. 'There's a pudding. Let's talk to each other.'

'Talk? What about?'

'Oh, I don't know. Life. Culture. What was the last film you went to see?'

'*Mission Impossible Three*. We saw it together.'

'So we did. OK. What is Katie going to do with the rest of her life?'

Ronan and Jess turned to look at her. 'Retrain as a tree surgeon?' Jess suggested.

'Don't be facetious,' Ronan admonished, doling out a portion of fruit trifle. 'Katie, what do you think?'

Katie sighed. 'I don't know, Ronan. I need to work out what I'm good at.'

'Borrowing my clothes,' Jess suggested.

'Remembering the lyrics to every song ever written,' said Ronan.

'Dealing with Richard downstairs,' said Jess. Richard was a marathon-running doctor who went to bed at ten, got up at six and became very angry when his routine was disturbed by Ronan, Jess and Katie dancing to old Abba records.

'Giving me advice about girls,' said Ronan.

'Giving me advice about boys,' sighed Jess. 'Not that I ever listen.'

There was no delicate way of putting it. Jess slept around. Casting directors, other actors that she met on location, her agent's assistant, several friends of Ronan. Basically anyone who'd asked.

Katie had the biggest bed in the flat, and Jess had an irritating habit of 'borrowing it' whenever her cousin stayed at Crispin's. Katie was fed up with coming home and finding pairs of Top Shop pants and huge lumpy 34DD bras tangled up in her duvet.

'I think the best thing about Katie is her kind heart,' Ronan said almost shyly. 'Maybe you should be a social worker. Or a nurse.'

'Wiping old men's bums? No thanks!' Jess yelled.

'Then I couldn't afford to live in London,' Katie pointed out, touched by her flatmate's tribute. 'Or so everyone tells me.' And as always, the subject was forgotten.

After dinner they watched *ER* and fantasized about Jess and Ronan both getting parts in it. Jess would marry Dr Carter ('He's already married,' Ronan pointed out; 'So?' said Jess) and Katie would move out to LA to be her personal assistant.

'Except I refuse to live in LA,' Katie said lightly.

'Why not?' Jess exclaimed. 'Sunshine all year. Amazing shopping.' Then she looked at her cousin's overly calm expression and remembered. 'OK,' she conceded. 'We'll live in New York.'

After *ER*, they got out the box of Belgian chocolates Jess had bought the previous day and squabbled over who would have the one with the hazelnut. 'The person who has the nut gets two,' Katie ruled.

'No, we should all have two,' Jess argued. 'The person with the hazelnut gets three.'

'Maybe we should all have three and the person . . .' Ronan began.

'Ronan!' Katie laughed. 'I thought you were watching your weight.'

'I am but . . .'

'The sooner we eat them, the sooner they'll be gone,' Jess interrupted. 'No more temptation.'

Impressed by the logic of this, they polished off the box

while discussing their plans for the weekend. 'Emily's party on Saturday,' said Jess.

Katie made a face. 'I should really see Crispin.'

'Well, bring him too,' said Jess.

'Maybe,' said Katie. She didn't really like going to parties with Crispin. She could never really loosen up. She brightened. 'He may be working. In which case, I *can* come.'

Jess and Ronan looked at each other significantly.

A few minutes later, Katie got up, yawning. 'My new life as a manual labourer has tired me out,' she grinned, kissing them both on the cheek. 'Sleep well, my darlings.'

She turned towards her bedroom and just then the phone rang.

'Aaargh,' Jess yelled. 'Katie. Can you get it?'

Katie sighed. She did this at least twice a week. Telling callers that Jess wasn't there, she didn't know when she'd be back and no, she didn't have a mobile (as if!) and yes, she'd take a message but she had a feeling Jess was filming in . . . Siberia! So, she might be out of touch for quite a while.

All the time, of course, Jess would be standing right next to her, mouthing obscenities and making 'Go Away' gestures with her hands.

'Can't Ronan do it?'

'No! You know he's a hopeless liar.' Jess thrust the cordless phone into Katie's hand.

'Hello?'

'Katie, darling!'

'Auntie Gillian!' Katie adored Jess's mum, who would die if she knew even one-tenth of the things her daughter got up to.

'Is my baby there?'

'She is,' said Katie, handing over the phone to a relieved-looking Jess. Ronan, now standing at the sink wearing pink rubber gloves, chortled.

As she lay in bed Katie thought some more about her cousin. She was twenty-nine, positively ancient by film star standards, and although she was indubitably sexy with her huge lips and enormous bust, she was also far too small and – they had to face it – too plump for the movies. Not that she was fat, only a size 12, perfectly acceptable in the British market, but by West Coast standards obese.

In fact, they all knew Jess's best days had passed her by already. She had a Catherine Cookson mini-series to her credit, a couple of West End plays and several abysmal Brit flicks, which had run for one week before being consigned to video land. Not bad, but hardly Dame Judi Dench.

Maybe Rebecca Greenhall was the answer? Katie would introduce her to Jess and Ronan, and she – or her business partner – would take them both under her wing and promote them. Katie's new job could turn out to be a blessing in disguise, sent to help all of them, to move them on to the next stage in their lives. It was time for a change. These days, Katie sometimes had the feeling she so often got at the end of a party, when the lights went up and she looked around the stragglers: too lazy, or too desperate for a snog, or too off their heads to leave. 'Why am I still here? Does this make me one of the losers?' she would wonder.

But she loved Ronan, she loved Jess. Sure, they had their eccentricities, but they rumbled along very nicely and even though Jess shouted and swore a lot they almost never fought. Katie had a horror of any kind of conflict. That was the main reason she'd said yes to Rebecca. Think how angry she might have been if Katie had explained the real situation.

Not that she and Crispin ever rowed, she thought, but then Crispin worked so late, so often. And while he was staying late at chambers, she'd get lonely and go round to the Elephant, so what was the point of moving out? And the prospect of becoming one of those tired-looking couples she used to show round houses was just too scary to contemplate. Surely life offered her more than that? With a little sigh, Katie rolled on to her left side. Tomorrow she would start looking for a proper new job. When she found work she loved, everything would fall into place.

3

That same night, Rebecca was holding court on a distressed leather sofa at Priory Street, a private club in Soho. Next to her sat one of her oldest friends, Suzanne Bell.

Rebecca was recounting the events of the previous night. 'Bastard!' she moaned. 'Bastard!'

Suzy sighed and surreptitiously glanced at her watch. Only eight o'clock. In a few minutes, she'd sneak off for a line. Otherwise, there was no way she was going to get through tonight.

Suzy was tiny and sleek. Rather like a cat, she liked to think. She had long shiny raven hair and always wore black, with an occasional flash of white at the throat. 'I'm in mourning for my life,' she would explain, if anyone asked her why, but actually her inspiration was an article she had once commissioned on the late, but eternally elegant, Carolyn Bessette Kennedy.

Suzy's ambition had been to become a Martha Gellhorn-like foreign correspondent, but somehow she had ended up editor of *Seduce!* 'The highest circulation magazine for ABC1 women in the twenty-five–thirty age range,' she would recite sarcastically. Her days were spent studying photos of celebrities in their swimsuits and proofreading articles called 'Is Your Makeup Past Its Sell-by Date?' Annoyingly for her, she was very good at this and her magazine kept winning awards.

'I was all set to go out when he called me,' Rebecca was saying. 'Said he couldn't make it, he had to stay in and work. I offered to come round and cook for him but he said it would be too distracting.'

Suzy and Rebecca had been friends for more than ten years. They'd met when Rebecca was still working in celebrity PR, and Suzy was an up-and-coming journalist, looking for people to interview. Since then their careers had soared, while their love lives had plummeted. Well, Rebecca's had anyway: Suzy had a married lover called Hunter in Philadelphia and – if she ever talked about it at all – always claimed she wouldn't have it any other way, and would rather go on a camping trip to Yorkshire than have him leave his wife.

There were two other members of the gang: Jenny and Ally. Jenny was Suzy's oldest schoolfriend. Rebecca met Ally when she was just twenty-two, new to London, and working in a call-centre selling life insurance. Ally had the seat next door and they soon bonded over the shame of being told to piss off 14,000 times a day.

Rebecca adored Ally, even if right now their friendship was going through a bit of a rough patch when they felt more like acquaintances than soulmates. The problem was they simply didn't see enough of each other – all Al's spare time seemed reserved for her new boyfriend, Jon. Although, Rebecca remembered uncomfortably, on the couple of occasions they had tried to meet recently *she* had been the one to cancel at the last minute. She had pleaded work, but the real reason was that Tim had suddenly called.

Still, they were seeing each other tonight. Rebecca felt quite excited as she saw her friend sashay into the room. Ally was tall and exotic-looking, with shoulder-length black curls and a hooked nose. Tonight she wore a denim pelmet and black jumper, designed to show her amazing figure to the max. Ally wore suits all day at the bank, but as soon as work was over she dashed into the loo, ripping off her civvies like Supergirl and emerging in some outfit that made Britney Spears look like a nun.

'Al!' Rebecca jumped up and kissed her on both cheeks.

'Becs!' They hugged each other.

'How are things?' Rebecca asked, after Ally had kissed Suzy and settled down.

'Oh, disaster, disaster,' Ally said cheerily. She had some astonishingly high-powered job and no one had a clue what she got up to all day. 'I got a call from Japan saying the Nikkei was in freefall and at just the same time Jon texted me to say our offer on the house had fallen through.' Just then her mobile bleeped loudly. 'Oh, talking of which.' She pulled her phone out of her bag and grinned at what she saw. 'Oh God, he is too much!'

'You're not allowed phones in here,' Suzy warned. However hard she tried, she could never completely shake off the traces of her former head-girl self.

Ally stuck her tongue out. 'Oh yeah? What are they going to do to me? Cut my rations of rocket? Look at this.' She thrust the phone under Suzy's nose.

'What?'

'Just read it.'

Want 2 fuck U up arse now.

'Al!' Suzy flinched. But Ally just laughed.

Rebecca rolled her eyes. She had fallen for this one before. One of the many things they all loathed about the Ally/Jon coupling was the way they flaunted their sex life, forever pawing each other and snogging with tongues out.

She realized that for several weeks she had been avoiding Ally, because right now she simply couldn't be honest with her. After all, how could she confess that she loathed her boyfriend? Mind you, Ally had been pretty silent on the subject of Tim. In fact all the girls had. Did they not like Tim, Rebecca wondered in surprise. But how could that be possible? More likely was that they barely knew him. After all, Tim wasn't around that much and he hated to make plans. Nearly all of their time was one on one, usually late, at Rebecca's after the pubs had closed.

'So you're still looking for a new house?' Suzy was asking. Another depressing topic. Ally lived in an adorable pink maisonette in Camden Town, but had recently announced she had put it on the market and was looking for a place in Hackney, big enough to accommodate Jon's two daughters.

'Yes, but having no luck so far. Either there aren't enough bedrooms, or the garden isn't big enough or there's a crack den next door.' She turned to the hovering shaven-headed waiter. 'Could we get a jug of water, please. Tap water.' Ally might earn a telephone-number salary, plus bonus, but at heart she was a Northumberland girl, who could never get over what a rip-off London was.

'And a bottle of champagne, Maurizio,' said Rebecca, flaunting the fact she knew all the staff by name. She was a bit pissed already, but sod it.

Maurizio smirked. In the two years since he'd arrived in

London from Brazil, he had seen enough women like these to fill Copacabana beach. Sexy, well-dressed and drunk. Or off their heads on cocaine. So undignified. No wonder he preferred men. Strong, silent ones.

'Oh my God, you'll never guess who I just saw!' They all looked up at a tall, busty woman with a halo of blonde curls like scrambled eggs. Jenny. Late – and as irrepressible – as ever.

'Victoria Beckham! Coming down the stairs in the stupidest shoes I've ever seen.'

'What were they like?' they all chorused like backing singers.

Jenny described every detail of Posh's outfit, while lighting a fag and pouring herself a glass of champagne, which she downed practically in one.

'She's got amazing hair,' she babbled. 'But she's still way, way too skinny. And those boobs, they're definitely not real, they . . .'

Rebecca smiled as she watched her friend trying to cram it all in. Jenny adored the glamour of Priory Street. She was a graphic designer and although she was the only one of the four with a decent boyfriend, she still had a permanent sense of inadequacy about her friends' flashier jobs.

'And do you think she's had Botox? I had a really good look, but then one of her bodyguards got in the way . . .'

'Are we going to eat?' Ally interrupted eventually.

'Ooh, yes,' Jenny cried. She snatched up the menu. 'Yummy! It's all so delicious here.'

'Some bread, ladies?' asked Maurizio.

They all shook their heads as if they had just been offered nuclear waste. But then Jenny cracked.

'Actually, I'll have one of these,' she said, grabbing a pumpkin-seed roll. 'I didn't have any lunch,' she excused herself.

'I'll have one too,' Ally said, to universal astonishment. She took a slice of wholemeal before doing something even stranger: *spreading it thickly with butter.*

'I thought you were allergic to dairy,' Rebecca gasped. For years Ally had claimed allergies to sugar, nuts, fat – in fact, virtually everything except lettuce. Suzy was almost as bad.

'I thought I was too! But Jon made me have a little nibble of his toast the other day and nothing happened.'

'That's amazing!' Jenny gasped. 'Because aren't you allergic to wheat as well?'

Bless her, she wasn't even being sarcastic. Rebecca tried not to smile, and Suzy smirked openly. But Ally serenely ignored them.

'Your tap water, ladies,' said Maurizio over-loudly. 'And are you ready to order?'

'God, I can't decide,' Suzy sighed. 'Maybe I'll have the burger. Or the pizza could be good. One of you go first.'

'OK,' said Jenny eagerly. 'I'll have the burger. Medium please. And lots of chips.'

'I'll have the roast chicken and pumpkin salad,' said Ally.

'Actually,' said Suzy, 'I kind of pigged out at lunch. So I think I'll just have the spinach salad. Hold the goat's cheese.'

'Me too,' Rebecca agreed.

Jenny gawped. How come she always ordered the most? 'Actually, could I have salad instead of chips?' she asked quickly.

'Oh no, keep the chips, Jen! We'll help you with those.' Suzy smiled winningly.

'And while we're waiting, maybe Ally will help me out with these.' Jenny held out her Marlboro Light pack to her naughty smoker accomplice. 'Here you go, babe.'

But Ally waved her away. 'Not tonight.'

'Not tonight!' As usual, Jenny expressed what they had all been thinking. 'Al! Are you pregnant?'

Ally laughed. 'Of course not.'

'Why are you drinking water then?'

Suzy cringed. Jenny had never learned the joys of subtlety.

'I've just got a bit of a headache. Big day today. And tomorrow. And I'm trying to cut down on the fags. Jon doesn't like it.'

The others exchanged glances. There were far too many things Jon didn't like about their perfect friend.

More drink arrived, followed by food, at which point Suzy got up and went to the loo. When she returned, she had a runny nose and was noticeably jollier.

'So how's Hunter?' Rebecca asked as Suzy sat down. Suzy was infuriatingly secretive about her love life, so the best time to strike was just after she'd done a line.

'He's very well. Coming over next week.'

'And will we get to meet him this time?' Jenny asked.

Suzy shrugged. 'I shouldn't think so. We don't exactly get quality time together as it is.'

'Doesn't that bother you?' Jenny asked, then giggled, answering herself. 'I guess it's not like me and Gords get much quality time, unless you count our trips to Homebase.'

35

Rebecca felt a pang. She would *love* to have someone to go to Homebase with, to discuss floor coverings and bathroom taps. She and Tim were nowhere near there yet. But Suzy smiled approvingly.

'That's the joy of being a mistress,' she said. 'You spend Sunday mornings at Homebase. I spend them licking chocolate off Hunter in a suite at the Ritz.'

Rebecca knew this was as much information as they'd ever get. She turned to Ally.

'So how about you, Al? How's it going with Jon?'

Once, Ally had been the queen of hilarious boyfriend stories. But now she just shrugged and took another nibble of her bread.

'Fine.'

Oh well, be like that then. Rebecca turned to Jenny. 'And Gordy?' Gordy was Jenny's boyfriend of four years.

'Oh, he's only being the most annoying git in the whole universe,' cried Jenny, who had been longing for her turn. 'Saying we can't go on holiday, because we need to replace the boiler.'

'And do you?' Rebecca asked.

'Oh, definitely. The hot water keeps going off when I'm in the shower. But . . . not having a holiday! I mean, why can't we do both?'

'Maybe you can't afford to,' Ally suggested.

'We can stick it on our credit cards, can't we? Gordy's such a killjoy. He can't see that a holiday is just as important as bricks and mortar, especially when you're as stressed as I am.'

'And what's going on with you, Rebecca?' Ally said hastily. They all loved Gordy for being neither a bully, nor a cad, nor a clingy neurotic, and hated it when Jenny attacked him.

And so finally, as Maurizio arrived with their dinner, Rebecca got to tell her Tim story and – since no one knew or liked him well enough to feel any loyalty towards him – they were all happy.

'I don't understand,' Rebecca wailed. 'Tim was the one who started all this. He pursued me.'

She paused for a moment, lost in reverie as she remembered how it had started. She was at Jake and Stella's housewarming, standing in the corner, bored out of her mind. Once parties had meant wild affairs where people copulated openly, the toilets were full of giggling gangs taking drugs and you danced until sunrise before catching the first Tube home. But then she had crossed into that strange hinterland of the thirties and parties had begun to mean fake champagne and small talk and everyone leaving at ten to relieve the babysitter.

All the same, Rebecca continued to drag herself out mostly for work reasons, but mainly because, as her mother said, you never knew when you were going to meet Mr Right. She was wondering how soon she could politely make her excuses and get home in time for the *Late Review*, when he walked right up to her. Some ugly bloke, with mousy hair, Joe 90 glasses and jeans that emphasized his long, skinny legs. He was smoking a Gitane. What a pretentious wanker, Rebecca had thought.

So how come, just two months later, it had come to this?

'It's just so weird,' she continued. 'I didn't even fancy him. When he sent me the flowers I couldn't even remember who he was. But then he begged me to see him.'

It was as familiar as a bedtime story. The others nodded dreamily. Ally filched one of Jenny's chips.

'Then we sleep together and it's surprisingly nice,' Rebecca continued. 'He tells me he loves me and he's never felt this way about anyone before. That he wants to get married and live in one of those big old houses in Hampstead that back on to the Heath. We'll have four children, who will grow up with terrible complexes because although we will love them, we will quite obviously prefer each other.'

'Aah,' Jenny sighed.

'Eurgh,' Suzy groaned. 'And what exactly did you find appealing about this?'

'Oh, Suze, don't be so contrary,' Ally said. 'You know that's every woman's dream.'

Suzy shrugged. Rebecca ignored her. 'So why's he doing this to me?' she asked fretfully. 'Why doesn't he want to see me?'

Jenny leaned forward and touched her arm. 'Becky, I'm sure he does want to see you. If he says he's working late, he's working late. He loves you. He said so.'

'But a couple of weeks ago, Tim wanted to be with me *every night*. And now I haven't seen him since Sunday. And then he didn't want to stay.'

'Anything else, ladies?' Maurizio asked unenthusiastically. He knew that with the slightest encouragement Jenny would be there all night.

Sure enough: 'Another bottle,' she cried, waving the empty one.

'And the bill?' Ally asked hastily. Jon would be waiting up for her.

'The bill? But it's only . . .' Jenny glanced at her watch. God, how did it get to be eleven-thirty so quickly? Oh well, she had nothing much to do at work tomorrow.

'Yes, I need to be making a move,' Suzy agreed. Time to get on the hotline to Hunter.

Maurizio had never added up a bill so hastily. Having never had truck with the London habit of simply slapping down your credit card, Ally picked it up and scanned it severely.

'A hundred and ninety-five pounds! Bloody hell. Does that include service?' she asked.

Maurizio grimaced. 'Well, ye . . . e . . . s. But is not service really. Is like . . . corkage. For the champagne!'

'Corkage! But we've already paid fifty pounds for that bottle. Plus,' Ally scanned the bill, but her superbrain gave up on her, 'far too much for food. So don't lie to me. Service is included and that's just an end to it.'

'Oh, don't be so embarrassing,' Jenny hissed.

'Embarrassing!' bellowed Ally. 'They're the ones who should be embarrassed. Bloody fifteen per cent service charge and then they try to rip you off for more.'

If she had been looking for a way to have Rebecca and Suzy on their feet, she couldn't have done it better.

'Well, I'm going to stay,' giggled Jenny. She had just caught the eye of a long-haired, Greek-looking man at the bar, who had beckoned to her to come over. Well, why not? It was only healthy flirting, she told her inner mother. She wasn't going to *do* anything. 'Sure I can't tempt you guys to another bottle?' she beseeched her friends. But they all shook their heads virtuously.

'Early start,' Rebecca said.

'God, you never used to say that,' Jenny complained, kissing her goodbye. She was right, Rebecca thought. Once they would happily stay out until two or three and stumble through work the next day in a hungover haze. But now it took longer and longer for her body to bounce back. Plus, she admitted to herself, she was kind of hoping if she made it out of here before midnight, she'd still have time to talk to Tim.

'At least we don't have kids,' she said. 'Then we wouldn't have made it out at all.' She noticed Ally grimace slightly. Oh God. She *was* pregnant. One by one they were abandoning ship.

'Rebecca's so right,' Suzy agreed, pulling on her Joseph sheepskin jacket. 'Kids spell the end of all human life as we know it. Goodnight, Jenny. Don't do anything I wouldn't.'

'Oh, you can be sure of that,' Jenny laughed, picking up her glass and making her way purposefully to the bar.

4

'God, what *is* Jenny like?' asked Ally, as she, Rebecca and Suzy stood on the pavement, waiting for the minicab man with the clipboard to assign them taxis.

'Oh, she's all right,' said Suzy. 'She's just bored, living in the sticks and going out with an IT consultant who's obsessed with DIY. Who can blame her for wanting more out of life?'

'But surely if you want more out of life the place to look isn't Priory Street,' Ally argued. Actually, she was playing devil's advocate – she hadn't been to Priory Street for ages and was surprised how much she missed her carefree girls' nights there.

Two cars pulled up alongside them.

'Primrose Hill?' said one of the drivers.

'Oh yes, that's us!' said Ally. She and Suzy always shared. Rebecca kissed them both goodbye, then climbed into a battered Escort. As soon as the door was shut, she fingered her mobile. She couldn't resist it. She pressed the redial button.

'Hi, this is Tim . . .'

Bollocks. She tried his landline. Answerphone as well. Where the hell was he? She flicked rapidly through her old texts – just in case she had missed one. Tim was a great believer in texting. He said it was because he was holed up all day in libraries, but, Rebecca was realizing, it was also a perfect way to blow her out. You couldn't argue with a text or make it feel guilty when it left you waiting like a lemon at a restaurant table for three-quarters of an hour.

She thought back to that first night with Tim. Or rather, the morning after when he had showered and she had lain in bed, picturing him waiting for her at the altar. Why did she always do that, she wondered, amused despite herself. Even when she was twenty-four and had spent a ludicrous, drunken – but career-boosting – night with Henry Bag-shawe, her bearded, middle-aged, married boss at Barter PR, she had still caught herself the following morning looking dewily at churches and imagining Mum in a hat looking proud.

Except now it was a bit more serious. She was thirty-six, for Christ's sake. Instead of laughing at the Lakeland catalogue like she used to, she now studied it intensely and had even recently sent off for a blow-up bed for the endless stream of backpackers constantly clamouring to stay. God, the other day she had even ordered a skirt from Boden. Whatever would Suzy say?

Rebecca had come to terms with some parts of the ageing process. She accepted that she might have to forgo getting married; in other words, forgo agonizing over headdresses, rows over seating plans and getting fleeced by a marquee company. But she did want children. And someone to share all the hassle with. All right, she had Tara to sort out most of her niggles and, she supposed, that new cleaner. What was her name? Rebecca's memory was not what it used to be. Too many Es in the early Nineties.

Yet even with those two, Rebecca was always the one who took ultimate charge. Wouldn't it be fantastic to hear someone say: 'I'm sweeping you off to Venice for the weekend. Don't worry, I've sorted the flights and hotels,' rather than having to phone round all her friends, begging them to abandon their partners and children for a weekend of fun.

The question was, why hadn't Rebecca married years ago? Although she was probably a little past her prime, she still looked fantastic – far, far better than she had in her teens when she had been frankly chubby, or in her twenties, which were littered with sartorial disasters. Her thirties, however, had kicked off with a bout of gastric flu that saw her lose two stone in a fortnight, which she had never regained.

What else was right with her? She was astonishingly successful – and no one seriously thought men were frightened by career women any more. And when she wasn't obsessing about Tim she was quite fun company, she knew she was.

It wasn't as if there hadn't been chances to settle down. Some of her relationships had lasted years longer than most marriages. There was Jack, her boyfriend from school, with whom she had acted out all the teenage clichés of sex in his bedroom with the door locked and all their clothes still on. That had ended when they both went off to college. Then Rebecca moved to Melbourne, where she spent two glorious years with Mike, whom she had loved with a passion but still not enough to turn down the offer of a job in London.

Lovely guys, but Rebecca couldn't honestly say she had

any regrets about finishing with either of them. At that point, men had been nothing more than a pleasant diversion in an eventful life. It was the ones who came later who had caused the real damage, she thought, as the car pulled up at Dartmouth Mansions. Especially Jamie, who had monopolized most of her late twenties, and who Rebecca complacently imagined was her future husband – because that's what boyfriends in your late twenties were all about. They had a lot of fun together, she and Jamie, shopping in Selfridges, going on lavish long-haul holidays, eating in the latest fashionable restaurant and enjoying sushi takeaways in front of the television.

And then one day Rebecca woke up, no longer with her whole life ahead of her, but on the verge of thirty, and conscious that, even though most of her friends were still unmarried, time was now at a premium. Not that she wanted to *marry* Jamie, but they ought at least to move in together.

Jamie had remained immune to all her hints, so in the end she had asked him outright. They were on holiday in Zanzibar, having dinner on the roof of their hotel. It was a balmy night, the lights were twinkling across the old stone town, the moon was nearly full and you could hear the hush of the ocean. Rebecca spent the whole of her starter trying to find the right words and eventually managed it as they finished their main courses.

'Do you think we should move in together?' It came out all in a rush.

Jamie stopped, his fork poised over a mouthful of fish curry. 'No,' he said finally. 'I don't.'

'Why?'

44

Jamie looked wary. 'I just don't want to.'

'But we're so good together.'

Jamie laughed faintly hysterically. 'You think so?'

Then, as if nothing had happened, he started talking about the book he was reading. Rebecca sat there stunned. He'd dismissed her out of hand. Hadn't even left any room for negotiation. In one of the most romantic spots in the world.

Later that night in bed, Jamie made love to her. She responded as enthusiastically as she could in the circumstances. She had, at least, to remind him that they had a textbook fabulous sex life.

'Go down on me,' she whispered in his ear.

Jamie sat bolt upright in bed and pushed her away.

'Christ, Bec. That is exactly why I don't want to live with you. You're so fucking high-maintenance.'

High-maintenance? Rebecca had no idea what he was talking about.

'All those fucking shopping trips. All the fucking restaurants. The posh hotels. These holidays. But we never talk. We never get to what's important. I don't know what makes you tick and you certainly don't know about me. You don't love me, Bec. The only person you love is yourself.'

After this diatribe Jamie rolled over and fell asleep as if nothing had happened. Rebecca lay awake, stunned and tearful. *Of course* she loved Jamie. How could he say such hurtful things? More importantly, what were they going to do now? They had three more nights in Zanzibar, then a week in Kenya. How was she going to spend the next ten days in the company of a man who didn't just not love her, but seemed to despise her?

45

Somehow, they struggled through it. Rebecca begged Jamie to explain exactly where she was going wrong, but he refused to discuss the matter further. Rebecca took her revenge by hogging the best seat in the safari minibus every day, so she got the best views of the lions and warthogs. Jamie sat looking sulky in the back. Once she would have offered to take it in turns, but not now.

Back in London, she braced herself for the break-up, but he said nothing and, astonishingly, their relationship limped on for another six months. In the hopes of making him see what he was missing, Rebecca bought her flat. Up to the moment she signed the contract, she expected Jamie to appear on the doorstep shouting that he had made a terrible mistake and they should get married tomorrow. Of course, he never did.

'Cut your losses,' some friends told her. 'Get out at once.' Rebecca knew they were right, but she kept putting it off, until one humiliating Friday night Jamie – after avoiding her calls all day – turned up late at her flat. She was waiting in her prettiest silk nightie.

'Why didn't you call me back?' she said softly. 'Don't you love me any more?'

There was a very long pause.

'Well, no, I don't,' Jamie said.

'What?' Rebecca screamed, although it was hardly a surprise.

'I'm not sure I ever have loved you,' Jamie said, looking very relieved. 'I liked you a lot because you were pretty and fun and had an interesting job, but it's never been love.'

And with that he left. Rebecca was devastated, of course,

though – she saw now – more because her pride had been so hurt than because her heart had been broken. People as gorgeous and glamorous as her simply didn't get dumped, she would sob into her pillow at night. To make it worse, Jamie found another gorgeous, glamorous girlfriend within weeks and six months later, *they* were living together.

But looking back, Rebecca realized she never cried because she missed rubbing her hands down Jamie's smooth, cool back or fighting over the popcorn carton in the cinema. Perhaps Jamie had been just as much an accessory to her as she had been to him. Perhaps she had never really loved him. Perhaps she had never really loved anyone, except Mike. Perhaps – and God, it was infuriating to admit it – Jamie had been right to end it.

She wished she'd bloody got in there first.

And then came Rebecca's thirties, when opportunities for steamy action were limited to teenagers, married men and deranged psychos. Not being quite that desperate, Rebecca suffered a drought of two whole years, broken by a brief fling with Giles, aged forty, who told her after their first blissful night together that his longest relationship had lasted three months. But Rebecca had convinced herself he was the one and spent another year painfully pursuing him.

Then another drought and then, two months ago, she had met Tim. He was the first guy in ages who could make her heart do cartwheels. He said he loved her and even if she wasn't entirely sure she loved him, she knew he was her last chance.

Rebecca was infused with determination to make it work. She did everything for Tim: had a Brazilian wax, took him out to beautiful restaurants (he never had any money), watched his porn videos and pretended to enjoy them.

But she still had no guarantee of a return on her investment. Tim was so up and down. One minute declaring his love, the next saying he needed space and disappearing for days on end.

Once, Rebecca would have told him to get lost. But at this stage in her life, she felt she no longer had that option. She was simply being too high-maintenance, she told herself. All successful relationships were built on compromise. Tim was a creative person and couldn't be bound by the normal rules. That was what made him so exciting and special, and she would just have to learn to be less uptight and go with the flow.

'And is he one of your clients now?' whispered a little voice in her head. Who had been rude enough to ask that? Katie! *That* was the cleaner's name. Frankly, Rebecca wasn't entirely sure about her: her standard of work was nowhere up to Alicia's. Still, at least she understood English for a change. But what a question to ask! *Of course* Tim wasn't her client; her job had nothing to do with their relationship. At least, Rebecca hoped not. Tim did ask a lot of questions about her links with the big publishing houses and how easy it would be to get a spot as a panellist on *Arts Roundup*. But that was inevitable – both of them working in creative industries. It didn't mean he was using her.

As she dumped her coat and bag on the floor, Rebecca noticed the red light on her phone was winking. A call! She ran to the answerphone and pressed the button.

'Hello, sweetheart, it's Mum. Just checking you're OK.

I know you're always so busy. If you have a moment, call me. I'd love to hear your voice. Bye, honey.'

No Tim, Rebecca thought bleakly, then slapped her head, enraged at her selfishness. That was Mum, for Christ's sake. And all Rebecca could think about was herself and her pathetic problems. She checked the time. Morning in Sydney.

The line to Australia crackled: *drrrrr, drrrrrr.* That monotone ring tone always made Rebecca feel sad. Rebecca missed her mum so much. She tried to go home once a year, but it wasn't enough. She was constantly offering to buy her mother a ticket to the UK, but she was frightened of flying and refused even to contemplate it.

Drrrr. Click. 'Laurel Greenhall cannot come to the phone right now . . .'

Damn. Missed her. Rebecca wished her mother would get a mobile. She'd pay for it, for God's sake. But whenever she suggested it Mum just laughed.

She breathed deeply. 'Hi, Mum. You're not there. Well, I guess I'm going to bed now. But I'll try you tomorrow. You take care now.'

Rebecca hung up but for a minute continued to grasp the handset, half-blinded with tears. Perhaps it was time to go home. But the business that she'd worked so hard to create was here. And her friends. And her apartment. And the husband situation was hardly going to be any better in Sydney, where men came in only two categories: redneck or gay.

Then the phone rang. 'Mum?'

The caller was amused. 'Is that what I sound like?'

'Tim! Hi!'

'Hello, darling.'

He was drunk. But hey, he was calling.

'What are you up to?'

It's one o'clock in the morning. I have a meeting at nine. What do you think I'm up to? What Rebecca actually said was: 'Nothing.'

'So I can come round and ravish you?'

'Of course you can.' She laughed with relief.

'Cool. I'm just around the corner. Be there in five.'

Five minutes! Five minutes to dig out her Agent Provocateur negligée from her chest of drawers, run into the bathroom, gargle with Listerine, brush her hair, wipe off her lipstick and replace it with gloss.

What now?

Oh yes. A candle! Light one. By the time the doorbell rang, Rebecca was panting like a marathon runner.

'Hello,' she breathed into the intercom in her best Felicity Kendal purr.

'Hi, babe.'

She positioned herself seductively by the front door. Tim emerged from the lift and rushed right past her into the loo.

'Bursting for a slash,' he shouted over a Niagara Falls-like roar.

The pee seemed to last about five minutes. Initially Rebecca posed on the sofa, but it was getting cold. She picked up the candle and moved into the bedroom. Shit. She'd forgotten to make the bed as usual. Never mind. She arranged the covers becomingly around her.

Tim appeared in the doorway, swaying slightly in his usual nylon parka. 'Babe,' he muttered. He pulled his shirt over his head and his trainers off his feet, unbuckled his jeans and stepped out of them. In his Daffy Duck boxer shorts he collapsed beside her on the bed. 'Good to see you.' He gave her a beery kiss, then rolled on to his side.

Within seconds he was snoring: comic little bleats. Except it wasn't funny. Rebecca couldn't believe it. What a fucking nerve! Here she was gone to all this effort, and here he was . . . using her. Like a youth hostel. This was not going to happen. She was going to wake Tim up and demand sex.

No, wait. Maybe she was being too high-maintenance. Poor Tim, he worked hard. He had a right to go out and get drunk with his friends.

Still, if Rebecca was to seduce him, he would remember how lucky he was. She started rubbing her body up and down against Tim's back. She covered his spine in feathery kisses, then reached round through the hole in his boxer shorts and cupped his flaccid penis in her hand.

The snoring grew louder.

Rebecca gave up. God, she didn't even want a shag anyway. She was exhausted. But God knows how she was going to get to sleep now with this noise.

For the next hour she lay there in the dark wondering what had gone wrong, if she was a controlling bitch not to want her boyfriend to fall asleep drunk on her. 'Why does it matter so much?' she asked herself. 'Why do I think I need a boyfriend? Why can't I be happy on my own?'

Then she thought of Mum, all alone. And she knew that she didn't want to end up like that. Rebecca had got everything else she wanted in life. She was *going* to make this work.

That first night at Rebecca's was nothing. It was on the second visit that Katie began to realize what she was getting herself into. By the third there was no escaping the truth.

Rebecca Greenhall was a triumph of style over sluttiness. In other words, a complete slob.

On day five of her new job, Katie opened the front door and turned off the burglar alarm, knowing pretty much what to expect. She had always thought people tidied up before their cleaners arrived, but – maybe because she was a foreigner – this concept appeared to have passed Rebecca by. Or maybe she *had* tidied? The idea was too frightening to contemplate.

Katie put on the tatty red apron she had discovered on her last visit stuffed at the back of a kitchen drawer and steeled herself for the work ahead.

Task One: Open windows to dispel the cigarette smoke, which hung over the room like a shroud. Rebecca didn't smoke – that must be her boyfriend. Run the dishwasher, even though it contained just three glasses and a dirty ashtray. Wipe down the counter and sweep the floor. Luckily, Rebecca didn't leave a lot of washing up. Either she ate out all the time, or she didn't eat at all.

Task Two: Enter bedroom. Pick up socks still in a concertina where Rebecca had ripped them off, and the shards of burgundy toenails on the bedside rug. Remove a damp towel from the bed and put a mascara-smudged pillow case in the dirty-clothes basket. Didn't Rebecca take her makeup off at night? Or had she been crying? Katie wondered if her boss had any idea how much she knew about her.

Task Three: Go into bathroom; rinse bath clean of splodges of sea-salt exfoliant. She glanced in the chrome cabinet above the loo. Thrush cream, a tube of Zovirax, athlete's foot powder, Clarins fake tan, a packet of razors and twenty-four miniature bottles of shampoo, conditioner and body lotion filched from hotel bathrooms around the world. If Rebecca were to lose all her money tomorrow, she would still have enough freebies to keep her clean-haired and smooth-skinned for the rest of her life.

She would also have enough clothes, enough books and enough aubergine makeup bags that had come as a free gift with two purchases, one to be skincare, from Estée Lauder. For Rebecca, to Katie's surprise, was a hoarder. Her cupboards bulged with crocheted day-glo pink headscarves and her desk drawers overflowed with Christmas cards that said 'Season's Greetings 1997 from All at Shlalwar Tandoori' and newspaper clippings listing the ten best romantic hideaways in Provence. Katie itched to chuck it all out. Perhaps in a couple of months when they knew each other a bit better. But in a couple of months she wouldn't be there.

For now, she decided she would make a start on re-ordering Rebecca's makeup collection. Happily, Katie began to rummage through the dozens of tubes and compacts in a basket by the sink. Prescriptives – maybe this was the perfect foundation she'd been talking about. Using the little triangular sponge, Katie dabbed some all over her face. Perhaps not her colour, but not bad.

What was this mascara? Shisheido. Katie swept some over her eyelashes. It was a pretty violet colour that made her brown eyes sparkle. Oooh. Now. How about trying some of this blusher . . .?

Her mobile was ringing. Katie jumped as if she had been shot. She pulled it out of her pocket. Oh, only Crispin. 'Hiya,' she said.

'Hi, babe.' There were traffic noises. Crispin was probably in a taxi. 'Busy?'

'Of course,' Katie said rather haughtily.

Crispin laughed. 'I thought so. Doing what exactly?'

Trying on her boss's personal possessions. 'Cleaning, obviously.'

Another laugh. 'Poor darling.'

The annoyance which Crispin's innocent remarks so often provoked rippled inside her. 'Just because you're a hotshot barrister and I'm unemployed,' she thought, 'no need to laugh at me.' Which was unfair, she told herself, instantly. Crispin wasn't laughing at her, he genuinely felt sorry for her.

'Look, what time are you finishing?' Crispin asked. 'Because I'm heading down to Mayfair for a meeting. It should end early for once, so I thought I could take you out for dinner. There's this really cool place in Shepherd Market I want to try. It's Mexican-Polish.'

What was it with men and food? Both Crispin and Ronan were obsessed with preparing Gordon Ramsay-style dinners and checking out every new restaurant before the doors had even opened. Katie would have been happy subsisting for the rest of her life on cans of tuna in brine.

'I'm not exactly dressed up,' she said now, looking down at her dirty jeans and trainers. Crispin was a rather traditional chap and although he never actually said anything he clearly preferred Katie in skirts to trousers and he had practically hyperventilated when she once went out in her knee-high patent white boots. 'They're a bit *flashy*,' he had winced, and Katie had put them under her bed and never worn them again.

Now, however, he seemed unbothered. 'Well, I knew you'd be in your cleaning outfit, sweetie. So when shall I see you?'

'I should be finished at six.'

'So, if I meet you in that pub in Shepherd Market? The one round the corner from the cinema where we saw that Bosnian film? Half six. OK?'

'Great.'

Katie cleaned the kitchen, changed Rebecca's duvet cover, dusted and hoovered, although she didn't like the way the red light on the vacuum cleaner winked at her. Her mobile rang again.

Jess.

'What can I do for you?' Katie hadn't seen her cousin since yesterday morning. She'd been stopping out again.

'Oh, Katie. I had the most incredible night.'

'Who with?'

'Well, his name is Antoine. Wait! I know it sounds poncey, but he was incredible.'

'Where did you meet him?'

'At Century.' Century was a club frequented by actors

on Shaftesbury Avenue. 'We were both standing at the bar and he offered to buy me a drink. We ended up getting totally shit-faced and then we went back to his place and it was fabulous.'

'So he could have been anyone?' Katie tried to keep the disapproval out of her voice. Jess swore she always used condoms, but that wouldn't stop her being raped and murdered.

'No, Kate, he couldn't have been *anyone*. He knows Petronella. So it's perfectly cool. *And* he asked for my number. I've got a good feeling about this.'

'That's great,' Katie said soothingly. As she spoke, she was wandering from room to room, emptying the overflowing bins into a black bag. Her call waiting bleeped. *Orla*. Oh shit, she really ought to speak to her.

'Jess, Jess, I have to go. See you later. Good luck! Hi, Orls, how are you?'

'Really well,' said Orla. 'I've just got back from my meditation course.'

'Oh yes, how was it?'

'Wonderful. We got up at four every morning and meditated on and off until lunchtime. I was in bed by nine every night. And we did a total detox, just wheatgrass juice for three days. I feel so much stronger.'

Orla was an old schoolfriend and one of the nicest girls Katie knew. And one of the flakiest too. She had a bit of family money, which meant she had never found a steady job, but instead spent her time on meditation, yoga and basket-weaving courses. Despite all this, Katie thought she was a bit lonely. She hadn't had a steady bloke for *seven years*.

'So I was wondering if you fancied a trip to the cinema?' Orla was saying. 'An early show obviously, because I have to get up at five-thirty for yoga.'

Christ. No wonder Orla was single. As well as the early mornings, she didn't drink or smoke and followed a strict macrobiotic diet which banned not only meat, dairy and wheat, but also tomatoes, aubergines and peppers because they 'came from the deadly nightshade plant'.

'That would be lovely,' Katie said absently. 'Tomorrow could be good. Why don't you check out the listings and call me back. Oh, shit!'

'What?'

The bloody sack had burst, spewing cigarette butts, coffee grounds, shampoo bottles, foundation-streaked scraps of cottonwool, cigarette packs (Peter Stuyvesant – Rebecca's man was obviously a complete pseud), the inside of a toilet roll and half a ton of plastic packaging all over Rebecca's pale floorboards.

'Bollocks, bugger, damn!' Katie cried. 'Orls, I've got a bit of a problem. Don't worry. Nothing serious, but I gotta go. Call me tomorrow.' There was nothing for it. Out with the Hoover. Katie glanced at her watch. She was going to be late for Crispin. Too bad. She pulled the Hoover from the kitchen cupboard, plugged it in and applied the nozzle to the filth.

Nothing happened.

Katie placed her hand against the nozzle. It breathed on her gently, like a sleeping baby. No suction at all. Fuck.

The red light was no longer winking, but on full beam. Katie had a horrible suspicion that the bag was full. But how on earth did she change it? She had never done such a thing in her life. In any case, she didn't remember seeing any bags under the sink. She ran to look. No, nothing. Worse, she had forgotten to buy any more rubbish sacks.

Help. What was she going to do with the garbage? She could sweep it all up and then run out and buy another bin bag, but by then she would be horribly late for Crispin. Worse, Rebecca might come home and catch her in the act. Katie didn't want to spend the rest of her life as a cleaner, but she *really* didn't want to be sacked again.

There was one solution. Katie grabbed a long-handled broom and began sweeping the rubbish towards the sofa. Shove it all under there and pray Rebecca didn't notice. She'd hoover it up when she next visited, on Friday.

Her mobile rang. *Mum*. She pressed the busy button. 'Go away.'

Immediately it rang again. Mum once more. 'Yes?' Katie snapped.

'Is that any way to speak to people?' her mum tutted.

'Mum, I knew it was you. It's called caller-ID.' Minette Wallace knew this quite well. She was the personnel officer for a big glass company in Solihull, in charge of five hundred people, but in the presence of her family she became an Amish housewife, who persisted in claiming coyly she had no idea how to set the video or go online.

'So you knew it was me and you still spoke to me like that?'

'Mum, I'm a bit busy at the moment. So if you don't mind . . .'

'Of course, darling. What are you up to?'

'I'm . . . on my way to a job interview.' There was no way she was telling her mother she was a cleaner.

Mum understood this. 'Oh, I won't keep you. Just reminding you that Dad and I are off to Vietnam on Monday, but before we go I wanted to be sure you and Crispin are coming for the Easter weekend.'

'Er, when is Easter?'

'Katie, I've told you a dozen times. It's April twentieth. So?'

Katie felt a little trapped. She hated the way Mum was always trying to commit her and Crispin to things. To be honest, she didn't entirely enjoy bringing Crispin home. Mum always laughed too loudly at his jokes, fluttered her eyelashes as she asked him to move a heavy table from the conservatory to the living room and oohed and aahed when he insisted on cooking something fancy for dinner. 'I wish you'd teach Katie to cook, Crispin,' she'd cooed once.

'No point,' Katie pointed out. 'Between him and Ronan I never get a chance to go into the kitchen.'

'Yes,' said Minette Wallace. 'But you won't be living with Ronan for ever.' And she had actually *winked*.

At least Dad behaved himself, all but ignoring Crispin, unless it was to discuss the football scores. For the first year of their relationship, he had called him Paul – that was, if he'd called him anything at all. At the time Katie had been furious, but looking back it was quite funny.

'So?' Mum prompted again.

'So I don't know, Mum. But I'm seeing Crispin tonight, so I'll ask him. Get back to you tomorrow, I promise.'

'Seeing him tonight? Well, send him my love.'

'What about my interview?' Katie asked, annoyed that

her mother had forgotten already, even though it didn't exist.

'Oh yes, good luck with that, darling. Speak tomorrow. Oh, and Elton sends his love. Bye.'

Elton was the family's elderly cocker spaniel and, Katie sometimes thought, the true love of her life. Crispin was a bit nervous around him, holding out his fist and mumbling, 'Good doggie.' He had been frightened of dogs since childhood, when he had been bitten by his neighbour's pug. Katie had made understanding noises when he told her this, but privately she couldn't help thinking he was a bit of a wuss.

Ten minutes later, the rubbish had been hidden and Katie could leave. She arrived at the pub sweating.

'What happened to Katie?' laughed Crispin, sitting in the corner with his pint of bitter. 'Your hair's all over the place. And why are your eyelashes that funny colour?'

Crispin. Once, the sight of his handsome profile would have been enough to cheer Katie instantly. They had met three years ago at a party. Katie had given him her number, then declined to return any of his calls for two weeks. When eventually she went out with him, she pecked him on the cheek at the end of the evening and rushed indoors.

She didn't snog him until the third date and didn't sleep with him for a month. And although the sex wasn't amazing – the first night Crispin couldn't get it up and the second he came in about five seconds – Katie told herself these things developed with time.

Crispin agreed. He had gone out and bought a pile of sex manuals, since when he had developed a fixation with finding Katie's G spot. They spent hours with him bending her into one position after the other, like members of the Moscow State Circus, until one night when she was lying on her back in relative comfort she had lied and said that he had it. Crispin was far too much of a gentleman to come before she did, so since then she had become an expert at faking it.

Sometimes Katie minded this but she reminded herself that the ripping-each-other's-pants-off-with-your-teeth phase never lasted more than a few months, and after that sex was only a cosy thing. Everyone knew that, even if they didn't admit it. Far more mature to embark on a relationship this way than in the heat of passion. It was the difference between taking a pizza out of the freezer and chucking it in the microwave or letting it defrost overnight and placing it in a pre-heated oven for twenty minutes. Actually, Katie couldn't see what was wrong with the first method, but Ronan assured her the second was much better.

Nearly three years later, much of Katie was still captivated by Crispin's beauty. Not that his looks were the only thing he had going for him. He was kind, he was clever and, best of all, he was *safe*. Katie knew that he would always love her unquestioningly and never betray her. Crispin was as faithful as a killer whale, as he frequently reminded her. 'They mate for life and so do I,' he would proclaim, looking deep into her eyes. 'I saw a documentary on Discovery.'

She hated herself, but when he said it she sometimes felt like blowing a huge raspberry in his face. Not that she didn't appreciate the sentiments, but the soppy expression on his face could be a bit much.

'So tell me about your day?' he asked now.

She told him and he laughed, and ruffled her curls and told her how cute she was, and admonished her for taking this job.

'I don't like Katie when she's stressed,' he said, kissing her. 'I like Katie when she's happy. Why doesn't Katie move in with me and stop this ridiculous cleaning nonsense. I'll look after her.'

'I can't,' Katie said sincerely. 'You know I've signed a lease until next June. We've promised the landlord that we three and no others will live in the flat until then. If I moved out the others would be seriously out of pocket.'

They had had this argument before and Crispin had offered to pay the rent on her flat until June, but Katie had said that would make her feel like a kept woman.

'I know, darling,' Crispin smiled. 'You're so independent. Now, what would you like to drink?'

'Vodka and tonic. And crisps. Salt and vinegar, please.' Crispin wrinkled his nose at her plebeian tastes, but still got up and pushed his way through the after-work crowd to the bar. Suddenly Katie felt tired. To be honest, she would rather be at home with Ronan and Jess, or in Pizza Express having dinner with some mates, than sitting in a pub bracing herself to hear all about Crispin's day.

Immediately, she reprimanded herself. She had a man who adored her, would make a great husband and a wonderful father. So what if it wasn't always perfect? Would she rather end up like Jess or Orla?

Still, there was one thing worse than not being in a couple and that was to be in a *couple* couple. Cuddled on the sofa in front of *Cold Feet*. Holding coupley dinner parties for other couples. The dullness of it made Katie shudder. Besides, you should never rely too much on another person. You had so much to lose if it went wrong. Not that Crispin would ever leave her, but suppose he . . . *died* . . . or something? One of the few things that had kept her going after she broke up with Paul, the love of her life, was that she hadn't ignored her friends and they were still there for her.

That was why Katie insisted she and Crispin both made plenty of time for their mates. When he spent Saturdays scouring antique markets for the perfect lampshade, she and Jess would be pursuing the ultimate pair of shoes on the King's Road. When she wanted to stay in and watch *Top 100 TV Personalities*, he went clubbing. That way, both of them enjoyed the benefits of the single life, with none of the horrors of one-night stands and waiting for the phone to ring. Katie couldn't understand why everyone didn't play it their way.

Crispin returned with the drinks and began talking about his day: clients, clerks, a new case dumped on him this afternoon that he had to have prepared by first thing Monday.

'So I'll have to work most of the weekend. Do you mind?'

'Of course not.' Katie was used to it.

'That's what I need,' she thought, as, loosened up by his second pint, Crispin continued to chat. 'A proper job. Then I'd have some self-respect. The only reason I pick holes in our relationship is because I'm not happy with myself. It's got nothing to do with Crispin. It's me.'

She resolved to spend the weekend scouring the

Guardian for jobs. In the meantime, though, she needed to remember to buy some more Hoover bags. And to learn how to bloody replace them.

'But I have got some good news,' Crispin was saying.

'Oh?'

'Guess who we're going to see?'

'Don't know.'

Crispin grinned, enjoying keeping her on tenterhooks. 'The Boss!'

'The . . . who?' She knew Crispin loved his work, but why was he getting so excited about going to see Colin Dickenson – was that his name? – the portly head of his chambers.

'Oh, Katie! *You* know. The Boss. Bruce.'

'Oh!' In the early days of their relationship, Katie had tried to make Crispin happy by pretending she loved Bruce Springsteen.

'That's great,' she lied now. 'When?'

'Easter Saturday. He's playing Wembley. The tickets were like gold dust, but I was determined to get them for my Katie.'

'Oh, Crispin, that's so sweet of you.' *Easter Saturday, so I can use that as an excuse to get out of going to Mum and Dad's. Every cloud had a silver lining.*

He grinned proudly. 'Shall we go and eat?'

Watching his excited face, Katie was suddenly overwhelmed with guilt. God she was an ungrateful old moose. She was very, very lucky to have this man.

'What would I do without you?' she said, planting a big kiss on Crispin's cheek.

6

When people met Crispin, a certain look would come over their faces. Katie recognized it well. It said: 'How did *she* manage to hook *him*?'

She didn't mind; in fact, she found it funny. Because while Katie had fairly average looks and brains, the one field in which she reigned supreme was getting her man.

It hadn't always been so. At school, Katie was not the girl everybody fell in love with – that role was reserved for long-legged Lisa Thomson. The teenage Katie had a nice smile and nice tits, but she had stumpy legs and greasy skin. She spent a lot of time shopping for trousers and applying spot creams that burned holes in her face and stained her duvet cover yellow.

Katie learned about playing hard to get two months after her fourteenth birthday, when she snogged Matthew Williams at a party. The following day she called him, but his brother said he was out. She left her number, then, after a few hours when he hadn't called back, tried again. Then again, and again. Matthew was always out, although once she thought she heard giggling in the background. After a week of it, she gave up. The next time she saw him at a party, he was standing with a group of his mates, drinking cider from plastic bottles. As she walked past they all started to laugh. 'Slag,' one of them whispered.

That was it. From then on Katie determined never to

open herself to humiliation. She learned always to be the one to back off first. Although her schooldays were marked by a series of passionate crushes, she never admitted them to anyone. At the school disco, when the school hunk Richard Bedford asked her to slow-dance to Spandau Ballet's 'True', then slow-dance she would. But as Tony Hadley's honking vocals faded into Lionel Richie bleating about Endless Love, she would smile, say she needed to get a drink, and disappear into the crowd.

When boys rang her after school, she got her little brother, Nick, to tell them she was out. When they turned up at the front door, she slipped out the back. She got back to them eventually, of course, but was vague about what she had been doing and where she had been (usually watching telly and eating her way through tubs of ice cream at Orla's house – in the days before veganism had struck).

Katie messed around the boys, but she was true to the girls. Boys came, boys went, but your friends were always there for you, and Katie was determined always to be there for them. If she had an arrangement with a friend, then it took priority over any night out with any bloke. Well, not Richard Bedford, she admitted to herself, but even he would have to book well in advance.

No one else was as strong-willed. Katie would fume when Orla blew out a trip to the cinema in favour of an evening sitting on the steps of the war memorial, sharing Marlboros, with some bloke from the year above. It wasn't personal – there was always someone else to go to the movies with. What got Katie was the fact that by dropping everything for a guy, Orla was playing right into his hands. It wouldn't happen the other way round, Katie pointed out, but she still tried hard to swallow the 'I told you sos' when a few weeks later Orla was dumped and sobbing. No wonder she had ended up having her most meaningful relationship with a yoga mat.

By the end of college, Katie had had two relationships of more than a year. She had ended both of them. In between, there had been the occasional fling. Sometimes the guy had wanted it to go further, sometimes Katie had. But if the call never came, she just left it. If it was meant to be, it was meant to be, she decided. And usually they did call her. Since Katie had gone on the pill, her teenage spots had gone and her bosom had become even more impressive. She was twenty-three, new to London, without a care in the world and in truth starting to be a little pleased with herself.

Then she met Paul.

The first time Katie encountered her nemesis was in the pub after work. He was a junior reporter at *Channel Update*, where Katie was working as a secretary. Eventually she planned to work her way up to presenter, but she was too young and optimistic to worry remotely about how she would climb the ladder. She was eager to enter the world of work, with its thrilling rituals of dropping off suits at dry-cleaners, buying sandwiches at Prêt and ringing friends to tell them self-importantly she was 'working late' and would have to cancel.

Paul was of average height, a bit plumper than Katie would have considered ideal, but then her last fling had had a big bum and she had found she enjoyed grabbing on to it. Katie liked the way Paul's brown curls clung to his forehead in damp tendrils. It wasn't love at first sight, although Katie was later to kid herself otherwise. But she did fancy him like crazy.

Which meant that when she was introduced to him by Jeevan, a jolly producer, Katie smiled, shook his hand, then turned her back and spent the rest of the evening deep in conversation with Marina, a researcher.

In the weeks to come, Katie observed Paul around the office. She liked his bouncy walk and the way that his tongue poked slightly through his lips when he grinned. She had no idea what he thought of her. Once she caught his eye and he smiled, but he smiled at everyone. Still, in her experience, only losers made it clear they liked you.

Before the Christmas party, Katie tried on at least fifteen outfits, before settling on a predictable black dress. When it came to clothes, Katie modelled herself on Rachel from *Friends* – pretty not trendy, sexy but not slutty. She could never understand girls who insisted on wearing high fashion: guys simply didn't get it.

She arrived deliberately late. As soon as she walked into the decorated boardroom, she spotted him, dancing badly in a dodgy brown leather jacket. Chemicals started stampeding round her body. She ignored him all night, laughed loudly with plenty of other men, and when the after-party crowd was milling around working out who could get them all into the Groucho Club, she slipped away.

Around the office, she listened for smidgens of gossip.

'Phwoar, just look at that girl,' moaned Jeevan. He and Katie were having lunch in the canteen, which *Update* shared with several other companies. His eyes were fixed on a round bottom bending over the salad bar. 'She's an account executive at the ad agency on the seventh floor. God, would I like to give her one. That lucky bastard Paul Grant's had her. He gets all the beautiful women. What's his secret?'

It was the kind of news that usually made Katie back right off. Lotharios. Who needed them? But, oddly, today it just made her feel competitive. She was prettier than her rival, younger too, and her arse was perfectly presentable.

'Paul Grant's in lerv,' said Marina a couple of weeks later, as they drifted round Hennes in their lunch hour. 'She's French. Lives in Paris. Apparently he's thinking of jacking it all in and going to live there.'

Still, Katie was strangely calm. Somehow she knew Paul was her destiny.

If she ever thought about it, she cringed. What had she been thinking of, setting out to steal another woman's man? But Paul had had that effect on her, of making her do insane things.

Her policy of doing absolutely nothing – not a flirtatious smile, not an email – paid off. About two weeks later *Update* had a reshuffle. Katie was moved on to the current affairs desk where Paul was sitting two chairs away. They couldn't have been spending more time together if they were married.

Katie's new job meant answering everyone's phone calls, giving her plenty of time to monitor Paul's love life. An annoyingly sexy French voice would ask for him at least three times a day. He spent an inordinate amount of time on the Internet, checking out cheap flights and deals on the Eurostar.

Katie never asked him any questions. When she knew

he was listening she would call up her girlfriends and have giggly chats about her plans for the weekend, making it quite clear that she led a fun and interesting life. When Paul spoke to her she was pleasant, but no more than to anyone else.

After ten days' working together he casually asked if she fancied a spot of lunch.

'Why not?' she said.

They went to Nino's brasserie, where she ordered a burger and chips.

'God, a woman who eats,' he said approvingly. 'I like that.'

Of course you do, that's why I ordered all this crap. By the same token, she nodded enthusiastically when Paul suggested a bottle of wine, although booze at lunchtime sent her to sleep.

Since all they had in common was work, that was what they talked about.

'*Update* is a pretty good place to work,' he told her. 'I actually took a pay cut to come here. Though naturally, it's not what I want long term.'

'What *do* you want?'

'A foreign posting,' he said, not catching her eye. 'Something with Radio 4 maybe. We'll see.'

'Plenty of time for that,' said Katie.

'Not that much. I'm getting on a bit, you know.'

'Why? How old are you?'

'I'm thirty-two.'

Katie was surprised and told him so. She had thought he was about twenty-seven. He accepted the compliment with a nod and a smile. He'd obviously heard it before.

She wasn't bothered by the age gap, in fact she liked the idea of an older man.

By the end of the meal she knew he fancied her. The clue was in the conversation. Done with work, they talked about books, films, television programmes, favourite holiday destinations.

Not once did Paul mention he had a girlfriend.

'Jackpot!' thought Katie. 'Friends talk about their other halves. Men who pretend to have no private life want to shag you.'

As they walked back, Paul was rather silent.

The following morning when she came in an email was waiting.

Would you like to go to the cinema tomorrow night?

Her stomach somersaulted but she sat perfectly still. She would not look at him, although she could feel his eyes studying her. She opened her other emails, dealt with her voicemail, went to the canteen to buy a round of teas and on her return replied:

Sorry. Busy tomorrow. Another time.

The reply came immediately. *Monday?* He could have suggested Friday, Saturday or Sunday, but such obvious date nights would be a bit too much.

After ten minutes, she wrote:

Wednesday would be better.

So Wednesday it was, giving Katie an entire week in which to depilate, exfoliate, apply fake tan and then remove it with toothpaste when it went streaky and orange. She went to the gym every night and ate nothing but brown rice and vegetables.

'Something's up,' Jess remarked.

'It could be,' Katie said coyly.

When Wednesday came Paul had to work late, so Katie hung around the office pretending she was busy too. It was a cold February night. They took a taxi from their offices in Kensington to the West End. They were running a bit late, but they decided there was still time to nip into the pub for a quick drink.

They drank and talked about work until half an hour later Katie glanced at her watch.

'Shit! The film! It's started.'

As if she would ever *really* forget the time.

By the time Paul suggested they got something to eat, Katie was pretty drunk. They climbed into another taxi and within a few minutes they were at the Café Flo in Islington.

Paul lived just round the corner.

So it started as these things always do with a suggestion, after dinner, of a nightcap. Paul's flat was on the second floor of a Georgian terrace, with high ceilings and a huge living room furnished with a tatty old sofa and a long, oak dining table covered in piles of paper and books. In the corner, Katie noticed the answerphone light was winking. Paul didn't look at it.

'Drink?'

'Beer, please,' Katie fibbed. It was the kind of thing men liked to hear.

'Sorry,' came Paul's voice from the kitchen. 'No beer. Bottle of champagne cooling nicely though.'

He must have put it there that morning.

They sat on the sofa, listening to Paul's Oasis CDs, smoking, talking more about the office and trying hard to appear nonchalant, as if it were quite normal to be drunk on a colleague's sofa at 2 a.m. during the week.

Normally at this point Katie would have announced she was leaving, but tonight she decided it was time to break her rules.

'So where do your parents live?' she slurred.

'They're divorced,' said Paul, getting up to put on a CD. 'My dad lives in the South of France with his girlfriend. Mum's in Suffolk.'

As he sat down again, his hand brushed against her arm. She didn't move away.

'Whereabouts in Suffolk?'

'Near Southwold,' he said.

Katie's mouth was completely dry. The only thing that would relieve it was Paul kissing her. 'Is it . . . pretty . . .' she couldn't remember the name of the place she was supposed to be talking about ' . . . there?'

Paul turned to look at her. 'It's . . . OK,' he muttered.

There was a long pause.

Katie struggled to keep her mind on the conversation. 'And what . . .?' She glanced up and caught Paul's eye. For a moment neither of them moved. Then they leaned towards each other and kissed.

That was it. Katie closed her eyes and ran her fingers through his damp hair. She could smell soap mixed with a faint overtone of sweat. His mouth moved in rhythm with hers, first slowly, then greedily. They stopped for a moment. Paul removed his glasses. Without them his face looked vulnerable. He blinked.

It was one of those miracles, where you like someone and they like you back. Katie started to laugh.

'What's so funny?' Paul asked, suddenly anxious.

She laughed some more. 'Nothing. I'm just happy.'

Paul looked at her intently. Then he smiled. 'Good,' he whispered.

They carried on kissing for what seemed like several hours. Katie was hypnotized. When she opened her eyes she was surprised to see a TV listings guide from a Sunday paper stuffed down the side of the sofa and to hear the boiler humming.

Suddenly the tempo changed. Katie pushed Paul back against the sofa, then straddled him. Paul undid the button on her jacket and it fell to the floor. She loosened his tie and fumblingly unbuttoned his shirt. He pulled off her T-shirt. Hastily Katie removed the less-than-flattering flesh-coloured bra she had put on that morning as part of a bargain with God ('If I wear sexy underwear, nothing'll happen'). He ran his hands up and down her body, massaging her hip bones, lightly stroking her breasts. He took off his shirt. She tugged at his belt, he pulled off her lycra skirt.

She wiggled out of her tights (no stockings had also been part of the celestial pledge) and he began kissing her again, then rolled her over so she was now underneath. She grabbed at his arse, he tugged so hard at her knickers (white and plain) that they ripped. Katie started to laugh again. After a second, Paul joined her.

Then the laughing stopped. Paul turned Katie over so she was kneeling against the sofa. She heard him unzip his trousers. Gently he pulled her legs apart. Suddenly he was inside her.

He was surprisingly small, Katie thought with a start. But it didn't matter. It didn't matter at all.

It was six in the morning when they stopped. For an hour they pretended to sleep. Then Paul reached out for her and slowly Katie felt his hand creep up her leg and brush her tummy.

'Hello,' he whispered.

'Hello,' she breathed.

He rolled on top of her and brushed his lips against her.

'Ministers say that asylum seekers must . . .'

'Shit,' said Paul, reaching over Katie to the clock radio. 'Bloody alarm. Not that I need to get up. I'm on the late shift.'

Katie, however, was due at work in an hour. She showered and pulled yesterday's clothes off the floor. Her chin throbbed. By the end of the day she would have a terrible stubble rash. But for now she glowed with excess endorphins. Paul came to the door in his dressing-gown and kissed her for a long time before he would let her leave.

She was half an hour late for work, but at *Update* they were fairly relaxed about that kind of thing. It was an all-male team today so nobody noticed she stank of booze and fags. Not that Katie cared. She should have been knackered but she had never felt more alert in her life. She laughed uproariously at her colleagues' jokes and charmed all callers. Her lunchtime sandwich was so delicious she could barely swallow it. As she was queuing for coffee in the canteen or drawing up the rota, a sudden flashback of

Paul's naked body entwined around hers would come into her head and she would gasp aloud.

Then, at about two, she took a call.

'Hello, *Update*!'

'Hellooo,' said a French woman. 'May I spik with Paul, please?'

It was as if Katie had been punched in the stomach.

'He's not in yet.'

'OK.' A soft chuckle. 'I try him at home.'

Katie had been pretty sure this woman – Aline, her name was – was still on the scene. After all, there had been no office gossip to the effect that she wasn't. But she had willed herself to forget about her. After all, Katie was here in London, while Aline was in Paris. After last night, Katie was even more confident that she was going to win.

She laughed and joked with the others some more, and was giggling when she picked up the phone again at half past four.

'*Update*!' She flicked a Hula Hoop at Jeevan who had his tongue firmly lodged in his left nostril.

'You're always laughing, aren't you?'

Paul.

'Just checking in. Anything I should know about?'

'Not really,' she giggled as Jeevan tried to snatch the Hula Hoop packet out of her hands. 'All quiet today.'

'Good. You must be shattered. Christ, I've been asleep all day.'

'Glad to hear it. See you later, Paul.'

This was the key time. She was going to keep her cool. She was going to act as if nothing had happened. And if bloody Aline called she would put her straight through, no questions asked. If she sat back and held tight, she and Paul would be together. It was fate.

Katie didn't usually believe in that kind of crap, but the problem was that although she would rather have gnawed through her own elbow than told him, she was in love with Paul. How did she know? Because in the months to come, whenever she thought about him, which was about 83 per cent of the time, it was like a fountain leaping inside her. Sometimes it was a good feeling, it gave her a spring in her step – but it also made her feel a bit sick.

For the next two years Katie was to spend much of her time in this state of nausea. At the end of them she was thinner, wiser, and her dreams of being a newscaster had long evaporated.

But there was another, more important change.

Katie Wallace no longer believed in love.

7

Looking back on it, Katie could never quite work out when the whole thing had turned sour. The last year of the relationship was misery, of course. But then the six months before that had been pretty dodgy too. Which left her and Paul six months of perfect happiness.

At least, they had seemed happy. At the time.

But in retrospect, those early days were tainted too. All the warning signs had been there; Katie had just been too young and naive to notice them.

Perhaps there had been a couple of days when everything had been perfect between them. The day after their first night together Paul strolled into the office at six. Katie had just wrapped a scarf around her blistered chin. 'Hi,' they said pleasantly to each other and Katie was out the door.

The following morning, she had email.

Sunday lunch?

Mercifully, Paul was on lates for the next couple of days so work was not the ordeal it might have been. Every evening Katie left shortly after he arrived. Regular applications of Eight Hour cream throughout the day got rid of the snog rash. As for Aline, Katie wasn't dumb enough to believe Paul had already broken the news to her, but she was certainly strangely silent. Or then again, maybe she just knew he was on nights.

On Sunday, Katie was ten minutes late to meet Paul at a café in Soho. She saw him through the window, reading the *Sunday Times*, and wearing his nasty brown leather jacket from the Christmas party. She was touched. It was obviously his results outfit and, to be fair, it had worked. They each had a plate of pasta and shared a bottle of red wine before going to see a very bad film starring Eddie Murphy and an alsatian. Not that it mattered, they could have been at the premiere of *Casablanca* and Katie would still have spent it listening to Paul breathing and trying to control her heartbeat when his elbow brushed hers.

Afterwards, there was no discussion. They got into a cab and went to his place. Paul unlocked the door and Katie walked ahead of him into the living room, throwing her bag on to the sofa as he switched on the light. As she turned, he caught her and they kissed awkwardly, her arm twisted into his body. Katie was heavy with desire, her head felt muffled with cottonwool. It was as if she was drugged.

And looking back on it, Katie realized that was exactly what she was. It was all bloody pheromones making her feel that way. Something in Paul's skin reacting with something in hers. They may have performed degrading and possibly illegal acts on each other but it wasn't as if they *knew* each other.

Paul's knees had carpet burn from last time, so he spread out a duvet on the living-room floor. They spent the rest of the evening there. In between energetic bouts of sex, they lay there and talked, once more about the office.

'Jeevan's nice,' Katie said.

'He's a bastard,' said Paul, stroking her hair. 'He's out

to shaft anyone who gets in his way. I've known him since university.'

'Where was that?'

'Oxford,' he said. It figured.

'Well, I like him. I'm a bit scared of Giles Plimmer though.' Giles was the station's boss and Paul often went drinking with him.

'Oh, Giles is a pussy cat. Don't be frightened of him.'

The question of Aline never arose, and there was no way Katie was going to ask. At about ten she went home. Paul asked her to stay, but it was too early in the relationship for that. Having slept with him far earlier than she intended, Katie was still struggling to follow her game plan.

But on Thursday night, she relented. On Saturday she did the same and she spent most of Sunday at Paul's too. She preferred to be at his place, away from Jess's inquisitive eyes.

Two weeks passed. Nearly every night they met each other after work, consumed a quick meal, then took a taxi back to his place. The love-making went on for hours. One Thursday, they lay next to each other in the dark, very still.

'I'll be away this weekend,' said Paul.

'OK,' she said.

It would be normal practice to ask where he was going. Katie refused. The best policy, she knew, was to remain completely unmoved. He would go to Paris, he would sleep with Aline because he was clearly too much of a coward to cancel their weekend together. But he would miss Katie. After this weekend he would be hers alone.

That weekend, she had a lot of fun with Jess and

refused even to think of what Paul might be doing. It was surprisingly easy.

'Did you have a good time?' she asked when he got back.

'Yes,' Paul said, looking troubled. He brightened. 'I went ice skating.'

What on earth was Katie supposed to make of all this? Did Paul seriously think she didn't know about Aline? Did he think she had no interest at all in where he disappeared to for the weekend? Did he honestly think she'd believe he had gone to some mysterious destination alone, in order to visit an ice rink?

She should have been upset; oddly, she was amused.

'Sounds like fun,' she said.

Her indifference worked. Paul seemed more smitten than ever. Men love women who don't nag, who don't ask questions, Katie thought. At work, whenever she looked up he was staring at her. He sent her suggestive emails. He asked her to go away with him for the weekend.

'Getting serious?' Jess asked excitedly on the Thursday evening as Katie – on an increasingly rare night at home – packed her weekend bag.

'Of course not,' Katie smiled. She hadn't told her about Aline: Jess would think she'd gone insane.

They went to Devon, stayed in a posh hotel, and spent all of Saturday in their room, much to the maid's frustration. On Sunday they finally ventured out for a walk. In a dreamy bubble, they wandered through the pretty village, then took a footpath out along the cliffs and climbed down a steep staircase cut in the rock to a deserted stony beach.

It was grey and chilly. Katie was wearing a long coat. Paul slipped his hand under the lapels and up her jumper. She unfastened his jeans. They put her coat on the hard ground and lay there, caressing each other. It was murder on Katie's back and bum, but she persevered. Paul was just about to enter her when they were engulfed in freezing salt water. The tide had started coming in. Giggling and soaked, they clambered back to their feet.

'I'm in love with you,' thought Katie, watching Paul's large bottom wobbling back up the cliff ahead of her. They sat in a tearoom and ate scones. She thought her heart might burst with emotion. But how could you love someone you had only slept with thirteen times? Katie didn't know Paul's friends or family, he didn't know hers. But how else could she explain this feeling?

Reluctantly she acknowledged it was time to talk about Aline. If she never mentioned it Paul would think she was an imbecile. It wasn't as if he was hiding the situation from her to deceive her. He was simply embarrassed to confess he already had a girlfriend, whom, to give Aline her due, he probably did like a lot.

Although not as much as he liked Katie. That much was obvious from the way he was with her.

In the car on the way home she sat in the dark watching Paul's snubby profile illuminated by the motorway lights. The radio was playing the Top 40. His eyes were fixed on the road. It would be easier to have this conversation if they didn't have to make eye contact. All the same, by the time she brought the subject up, they were getting dangerously close to London.

'Paul, I know you have a girlfriend.'

Her voice sounded squeaky and faraway. His profile was quite still. The songs continued to play.

'Paul?'

'Yes?'

'Did you think I didn't know? Everybody knows.'

Silence.

'What happened when you went to Paris last weekend?'

There was another long pause. For the first time since she had known him Katie felt her feet turning to blocks of ice. In the months to come she would get used to it.

'I'm sorry, Katie. I've behaved like a twat. I should have talked to you. But I didn't want to spoil things.'

The music played on.

'When I met Aline I thought I was in love with her. But then I met you. And it was amazing. Katie, you're bright. You're caring. You make me laugh – and that's important, you know.' He glanced at her. 'And the sex is the best I've ever had.' His gaze returned to the road.

'But?' Her heart was headbutting against her ribcage.

'No but. You're the person I want to be with.' He gave out a high-pitched giggle like a girl. 'But I'm scared. Aline wants to marry me. She's in her thirties. Other guys have let her down. I don't know what she'd do if I ended it.'

'So you thought you'd just screw me behind her back?'

He looked at her again. This time there was genuine anguish in his round face. Suddenly Katie could see what he would look like when he was an old man.

'No! Katie, it wasn't like that. When I met you I knew I wanted to be with you all the time. But I just can't bear to hurt Aline. I'm a very sensitive person.'

'But Paul,' said Katie, 'you're going to have to tell her some time.'

'I know. But she's coming over here the weekend after next. She's bought her ticket and everything. I don't know how I can put her off.'

'But you have to!'

'I know,' he sighed. 'I will. I'll do it on the phone.' His voice brightened. 'Or maybe by email.'

'Paul, you can't do it by email!' A thought occurred to her. 'How come Aline gives you so much leeway? Why does she never call your mobile? Where does she think you are this weekend?'

'She doesn't call my mobile because she doesn't know I have one. And she thinks I'm spending this weekend at my mother's.'

Katie couldn't remember exactly how the conversation ended, but basically Paul promised he would tell Aline as soon as possible. Then they decided that rather than return to their flats that night they would check into a hotel and spend the night there. In the morning, they would get up early and go straight to work.

Years later, when it was all over, Katie realized why Paul did not want to take her home that night. God knows how many messages Aline would have left for him.

In the tiny bedroom of the Brewer's Motel on the A40, Paul tore Katie's clothes off and threw her on to the slippery brown duvet, kissing her more passionately than ever.

She couldn't help it, she really couldn't. It popped out of nowhere.

'Oh. I do love you.'

Paul stopped kissing her. For a long time he looked searchingly into her face.

'And I love you,' he whispered eventually. 'From the first moment I saw you.'

For the whole of the following week Katie was very, very happy. Paul told her he had some difficult phone calls to make. Jess was off filming a mini-series in Northumbria, so they fell into a new pattern where he would turn up late at her place, looking stressed. Katie never asked, but it was clear he had been on the phone to Aline. It couldn't be easy. But after a few moments in bed with her, Paul would know he was doing the right thing.

They spent the weekend holed up at her place, watching videos and shagging.

'By the way,' whispered Paul as they lay intertwined on Sunday night, 'I won't be around next weekend.'

She said nothing. *Men like a woman who's restful, who never makes a fuss, who doesn't interfere.*

He blustered on. 'I have to go and see my mum.'

8

It was Monday. Katie had spent the weekend circling promising-sounding jobs in the *Guardian* and the morning sending off her CV to potential employers. Not that she'd spotted anything particularly appealing, but a girl needed a job.

Because she couldn't carry on doing this much longer, she thought, opening Rebecca's front door.

'Oh my God!' shrieked Jess. 'It stinks in here!'

So much for Katie's attempts to keep Jess out. Her cousin had been adamant that if she wanted to learn how to change the Hoover bag she would have to demonstrate in person. Annoyingly, Katie had been unable to practise at home, because they had a Dyson.

'It doesn't need bags,' Ronan had explained with a grin. 'As you might know if you had ever used it.'

So Jess had got what she wanted, a snoop round Rebecca's fabulous pad. Not that Katie really minded. It was no fun working for Rebecca unless you had someone to share the experience with.

After the weekend, the place was even worse than usual. There were overflowing ashtrays everywhere. The kitchen sink was full of cold water. A scummy layer of fat floated on the top, beneath lay assorted knives, spatulas and pans. Tim had clearly enjoyed a monster Sunday fry-up.

'Do you think Rebecca ate any of that, or did she just

watch?' Katie asked, but Jess wasn't listening, having just opened the fridge door.

'Jesus!'

'I know,' said Katie, standing behind her. Rebecca's fridge contained twenty eye and lip pencils, a dozen face creams, two eye masks and seven bottles of perfume. There were also three bottles of vodka, two of white wine, an elderly jar of mango chutney, some curry paste, a bluish lump of parmesan and – in the vegetable drawer – a bag of rotten spinach.

'Sell-by date: 19 March. That was nearly a month ago!'

Katie shrugged. 'Now do you envy me my job?'

But Jess had rushed out of the kitchen and into the living room, where she was inspecting the rows of thick white invitations on the mantelpiece. Most were to weddings and christenings: a good number, however, were to exciting parties.

'Christian Dior,' she read. 'Wow! That party's in Paris. Do you think she'll go?' She picked up what looked like a parking ticket. 'The Twigz album launch! How cool is that? And to just leave it lying around, like that! It's like she's so popular she doesn't *care*.'

'It's not about popularity, it's her job. And I shouldn't think for a second she does care about Twigz.'

'Do you think she won't go then?'

'Well, the invite is for Friday night and if you look carefully you'll see that's also the night she's been invited to Celine Harper's birthday party. Now, which one would *you* choose?'

'But that's brilliant. That means the Twigz invitation is up for grabs.'

Katie looked at her suspiciously. 'Meaning?'

'Well, if Rebecca isn't going to use it then we might as well take it.'

'Jess, we can't! It isn't ours.'

'But if Rebecca doesn't want it . . .'

'*You* can't have it.'

Jess gave her cheekiest grin. 'Oh well.' Her eyes fell on her cousin who was piling cocktail glasses into the dishwasher. 'Katie, what are you doing?'

'Loading the dishwasher.'

'You can't put cocktail glasses in there, idiot. They're far too fragile.'

'Oh, OK.' Katie removed them, put them into the sink and started running the hot tap.

'No! That water's boiling!' Jess was too late. With a sickening snap, the glasses split in two.

'Oh, Kate! Now you're going to have to replace them.'

Katie was stunned. 'How did that happen?'

'You can't put delicate glasses in hot water. They're like dry-clean only. You have to take care.'

'God, rich people!' Katie exclaimed. 'Imagine buying glasses you can't wash up.'

'You're crap at this. Why isn't it my job?'

'As soon as I get some proper work, you can have it. Anyway, you've got to prove you can do it yourself. Show me how to change the bloody Hoover bag.'

'In a minute. First I want the grand tour.' Jess wandered into the bedroom. 'Oh, hello!'

Katie followed her. 'Jess!' Her cousin was leafing through the wardrobe with the practised hand of a car boot sale regular. 'Don't!'

'Why not?' asked Jess, wrapping an embroidered pashmina around her neck and using it to give the mirror a polish. 'It's such a dump in here. She's hardly going to notice.'

Katie snatched the pashmina away. 'Those are so last year, darling. I'll give you a tip. Rebecca never puts away anything she actually wears. All her favourite things are in a pile on the floor. The wardrobe is strictly for fashion mistakes.'

Ten minutes later Jess was a vision in a black Vivienne Westwood bustier and a Gucci leather skirt, even if her face was a little purple from holding her tummy in. 'Shoes, shoes, I need shoes,' she cried, scrabbling under the bed where an Imelda Marcos collection was housed. 'What size is Rebecca?'

'Five. Smaller than you.'

'Bugger. Well, I should be able to squeeze my feet in. I . . .' Jess let out a bloodcurdling shriek.

'What?'

She emerged from under the bed, her face wrinkled in disgust. 'Oh my God, Katie. Look what I *found*.'

She held out a used orange condom. Katie burst out laughing.

'It's not funny. Where's the bin? I put my hand on it. It was all slimy. Yuk. God knows how old it is. There's probably a prime specimen of Kurt Cobain's sperm in there. If you found a turkey baster you could have his love child.'

They giggled. And then they heard the door slam.

They froze.

'Who is it?' Jess whispered.

'Must be Rebecca.' Katie looked desperately around the room for a hiding place.

'What are we going to do?'

Through the half-open door they heard keys flung on the floor, then the thud of Rebecca's leather coat landing beside them. Then came the low sound of sobbing.

'Stay here,' Katie mouthed. Jess nodded in terrified agreement. Slowly, making as much noise as possible to give Rebecca maximum warning, Katie walked out into the living room.

Rebecca was sitting on the sofa, weeping into a velvet cushion. At the sight of Katie she looked up briefly, sniffed loudly, then continued to cry.

'Rebecca. Are you all right?'

From the depths of the cushion came a snuffle.

'Rebecca, what is it?'

A few more sobs and then, 'Ti- i-im.'

'Oh, Rebecca. What's happened?'

Rebecca's face contorted with anguish. 'He ... he ...'

'He what?'

'He was going to see me tonight. But now he can't.' A yelp of pain.

Instantly, Katie's heart went out to her. 'Oh, you poor thing.'

From the depths of Rebecca's Tanner Krolle bag a mobile started to play 'Waltzing Matilda'.

'Fuck.' Rebecca grabbed the bag. Some tights landed on the floor. Sunglasses missing an arm. Pens, tampons, lipsticks, receipts, a battered iPod. Katie tried not to gape. There was about twenty-grand's worth of accessories here.

Finally, the Motorola emerged. Rebecca peered at it, then exhaled like a diver coming up for air.

'Hello? Tim? I . . . Yes. OK . . . OK.'

The phone jabbered.

'No, that's cool. It's just . . . I thought we had an arrangement.'

Jabber.

'No, that's fine,' said Rebecca. 'If you forgot about the party invitation, you forgot about it . . . I understand, darling . . . No, go, go, don't worry about me! I know it's your career.'

More squawking at the other end.

'Well, but maybe you could come over afterwards . . . I don't mind if you wake me up. We'll just go back to bed again . . . Yes, you're right . . . I do need my sleep. Well then, maybe tomorrow?'

Katie glanced over her shoulder for signs of Jess.

'Well, if you're going to be tired, why don't you come round and be tired with me? We can watch TV and chill. Tim? Hello? Hello?' Rebecca jabbed at some buttons. 'I don't believe it. Voicemail. He must have lost his signal.'

Katie felt her stomach squeeze tight with familiarity. She knew exactly what Rebecca was going through.

'Or maybe his battery ran out.' Rebecca stared at the phone, willing it to ring. It stared back at her, unmoved.

Katie felt a swell of anger against the mysterious Tim for doing this to Rebecca and with Rebecca for doing it to herself. If this was Jess crying, she would have told her what to do. But Jess would never waste her energy on some Peter Stuyvesant-smoking toerag. And she could hardly tell Rebecca to get herself a life.

'I'll try his landline,' said Rebecca.

She dialled the number. Katie heard a faint, tinny voice: 'Hi, it's Tim . . .'

Rebecca hung up. 'Fuck. I'll try his mobile again.' She pressed the button and listened. 'Oh fuck!'

She flung the phone down and began to weep again. 'OK,' she sobbed. 'I'll leave him another message.'

That did it. Katie took a deep breath. 'Um, I really don't think you should do that.'

'Why not?' barked Rebecca, phone to ear. 'I need to talk to him. We've got to sort this out. I was so looking forward to seeing him tonight.'

Nervously, Katie blundered on. 'I just don't think it's a good idea. You've made it obvious how you feel. You've left all the power in his hands. If you call back and beg, or leave messages, he's going to feel persecuted. Leave him alone. Go out anyway. Have a good time. If he wants to see you, he'll call in a day or two. If he doesn't, you should get out.'

Slumped back in the sofa, Rebecca looked at Katie as if she had just told her to check out the sale at BHS.

'But I have to sort this out! I don't feel in control here.'

Katie sat down beside her and patted her on the hand. 'Don't be so upset. You're taking this terribly personally. Just because he can't see you tonight doesn't mean he doesn't like you.'

'But . . . I never know if he likes me or not. Sometimes he acts so sweet and funny and loving, and then I don't hear from him for days on end. When we arrange to meet I never know if he'll turn up or not. It's like living on a cliff edge. It's driving me insane, Katie.'

Glancing up, Katie caught sight of Jess's freckled face peering excitedly round the bedroom door.

'Fuck off,' she mouthed before getting back to the task in hand.

Fortunately, Rebecca was too immersed in her woes to notice. 'I don't understand. Why can't I keep a man? I do bloody everything for them. I send their mothers birthday cards. I book tickets for plays. I sew on buttons. And they still dump me.'

And now Katie knew why. She took a deep breath. 'Rebecca, I hope you don't think I'm being out of order here. But you said before you've only been with Tim for a couple of months.'

Rebecca sat up straight. 'Yes,' she said suspiciously.

Katie stumbled on, her fear of Rebecca's wrath overcome by a more pressing compulsion to set her on the right path.

'So first of all it's early days. You shouldn't be sewing on buttons until you've been with someone for at least a year. But more importantly, I don't think Tim is treating you with enough respect. Men shouldn't cancel on you at the last minute. Men shouldn't leave you with butterflies in your tummy, not knowing if they're ever going to call.'

'But that's *love*,' Rebecca bellowed. 'Excitement. Anticipation.'

'It's love when they actually do call,' Katie said. 'But if they don't, then forget them. And you know, Rebecca . . .' Oh God, she was beginning to sound like a country and western singer. 'You know, you're such an amazing woman. You're beautiful and successful and dynamic and that was the Rebecca that Tim bought into. He probably can't

94

understand who this other Rebecca is, the one who wants to spend every second of the day with him and mend his clothes.'

'But isn't that love? Caring for someone? Wanting to be with them?'

'Of course. But you can't let that side show too much. Not in the early days. Men might want a woman who'll mend their socks for them, but more than that they want someone sexy who . . . dances on tables and has millions of friends and will drop everything on the spur of the moment and run off to Rio for the weekend.'

'I used to love dancing on tables,' Rebecca said wistfully.

It was time to change the subject. 'So what are you going to do tonight?'

Rebecca brightened marginally. 'Well, there's a party I could go to at the Roundhouse.'

'Lovely. And what will you wear?'

'Oh God. I've got this dress from Miu-Miu which I *love*. Or there's my Vivienne Tam trouser suit. Why don't I show you?'

No! But before Katie could stop her, Rebecca had rushed into the bedroom.

'Hello,' said Jess, stretching out her hand. 'Jessica Harrison. Wardrobe consultant. We had an appointment, remember? You were a bit late so this . . . lady,' she nodded at Katie, 'let me in.'

The cheek of the girl, thought Katie. How on earth did she think she was going to get away with this one? Another job was going to bite the dust. At least Jess had managed to change back into her own clothes.

For Rebecca was not fooled for a second. 'What wardrobe consultant? I never made any appointment with you. What's going on?'

Katie didn't know where she found the inspiration. 'It was my idea, Rebecca. You know, as part of the service. I thought I'd get my friend – er – Ms Harrison to come and give you some advice on decluttering. You know, feng shui, that kind of thing. There's no fee,' she added hastily, noting Rebecca's outraged expression. 'You're such a prestigious client you get her advice for nothing.'

Rebecca might be pathetic over men, but in other ways she was right on the ball. She went over to the bed, where Jess had hastily discarded her clothes, her eyes narrowed scarily.

'I *like* this bustier,' said Rebecca, picking it up. 'It's Vivienne Westwood, you know. I'm not going to throw it out. But the skirt you're right about. I knew it was a mistake as soon as I got it home.'

Jess gave her most oily smile. 'Quite right, Rebecca. Shall we start on the rest of your wardrobe now? There are so many beautiful pieces, it *is* going to be hard. But you'll feel so much lighter without all that clutter on your psyche.'

'Oh, don't be silly,' Rebecca snapped. 'I hate all that airy-fairy bollocks. Basically, I've got too many clothes and I need a kick up the arse to get rid of some of them. But I'm not going to do it now. I only popped back from the office to . . .'

'Howl like a banshee,' Katie thought.

'Pick up my Psion. So although I appreciate your efforts, in future could you call to make an appointment?'

She turned on her heel and left the room. Katie and

Jess had a moment to swap relieved glances before Rebecca called from the living room.

'Katie! Come here!'

She was going to sack her. In private, away from Jess the wardrobe consultant's prying ears.

Rebecca was brushing her hair. She didn't turn round but addressed Katie's reflection in the mirror.

'Look, sorry about that scene,' she said. 'I feel like an idiot.' She dipped her head, so Katie couldn't see her expression. 'I just really want to make this work.'

Katie felt a pang of empathy.

'Rebecca,' she said, 'I can tell you really like this guy. But isn't a bit of it too that you feel you have to be with *someone*? I know you think you love him. But can you really love someone after such a short time? And more importantly, does he love you?'

'Does he love me?' Rebecca said thoughtfully. She bent down, picked up her red coat from the floor and pulled it on. 'He says he does.'

'It's an easy thing to say,' Katie blurted out, then wished she'd stayed silent.

Katie thought Rebecca was going to reply, but instead she headed to the door. On the threshold, she turned round. 'Thanks for the advice,' she said. 'I appreciate it. But Katie . . .'

'Yes?'

'Could you please just do a little bit more cleaning?'

9

The week passed. It was Friday night and Rebecca was arriving home from work in a very bad mood.

She'd had a fucking awful day. All morning grief, grief, grief from one of her most high-profile clients, Jeremy Jackson, presenter of *Breakfast Today*, about his autobiography proposal. Rebecca had been trying to explain that they would only get serious money if he put in all the details about his failed first marriage and his long-running feud with his former co-host, Christina Minns. Jeremy refused to do anything of the sort, saying the public would be happy enough reading about his idyllic childhood in Doncaster and would not listen to Rebecca's repeated pleas of 'No dirt, no book deal.'

Then in the afternoon, crisis upon crisis. Some party invitations had returned from the printers with the typeface two points too small. Angélique Brown, one of Ben's actress clients, had gone back into rehab. One of her presenters had been slagged off by the *Mirror*'s TV critic and had been on the phone in tears.

Fucking awful, Rebecca repeated to herself, as the lift carried her up to the top floor. It was seven o'clock, fantastically early for her to be home. Terrible day.

Except that it hadn't been really. The truth, and Rebecca knew it, was that today had been quite normal. Nothing she couldn't handle.

The truth was it was Friday night and Tim still hadn't called.

It wasn't, she thought furiously as she scrabbled in her bag for her keys, as if she hadn't plenty to do. Tonight, as on every night of the week, she had been invited to half a dozen events. But she'd turned them all down, in the hope, in the hope . . . she'd be spending tonight with Tim.

Who was silent.

Who'd been silent since that embarrassing afternoon with the cleaner, despite Rebecca's two emails and three increasingly pissed-off messages on the mobile demanding to know what was going on.

She couldn't even kid herself that he was lying somewhere in a coma, because when she called him at home he picked up. Luckily her fingers were already poised for a hang-up. And of course she had withheld her number. So the bastard was alive and in the country. He was just showing no sign of wanting to see her.

Rebecca turned on the light, pulled off her coat and threw it on the floor. She looked around the room. At least Katie had been today. Good, she had bought flowers (Rebecca had left £60 extra for them in the hope that Tim would see them and think she was a Domestic Goddess), even if she had dumped them in some ugly porcelain vase she must have found at the back of the cupboard under the sink.

The black demon inside her rose up. For the first time in several days, she was not thinking of Tim but of how useless Katie was. All that crap with the wardrobe consultant – clearly she was hoping for a commission – and then her confession that she'd broken five of Rebecca's cocktail glasses. She'd offered to replace them and Rebecca had curtly pointed out that Katie would have to work for her for about three months to do this – and told her to forget it.

Now, however, Rebecca was in no mood to forgive. She stormed into her bedroom. OK, the bed was made (well, the duvet was smooth) and – she sniffed the pillows – Katie had remembered to spray it with Chanel No. 5. But Christ! She had rearranged her Shisheido bottles on the dressing-table!

Calm down, calm down, Rebecca told herself. You're being a control freak. Katie was dusting the table. She couldn't have put them back exactly as you left them unless she took a bloody Polaroid first. Though that wasn't too bad an idea.

Rebecca had been so distracted she had almost forgotten to look at the phone. Her caller ID should have logged any calls she'd missed – although why anyone would call her at home instead of on the mobile was incomprehensible. Still, it would be just Tim's style to leave a message when he knew she'd be in the office. The phone sat on the bedside table. The little red light that winked when someone called was still.

'So that's that,' Rebecca breathed.

What was she going to do? She wandered into the kitchen, opened a couple of cupboards and listlessly studied the contents – a tin of mustard powder, some dried mushrooms and a jar of Vegemite. She'd have to order in again.

What was on telly? She turned it on and flicked down the listings. *Top of the Pops*, *Coronation Street*, a repeat from the third series of *Friends*, snooker. Great. A DVD? She wasn't in the mood. A long hot bath? That was a better idea. Pamper yourself, as the magazines said. Plus it was good reverse psychology. Make yourself unavailable and he was bound to call. She could keep the mobile close at hand, but the landline cord didn't reach into the bathroom.

The bathroom was pretty clean, she had to admit. She remembered how she'd shaved her legs in the shower that morning and left the hairs for Katie to rinse away and almost blushed. Still, she was paying her, wasn't she? Rebecca turned on the taps, poured lavender revitalizing oil into the water and sat on the edge of the tub inhaling the scent.

Brrr, Brrr. Brrr, Brrr.

Rebecca's adrenalin soared. She hurled herself across the room, dashed across the bedroom and grabbed the handset by her bed. She paused for a moment before speaking.

'Hello?'

'Rebecca, it's Tara.'

Damn.

'Did you get my message?' Tara continued.

'No. On my mobile?'

'No, on your answerphone. I knew you were going straight home after work.'

'But there weren't any messages.'

Tara was flustered. 'Shit. I'm sure I got the right number. I did! The message said: "This is Rebecca . . ." Anyway, whatever. The thing is, Jeremy now wants . . .'

Tara talked on. Rebecca wasn't listening. She was itching to go to her desk and check her answerphone.

'So what shall we tell him?'

'Uh? Look, Tara, I'm just going to change phones. I've got a Jeremy file on my desk in the other room.'

She ran into the living room. The answerphone was sitting on the desk. Its little light winked at her coyly. You have messages. Three, in fact, according to the counter. So why hadn't the bedroom phone flashed? Rebecca didn't understand. Was it broken? Christ, if Tara hadn't called she would never have known a message was waiting for her. It could have been catastrophic, like when Tess of the D'Urbervilles' letter to her lover gets lost under the doormat. He never gets it and she dies. God, that was a sad film. Why hadn't the phone flashed?

'What do you think, Rebecca?'

'Um? Oh, tell him to chill out. Send him flowers. I'll call him. What's his mobile number?'

She was writing down the number when a voice in her head said: *Katie.*

Of course. Katie. Miss Zealous Knickers had bloody punched the button on the phone while she was dusting so the light had stopped flashing. God knows how many calls Rebecca had not been alerted to. She could have lost important business this way.

'Tara, darling. Don't worry about it. Go home. Enjoy your weekend. I'll sort this out.'

She slammed down the phone and pressed play on the answerphone.

'Rebecca, it's Tara. Sorry to . . .'

Erase.

'Rebecca, Tara calling . . .'

Oh, for God's sake.

102

'Rebecca, hi. It's Tim. Sorry I haven't got back to you earlier. Work has just been mad. Look, I'm away all weekend. I'll try to call Sunday. We'll hook up. Bye.'

Rebecca stared at the machine as if it held the secret of eternal youth. She pressed play again. 'Rebecca, hi. It's Tim . . .' 'Rebecca, hi. It's Tim . . .' 'Rebecca, hi . . .'

The initial relief she had felt at hearing his voice was beginning to harden into a quite different emotion. What the hell was this she was hearing? Where was he going all weekend? What did 'We'll hook up' mean? Was she dumped or not?

'I'll try to call Sunday,' she imitated. 'Fuck off, Tim.'

Shit, the bath! The water was just up to the brim. At least one disaster had been averted. But what would she do now? Her instinct was to curl up on her bed and bawl the house down. But she refused. 'Get straight back on the horse,' she told herself. At her age, she had no time to waste. She would have a bath, make herself look fabulous and then go out and find a new man. What party could she go to? As she pulled her clothes over her head, she racked her brains. There was the Christian Dior party in Paris – she would've gone except she needed to be in London first thing tomorrow morning for a session with her personal trainer. There was Celine Harper's birthday do – well, she wouldn't be seen dead at that since the little bitch had dumped Greenhall and Graham and gone over to a rival agency.

But, she remembered as she unfastened her bra, there was the Twigz bash somewhere in South London. Rebecca hated Twigz but there'd certainly be lots of people – well, men – there. She knew she had an invite. Naked, she wandered into the living room and over to the mantelpiece.

It wasn't there.

Katie.

For God's sake. This really was getting a bit much. Katie had obviously moved it. Or thrown the bloody thing away. No point searching the bins, they had been emptied. Down the rubbish chute. Rebecca was not going down to the basement to root around amongst God knows what for a piece of paper.

There was only one thing to do. Swearing under her breath, she picked up the phone and called Suzy.

'Suze, darling, it's me,' she gabbled as soon as her friend picked up. 'Listen. Do you know where the Twigz party is taking place tonight?'

'Why are you going to *that*?' Suzy asked. She sounded as if Rebecca had asked for directions to the Bromley knitting circle AGM.

To get laid. 'There's a client I'm pursuing who might be there,' Rebecca said haughtily.

'I see,' said Suzy. Rebecca knew she was laughing at her.

'So where is it?'

'Where's what? Oh, the party? Hang on a sec . . . So who is this client, Rebecca?'

'You'll see.'

'Sure . . . It's at Sud. In Kennington. You know that converted abattoir?'

'Cool. Thanks, Suze.' She hung up. 'Grrrr!' she shrieked. Kennington was the arse end of nowhere. And her bed looked so inviting. 'No time to waste,' she told herself firmly. She would make herself irresistible.

As she lay in the bath, she felt oddly calm. So Tim was

messing her around. Well, it had only been two months. Like Katie said, it took longer than that to fall in love. Better to end it now before any more damage was done.

Funny that Katie had even said that, she thought. She was obviously quite a perceptive girl. Pity she was such a diabolical cleaner.

Rebecca hauled herself out of the cooling water and did her makeup wrapped in her bathrobe. She could see what other people saw, she decided, peering into the magnifying mirror. A five-foot-eleven woman with auburn hair, blue eyes and white teeth. Sexy and cool, and thanks to Dr Lumet, her Botox man, and Dr Knight, the implant impresario, flawless, even if that impression was getting harder and harder to maintain as the years flashed by.

It always surprised her though that people couldn't see the other Rebecca, the skinny seven-year-old with braces, whose father had left, probably because she wasn't pretty enough. Or because she wasn't good enough at school. Of course Rebecca's shrink had told her that Dad's leaving had had nothing to do with her, and everything to do with Monica, their next-door neighbour but one. But her beautiful, funny, kind, loving mum who had never shown a hint of bitterness, must have been lacking somehow. If Mum couldn't keep a man, who could? Rebecca started all relationships knowing that sooner or later the man would see through her and leave.

But perhaps not tonight, if she chose her outfit carefully enough: Earl jeans, a pink shirt open to reveal a hint of bra, kitten-heel ankle boots. The effect was very slimming. Not bad, Rebecca said to herself, glancing in the mirror. Not bad at all.

She didn't really believe it.

She looked again. What was this? Oh, for fuck's sake, her shirt had a big black splodge directly under her right breast. How had she done that? It looked like ink. Cursing, Rebecca ripped it off and peered at the label. Dry clean only. Well, bugger that. This stain needed a boil wash.

In her bra and jeans, she hurried into the kitchen and opened the washing machine. A jumble of elderly-looking bras, faded knickers and scraggy T-shirts was waiting for her.

'What the . . .?' Rebecca didn't recognize any of these manky clothes. Whose were they?

Katie.

Bloody Katie had been using her washing machine.

In cold fury, she chucked the pink shirt on the floor, returned to the bedroom and calmly buttoned herself into a tight, petrol-blue number. The wardrobe consultant, the cocktail glasses, and now this . . . Was there no one she could trust? In the morning that girl was bloody getting the sack.

She went outside and hailed a cab. Twenty minutes later it deposited her at the entrance to a hangar in the middle of an industrial estate in darkest South London. Rebecca felt as if she had just arrived for a night-shift packaging pork pies. The only indication she was at a party was a bald man in a suit mumbling into a walkie-talkie and a tall black girl with a pony-tail and wire-rimmed glasses brandishing a clipboard.

'My name's on the guest list,' Rebecca told her.

After some scrutiny, the girl agreed it was. Rebecca passed into the club. It was, of course, a dark and noisy hellhole. Hundreds of people all younger, cooler and prettier than her yelling and brushing her with their cigarettes. Desperately, she looked around for a waiter. No one. She forced her way to the bar. As she stood there, her eyes flicked around the room. There was Dempster Preston, one of the hottest Brit artists, slumped back in a sofa being entertained by two pieces of jailbait. Nearby stood Janine Palmer, agent to a host of stars, head back and laughing like a fool. God, she was going to need a drink before she launched herself into this lot. 'Excuse me!' she barked. The barman looked straight past her at the pretty little Portuguese boy nestling under her right armpit.

This was getting embarrassing. To save face, she turned her back to the bar and once again scanned the room.

What? Rebecca's faked nonchalance deserted her. She could not *believe* what she had just seen.

Katie.

Katie looking vaguely presentable, sipping a cocktail and laughing with a girl who looked vaguely familiar.

What the fuck was she doing here? A nasty suspicion was forming in Rebecca's brain. No time for a drink now. She began to push her way through the crowd. Across the room, she saw Katie and the girl deposit their glasses on a passing tray and walk off in the direction of the dance floor.

A wiggle of the other girl's bum made Rebecca remember. That was the bloody wardrobe consultant, what was her name? Harrison! What was she doing with Katie?

It wasn't looking good.

Like a cat stalking a mouse, Rebecca pursued Katie and Jess through the crowd. Katie had stolen the invitation.

She was getting the sack. Now. The two girls had moved into the middle of the dance floor and were gyrating vigorously to Kool and the Gang.

Rebecca had almost reached them when she saw something much more terrible. A tall man in a Fred Perry top and skinny Levis. A small woman in a candy-pink slip dress and a blonde bob. They were talking intently. He laughed, bent forward slightly and gently removed a strand of hair that had fallen over her eyes.

Tim.

Something snapped in Rebecca's heart, like an elastic band. She pushed through the crowd towards him. He continued flirting and would have carried on that way for hours had he not been interrupted by a glass of cold white wine flung straight in his face.

'You bastard!' Rebecca cried.

10

Even as she was doing it, Rebecca knew she was making a big mistake. She turned and started pushing through the crowd. 'Excuse me. Excuse me.' Tears blinded her. She didn't know what was worse: what she had just seen or how she had reacted. She didn't even have the excuse of being pre-menstrual. She was just a psycho who should be locked up.

A hand tapped her shoulder. 'Rebecca . . .'

She turned round. Oh, for heaven's sake. It was the cleaner. God, there was no one in this world she could trust.

'Fuck off,' she snapped. 'You're fucking sacked.'

She pushed on, past the VIP ropes and out into the courtyard. The bouncers looked at her curiously.

'Get me a cab,' Rebecca ordered.

They smirked. 'Sorry, *madam*,' said one. 'No cabs. A fleet of limos has been ordered for midnight. You'll have to wait until then. Or call one.'

'Do you have a number?' Rebecca said with as much dignity as she could muster.

'No, madam.'

'You liars,' Rebecca thought but she didn't have the energy to argue. She felt as deflated as a popped balloon. She pulled her mobile from her bag. 'Oh, no!'

The battery was dead.

'Is there a payphone inside?'

They shrugged. What the hell was Rebecca supposed to do? She couldn't walk round these streets in these heels looking for a cab. She'd have to go back into that building where she had just humiliated herself and beg to borrow someone's phone.

'Rebecca?'

She glanced round. Christ! It was the cleaner, *again*. What was she doing following her? Couldn't the girl get the message?

'Would you like to use my mobile?'

Rebecca was astonished. 'No, thanks!'

'Are you sure?'

Rebecca felt a sob well up. 'Yes.'

'Well,' said Katie, who really was trying hard, 'I'm going to call a cab. So I might as well order one for you.'

There was no getting out of this. 'OK!' Rebecca huffed. She wrapped her arms around herself as she heard Katie talking on the phone. 'No. Two cars, please. *Two*. One to Elephant and Castle. One to Bayswater. *Bayswater*. You know. Between Notting Hill and Hyde Park. Nice area. Good tip.'

She hung up. 'It'll be about five minutes,' she announced. She exhaled deeply. 'Rebecca, I'm really sorry.'

'Why? It's got nothing to do with you!'

For a moment Katie was confused. 'Yes, it has!' Then she realized what Rebecca was actually saying. 'Oh, that . . . business inside? No, that hasn't. Although I'm sorry about that too. No, what I meant was my behaviour. I took the invitation. I thought you didn't want it. I'm really sorry.'

'It was stealing,' Rebecca snapped.

'I know,' said Katie. 'And I apologize. Sincerely.'

'Becs,' panted a voice behind them. 'I'm *so* sorry.' It was the man from the party, in a stained Fred Perry T-shirt. He reached out and tried to grab Rebecca's arm. 'Honey.'

Rebecca pulled herself away. '*Don't* honey me!'

'Rebecca,' he said, 'what's the deal? We were only talking. Chrissie's an old friend.'

'That's not the point. The point is you told me you were away all weekend.'

Tim reddened. 'Well, there was a change of plan.'

'Oh? And did you not think it might be polite to share that change of plan with your *girlfriend*?'

'I thought we were finished. I thought you didn't want to see me any more.'

Rebecca's face was full of confusion. 'How the *hell* did you think that?'

'Last time I saw you. You were so cold. I thought you didn't want to be with me any more.'

'But . . .?'

'I was angry. I went out tonight trying to forget everything. I was so hurt by how you had treated me.'

What? Now Rebecca was confused. Had she treated Tim badly? Maybe. Why couldn't she ever get it right?

A battered Volvo drew up. The Ghanaian driver leaned out of the window. 'Elephant?'

'Yes, yes,' cried Rebecca. Then she spotted Katie standing there meekly. 'Oh. No. I'm Bayswater. Where's your colleague?'

'Colleague?' said the driver.

'Yeah. There should be two cars.'

'No,' Katie said hastily. 'You take this one, Rebecca. I don't mind waiting.'

'OK.' Rebecca opened the door.

'No, madam,' objected the driver. 'I am not going up west. South London only.'

'Oh, come on,' said Katie. 'She'll give you a big tip.'

The driver was offended now. 'No, love. This is my last job. I am going home to Catford. Elephant is on my way. Bayswater is not.'

Tim stepped forward. 'Baby, you're being silly. Let this . . .' he looked at Katie ' . . . person take the taxi. We need to talk.'

'When's my taxi arriving?' Rebecca asked.

The driver looked up from his radio. 'Sorry, darling. No more taxis. They're all busy right now. We're talking maybe an hour, hour and a half?'

'Look,' said Katie. 'Please take her home.'

'No! I may just be a taxi driver, but I have a life, you know? I want to see my wife tonight, not get stuck in all that West End traffic.'

Rebecca's lower lip wobbled. Katie swallowed. 'Rebecca, listen,' she said. 'Why don't you get in the cab with me and I'm sure when we reach a main road we'll see a black cab and you can take that.'

'No,' Tim said. 'Stay here.'

Rebecca looked at them both. She desperately wanted to fling herself into Tim's arms, to believe what he had just told her. But she knew she couldn't.

'Goodbye, Tim,' she said haughtily and climbed into the car. Katie followed.

'Whatever,' said the driver. 'But I am not taking you to the West End.'

'Can we just go, please?'

Tim tapped on the window. 'Darling, wait.'

'Go!' The car pulled away. Rebecca sat back in the torn leather seat and tried to choke back more sobs.

'Are you OK?' Katie asked gently.

What kind of a stupid question was that? Rebecca bit her lip. 'I'm fine,' she choked. 'Thanks.' Why was she always crying in front of the bloody cleaner? It was all too humiliating.

'Tosser,' Katie mumbled under her breath.

'Excuse me?'

'Nothing.'

'Did you just say tosser?'

'Yes. But I didn't mean you! I meant your boyfriend.'

'How dare you call my boyfriend a tosser!'

'Some boyfriend,' Katie said. The fear that Rebecca had once instilled in her had vanished. Fuck it. She had been sacked. She could say what she liked.

'And what would *you* know about it?'

'Well, I've only met you three times and twice you've been upset because of this guy. It doesn't seem right.'

Rebecca gave a haughty sniff. 'So? We've been going through a rocky patch. We'll work it out.'

'What kind of rocky patch? The other day you were crying because he didn't want to see you. And now you've caught him at a party he didn't invite you to, flirting with another woman. It doesn't look good.'

'He explained. It was a mistake. He thought I didn't love him any more.'

'And how exactly did he get that idea? You're obviously crazy about the guy.'

'I don't know. I must have given out the wrong signals. Been too high-maintenance. Now can we not talk about this any more?' Rebecca folded her arms and turned away.

Katie was beginning to feel positively aggressive. 'Well, which one is it, Rebecca? Did he think you didn't love him any more? Or were you being too full on? Because it can't be both. And why are you blaming yourself anyway? It's Tim who's the fuckwit here.'

'Please,' said the driver, crossing himself. 'Avoid such language in my cab.'

'Sorry! Look, Rebecca, I know you think I'm out of order. But you're so beautiful and this guy is just crapping all over you. Sorry!' she said as the driver gave her an outraged look over his shoulder. 'But he is. He's playing stupid games. I really can't bear to see it.'

They had been driving fast and had already reached the giant pink shopping centre that signalled Katie's manor. It had started to rain and there was not a taxi in sight. Welcome to London on a Friday night.

Katie leaned forward. 'Er. You should take a right here, then left at the lights. And then *please* can't you just take this lady home? She's having boyfriend problems.'

'So I heard,' said the driver, flicking on his radio. 'Sorry, love, but no.'

They were outside King Kebab. 'You'll have to come in,' said Katie. 'We'll call you another cab. I'm sorry about this.'

'It's not your fault,' Rebecca muttered through clenched teeth. She hated that this person she'd just sacked was being so sodding nice to her. It made her feel even more of a loser than ever.

Katie paid the driver – although she could ill afford it – and they went inside. Even though her relationship with Rebecca was now at an end, she felt horribly embarrassed at having her in their tatty little flat. She glanced at her watch. Five minutes past midnight. At least Ronan was out. And since Jess had been last seen snogging the bassist from Twigz, it was fair to assume she wouldn't be coming home tonight.

Rebecca looked around. She took in the film posters on the wall; the mismatched plates drip-drying in the rack by the sink; the itemized phone bill on the table, with sums scribbled all over it. Scruffy, but cosy. And immaculately clean, she had to admit. God, now she would have to find a new cleaner. As if she didn't have enough problems.

'How student!' she said briskly. 'Now, can I call a cab?'

'The phone's over there. There are some numbers on the board.'

Rebecca dialled six firms in a row. The shortest wait was an hour.

'You can always get the night bus,' Katie was tempted to say. Instead, she said brightly: 'Would you like a cup of tea while you're waiting?'

Christ, these English and their insufferable cups of tea. But what the hell. 'Yeah. Camomile.'

And so it was that Katie found herself drinking tea at her kitchen table over the kebab shop with one of the most glamorous women in London.

And actually having rather a good chat.

'I just feel so confused,' said Rebecca. 'Did I push him

away? Should I give him a second chance? I wonder if he's been trying to call me. You don't have a phone charger, do you?'

Of course Katie did – she wasn't a total peasant – but neither hers, Jess's nor Ronan's was compatible with Rebecca's superior model.

'Sorry about that,' Katie said, after they had finally ascertained this. 'But honestly, Rebecca, even if he has called you, you should ignore him. He's making you miserable. From what I can tell, he always has done. Is that any way to lead your life?'

It was Katie's favourite rant, much practised on drippy girlfriends over the years. They'd listen to her, after which they'd stop crying, shout, 'Yeah, yeah. What a wanker.' Then they'd drink a bottle of vodka, put on 'I Will Survive' and dance around until they passed out in an armchair.

Two days later, the boyfriend would ring and they'd go running back to him.

Pathetic.

'Yeah, yeah,' said Rebecca now. 'It's no way to live, is it? Tim has always made me unhappy. I can do better than this. I can find someone who treats me with respect.' She looked curiously at Katie. 'How does your boyfriend treat you?'

'Really well.'

'So you were lucky, huh?'

'I suppose.' But then Katie sat upright. 'Actually no, Rebecca, I wasn't lucky. My boyfriend treats me well because that's the way I trained him.'

'Trained him?' For the first time that evening Rebecca laughed. 'He's not a dog.'

'No, of course he's not. But he's a man. Practically the same. Although dogs are much nicer. Obviously.'

Rebecca laughed. 'Obviously.'

'No, seriously,' Katie said. A memory flashed into her head: her taxi pulling into her parents' driveway and Elton running out to greet her. 'What Elton and I have is perfect love. Perfect devotion. If Elton was your boyfriend he would always call when he said he was going to and never forget to pick you up from the airport.'

'Who's *Elton*?'

'My dog. Well, my parents' dog. But even Elton didn't get that way all by himself. We had to train him to be a good boy.'

Rebecca rolled her eyes incredulously.

'No, seriously, Rebecca!' Katie's teenage reading of Dr John Fretton's *The Complete Dog Trainer* was slowly returning. 'Men and dogs are very similar. They're hunter-gatherers. It's in their DNA. For thousands of years they had to use their bodies and their brains to survive. But now they live in cosy houses and their dinner comes from Tesco's. They're safe, but they're bored. They still need something to chase. That's why Elton has his squeaky toys.'

'So you think I should buy Tim a squeaky toy?'

'Of course not!' Katie was inspired now. This was what Einstein must have felt like when he cracked gravity! Or was that Newton? Anyway, 'The point is you have to make the chase as interesting as possible. If he just catches you and you give up, it's no fun. I think it's excellent that your battery's dead. Tim probably thinks you're umbilically attached to your phone. And it's probably quite a good thing you're here and not at home. He's not going to get hold of you and he'll be wondering what you're doing. It'll drive him crazy. Serves him right after all the shit he's put you through.'

'But that's game-playing!' Rebecca said. 'I grew out of that when I was sixteen. You can play hard to get, but he's going to get you eventually and then he'll realize you're just an ordinary woman and he'll lose interest. Bam.'

'Perhaps,' Katie said. 'So that's when you move on to the next stage of inspiring devotion. Showing them that you're leader of the pack.'

'Leader of the pack?'

'Well, as I remember, dogs are pack animals. They don't appreciate democracy. They like to have a boss to look up to and who sets the rules.'

'How can I set the rules?'

'Well, you can't set rules as such. But you can basically make it clear you're the boss, by just getting on with your own life rather than letting your world revolve around him. Men don't waste time worrying about how to please women. They go to work and watch football and enjoy themselves with their mates.'

'But I can't be like that,' Rebecca exclaimed. 'When I'm in love I think about my boyfriend all the time. I read his horoscope. I looked us up in Linda Goodman. Gemini male, Libra female. Quite a good combination, actually.'

'Are you Libra?' Katie asked, momentarily distracted. 'Me too!' Rebecca looked totally unimpressed. She stumbled on. 'Look, looking your boyfriend up in Linda Goodman is normal. But you don't need to let him know anything about it. As far as he's concerned you're a cool woman who had a life before he came along, and will go on having a life *long* after he's history. You don't read Linda Goodman, you read . . . the *New Yorker* and James Joyce.'

'I never told Tim that I checked us in Linda Goodman. I'm not *that* stupid.'

'Yes, but you made it clear that your life was meaningless without him.'

Rebecca thought for a moment. 'So what do I do now?'

'You don't see him any more!'

'Even if he's genuinely sorry?'

Christ! Katie was on a roll now. Time for some of Jess's choicest phrases. 'Rebecca. He's a wankstain.'

'But maybe if I take what you're saying on board, things can be better.'

Katie sighed. 'No. It's too late. The damage has been done now. And anyway, even if you didn't behave brilliantly, the person at fault here isn't you. It's Tim.'

'But I love him. He said it was a mistake.'

'Rebecca. Actions speak louder than words. Don't listen to what he tells you, watch how he treats you.'

'And if his actions change?'

'They won't.'

'But if they do . . .?'

Katie was saved from this ridiculous exchange by the doorbell ringing. She leaned out of the window.

'Minicab!'

'God, is it here already?' said Rebecca. She blinked and rubbed her eyes. Thank God for waterproof, smearproof mascara. Suddenly she really didn't want to leave at all. Katie might be an invitation thief, but for some reason she liked her. At least, unlike her real friends, she was *there*. She'd never have dared call the others at this time of night.

She got up and stood there, feeling a little foolish. How the hell was she going to say this? 'Look,' she began. 'I feel bad. I've been pretty harsh to you. And all you've done is be nice to me and tell me a few home truths.'

Katie smiled, embarrassed.

'So . . . I'd like to give you your job back. But perhaps sometimes you could come over when I'm there. Then we could talk and I could help you clean!'

Rebecca wanted to pay her for her advice. It was the most ludicrous idea Katie had ever heard.

'Isn't that what you pay a shrink for?' she asked.

Rebecca laughed, for the second time. Easy, tiger, she thought with surprise, you're supposed to be heart-broken.

'Not exactly. You just said it. I pay my shrink to let it all hang out. I'm paying you to help me keep it all in. Plus, she wants to know all about my childhood and did my father ever touch me inappropriately and was I bullied at school. I haven't got time for that. I need a quick fix.'

'Well, what about your friends?'

Rebecca considered. 'Well, that's the issue really. I mean, I used to tell my friends everything. They were definitely like my family, especially as my mum lives so far away. But in the past couple of years everything's changed. Everyone's so busy, it's hard to get them on their own, and if you do they want to talk about *their* problems. And besides . . .'

'Besides?'

'Talking to my friends makes me feel like a failure. I mean, they're all in relationships – even if some of their boyfriends are toilet brushes. I don't know why they can do it and I can't. So usually I just keep it all in and pretend everything's perfect.'

Katie gave up. Rebecca was a basket case. But she wanted to help her, like she wanted to help anyone who'd had their heart dashed on the rocks.

'So when shall I come next?'

Rebecca pulled her Palm Pilot from her bag and began studying the diary.

The doorbell rang again.

'She's coming,' Katie shouted out of the window.

'Monday night, I'm out. Tuesday, same. Wednesday, yup. Thursday – I could do next Thursday if you came in the evening.'

Katie looked stricken. 'Oh, I can't. It's Ronan's birthday.'

Annoyance flitted across Rebecca's face, but then she remembered what an absurd request she was making.

'Well, look. Maybe you could come tomorrow? I'm free and I'll have spoken to Tim. *And* you have some washing to pick up,' she added, suddenly remembering.

Katie went scarlet. 'Oh my God! I'm so sorry, I forgot all about it.' Actually, she'd remembered on the way home, but she'd consoled herself that the chances of Rebecca checking the washing machine over the weekend were about as likely as Ronan playing Hamlet at the National.

Rebecca waved her apology away. There were other things to think about. 'My personal trainer's coming at ten,' she said. 'So how about the afternoon? Say two?'

There was the sound of keys in the lock. 'Hello?' said a male voice. 'You're back early.'

'Oh, hi,' said Katie, looking a little flustered.

Rebecca looked at this fine specimen with admiration. So *this* was Katie's man.

'Hi,' she said, sticking out a hand. 'Rebecca Greenhall.'

Ronan tried to look casual. 'Ronan Waters.'

'Nice to meet you, Ronan.' Rebecca's respect for Katie was increasing by the minute. How had she managed to pull such a gorgeous guy? She wasn't *that* pretty and she'd obviously never heard of John Frieda's Frizz-Eeze. It must be the way she had . . . trained him.

The doorbell rang for the third time.

'Better go,' said Rebecca. 'Katie, I'll see you tomorrow. Thanks for tonight.' As she opened the door, she honked with sudden laughter. 'In the morning I'll see my personal trainer. And in the afternoon my love trainer.' The thought had her chuckling all the way down the stairs.

11

So now Katie had to contend with more mirth from her flatmates.

'Love trainer?' Ronan spluttered. 'It's the maddest thing I ever heard. Rich people really do think they can buy everything. Fat arse? Have liposuction! Rubbish love life? Get someone in to sort it out!' He put down his cup of tea. 'And anyway, Katie, why you? I mean, no offence but if I was rich I think I'd go a little bit more upmarket. I'd get in someone like that Dr Raj bloke from the telly.'

Despite herself, Katie felt a bit huffy. 'Excuse me! Who said I'd make a brilliant social worker? *You*. And this is practically the same thing. At least I have a love life, unlike *some* people I could mention.'

Ronan looked like a puppy who had trodden on a thorn.

'Sorry!' Katie cried, stricken. 'So how did it go tonight? How come you're back so early?'

'It's not that early. And actually tonight was good. I met a gorgeous girl. Her name's Claire. Friend of Charlie's. We talked for ages. I'm going to get her number.'

'Didn't she give it to you?' Suddenly Katie was on alert. She tried to keep the sharpness out of her voice.

'No. I was going to ask, but I didn't notice her leaving. But Charlie'll have it. I thought I'd call her in the morning. See if she fancied a film, or a walk in the park maybe.'

'Oh, Ronan! *Not* in the morning. I've told you about this. Wait until Tuesday at least. Otherwise she's going to think you're a stalker.'

'You always say that,' Ronan protested. 'But what's wrong with being honest? Letting someone know you like them?'

'Women love bastards,' Katie admonished.

'*Your* boyfriend isn't a bastard.'

Suddenly an image of Paul laughing entered Katie's head. Where the hell had that come from? She hadn't thought of him for weeks.

'You're right,' she agreed. 'My boyfriend is lovely. But you're still playing it too keen, Ronan. Back off. If she liked you tonight, she'll like you even more after four or five days waiting by a silent phone.'

Jess returned home with faint smudges of mascara under her eyes and a Starbucks cup in her hand.

'Oh God! What have I done now?' she groaned, curling up on the sofa.

'The Twigz guy?'

'Rowley. Oh, Katie. I'm not even sure I fancied him. He was coming on to me and I thought it'd be fun to snog a rock star and then I ended up going home with him. I wasn't going to shag him. But then I just did.'

'And how was it?'

Jess wrinkled her nose. 'To be honest, it didn't last long. Either time. And then it was a bit embarrassing. I got the vibe that he wanted me out of there, but it was four o'clock and I couldn't afford a cab. So I went to sleep, although I'm not sure he did. When I woke up, he wasn't there. He was in the next room reading a book. Fully dressed. He didn't ask for my number.'

'But Jess, you didn't even fancy him.'

Jess looked grumpy. Well, I didn't *at first*, but then I began to quite like him. He seemed to like me.'

'Jessica. Just because someone likes you does not mean you have to like them. If Jeremy Beadle said he liked you would you suddenly want to jump into bed with him?'

'Of course bloody not.' From the look on her face, Jess didn't seem convinced though.

After dealing with such a pair of dysfunctionals, Katie felt almost relieved to be returning to Rebecca's. Judging by Rebecca's face when she opened the door, the feeling was not mutual.

'Oh, hi,' she muttered. She was wearing a pair of Maharishis and a pink fleece. She looked sporty and girlish. The same outfit would have made Katie look like a lesbian window cleaner. 'I suppose you'd better come in.'

Katie followed her into the kitchen. Rebecca seemed to be struggling with what to say next. 'Would you like a coffee? I'm not actually allowed it,' she gabbled. 'My nutritionist has me on a strict diet of teas. But today is an exception. My nerves are shattered. I'd offer you milk but I haven't got any.'

Rebecca's coffee was like swamp water. Katie hoped it wouldn't give her dysentery.

'So look,' said Rebecca. 'I behaved pretty stupidly last night. I was stressed out. I'd had a bad day at work and over-reacted. You helped me out. But when I got home I found this.'

She walked over to the desk and pressed play on the answerphone. 'Rebecca? It's Tim. Where are you? Baby, I am *so* sorry. Please. We need to talk. Call me as soon as you get in.'

A rueful smile passed over Rebecca's face. 'Rebecca,' said the machine. 'Pick up! You should be home by now. I'm worried about you. Oh God. Please call me.'

By the third message, he was sounding irate. 'Rebecca! Where are you? Please. I need to talk to you. To explain.' There was a pause. 'I love you.'

'*And* he left a message on my mobile too,' said Rebecca, waving it above her head like the World Cup. 'He was frantic. So thank you, Katie, for telling me not to call him. It obviously worked.'

'And have you called him since?' Katie enquired.

Rebecca shrugged. 'Well, yes. Of course. I called him this morning. I mean, he was out of his mind with worry. I had to let him know I was OK.'

'And?'

'And so we're meeting tonight.' Rebecca spoke hastily, as if hoping Katie wouldn't catch what she said.

Just don't go there, Katie said to herself. *If she wants to ruin her own life that's her business.* 'Well,' she said, smiling. 'That's great.'

'Do you think so?'

Katie took a gulp of coffee, then tried not to gag. 'Um, yes! I think it's fabulous news.'

'That's not what you were saying last night.' Rebecca eyed her suspiciously.

God, why was she always so contrary? 'Rebecca, I was probably a bit out of order last night. It's your life, you're older than me, you're far more successful and I'm *sure* you know what you're doing. I really don't think I'm the best person to be giving you advice.'

A slow grin spread over Rebecca's face as she sat down. 'Well, you say that. But you do have that gorgeous boyfriend. So you're obviously doing something right. Why can't I get someone like him?'

'Crispin? How do you know he's gorgeous?'

'Well, I saw him, didn't I? You are seriously lucky.'

'You've never seen . . .' The balls fell into place. 'Oh! You mean Ronan? He's not my boyfriend, he's my flatmate.'

'Oh!' Rebecca felt strangely relieved. 'But you do have a boyfriend, don't you?'

'Yes, that's Crispin.'

'Do you have a photo?' She was as shallow as a puddle, she knew, but Rebecca's image of Katie had just taken a blow. She didn't want to take love training from a girl whose man looked like Barry in *EastEnders*.

'Sorry. No.' As far as Katie was concerned, carrying round pictures of your boyfriend was only one step removed from sleeping with a teddy bear and ordering china dollies in frilly pinafores from the back of colour supplements. After all, she'd carried Paul's and look what such soppiness had brought her.

'Oh. Well. Anyway, I'm seeing Tim tonight. He's cancelled his dinner party for me, which was really sweet. Because, whatever you may say, I have made some mistakes. I'm probably not the easiest of girlfriends. I work so hard, I'm not a good cook, and I . . . certainly need you to clean up around me. Maybe if I was a little softer, more feminine, Tim would like me more.'

It was impossible. However hard Katie tried to be patient with Rebecca, there always came a moment when she reached breaking point.

'Rebecca! You don't need to be softer, you don't need to be more feminine. You are fine as you are. Stop thinking about how to make yourself better for him all the time. Think about how he can make himself better for you.'

Rebecca looked impressed. 'That's a good one.' From a desk drawer, she took a Smythson notebook and a Mont Blanc pen. 'I'm going to write that down. And last night you said something else I liked. What was it? I know! Actions speak louder than words!'

'It's hardly the Desid . . . the Desiday . . . Oh, you know, that thing people hang on their loo walls about going in peace.'

'Doesn't matter! It works for me. It's one thing for Tim to *say* he loves me and wants to have babies with me, but what's he doing about it?'

'Good!' For a second Katie tingled with the same glow she always felt on hearing the first bars of 'Come Up and See Me' on the radio. They were making progress. She seized the moment.

'Rebecca, what if I was to tell you that you're a stone overweight, your roots are a mess and that with legs like that I would never wear combats?'

Rebecca winced.

'Well, I could do with losing half a stone. And I am going to the hairdresser's next week. Do these combats make me look fat? Shit!' She studied her long limbs in disgust.

'I was joking,' Katie said hastily. 'I don't think any of

those things. I think you are completely gorgeous. Your body's amazing, your hair's perfect. But this is what I'm saying. All women hate themselves. We're convinced we're hideous, and we – well, you – are just not! So don't think about what Tim doesn't like about you. Think about what you don't like about him.'

Rebecca wrinkled her nose in concentration. 'What's wrong with Tim? What's wrong with Tim?' she muttered. 'OK! I've got one! He's got a stupid laugh.' She made a wheezing sound like an air bed expiring. 'That bugs me.'

'Good! What else?'

'He talks Cockney.' Rebecca leaned forward confidingly. 'But I don't think he's anything of the sort. He goes on about how I have nice Bristols, but his parents live in Gloucestershire and I'm pretty sure they're loaded.'

What a knob, Katie thought. 'That's great, Rebecca. And another thing?'

'His clothes are stupid. He goes shopping in Carnaby Street and has a thing about the joys of man-made fibres. *And*,' she remembered triumphantly, 'he wears those cool glasses, but the glass in them is clear. I know. I tried them on.'

Katie leaned forward. 'OK. That's loads of bad things. And I think there's another you've forgotten.'

Rebecca looked puzzled.

'Rebecca, you caught him with another girl last night. He was behaving like a complete arse.'

'But he's sorry.'

'Are you sure about that? It's actions and words again. He *says* he is, but maybe he feels like an idiot because you caught him in the act. I just think you can do better than this. Stop wasting your time.'

'But Katie, we had a lot of fun. I really liked him. I thought he really liked me. We need to talk – that's clear. So let's see how it goes tonight.'

'I don't think you should be seeing him tonight.'

Rebecca stood up. 'Well, I'm going to.' She carried her coffee cup over to the kitchen. 'I can't just leave it like this.'

'OK,' Katie said, following her. 'But look, Rebecca. Don't see him for too long. Don't spend the night with him. Don't let him into your flat. Have a drink with him, talk, and then tell him you have to be somewhere else. Even if you are going to get back with him, don't make it too easy for him. Make him fight for you.'

Rebecca leaned back against the unit to face her.

'Where are you meeting him?' Katie persisted.

Rebecca looked evasive. 'I don't know. I guess I'll call him in a minute and find out.'

'No!' *Calm down*, Katie told herself, *why do you care so much?* 'Don't. Let him do all the work from now on.' A plan started formulating. 'Rebecca, I know what you should do. You should go to the cinema. Or the theatre. Somewhere where you have to turn your phone off, any-way. Then if Tim does call, he won't be able to get hold of you. That will freak him out. If he doesn't call, you don't call him. Go out. Leave your phone at home. We want him to think that you're having a great time, that you don't need him.'

'I can't go to a movie on my own,' Rebecca exclaimed. 'That's what old men do! Someone might see me.'

'Well, then go with a friend.'

As if anyone would be free, at such short notice! Katie simply had no idea what busy lives her friends led. But a movie could be fun. Rebecca smiled at Katie, as sincerely as she could muster. 'Would you like to come?'

'I'd love to,' said Katie. She looked around anxiously. 'But what about the cleaning?'

'Oh. Yeah!' Rebecca also looked around anxiously.

Katie had another revelation. 'Rebecca! I don't mind doing the cleaning. Honestly. But I actually think it might be better if you left the place looking a . . . bit untidy. Then you won't be tempted to bring Tim back here. I'll come and clean tomorrow if you like, but maybe today we should leave it.'

To Katie's surprise, Rebecca was getting it. 'OK,' she said. 'And maybe I should wear like really disgusting underwear as well. I have this sports bra Mum gave me. You have to see it! It's so disgusting! I'll put it on. And the knickers I save for my period. Unfortunately, I shaved my legs last night, so there's nothing I can do about that.'

She ran into the bedroom and emerged two minutes later, her hair slightly dishevelled and her face pink. 'Revolting bra, scary pants. Now, what shall we go and see? I haven't been to a movie that I chose for ages.'

Five minutes later, giggling, Rebecca and Katie were hurrying down the road to catch the two-thirty showing of *The Wedding Day* – the story of three different women getting married on the same day, who triple-book the same registry office – and then end up going off with one another's fiancés. Rebecca had been dying to see it for ages, but because it didn't have subtitles and starred J-Lo, she had never dared suggest it to Tim. This afternoon was going to be fun.

12

For a couple of hours in the cinema, Rebecca had been perfectly happy wondering if the second bride would get it together with the third groom. It was a shock to emerge from the cosy foyer on to the bustling, neon-lit Edgware Road that constituted the real world. Immediately, Rebecca turned her mobile back on. (Katie, with surprising force, had made her switch it off in the cinema. She wouldn't even allow her to put it on vibrate.)

It rang immediately.

'Hello,' gasped Rebecca, then tried to look cool when she realized she was talking to her voicemail.

'You. Have. Three. Messages.'

And so Rebecca listened in decreasing excitement to the dry-cleaner telling her that her leather coat was ready for pick-up, Suzy asking if she'd enjoyed the Twigz party – the gossip had clearly filtered through then – and Jeremy Jackson telling her that he *loved* the diary piece about him that Rebecca had planted in today's *Telegraph* and she was a sweetheart and he was going to make it up to her for being such a prima donna.

'Pants!' Rebecca bellowed, to the alarm of two veiled Arab ladies walking arm in arm. 'The bastard hasn't called. After all the trouble I took to avoid him.'

It was half past five. Still early. Plenty of time for Tim to call. But they both knew he wouldn't.

They travelled back up to the flat in thoughtful silence. Rebecca stood and watched as Katie nervously filled three plastic bags with her by now slightly mouldy washing.

'Anyway, Katie. Thanks for your time this afternoon. I'm sure you have things to do.'

Katie thought of Crispin. 'Well, yes, but . . . are you going to be all right?'

'I'll be fine.' Rebecca smiled. *I'll call Ally*, she thought. Oh no. Ally would be with Jon. And Suzy was bound to be busy. But Jenny was always up for a laugh. Yes, she'd try Jenny.

'I'll call you tomorrow,' she said to Katie. 'Work out when you're next going to come and . . . er . . . clean.'

As soon as the door shut she picked up the phone.

Jenny Mullins was in the kitchen of her terraced house in Balham, stirring her Jamie Oliver bouillabaisse, sipping from her glass of Pinot Noir and singing along to her Misteeq CD (Jenny thought it was very important to keep in touch with the latest sound) when the phone rang.

'Hello?'

'Jen. It's Becca.'

'Hello.' Jenny kept her tone frosty. Rebecca hadn't called her for three weeks. Probably busy with other, more glamorous friends, who didn't live near the end of the Northern Line.

'How are things?'

'Fine, great! Really, really busy actually.'

'Just wondering if you'd like to hook up tonight?' Rebecca blurted. She knew that in London last-minute arrangements were as rare as white tigers, that friends had to be booked three weeks in advance, then cancelled at least four times before anyone got to see anyone. But hey, she had just split up with her boyfriend. Normal rules had been suspended.

Jenny paused, but then her kind heart got the better of her. 'Well, Gordy and I were having a few people round for dinner. You're welcome to join us. And Tim, of course.'

'Well, Tim and I, we're . . . over, actually.'

At this, Jenny's reserve dissolved like an Alka-Seltzer. 'Oh, babe! Are you OK? Listen, why don't you come round right now and tell me all about it?'

'Would that be OK?' Rebecca asked pathetically.

'Of course. I'll pour you a massive glass of wine and you can talk while I cook.'

This arranged, Jenny put down the phone happy. She loved to feel wanted.

'Was that Carl?' enquired Gordon, sticking his head round the door. Carl was one of the builders Gordon was constantly employing in an effort to upgrade their property.

Jenny sighed. 'Yes, that was Carl. We were arranging a secret love tryst.' Gordon looked bewildered. 'Of *course* it wasn't Carl. I'd have called you, wouldn't I?'

'I suppose so.' Gordon was covered in dust. 'God, it's hot up in the attic. But I'm really making progress today.'

'You will shower before the guests get here?' Jenny lived with a constant nagging terror that Gordon was somehow going to let her down. She waved a forkful of bouillabaisse under his nose. 'Taste this, tell me what you think,' she urged.

He tasted and wrinkled his nose. 'Mmm.' Gordon had

gone to boarding school and unquestioningly ate whatever he was given.

'Is it horrible?'

'No, it's lovely,' Gordon reassured her, his mind far away on the water-tank lagging. He saw her strained expression. 'Maybe you could . . . add a little salt or something.'

Jenny started rummaging through her thousands of dusty spice jars. Cinnamon. That should do the trick. 'June 1999' read the sell-by date. Oh well.

'So who *was* on the phone?'

'Oh, Rebecca. She's coming round. Just broken up with her man.'

'Not again,' Gordon groaned. He was very fond of Rebecca.

'I *know*,' Jenny said. 'It's amazing, isn't it, how someone so beautiful and successful and skinny just can't keep a boyfriend. Makes you wonder what hope there is for the rest of us.'

This was Gordon's cue to say: 'But you're far more beautiful than Rebecca.' But he had never been one for compliments. His nickname for Jenny was 'porker'. Once she had worked out that in four years together he had told her she looked nice seven times – and on five of those he had had a raging erection. Still, at least he never told her she was looking rough, which was the kind of thing Rebecca's boyfriends did.

Rebecca arrived within the hour. 'That was quick,' Jenny smiled, flinging open the door. 'What did you do? Charter a helicopter?'

'Great highlights,' Rebecca replied admiringly.

Jenny looked annoyed. 'What highlights?' Too late,

Rebecca remembered that Jenny regarded all beauty treatments as a shameful secret.

'It must be the sun,' she cooed appeasingly. 'Where did you get that skirt?'

'New Look!' Jenny glowed.

'Well *done*.' She followed Jenny into the kitchen and watched passively as her friend poured her a huge glass of red wine. 'Are those new?' she asked, gesturing at four primitive-style paintings behind the dining table. Jenny's house always looked so lovely. Perhaps if Rebecca lived with someone she'd make more of an effort. The thought made her bite her lip in self-pity.

'Yeah, me and Gords got them in Colorado last summer. Shows how long it is since you were last round here.' Her tone was a little tart, but then Jenny saw the misery on her friend's face. 'Oh, Becs! Now tell me all about it.'

'Oh, Jen, I've had such a horrible night. I went to a party and Tim was there flirting with another woman.'

In spite of herself, Jenny glowed even more. She loved it when her friends had problems. It reminded her that however much Gordon irritated her with his work and his indifference and his leaving the loo seat up, at least she had something that beautiful Rebecca never seemed to have any luck with.

'Tell me all about it,' she cooed.

So Rebecca recounted the whole story, although she did miss out the chucking wine bit and the whole love-trainer episode. Even Jenny might find that a bit too odd.

'So are you sure this isn't just a blip, babe?' Jenny asked as Rebecca finished speaking. 'Maybe he was just confused. It sounds like he'd like a second chance.'

'Well, why hasn't he called me this evening then?'

Jenny frowned, as if she was doing her accounts.

''Ullow, 'ullow,' said a growly voice behind them.

'Gordon!'

Gordon was slightly shorter than Jenny, stocky, fair and utterly amiable. Of all Rebecca's friends' boyfriends, he was the mile-long favourite: jolly, bright and incredibly handy around the house. If he couldn't fix something then he knew an army of people who could – for a fair price.

'If that's not perfection, I don't know what is,' Rebecca would tell Jenny, after a few. 'As long as Gordon exists I can go on believing in true love.'

She kissed him enthusiastically. 'Great to see you! Urgh, your hair's all dusty.'

'Oh, go and have a bath, Gordy,' Jenny snapped. 'The others'll be here in an hour.'

And indeed an hour later, Rebecca was perched on a footstool in the front room, stroking a cat, smoking a cigarette, drinking her champagne and flirting outrageously with Freddie, who was tall, dark, handsome, thirty-nine, single.

And gay.

'Ah ha, ha, ha, ha,' roared Freddie, clapping his hands together like a performing seal. 'Rebecca! You are *so* funny. Gorgeous girl. I tell you, if I was any other way inclined I'd marry you like a shot.'

The living room reeked of Jo Malone candles. The other guests were lounging around drinking wine out of huge goblets and picking at herby olives.

Jenny entered the room, followed by a tall man with a beaky nose and an earnest expression.

'Rebecca, Freddie, this is Andrew, our neighbour,' she cried. 'Have you met?'

'Yes, yes, I think we have,' Rebecca said.

'And Laura?'

Laura, clearly his wife, wore a long green tunic and was hugely pregnant. She waved at them all regally, then sank into the sofa, her eyes half closed. Rebecca hated her on sight.

'Lovely to meet you,' she lied.

'And this is Ludo, who used to work with Gordy,' Jenny yelled, dragging another man across the threshold.

'How do you do?' said Rebecca and instantly regretted sounding so formal. Ludo was tall and tanned with cheekbones like stubbly wing-mirrors. Bound to be gay too. Otherwise Jenny would have told her all about him. Rebecca sat up straighter and sucked in her stomach.

'And you guys don't need any introduction.'

'Ally!' Rebecca jumped up at the sight of her friend. Alone! 'Jon not here?' she asked carefully.

'Oh, yeah, he's just hanging up his coat.' Ally glanced over her shoulder. 'Jon-ny! Come and say hello.'

Jon had dishwater hair and a doughy face. He wore a grey sweatshirt, combats and an aura of affronted superiority.

'Sweetheart,' said Ally. 'Remember Rebecca?'

'Uh,' he said.

'Hi, Jon,' Rebecca smiled. 'How are you?'

'Uh. OK.' *And how are you, Rebecca?* But that would be too much to ask.

'I think that's everyone,' Jenny said, turning to Gordon. 'Is the wine chilled, darling?'

'Yup, practically horizontal. It must be Jamaican,' Gordy joked in an atrocious Caribbean accent. Jenny rolled her eyes to heaven. He turned to Rebecca. 'Did you watch *Brewster's Bingo* last night? Hilarious.'

'Gordy! Becca's got better things to do than stay in watching trash.'

'No I don't,' Rebecca insisted. 'Tell me about it.'

So Gordy did and she nodded and smiled, trying to tune into Ludo's conversation with Laura.

'So my ex-wife said . . .'

Ex-wife! Perfect! Not gay and not married. Rebecca had recently begun to accept that at her age she was probably going to have to settle for a second-hand husband – or 'vintage' as they called it these days. Put that way, it sounded positively chic.

'Ah, ha, ha,' she laughed in relief.

Gordy looked puzzled. 'It wasn't *that* funny.'

'So now we're all here, let's eat!' Jenny cried. She grabbed Ludo's hand. 'You're next to me, sweetie!' Typical. Not only had Jenny found the only decent man in London, now she was monopolizing Rebecca's only chance for future happiness.

Ally saw Rebecca's scowl. 'He's thirty-eight and divorced,' she whispered, nodding at Ludo's back. 'Decree nisi came through about a week ago. Which makes him about as desirable a commodity as Perrier in the Sahara Desert. And doesn't he know it.'

Rebecca put on her best bored expression. 'Yeah, he does seem a bit full of himself.'

Ally smiled sympathetically. Rebecca knew what she was thinking: thank God she was with Jon and no longer had to put herself out there. But surely it was better to be alone than with Jon?

Although wasn't that what Katie had said to her about Tim?

'So who are you seeing at the moment, beautiful?' asked Freddie as they made their way into the kitchen.

'Oh,' Rebecca shrugged, 'nobody.' She spoke as loudly as possible, hoping Ludo would hear. Otherwise he was bound to think she was in a couple. After all, everyone else was.

At that moment, in the other room, 'Waltzing Matilda' started to play.

'Who does that belong to?' Jenny laughed.

'Not me!' cried Freddie, patting his jacket pocket. The others agreed.

'I have the "Bob the Builder" tune on mine,' Laura announced. 'Jago adores it.'

'I don't have a mobile,' said Jon. 'We got along fine without them for years, didn't we?'

'But you give my number out to everyone,' Ally laughed. 'I'm always . . .' Suddenly, she stopped.

'It's mine,' Rebecca confessed. Stealthily, she approached her bag like a ticking land-mine and extracted the phone just as the ringing stopped.

One missed call. *Tim.*

She looked at her watch. It was a quarter to nine. What the fuck?

'Who is it?' enquired Freddie, peering over her shoulder.

'Whoever, they're not invited!' Jenny yelled from the kitchen.

Once again, the jaunty tune started. It wasn't voicemail, it was Tim again.

Don't do it, Rebecca told herself. Turn it off. Why is he ringing so late? He can get stuffed. Who needs a man anyway? Remember you're wearing your sports bra. Think of the state of your flat. She glanced over her shoulder at Freddie. Suddenly his giggling and wiggling annoyed her beyond reason. The choice was stark: answer the phone or be doomed to a life of fag-haggery.

'Hello?'

'Rebecca!' Loud music and voices in the background.

'Tim.'

'Becca, where are you? I thought I was going to see you! What happened? Why didn't you call me?'

'Er, why didn't you call me, Tim?' Freddie made another of his delighted seal gestures. 'Fuck off,' Rebecca mouthed at him.

'I want to talk to you, Rebecca. I love you.'

'Tim, I'm busy. You said you'd call and you didn't. I'm at a dinner party and it sounds like you are too. We will talk in the morning. Goodbye.'

She hung up. 'Ice maiden!' cried Freddie. 'You *are* the weakest link!'

The phone rang again. Freddie snatched it. 'Now listen,' he said in a deep John Wayne voice. 'Rebecca's here with me. She doesn't want to talk to you. Ow! Rebecca, get your hands out of my pants. Got it, buddy? So see ya. Wouldn't want to be ya!' Tittering, he turned off the phone and slipped it into his jeans pocket.

Laura howled with laughter. Rebecca did not. 'Why did you do that?'

'To put him in his place! The bastard! He's not giving you the respect you deserve – and I don't like that.'

Would people *stop* saying that?

'Your soup's getting cold,' Jenny shouted.

And so Rebecca ate a dinner of watery-tasting broccoli and coconut soup, bouillabaisse and burnt saffron rice, followed by pistachio ice cream. She was seated next to Gordon, but he kept running into the kitchen to help Jenny, so she was forced to make conversation with Laura, who, she discovered, used to be a gynaecologist.

'I know,' Laura smiled, seeing Rebecca's face. 'Once I had a life.'

'Oh, that wasn't what I was thinking!' Rebecca lied hastily. Even though she was dying to have a baby, she still regarded all mothers as robotic milk machines.

'But I don't regret giving it all up for *one second*. My family mean everything to me. Do you have children?'

'No.' *You know I don't.*

Laura's eyes narrowed. 'And how old are you now?'

She was doing this on purpose. 'I'm thirty-six,' Rebecca muttered through clenched teeth. She prayed Ludo hadn't heard her. Luckily Jenny had him locked in intense conversation.

'Thirty-six!' Laura screamed. 'Gosh, I didn't realize you were that old. Rebecca, don't take this the wrong way but you should really think about freezing your eggs. I could put you in touch with the right people, if you want.'

Silence fell on the table. Rebecca's dreams of heading straight to the East End and the scaggiest pub she could find in search of a contract killer were interrupted by Jenny.

'God, everyone's having babies right now. There's you, Laura, and Marie who I work with and Joanna Tarbutt. Must be something in the water.'

'Joanna Tarbutt?' said Ally in a slightly strained voice. 'Who's the father?'

'Her boyfriend,' said Jenny, surprised. 'I didn't know you knew her.'

'I was at uni with her. Didn't know she had a boyfriend.' Ally looked tense, Rebecca thought, *Oh God. Freeze your eggs, Al. Anything's better than him as a father.* She checked that her friend's glass was full of wine. Yes. So at least the danger could still be averted.

'Yes, there is a bit of a baby boom.' Laura smiled. 'I think women are realizing that no career, however satisfying, can make up for the love of a child.'

Ally got up and rather noisily started gathering plates.

'So what do you do, Jon?' Gordon was asking.

'I make films actually,' Jon said.

'Oh? I love movies. Anything I might have seen?'

'I doubt it,' Jon said witheringly. 'I don't go in for *commercial* cinema. I'm trying to do something a little bit more difficult. But it's not easy, government funding for arts in this country is a fucking scandal. I mean, when you think what they pay Ally just to buy and sell euros . . .'

'But a good proportion of Ally's wages goes into funding your films,' Rebecca said. 'So it all works out nicely in the end.'

'Did Ally tell you that?' Jon sounded threatening.

Jenny hastily raised her voice. 'Now, who's for coffee? Or tea?'

'Do you have any peppermint?' everyone asked.

Jenny assured them she did. 'And now why don't we all swap places? Everyone move up a slot.'

And suddenly Rebecca had a new neighbour, Ludo. Automatically, she ran her fingers through her hair and put on her most sympathetic smile.

He was quick to start telling her about the divorce.

'Oh, how sad,' said Rebecca, brushing her hand against his as she reached for the teapot. 'Any children?'

'No, thank God,' Ludo said bleakly.

Bingo! 'And where are you living now?'

'I'm sleeping on a friend's floor in Dalston. My wife is keeping the house.'

'Oh, poor you!' Rebecca tried hard to sound genuinely sorry.

'Well, it could be worse. My boyfriend stays over most nights. I'd stay with him, but he still lives at home with his mother.'

It was just as Freddie had always said, all men were gay. Rebecca spent the rest of the evening pretending she had known why Ludo's marriage had broken up all along. As soon as she could she made an excuse about work to catch up on tomorrow and called a minicab.

'Aren't you coming to Heaven with us?' Freddie asked, handing back her mobile. He caught Ludo's eye and winked.

'Could be fun,' Ally teased, but she squeezed Rebecca's arm. Rebecca looked at her gratefully. She adored Ally. Please don't let her get pregnant by that bog troll.

On the way home, Rebecca contemplated her life. She felt strangely fatalistic. This was it. Her dating days were over. From now on she was going to live a life of celibacy. She would channel her energies into visiting exhibitions and helping the poor and sick. As for children, she would adopt. A little Chinese girl, perhaps. She'd dress her in cute Jigsaw dresses and bring her up to be trilingual, a brilliant ice skater and a ballerina. All the advantages Rebecca never had.

It wasn't as if her own dad had been around a lot.

Rebecca realized she'd forgotten to turn on her mobile. God! She might as well have left the house stark naked. This was fantastic. Katie would be so proud. She was following her advice without even trying.

She took it out of her bag. She'd just turn it on quickly. Mum might have called. It rang straight away. How satisfying. A message. It was true. As soon as you stopped caring they all came running after you.

'Rebecca, it's Jenny. Listen, I think you've gone off with Laura's scarf. Her Graham and Greene one. Obviously a mistake, but she's a bit pissed off. Call me back.'

Oh, for heaven's sake. Rebecca had *not* gone off with anyone's scarf. As if. It was just Jenny longing to hear what a brilliant hostess she was. Well, she could wait.

As for the lack of other messages, Rebecca didn't care. Maybe she would even give her mobile phone away. They were a burden, a weight on her chi. Or was it her chakra? Rebecca gave up one of her regular prayers of thanks that they hadn't had mobile phones or email when she was at school. If they had she'd still be sitting behind the bike sheds, waiting for Billy Worcester to get back to her.

Her thoughts turned to the morning. Sunday. No one to snuggle with, again. What on earth was she going to do all day? Perhaps she could go to church. Then she could book a holiday in a Himalayan retreat. Lots of yoga and vegetarian food. If she drank the tap water she'd probably catch a disgusting bug and lose at least a stone. Would there be any single men there?

The car drew up at Dartmouth Mansions. Tim was sitting on the steps.

Rebecca's heart rollercoastered. Immediately she pulled herself together. She'd been disappointed too many times. He'd probably come to ask if he could have his DVDs back or something. Whatever. He could whip out a ring, she wasn't interested.

Hands shaking, she paid the driver and slowly got out of the car.

'Rebecca!' He grabbed her arm. He was dishevelled, he stank of booze and he was delicious.

'It's a bit late, isn't it, Tim?' She pushed past him and put her key in the lock.

'Why are you doing this to me? We have to talk.'

'I don't think so. Now, have you come to pick up your things? Because I'd rather you came when I was out. When the cleaner's here.' The thought of the cleaner made her sound fiercer than she felt.

'But Rebecca, this is different. I'm sorry. Why won't you let me see you?'

Her mouth felt very dry. She turned to face him. He was pale and his mousy hair stood up in a pointy quiff.

'Tim, I need to sleep. Go home.'

'I can't get a cab at this time of night. You wouldn't want me to walk, would you? All the way to Dulwich? I'm hardly a top physical specimen, am I, Rebecca?' He flexed a non-existent muscle and grinned winningly.

She said nothing.

'Oh, I see. She's cross with me. Oh, you're a hard woman, Rebecca. And I'm so soft about you. Please.' He reached out and brushed her hand. 'Just let us talk.'

'We can talk tomorrow.'

'Tomorrow! Where's your spontaneity? Tomorrow is another day. I'm here *now.*'

She didn't know if he meant it or not, but the threat was there. Don't let me slip through your fingers. Tomorrow I might be gone again.

'God, you look gorgeous,' Tim said, brushing her hair away from her face.

'OK,' she said. 'You can come in. But you're not spending the night.'

They both knew she didn't mean it. And so Tim Beaumann saved £22 on a taxi fare, got a free bed for the night and a blow job from Rebecca Greenhall.

13

That Saturday evening Katie and Crispin went to an Ethiopian restaurant in Cricklewood.

'So what have you been up to for the last couple of days?' he asked, once they had ordered.

'Oh, not a lot,' said Katie, who knew what he would think of love training. 'What about you?'

As usual, Crispin had been busy. 'Last night Hugh and Anthony and I went to this new club in Brick Lane,' he told her. 'It was really cool, they had this room full of amazing installations and we got into a fascinating conversation with a group of Colombians we met about the drug trade.'

'Theoretical or practical?'

Crispin waved his fork at her. 'Katie! Naughty!' Crispin was far too paranoid about his standing as a barrister to ever dream of getting involved with illegal substances. He didn't even really like being in the room when people were smoking dope.

'And today?'

'Today, I got up early, I went to my Tai Chi class, then on the way home I checked out this fabulous new Portuguese deli. I made a delicious lunch of salt cod and various cheeses. Maybe we should go to Portugal this summer. And in the afternoon I read the *Guardian* and did some work.'

It was Crispin's best quality, the fact that he was a walking *Time Out* guide, determined to cram every minute with activity, to make the most of what London had on offer. On the surface Katie shared his enthusiasms but secretly she felt guilty that she didn't always feel like attending an Urdu/English poetry reading in Southall, that sometimes she would just like to spend Saturday nights chilling out with a bottle of wine and a really bad film.

For the second time that weekend an image of Paul floated into her head. Paul naked, his legs crossed to hide the vital bits, sitting on the bed in their hotel room in Morocco, wearing shades, holding up a hardboiled egg and laughing. It was her favourite photo of him, which she kept hidden in a P. D. James paperback in her bedroom.

To her surprise, her throat began to ache. She could remember that holiday so well. Laughing at a group of Italians dancing in the hotel disco. Her fury – and Paul's amusement – when they'd returned to the pool after lunch one afternoon and found some Germans had snaffled their loungers. Paul being late for their pre-booked jeep excursion into the desert, because he suddenly decided he needed to go to the loo. The guide said they'd leave without him. Katie had been in tears, begging him to wait just another five minutes, and the Norwegian couple they were going with were mumbling disapproval, when she had seen Paul ambling towards them completely unperturbed.

Paul had always been late for everything, she reminded herself. And he had always been making her cry, especially on that holiday, their last one together before he took the job in LA.

Naturally, Paul had waited until the last possible moment to tell her he was leaving.

'So I had a meeting with Giles this morning,' he said. 'He says the LA job's coming up in the autumn and he'd like me to take it.'

'Well done,' said Katie, almost sincerely. 'That's fantastic. We'll have to go out and celebrate.' If she was calm it was because she had been hacking into Paul's emails for the past few months and was well aware of every detail of the tortured negotiations to win this plum post.

And so that evening they sat in a nasty steak house off Regent Street, where they ate rubbery fillets with flabby chips and toasted Paul's departure with red wine that scoured the inside of your mouth.

'So when did you find out you were going?' Katie asked. *Four days ago*, she thought.

'Oh, just this morning.'

'What, Giles just sprang it on you?'

'Yes.' Paul shook more ketchup on to his plate.

'And you made up your mind just like that?' It was as if there was a cold rock in her chest keeping down the tears.

'Katie, it's what I've always wanted.' He leaned forward and stroked her cheek. 'You can come and visit me.'

Perhaps Katie should have made more of a fuss: demanded to know how Paul thought he could have it both ways – his dream career half a world away and his devoted girlfriend back home. But Katie's self-imposed rules stopped her from asking. She'd won him from Aline (well, sort of) by refusing to make a fuss, by setting him free. Now she would just have to suppress the pain and let him go.

Katie had always been a hopeless diva, unlike Jess who slammed doors, banged her fists against walls and screamed the place down every time she was dumped from a great height or mislaid her housekeys. But there was no doubt she was suffering.

'Katie, you've lost so much weight,' Orla exclaimed as they queued for the cinema the following night.

'Well, there has to be some advantage in going out with a bastard,' Katie laughed.

'So he didn't ask you to come with him?' Orla said as they took their places in the stalls.

Katie stared straight at the screen. 'Well, to be honest, I'm not sure I'd have gone. I mean, Los Angeles! I'd have to find a new job. Make new friends.'

'But he didn't ask, did he?'

Katie continued to avoid eye contact. 'Orls, if he'd asked me a year ago I would have gone. No question. But now I'm really not sure. I love him more than anything, but I don't trust him. I should use this as a chance to end it. Get away from him.' She squeezed Orla's arm. 'Shall we check out that new club on Wardour Street later? It's meant to be really cool.'

But although she managed to keep up her self-contained front with her friends, with Paul she was daily growing more paranoid and obsessive.

Every morning of their holiday, she promised herself she would stay breezy, yet a few hours later she would be crying helplessly, begging him not to leave. Sometimes he got angry.

'You're making me feel so guilty,' he'd say, storming into the bathroom and running the taps.

Other times he cried too. 'I'll miss you so much,' he'd whisper, running his fingers along her arm. 'Do you know what's the first thing I'm going to do when I get there?'

'What?'

'I'm going to send you a ticket. We'll only be apart for a couple of weeks.'

But why, what's the point? Katie thought. How can it last when we're 6,000 miles apart? How can I live without you?

But then Paul had always been a master at evading reality. Ever since that weekend when he'd said he was going to his mother's, then sneaked off to see Aline, she'd known he was a liar. She forgave him, because she saw his behaviour as more of a weakness than a crime. He just wasn't brave enough to face the consequences of his actions.

It was weird, but in some way it almost helped to know that he wasn't perfect. And she knew he loved her. How wrong could you be? Now, she knew it was a sort of craziness they had, a physical obsession, but not love. After all, Katie thought furiously, how could you love someone and plan to leave the country behind their back?

Still, he definitely preferred her to the other women. And there had been plenty of them, although at the time she had tried to ignore the signs. For a start, she stayed over at his less and less. And once when she had rung his flat early one morning a girl had answered, for Christ's sake!

'Who are you?' Katie asked.

'I'm Marion,' the girl said smugly. Marion was a Paris-based freelancer. 'Paul's gone to work.'

'Why was Marion staying at your flat?' she asked Paul politely, when she tracked him down on his mobile. He wouldn't answer her calls, so she'd ended up withholding her number so he'd think it was the office calling.

'We'd had a drink. She needed somewhere to crash,' he replied with equal equanimity.

'It made me feel funny, her answering the phone,' Katie said, declining to make a scene.

'Yes,' said Paul. 'I'd feel pretty funny if I rang your flat and some bloke answered.' And they left it at that.

A few weeks later she met Jeevan for a drink.

'How's it going with Paul?' he asked gently. Katie knew that the whole office gossiped about nothing else, like the court of Charles and Diana.

'Fine,' said Katie stiffly.

Jeevan's tone could not have been more gentle. 'You know there's a rumour around that he's been seeing Marion?'

Katie didn't know. 'Yeah, yeah, I've heard that. It's not true.'

'Of course it isn't,' Jeevan smiled.

She couldn't help wondering how she could have done things differently. *Why* had she been the first to crack and say 'I love you'? *Why* had she made her pain so obvious? And why had she given Paul such a ridiculously long leash: tolerating his lateness, his unreliability, his obvious infidelities? She should have left him, but she couldn't. She loved him too much.

Oh well, she'd been very young. And she'd learned a lot.

It was a situation the much older Rebecca could learn

from too. Katie wondered how her evening had gone. She thought of texting her, but that would be ridiculous.

'So what shall we do tomorrow?' Crispin asked. 'There's a South American festival on the South Bank.'

'Actually, tomorrow I may be working.'

'Working?'

'For Rebecca. I said I might go round and do some cleaning.'

'On a *Sunday*? That's exploitation!'

'Well, not really, it's as good a day as any other.'

'But it's *our* day, the day we spend together,' Crispin pointed out, his voice rising in indignation. 'Katie, you can clean Monday to Friday, when I'm at work. But don't do this to me at the weekend.'

'You're always bringing work home.'

'Yeah, but mine's a *proper* job.'

Instantly, he was sorry. 'Oh Katie. I shouldn't have said that. That was so mean of me. Sorry, baby. Of course you can work tomorrow. Or any day. I shouldn't belittle your job. I just know you can do better than this.'

But on Sunday, Katie's phone never rang although she kept it switched on all day. Once she even tested it by calling it from a landline. Nothing. Rebecca had forgotten all about her.

14

On Sunday, Rebecca woke up with Tim beside her. She wriggled around a bit hoping he would stir, then when she realized he was out cold, slid out of bed and into the shower. She spent a lot of time in there, soaping her body luxuriantly, piling her wet hair on the top of her head, arranging a cute blob of shampoo on her nose for when Tim surprised her.

Twenty minutes later she was wrinkled all over and had to get out. She dried herself and squeezed the tube of body lotion. It was nearly empty and made an awful farting sound. God! Perhaps Tim would think *she*'d done it? Scarlet, she poked her head around the door. He seemed still to be sleeping.

Rebecca slipped naked under the duvet again. She leaned over and gave Tim a featherlight kiss on the cheek. He slept on.

Oh well. Rebecca rolled out of bed again, dug around in her drawers, found a sexy black Janet Reger camisole and pulled it on. Fuck, she was freezing but she wanted to be looking delectable. In the kitchen, she made a pot of fresh coffee and put some bacon into a pan. Thank God she had gone shopping yesterday. The smells would seep into Tim's unconsciousness, slowly waking him, when he would be in the most fantastic mood.

She licked her lips and grinned, wandering over to the

mirror to rearrange her damp locks. Perhaps she should put on some makeup?

Nee-naw, nee-naw, blared the smoke detector.

Fuck, the bacon was burning! Rebecca sprinted over to the cooker. Yawning and unshaven, in his baggy boxer shorts, Tim appeared in the doorway.

'Rebecca!'

'Sorry, sorry, sorry, honey!' Rebecca dashed around the flat opening windows. 'Sorry! Did I wake you?'

Tim gave her a withering glance. 'What time is it?'

'Uh. About ten.'

'Christ, it's still the fucking middle of the night.' He retreated into the bedroom.

Rebecca spent the next half-hour slouching around the kitchen and flicking through magazines before she made her next move. Sneaking into the fetid bedroom, she pulled last night's top off the floor (OK, it stank a bit of cigarettes but it did show her tits to their best advantage) and fumbled around in the wardrobe for some jeans.

'Uurgh!' came a sound from the bed.

Encouraged, Rebecca sat down and tenderly stroked Tim's brow. 'Honey, I thought I'd just get the papers and some croissants.'

'Cool,' Tim groaned. 'Make sure you get the *Sunday Telegraph*. It's got the best sport.'

Much cheered by this exchange, Rebecca went down to the corner shop and bought all the papers. They were out of croissants (well, it was getting on for lunchtime), so she settled for sliced bread and a pot of jam. They would have toast and get crumbs all over the sheets.

When she got back, Tim was in the shower. When he

emerged, he seemed quite happy to sit at the breakfast bar munching toast and reading about football.

'Actually,' he said, glancing at his watch, 'the football's on now. You've got Sky. Do you mind if I watch some?'

'Of course not!' said Rebecca, thrilled to be able to keep him there. For the rest of the afternoon she sat snuggled beside him on the sofa trying to look absorbed, even though she was yearning to be tucked up in bed studying the Style sections. She tried asking some questions: 'What's a corner?' 'What's offside?' and Tim would patiently explain. *For God's sake*, she thought at one point, *Tim doesn't pore over Lancôme adverts to try and please me.* But she checked herself. Relationships were all about sacrifice. This was where she had gone wrong in the past.

In the ad break, she tried, once or twice, to grapple playfully with his belt buckle, but Tim, transfixed by a little boy frolicking on the lawn with a dalmatian puppy, didn't seem to notice.

At about five, the football ended and a film, starring someone who used to be in *Dallas*, began. They watched this too. Rebecca glanced occasionally out of the window. It had been a glorious spring day. Now it was getting dark. So much for the walk in the park she had been looking forward to. 'Could you make us a cuppa?' Tim said at one point. A little later, he turned to Rebecca. 'Anything else to eat?' he asked hopefully.

At the back of the freezer Rebecca found an oven-ready curry. She remembered buying it for her ex, Jamie. Well, it was only three years past its sell-by date. She looked over at Tim, absorbed by the television like a child at the circus.

'He won't fucking notice,' she thought, with a sudden flash of bitterness, stabbing the plastic cover with a fork.

And he didn't, eating it enthusiastically, then placing the empty plate on the sofa beside him. Rebecca picked it up and put it in the dishwasher. *What is this?* she thought. *Have you lost the use of your legs?*

Beep beep. Oh goodie, a text. At least someone loved her. She snatched up her phone.

Call 08987 444444 b4 6 and you cd win a gr8 prize!

She deleted it in disgust. 'Christ, that's about the fourth junk text I've had this week. It's driving me crazy. I mean . . . how dare these people think they can invade your life like that?'

Tim barely looked at her. 'Could you save the chatting? I'm trying to *watch* this.'

Rebecca felt as if she had been bitten by a chihuahua. Suddenly, something Katie had said came back to her. *Dogs are pack animals. They don't appreciate democracy. They like to have a boss to look up to and who sets the rules.* Maybe she should just tell Tim to turn the bloody telly off.

She stopped herself. Probably she *was* being annoying. Anyway, she had been attracted to Tim because he was wild and different. Why on earth should he care about the navel fluff of her life?

Anyway, Tim *did* love her, and the proof came after the news and with the opening chords of the *Antiques Road Show* theme. He seized the remote and switched off the television.

'Rebecca Greenhall,' he said. 'I want to take you to bed.'

And so they made love in last night's rumpled sheets.

159

And it was . . . quite good, although Tim did come rather more quickly than Rebecca would have liked.

Still. 'You're an amazing woman,' he said afterwards, kissing her on the top of her head. And then rolling out of bed and pulling on his boxers. 'Got to go now, honey. It's a school night, you know.'

Once, Rebecca would have protested. But that was before she had taken at least some of Katie's words on board.

'OK,' she shrugged.

Tim looked faintly surprised. 'Well . . . thanks for a top day.'

Rebecca smiled. 'My pleasure.'

'And . . . see you.'

It was her cue to say 'When?' and whip out her Palm Pilot to fix the next date. But now she knew better.

'See you.'

'Are you OK?' Tim asked.

'Yeah, I'm cool. But . . .' She jumped out of bed and quickly pulled on her dressing-gown. 'I'm kind of busy. You know, it's been great hanging out with you today. But now I have things to do.'

Still looking confused, Tim kissed her on the doorstep. 'Well, goodbye.'

'Goodbye,' she said more firmly than she meant it, and shut the door.

And when he was gone, Rebecca realized that she meant it: that she did have things to do: applying her Sunday fake tan, reading the papers properly for mentions of clients, phoning the girls for a gossip and ordering in some sushi. Time to detox after all those carbs.

Katie's advice had been good, she realized, as she ran her bath. It was such obvious stuff: step back and they come running forward, but it had been incredible to see it in action. She paused for a moment, hand over the hot tap, as a tiny idea began to form at the back of her mind.

Hmmm. Interesting. These days, much of Rebecca's career ran on auto-pilot. Sure, there were crises, but she knew she could weather them. As for innovations, she left most of those to Ben. He was the creative one in their partnership, she was more practical. But perhaps this could be *something* . . .

She ran to her desk, scribbled a note on her jotter, then ran back to the bath, threw off her robe and climbed in.

In the hot, oily water, she luxuriated in the joy of being back with Tim. The thing about him, she decided, was he was a free spirit. Just because he was always late, or abandoned her for hours at his friends' parties where she knew no one, in order to have an intense conversation with some model, didn't mean he didn't care. She would just have to try to be more like him. Follow her own path. Because it was great to be back together. Great to be in a couple. Great to know she was no longer doomed to a lifetime of gay and married men.

15

A month passed and Rebecca and Tim were really very happy. Summer was coming to London and they spent the evenings sitting on Rebecca's tiny roof terrace, smoking spliffs and drinking wine, looking down at the people strolling in Hyde Park.

Rebecca had a rather stilted conversation with Katie, when she told her she was welcome to keep cleaning the flat, but the love-trainer idea was a bit silly – didn't she think? At heart Rebecca knew she had used some of Katie's advice and that it had worked, but the thought of Katie hovering over them searching for flaws, like a wasp at a picnic, was more than she could take.

But Katie seemed fine about the whole thing. In fact, she was relieved to leave Rebecca's love life alone. She was still certain Tim was a twat and Rebecca was going to end up hurt, but why involve herself in the car crash?

So Katie continued to clean the flat. In the meantime she applied for forty-six jobs, which led to eight interviews and one offer as deputy head of human resources for a chain of pizza restaurants. Katie knew she was being a spoilt bitch, but she just couldn't bear it. She decided to keep looking. There was still just about enough in the bank for that.

Meanwhile, she had absorbed herself in the lives of Jess and Ronan. Jess, as usual, had been shagging another actor and things had been going swimmingly for three weeks, but when he got a new job, he dumped her out of the blue. 'When I love something or someone I have to give myself to it fully,' he had said. 'And I love you, but I also love my work. And there isn't room for both of you in my life.'

'Sounds like a poor excuse to me,' Katie said, and Ronan agreed. Jess wasn't so sure – 'He did really like me, I could tell!' – but since it had only been three weeks, she couldn't be upset for more than half a day. Then she went out and slept with a man from *Holby City*'s props department, whom she'd met when she had a small part as a drug dealer six months earlier.

As for Ronan, he had called Claire from the party and she had agreed to go on a date with him. They went out twice but didn't snog. When Ronan called her for a third date her flatmate told him she had gone to live in Manchester for the foreseeable future. Ronan called her on her mobile a few times but she never answered. Eventually he got the hint.

One June weekend, when the forecast was particularly brilliant, Katie, Jess and Ronan decided to visit Katie's parents in Solihull.

'It's not exactly Barbados,' Katie said. 'But they have got a massive garden and a fridge full of ice cream.'

The others thought it sounded an excellent idea. They packed into Jess's beaten-up Toyota Corolla and headed off down the M40. 'But you don't actually give a flying fuck about seeing your parents,' Ronan said, just as they turned on to the M42. 'You just want to see Elton.'

'Too right,' Katie yelled over the strains of some boy

band Jess was insisting on playing. 'It's been bloody months. I've missed him so much.'

'If you were on a desert island and you had the choice of Elton or Crispin for company, who would it be?' Jess asked, giving the finger to a yellow Porsche that had just overtaken her on the inside.

'That's so tough,' Katie wailed. 'I mean, normally I'd say Elton but he can't have many years left. So I guess it would have to be Crispin.'

Jess grinned at her in the mirror, then realized, from her cousin's pained expression, that she was completely serious.

'How old is Elton?' Ronan asked.

'He's fifteen,' Katie said proudly. 'Which makes him . . .' She failed to do the maths. 'Very old in dog years.'

'Older than a hundred,' Ronan agreed solemnly.

As their car backed into the Wallaces' driveway, Elton was waiting to meet them, waggling his stubby little tail and barking his old lungs out.

'My baby,' said Katie, falling upon him. His long silky ears bounced up and down as he slobbered all over her face with his raspy tongue.

'Now, that is what I call true love,' laughed Minette Wallace, kissing her daughter and niece.

Minette turned to Ronan. 'Handsome boy! How are you?' Katie's brother, Nick, lived in Hong Kong, so Minette used Ronan as a substitute son.

'God, you're looking gorgeous today, Minette. That outfit really suits you.'

Katie and Jess caught each other's eye and made discreet gagging gestures.

'Hello, sweetheart,' said Geoff Wallace, giving his daughter a friendly hug. He patted Jess helplessly on the head and waved shyly at Ronan. Geoff was fond of his daughter's flatmates, but at the same time slightly baffled by their *ménage à trois*. He would never have dropped in uninvited at the flat in the Elephant for fear of disturbing something he would rather not know about.

'Hello, Geoff. How are you? How was Vietnam?' Ronan said. Katie was almost regretting bringing him. He was such an arselicker.

But her dad just looked at Ronan with faint hostility. 'Fine,' he said and delved into the boot for his daughter's bag.

'Such a shame Crispin couldn't make it,' Minette sighed as they followed her into the kitchen for cups of tea. 'Working again is he? He works too hard.'

'That's how he makes his money, Mum.'

'Well, money isn't everything. Tell him we miss him.'

God, sometimes it was like Mum loved Crispin more than she did. Katie had never minded him working too hard. It meant when they did see each other they had something to talk about and it kept that clinginess Paul had induced in her at bay. Which reminded her of something she'd planned to do this morning. She'd wait until after lunch.

Despite the minor family irritations, it was nice really to be home. Minette had made no effort to cook, but had stripped M&S of cold meats and salads, which they ate in the garden, in the shade of the old willow tree. It had been cloudy during the drive, but now the mist had been burned away and the sun shone fiercely.

Elton watched the table with baleful eyes. Ronan tried to slip him a scrap of cold beef.

'Stop that now!' Geoff roared.

'But he's so adorable,' Ronan pleaded, red-faced.

'He's a fat slob and you are making him even fatter,' Geoff retorted. 'Do you want him to have a heart attack?'

The conversation turned to Geoff and Minette's next holiday, to Argentina. It was slightly galling, Katie thought, that her parents were always travelling, while she – having never had a gap year – had never done India, or Thailand. In fact, the most exotic place she had ever been to was Los Angeles. At the memory, she shivered slightly. But maybe it was just the sun passing behind a cloud.

After lunch, they snoozed on loungers: Jess right out in the sun without even a hat on, the others in the shade. It took all Katie's energies to steel herself to go into the house and upstairs to her old bedroom, a spooky shrine to Katie Wallace aged eighteen with its faded poppy duvet and Lou Reed posters on the wall. On the dressing-table sat a collection of nail varnishes, untouched for a decade. She should throw them out, she thought, but somehow she liked knowing this old part of her was still there.

She turned to the bookshelf and ran her eyes along the battered paperbacks. *Ballet Shoes*, *Claudine at St Clare's*, *National Velvet*. Occasionally she picked one up and lost herself for a few moments in her eleven-year-old self, whose three ambitions had been to dance at Sadler's Wells, go to boarding school (preferably the Royal Ballet School, although everyone knew it was fiendishly difficult to get in) and win the Grand National. Boys hadn't figured then and the whole world had been at her feet. Where the hell had it all gone?

'Katie,' Ronan bellowed up the stairs, making her jump. 'What are you doing? We're all having Magnums.'

Katie snapped back to the present again. She continued running her finger along the spines. Aha! Here it was. *The Complete Dog Trainer* by Dr John Fretton. On the cover, a labrador puppy grinned imploringly, holding a lead between his teeth. It was exactly the kind of look Paul used to give her after he had stayed out all night or not called for three days.

She heard Ronan's voice again. Fussing as usual. 'Kate?'

'Coming!' She hurried down the stairs. Ronan was standing at the bottom, holding a teapot.

'Your parents have gone for a walk, but we said it was too hot to move,' he explained. 'Minette's left your Magnum in the freezer.'

'That's good,' said Katie absently, sitting down on a lounger and opening the book.

'What's that?' Jess asked.

'My old dog-training manual.'

'Are we going to get a dog?'

'Unfortunately not. Unless you're volunteering to scoop the poop.'

'Yuk.' Jess lay back in her deckchair, exhausted at the very idea.

Katie flicked through the pages. Photograph after photograph of adorable dogs and their less endearing owners – with Eighties mullets and lime T-shirts – instructing them to sit, stand, lie and fetch. Towards the end of the book, hounds were jumping through hoops and running along narrow beams.

'That's probably a bit ambitious for Elton,' said Ronan, peering over her shoulder. 'I think he's more beauty than brains.'

'Takes one to know one.'

'Ah, ha, ha!' Ronan whacked her over the head with the *Daily Mail* Weekend Magazine. Katie, absorbed in the preface, ignored him.

'Guys,' she said slowly. 'Do you remember what I said about men needing to be trained, like dogs?'

'Mmm-hmm,' Jess yawned. She had no idea what her cousin was talking about.

'Well, it works! I can't believe it. Virtually any rule in this book could just as easily be applied to people.'

'Such as?'

Katie came straight back at her. '*Female dogs' moods change according to the time of year.*'

'The time of month,' Jess corrected.

'Or day in your case,' Ronan sniggered.

Katie cleared her throat. '*Female dogs are easier to obedience-train, easier to house-train and more demanding of affection.*'

'Not sure about that,' said Ronan. 'You're not house-trained, are you, Jess?'

'Nope! And my obedience is rubbish.'

Katie ignored them. *More demanding of affection.* She'd never forgotten the way she used to snuggle up to Paul in bed and he'd push her away saying he was too hot.

'*Male dogs are more likely to be dominant, aggressive and destructive.*'

'Except for Ronan.'

'Maybe Ronan was neutered,' said Katie, and was rewarded with a thump from a cushion. She skimmed down the page.

'OK. This one works for men and women. *Dogs respond to rewards and develop bad habits when bored.*'

'That's true,' Jess agreed. 'When I'm bored I go out and take drugs and then I pick up ugly men and shag them.'

'Carry on,' Ronan urged, slathering his six-pack with sun cream.

'Ummm.' Katie flicked through the pages. 'Well, not all of it's relevant. I mean, there's this bit about leashes.'

'Sounds very relevant to me,' Jess chortled.

'You can go to Soho if you want that kind of training.' Katie carried on flicking. 'OK, so here's a list of dos and don'ts.' She read for a minute, then shrieked, 'Listen! Listen! They all make perfect sense.'

'OK,' said Jess, rolling on to her tummy.

'Right. Number one. *Do* be realistic with your expectations of your dog. Two. *Do* treat your dog as someone who should implicitly do as it is told. Three. *Do* be leader: you initiate all activity. Four. *Don't* give in to your dog's demands to be stroked and cuddled. Five. *Don't* let your dogs go through doors or downstairs before you.'

'I always let the lady go first. It's just basic gentlemanly behaviour,' Ronan said.

'It's about reinforcing that you're leader of the pack. Six. *Do* teach your dog to eliminate on command.'

'That would be good,' said Jess. 'Then maybe Ronan would stop hogging the bathroom for hours on end.' Ronan's toilet habits were a source of great wonderment to his flatmates. As Jess put it: 'When I want to do a poo,

I go into the bathroom, I pull down my knickers and I do a poo. But when it's Ronan he announces it to everybody, he searches around for a magazine to read, he locks the door and he stays in there for about an hour, while the rest of us have to cross our legs.'

'Seven. *Do* train the dog to walk nicely by your side.' Katie continued. She was enjoying this. She could just imagine Rebecca laughing her head off as she listened to the list.

Sadly, Rebecca didn't seem to want her advice any more. Katie wished she'd had a rule book like this for her Paul days. The problem was that even though she knew intellectually how to act around him, her emotions had kept getting in the way. She loved him so much, she kept saying stupid things, letting her feelings show. He'd always been the leader in their pack.

She felt a warm, furry head butt her leg. She looked down. It was Elton looking up at her with huge, imploring eyes.

'My darling,' she gasped, holding out her arms and pulling him on to her lap – no easy task. She remembered when Elton had stayed with them, when Mum and Dad were in Borneo and the Claverings next door were unavailable to dog-sit. Every night he would listen for her key in the lock. As she walked in, he would bound over excitedly, cover her in slobber and beg for his dinner.

Mum was right. It was perfect love. She wished everyone could experience it. Especially Rebecca. She didn't know what she was missing out on.

16

Suzanne Bell met Hunter Knipper a year and a half ago in the lobby of the SoHo Grand Hotel in Manhattan. Both were waiting to check out and getting more and more impatient at the ineptitude of the pretty, designer-clad Latino boy behind the desk who had no idea how to swipe credit cards.

'I'm going to miss my flight,' Suzy hissed, and caught herself actually slipping her fingernail into her mouth to chew off a chunk.

'Me too,' said the tall, silver-haired man next to her. He looked a bit like Paul Newman and wore a beautiful navy cashmere overcoat. 'Where you flying to?'

'Heathrow.'

'Me too. Want to share my limo?'

Suzy was impressed. *Seduce!* was far too mean to provide her with a limo and insisted she took grotty yellow cabs driven by psychopaths. But she didn't want this man to know that, so she hesitated.

He saw her pause. 'I'm safe, honest!'

'But how do you know I am?' she replied, and when he laughed she felt her nipples go hard.

So they travelled to JFK together, where Hunter – who turned out to be a very important banker – got Suzy upgraded all the way to First (*Seduce!* were so damn stingy they insisted she sat with the plebs at the back). Normally, on the red eye, Suzy pulled on her sleep mask, took a couple of valium and knew nothing until they hit the tarmac at Heathrow. But this time, she chatted wittily to Hunter all night. At Heathrow they made plans to meet the following evening, and the following night Suzy officially became Hunter's mistress.

It wasn't the first time Suzy had been the other woman and to be honest, she couldn't imagine life any other way. Marriage had never appealed to her – you just had to look at her parents to see why. After thirty-seven years they were still together, but their relationship had always been strained and cold. Dad worked long hours running his own business manufacturing calendars and diaries. Mum had stayed at home and, once Suzy was off at boarding school, hit the gin bottle. After two decades of drying-out clinics, interspersed with neighbour-shocking benders, she was sober now, but husk-like and subdued.

'My problem was I never had enough interests,' she told Suzy once. 'You had gone and the house was perfect, I was bored out of my mind. Never make that mistake, darling.'

Suzy had no intention of doing any such thing. She had filled her life with her job, her friends, her yoga, but decided to give as little as possible to long-term relationships.

Only once, in the very early days of their affair, had Hunter disappointed her. They had had dinner in an Italian restaurant in Soho. When the bill arrived, he made no move to pick it up.

'You are getting this, aren't you?' Suzy had said eventually.

Hunter sighed. 'You know, Suzy, I'm getting a bit tired

of picking up the tab. I feel you're just using me as a meal ticket. Sometimes *I*'d like to be spoilt for a change.'

'*You*'d like to be spoilt!' Suzy screamed. 'Excuse me. I am your kept woman, your bit on the side. The rule is you pay for everything. Where are my chocolates? Where are my flowers?' There was a sudden hush in the restaurant and the Latvian waitress giggled. Then Hunter had laughed too and slapped down his platinum Amex.

Hunter was obliged to spoil her, and he was also banned from burdening her. When he moaned to her about his job or his nightmare marriage – no wonder it was a nightmare when he was seeing someone else – she would make sympathetic noises, but her mind would be far away on her own career niggles. When she saw her friends like Jenny worrying about what to wear for dinner with Gordy's clients, she couldn't help but laugh.

'Mistresses have all the glamour,' she would tell her friends. 'Christine Keeler, Madame de Pompadour, Nell Gwynn . . . Everyone remembers them. No one remembers the wives they supplanted, do they?'

And no one could.

Suzy was very careful to let Hunter know she had no desire for him to leave his wife, Justine. She was much given to making Glenn Close jokes and asking him if his daughters had any pets they were especially fond of.

Once, in the early days, they had been in bed in some hotel where he was attending a conference.

'Whatever you do, don't pick up the phone!' Hunter kept reminding her. 'It might be Justine!'

No kidding, Hunter. They had been lying there, sleepy

after sex, when his mobile had started ringing on the bedside table.

Suzy lunged across the bed for it.

'Helloooo,' she breathed. 'Suzy here, Hunter's bit of fluff. Would you like to speak to him?'

Before he had a heart attack, she confessed that she had dialled him with her mobile, hidden under the sheets. Hunter had not appreciated the joke.

Justine had nothing to fear. Suzy couldn't understand why you would want a man living with you full-time. Filling the fridge with horrors like frozen pizzas. Rucking up the rugs on her beautiful wood floors. Wrinkling her cushions. Leaving mugs on the table. Just the thought of it made Suzy feel as if ants were crawling up and down her spine.

Of course she missed Hunter sometimes: when she had had a bad day at work, or there was a spider in the bath. And sometimes she just wanted sex – but on those occasions there was always some pushy photographer or male model panting to be accepted into the *Seduce!* fold, who was more than happy to sleep with the boss to get there.

Suzy was thinking about this on Monday morning as she sat at her breakfast bar, nibbling on the passion-fruit that constituted her breakfast.

It was 7.15 and she had already done an hour's ashtanga yoga – double her normal session because yesterday she had skipped it altogether and spent most of the day in bed with a twenty-two-year-old wannabe stylist called Seamus Van-Huskins, whom she had picked up at a fashion party in Brick Lane. It had been so relaxing, she mused, just lying there while little Seamus tried every trick in the book to impress her. She hadn't even touched his willy, just barked instructions as to where he should put it. She had booted him out at six, after three lovely orgasms.

'So shall I . . .?' he had asked tentatively on the doorstep.

'Email your CV to my assistant, Gemma Martin, and she'll pass it on to the right people,' Suzy had yawned.

She was pulling her black slip dress over her head and giggling at the memory of his stricken face when her phone rang.

'Honey?'

'Hunter. What are you doing up so late?' She glanced at the silver watch on her slim left wrist – one of his many tokens to her. 'It's the middle of the night in Philadelphia.'

'But I'm not in Philadelphia,' Hunter said. 'I'm here.'

'In London?' Suzy tried to sound delighted.

'Of course in London. Where else? I'm staying at the Vanderton, honey. Your favourite.'

'So what time shall I come round?' Suzy said. She was already pulling off her comfy, white cotton M&S granny pants. Time to replace them with the La Perla Hunter always bought her.

'My meetings should be finished by seven-thirty, baby. As soon after that the better.'

'I can't wait,' whispered Suzy. She hung up. Oh damn. This meant she was going to have to stay up all night drinking champagne and having sex. She'd been really looking forward to the *EastEnders* omnibus that she'd taped yesterday, followed by an early night. She could blow Hunter out, she supposed, but he would be so hurt.

Her phone rang again. Oh, what now?

Rebecca.

'Why are you calling so early?'

'And it's lovely to hear from you too.'

'Yes, but what do you want?'

Rebecca was fizzing with excitement. 'I've had a great idea. I'm going to have a *dinner party*. A week Friday. Are you free?'

'Becs, I hate to break it to you, but the concept of a dinner party is not a new one.'

'Oh, piss off! The point is *me* having a dinner party! You know I never cook. But things are going so well between Tim and me right now, and I really want to give him a helping hand with his career, so I thought I'd get Roddy Bannister over and you and some other fun people.'

'I'm not fun.'

'Oh, Suze! Yes you are. And I thought I'd get Ally and Jon . . .'

'Ally and Jon! They're about as much fun as a holiday in Iraq!'

Rebecca sighed. 'I know, but we can't just dump her.'

'I wish she'd dump her boyfriend, though.' *Not that yours is any better*, Suzy thought, as she pulled on her sexy Grace Kelly raincoat that Hunter loved. Roddy Bannister indeed. He was the chairman of the prestigious Collins Prize for fiction and was as accustomed to bribes as a Colombian police chief. Did Rebecca really think that plying him with a few glasses of champagne and a Nigella recipe would bring Tim within a million miles of the prize? Worse, did she really think that hosting a dinner party for that pathetic specimen was going to lead to Tim coming up with an engagement ring?

'So are you free?' Rebecca repeated. She paused before adding, 'And Hunter too if he's around.'

'Yeah, I'm free,' Suzy said grudgingly. 'But Hunter'll be in Philadelphia.' Actually, she had no idea where Hunter would be, but she had no more intention of bringing him to Rebecca's than of arriving on the arm of Skippy the kangaroo.

'Brilliant!' Rebecca squawked. 'I'm so excited about this. Eight for eight-thirty, OK?'

'OK. See you.'

Suzy slipped her phone into her Furla bag and looked out of the window to check her minicab was waiting. After months of wrangling with management, they had finally agreed to pay for this. After all, how could Suzy be expected to wear the latest footwear *and* travel on the Tube?

Tony, her regular driver, saw her and waved. She smiled. Not bad for a girl from Godalming. She glanced around the room, quickly straightened a picture frame, then headed out the door to conquer the world.

As she got into the battered Volvo (she would have liked a Jag of course, but never mind) she thought of Hunter gagging to see her tonight, then she thought again of Rebecca, running herself ragged to please that ungrateful twat. Somehow it didn't seem fair. Suzy didn't understand. How come if she could run her life perfectly, nobody else could?

17

On Monday afternoon, Katie unlocked Rebecca's front door to find the usual tip. Worse in fact now Tim was virtually living there. Katie picked up some boxers from the floor, emptied two overflowing ashtrays and crumpled up an empty pizza box.

Today Rebecca had left a note, along with her cash.

Dear Katie,
　　I was wondering if you happened to know any caterers? Planning dinner party for six – Friday week. Would ask Tara but she's on honeymoon!
　　Best
　　Rebecca

Oh sure, Rebecca, Katie muttered to herself. How about darling Pierre? I always find he's excellent for intimate little dinners. He can rustle up a *lovely* vichyssoise. What planet did this woman live on?

Her ranting was interrupted by her phone ringing. Ronan.

'Just calling to see if you wanted to come and see the Arnie movie with me and Jess tonight? I'm booking tickets now.'

'Ronan, you old fusspot. We don't need to book!' She

picked up a vase of dying flowers. 'God, you'll never guess what Mrs Bossy wants from me now. She's asking me to find a chef for a dinner party.'

'Wicked,' said Ronan. 'I'll do it.'

'Yes, very funny. I'm going to tell her to fuck herself. Although maybe not in so many words.'

'No!' Ronan bawled. 'Seriously, Katie! Let me do it. You know I love cooking. And that way I'd get to see the inside of Rebecca's flat.'

Katie really wasn't sure about this. Her flatmates and Rebecca equalled certain trouble.

Ronan understood her silence. 'Jess will have nothing to do with this. It'll be just the two of us. I'll cook, you serve. I need the money, Katie. And I promise I won't use the washing machine or try on Rebecca's clothes.'

Katie snorted with laughter. 'I don't think they'd fit you, love.'

It was a good idea. Ronan *was* a fabulous cook and he'd love catering for Rebecca's rich and famous friends. The only problem was Rebecca had seen him before, that night at the flat. Katie was not going in for any more deception. She'd suggest Ronan and if Rebecca said no, there would be no more discussions.

But Rebecca said yes. To tell the truth she was desperate: naturally before she asked Katie she had gone through the Yellow Pages and asked friends for recommendations, but the companies she had rung had all been booked up – and ludicrously expensive as well. But the idea of Katie's gorgeous flatmate doing the cooking appealed. It would be less corporate that way, more *homey*.

Dear Katie,

Just so you know — one of the guests is vegetarian and one thinks he may be suffering from a wheat intolerance, so please bear all this in mind.

Perhaps Ronan could prepare a menu for me to have a look at, about a week in advance?

We'll discuss the fee later.

Best wishes,

Rebecca

Despite the restrictions, Ronan was very, very excited about the dinner. His first choice was a spinach lasagne, until Jess — who was miffed at being kept out of the fun — pointed out that lasagne contained wheat. His next choice was a lentil bake, but that was rejected by both Katie and Rebecca on the grounds of it being too Greenham Common. Finally, everyone settled on a Thai vegetable curry.

'That sounds lovely,' said Rebecca, when Katie told her over the phone the night before. 'But vegetables on their own — it's a bit peasanty, isn't it?'

'But what about the vegetarian?'

'Oh, that was Jon. Didn't I tell you he and Ally had cancelled?' Rebecca sounded breezy, but in fact she was furious. Ally's excuse had been: 'Sorry, but Jon will have just got back from visiting the girls in Cardiff and he says he'll be too emotionally drained.' She sounded incredibly apologetic, but that made it even worse. Why couldn't she just have left Jon at home? And Ally had cancelled so late it was impossible to invite anyone else without it being obvious they were a fall-back. Oh well, Roddy was the guest who really counted. And Suzy was always good, bitchy value. An evening *à quatre* would do Tim's literary prize chances no harm at all and show him what a fabulous hostess she was.

The first blow came at 6.30 p.m. that Friday. Rebecca had left work early to supervise proceedings. It was all very satisfactory: that handsome Ronan was in the kitchen chopping galangal and crushing lime leaves. Katie was ironing a linen tablecloth. Rebecca tried and failed to put her hair in curlers – why hadn't she left enough time for the hairdresser's? – so settled instead on a bath. Relax, relax, everything was in order. She smeared her face with Marcella Borghese mud.

Someone was knocking on the door.

'Rebecca, the phone's ringing! Shall I answer it?'

'Wha'? Oh yes, yes. Please.'

When she emerged from the bathroom twenty minutes later, Katie was standing in the hall looking awkward.

'Um. That was Roddy. He apologizes but says he isn't going to be able to make it.'

'*What?*'

'Apparently he's double-booked. He completely forgot about the other event until half an hour ago, but he really has to go because all the other Collins Prize judges will be there.' Katie didn't look as if she quite believed this.

Rebecca was outraged. That was bloody London life for you. Everyone waiting until the last moment to work out which was their best offer for the night. Now her friends had started to breed, it had got even worse – the au pair was always having a nervous breakdown or little Archie had done a green poo-poo and his mother really didn't feel she could leave him. Anyway, far too late to drag up any new guests.

'Well, it's just going to be me and Suzy and Tim then.'

Katie felt very sorry for Rebecca, but she tried not to show it. 'Well, shall we pack up and go home?' Delicious odours wafted through the flat.

'Huh?' Rebecca thought. 'Oh, no. Ronan might as well finish what he started. It smells so good.' She tried to brighten. 'It'll mean bigger portions all round.'

Katie was relieved. At least Ronan would get paid. 'Well, do you mind if I wait until he finishes? Because then we can travel home together?'

Rebecca's mind was on what she was going to wear. 'No problem,' she said absently.

So Katie went to help Ronan in the kitchen, who rather than being disappointed was delighted by news of his diminishing audience. 'If I fuck up now it won't matter so much.'

'You won't fuck up,' said Katie fondly, inspecting the cheese board.

By 8 p.m., everything was perfect. Katie laid out a small bowl of olives and another of organic sea-salt-encrusted potato chips. In the corner, the dining table had been relaid for three. Candles burned in silver sticks. The champagne was in the fridge. Ronan had prepared a green salad, with a jug of dressing on the side. The curry simmered gently on the stove, with basmati rice in a casserole beside it. The music had changed to David Gray and Rebecca was sitting decoratively on the sofa, pretending to read the *Evening Standard* and occasionally glancing at the clock on the DVD.

At 8.33 p.m. the doorbell rang. Rebecca ran to the intercom.

'It's me!' Suzy announced. Two minutes later she glided into the flat, wearing a tight black sheath dress and high boots. Anyone else would have looked as if she were about to set off for an evening's work at King's Cross, but on Suzy it looked elegant.

She and Rebecca kissed. 'Christ, I've had a god-awful week,' Suzy said. 'I had to spend three days in a hotel near Luton with a focus group. Twelve *Seduce!* readers all asking me if I'd ever met Madonna. Or Beckham. Moaning because their useless boyfriends won't marry them. I mean, have they looked in the mirror lately?'

Rebecca broke the news that Roddy wasn't coming.

'Oh, right. Well, no harm done there. The last time I met him he cracked a series of jokes about how if my readers had their way Geri Halliwell would have won the Collins Prize for fiction. Condescending arsehole.' But Suzy was annoyed. Friday night in with a couple – especially one as ill-conceived as Rebecca and Tim – was never her idea of a good time. Suzy couldn't be bothered being nice to her friends' boyfriends. You made an effort to get to know them, you even started to like them, and then they disappeared and the whole cycle started again.

Katie appeared, bearing two hot, crusty baguettes and a dish of cold, salty butter.

'Suzy, this is Katie who's helping me out tonight. Katie, Suzanne.'

'Hello,' Suzy said.

Katie recognized her from the pictures dotted around the flat. There was one of her and Rebecca on a balcony in some exotic location, drinking cocktails. Suzy had on a beautiful black halterneck swimsuit. Did Rebecca pick all her friends from catalogues? Suzy, in turn, recognized a typical *Seduce!* reader, young and unsure enough of herself to be taken in by all the myths she peddled. She'd better turn on the charm – she was the magazine's ambassador.

'Smells good,' she said in a more friendly tone. Suzy was ravenous, but she wasn't going to admit it. Like the Queen, she preferred to deny all bodily functions. It was a source of wonderment to her staff that they had never spotted her in the office toilets. Only Suzy's PA, Gemma, knew about the little room off the fire escape that her boss had seconded for such purposes.

The only weakness Suzy would admit to was her fondness for cocaine, although she took great care to stay in control of this. After all, it turned most people into inane gibberers – Jenny was the worst. Whenever Suzy took it she went to great lengths to act more self-possessed than ever. As far as she was concerned, coke was merely an appetite suppressant that also kept her awake during endless meetings with advertising reps.

She could do with some now, she thought, digging into her Furla purse.

'Want some?' she asked Rebecca, waving a wrap under her nose, but her friend shook her head. Rebecca loved coke and the powerful feeling it gave her but normally she reserved it for depressing occasions like weddings and birthdays. Still, tonight she might make an exception as Tim would be bound to want some. She'd wait until he got there.

By 9.23, they had exhausted the gossip on everyone

they knew, Suzy had done three fat lines off Rebecca's dressing-table, Rebecca had drunk three glasses of champagne and Tim was officially late.

'Does he always do this?' Suzy asked.

'He'll be on his way,' Rebecca retorted, although inside she felt less confident.

'Well, give him a call and find out what's happening.'

Rebecca needed no encouragement. She hit speed-dial. Voicemail. 'Tim, honey. It's me. Just checking you're on your way. You're probably on the Tube. See you soon.'

Suzy was flicking through an old copy of *Vogue*. 'God, these features are dull! I know for a fact they lifted that idea from *Harpers Bazaar*. So, what's the problem?'

He probably didn't realize you meant eight-thirty literally, Rebecca told herself. *An hour is nothing. There must be problems on the Tube. Or his cab's stuck in traffic and his battery's run out. Tim can be a little scatty. That's why you love him.*

At 9.45 p.m., with Suzy growing more impatient, she tried him again. Still voicemail. She didn't leave a message. She knew now that he wasn't coming.

She went into the kitchen. Ronan and Katie were sitting at the table, looking apprehensive.

'I think we might as well eat now,' she said. She tried to stop her voice from wobbling. 'Tim's been delayed.'

'OK,' said Katie. She knew the truth.

Just then the phone rang. They all started. 'Do you want me to get it?' Katie asked.

'No! No! I will.' Rebecca walked towards it slowly, took a deep breath, then picked it up.

'Hello? Oh, hi. Hi, Roddy. Yes, I'm sorry too . . . Yes, shame you couldn't make it. But never mind. It was totally casual . . . yes, just a few friends I think you'd have enjoyed meeting . . . Yes, we can do it another time . . . OK, well I'll get my PA to call your PA on Monday to rearrange . . . No, I totally understand, these things happen . . . Byeeee.'

Gingerly, she replaced the handset in its cradle.

'Well, thank fuck he isn't here to witness my humiliation,' Rebecca said. Softly, she started to cry.

Ronan was crimson with embarrassment. Katie felt a wave of *déjà vu*. 'Would you like us to go, Rebecca?' she asked.

Puffy-faced, Rebecca shook her head. 'Just excuse me,' she mumbled and disappeared into the bedroom.

'What do we do?' Ronan asked.

'I don't know.' Katie could feel herself shaking with fury. 'I guess we serve up dinner to Rebecca and her Goth friend.'

'Maybe he forgot,' Ronan said hopefully. 'Maybe he thought it was tomorrow night!'

Katie, removing hot plates from the oven, said nothing.

'I can't do this!' she said suddenly, straightening up. 'I can't watch such a woman get so royally fucked over.' She could remember herself, aged twenty-five, in a black lace nightie with suspenders underneath, waiting up until after midnight for Paul to arrive. He never came. As their relationship had soured, it happened more and more, but every time she steeled herself to dump him, he told her he loved her and promised her everything would be different.

'Do you think she'll be all right?' Ronan asked anxiously. He hated scenes.

'Probably not,' Katie said grimly. 'Which is why I'm going to help her.'

She opened the kitchen door and poked her head around it.

'He's stood you up,' Suzy was saying coldly. 'Rebecca, call him now and dump him. Salvage some pride.'

Katie couldn't have agreed more. But Rebecca sat there numbly.

'He's not worthy . . . to lick the dirt from the soles of your shoes,' Suzy continued. Creative writing had never been her forte, that's why she'd gone into journalism.

Rebecca was too depressed even to smile. 'I'm sorry I wasted your evening. Shall I call you a cab?'

Suzy sat on the sofa beside her and placed a skinny arm round her shoulder. 'Hey. I can't leave you until we've worked out the best way of killing Tim.'

Rebecca sighed heavily. 'Suzy, just go. Get to Priory Street and enjoy yourself before the evening is a total write-off. I'll stay here.' She turned to Katie and smiled. 'You and Ronan go too. Just leave the food in the fridge or something. I'll eat it tomorrow.'

But in her current militant mood Katie was having none of this. 'Rebecca, I don't think you should stay in alone. You'll just sit here and torture yourself wondering when Tim's going to arrive and checking the phone, to see if it's not out of order. You need to go out and keep busy.'

'She's right,' Suzy agreed. She looked at Katie with approval. Maybe she wasn't as dumb as she appeared. 'Take control of the situation. The night's not over yet. You can still have fun.'

Yeah, right, thought Rebecca. 'But suppose Tim arrives?'

'Tim is . . .' Katie looked at her watch. 'More than two

hours late. I *sincerely* doubt he's going to turn up now, but if he does why should you be waiting for him?'

'Exactly!' Suzy nodded. 'Come on. Let's go to Priory Street.'

Rebecca shook her head. 'Too many people I'll know there. I'm not in the mood for social chat.'

'Well then, we'll go to a club,' said Suzy. Suzy hated dancing because – like all things athletic – she was no good at it. On the other hand, she adored laughing at other people making fools of themselves. Besides, part of the job was to check out the scene occasionally to see what nonsense her readers were getting down to and what fashion crimes they were wearing.

Rebecca perked up. She *loved* dancing but Tim – for much the same reasons as Suzy – hated it, and in recent months she had hardly done any.

'All right,' she smiled. 'We'll go dancing. How about the Met Bar? It's just down the road. We can walk there.'

Suzy clapped her hands in delight. 'Excellent! Stuffed full of Eurotrash and wannabes.' She took her wrap from her wallet. 'Just wait until I have a line.'

'Suzy!' Rebecca gestured at Katie, still standing there unsure what to do.

'Oh, like Katie cares! Would you like some, darling?' Suzy checked herself. Enough gushiness, already! Perhaps she should slow down?

'No, thanks,' Katie said primly. 'Ronan and I will be off then?'

'I'll pay you,' said Rebecca. 'Just wait until I find my purse.'

'No, no, don't go!' protested Suzy, rubbing her fingers

along the top of her gums. She didn't want to be stuck alone at the Met Bar with a weepy Rebecca. 'Come with us.'

'Suze!'

'Come on, Becs!' Suzy marched towards the kitchen. 'Chef! What's your name? Fancy a night out clubbing?'

Ronan, who had been pretending to do the washing up, while listening to every word, smiled sheepishly.

'Um, thanks, but I don't . . .'

But Suzy had done a double take. Why hadn't Rebecca told her that Adonis was hiding in the kitchen? This night might turn out all right after all.

'Pleased to meet you. I'm Suzanne Bell. You must be Ronan. Sorry we didn't get to taste your food. Some other time, perhaps. To make it up to you, let me take you and your friend to the Met Bar. All expenses paid.' Of course *Seduce!* would pick up the bill.

Ronan glanced at Katie hopefully. He had always dreamed of going to the Met Bar. Imperceptibly, she smiled and nodded.

'Sounds like fun,' he said.

Rebecca wasn't thrilled to be going out with the staff, but she was too sad to argue.

Instead, she reached into her purse and pulled out a £20 note.

'Suzy. Hand over that coke.'

18

And so, just fifteen minutes later, Rebecca was ushering her three accomplices past the Met Bar's red velvet rope and into a place which until now Ronan thought he had about as much of a chance of entering as a nun's bedroom. Although even now it looked for a moment as if they wouldn't make it after Rebecca haughtily waved her Boots Advantage Card at the doorman and had to leaf through her bag for about five minutes before she found the right piece of plastic.

'Oh,' said Ronan, looking round the dark, half-empty, red-walled room, with a bar along one side and a DJ desultorily spinning decks in the corner. 'It's not very big.'

'That's what everyone says,' laughed Suzy, a woman of the world.

They settled into a red leather banquette. 'Cristal,' Suzy commanded, to a hovering male model masquerading as waiter.

In her waitress outfit of black trousers and a white shirt, Katie felt distinctly overdressed. All around her girls of about sixteen in low-cut tops were sipping cocktails and gesticulating wildly to one another. The men, meanwhile, were portly, wearing suits and aged on average about forty-five. They sat on low stools, eyes level with the girls' perky buttocks and looked very satisfied.

'That's the great thing about coming here,' Suzy

explained. 'If you're not a hooker no one pays you any attention. You're left totally in peace.'

'Those girls aren't hookers!' Ronan exclaimed.

God, why were men so gullible? 'Hello! Do you think they work for Save the Children?'

'She's not a hooker,' Rebecca stage-whispered. 'That's Emma Cornish.' And indeed, there was the supermodel *du jour* settling into the next-door banquette surrounded by a giggling entourage.

'Not a hooker!' Suzy snorted. 'I'm not sure about that. The first time she did our cover she managed to service the whole crew, including the girls.'

Katie hugged herself. She couldn't wait to tell Jess the gossip. She wished she was here.

'"Groove is in the Heart"!' Ronan, who had been looking faintly shocked at such loucheness, perked up. 'Come on, let's go and dance!'

'Not yet,' said Katie, who was feeling a bit self-conscious.

'I'm going to the loo,' Suzy announced. Taking drugs at the Met was a nightmare. There were no flat surfaces in the cubicles apart from the top of the bin, which was covered with some kind of sticky gunk. If you didn't come prepared with your own mirror, then you could end up snorting it off the floor. Suzy had been reduced to that once, an incident that would go with her to the grave.

'I need to get a bit more tanked up first,' said Rebecca, waving her glass in the air, her Australian accent distinctly stronger. Apart from a few organic crisps, she realized, she hadn't eaten. So what? She would just have another line.

Two boys sidled into the booth next to them. Tall, dark, dressed in Armani suits and both about seventeen.

'Hi, ladies. I'm Abdul and this is Chitwe. Can we buy you ladies a drink?'

'No thanks,' said Katie haughtily.

They slunk away like a pair of chastened puppies. Treat them like dogs, Katie thought.

Rebecca looked after them anxiously. 'That was a bit rude.'

'No it wasn't. Do you want to be bought a drink by Beavis and Butthead's stupid younger brothers?'

'They might have been all right.'

Katie looked at Rebecca in confusion.

'Hello, ladies,' said a voice behind them.

They turned round. Two middle-aged men, with thinning grey hair and chubby, rosy cheeks, stood beaming at them in their flannel suits.

Katie sighed and turned her attention back to the dance floor.

'Hello!' said Rebecca.

'I am Ingmar, this is Johan. We are here in London on business from Sweden. May we buy you ladies a drink?'

'No thanks,' said Katie in her best snooty voice.

'That would be lovely,' Rebecca purred, moving up the banquette and patting the space beside her.

They sat down instantly, clearly unable to believe their luck.

'So, Johan,' said Rebecca. She was leaning forward, displaying maximum cleavage. 'What are you doing in nasty old London?'

'I am just completing a business deal with Telebrite,' he

replied eagerly. 'It is most fascinating, discussing the views on broadband with their deputy head of marketing.'

Ingmar looked glumly at Katie, the booby prize. 'So,' he said dubiously. 'Do you come here often?'

'Er, no, first time,' Katie replied, scanning the dance floor for her friends. 'And you?'

'Always I stay in the hotel,' Ingmar told her. 'It is very good for frequent-flyer miles. And like this I have entry to the bar. The coolest in town.'

Katie wasn't listening, distracted by the sound of Rebecca laughing loudly at Johan's jokes. What on earth was going on? Why was this sex bomb coming on to a telecom salesman from Malmö?

Johan too was bemused by his unprecedented success. He decided to strike while the woman was hot. 'So maybe we can have dinner sometime while I am over here?'

'How about tomorrow?' Rebecca yelled over the pounding beat.

Even Johan thought this was a bit full-on. He recoiled slightly. 'Actually, tomorrow I have an engagement, but Monday night could be fine.'

'Monday's great!' She pulled a card out of her jeans pocket. 'Here's my number.'

Katie could take no more. 'Come on,' she bellowed as the music changed to Public Enemy. 'Let's have a dance.' She grabbed Rebecca's elbow and dragged her on to the floor.

'What are you doing? We'll lose our table!'

'I just think you were giving that guy the wrong idea. You don't seriously want to have dinner with him, do you, Rebecca?'

'He's OK. We could just have a friendly meal. I love Sweden. I went to an Eel's gig there a couple of years ago.'

'I can't believe we're even having this conversation. There's no such thing as a friendly dinner. He wants to get in your pants. Is that seriously what you want?'

'Well, no . . . Not yet. But the physical attraction could come. He looks kind and reliable and honest. And Sweden would be a great place to bring up children. No pollution. No crime. Though I suppose it might get a little cold in winter.'

Katie stared at her, as understanding slowly dawned. No wonder Rebecca ended up with losers when she made it so easy for them. Talk about low self-esteem. Her boss was nothing more than a slimmer, better-dressed version of the trailer-park women on Jerry Springer who had five children by three different wife-beaters.

The music changed to Michael Jackson and they were interrupted by Johan and Ingmar, hips gyrating wildly.

'I loff this song!' Johan yelled, waving his arms over his head. 'Billie Jean is not my loff-er.'

'Me too!' screamed Rebecca, thrusting her hips towards him.

Katie could not bear to be part of this. She fought her way through the whooping crowd to the bar, where Suzy and Ronan were drinking caipirinhas and laughing at the bad dancing.

'I can't believe it!' Katie yelled. 'Rebecca is getting off with a Swede.'

Suzy laughed and sniffed loudly. 'It's the marching powder. It always turns Rebecca into a sex-mad vixen.'

She shrugged. 'I probably shouldn't have given her any. She'll snog anyone when she's on drugs.'

Ronan looked horrified. 'Even him?' Rebecca and Johan carried on grooving as the music segued into 'Disco Inferno'. With a yelp, Johan removed his tweed jacket and flung it on to the floor before launching into an inspired version of the mashed potato. Rebecca leaned forward and whispered something in his hairy ear.

'Do something about it, Ronan. Rescue her!'

And like a superhero Ronan pushed his way across the floor and into Johan's space. The music changed again, this time, to S Club Seven, 'Don't Stop Moving', and with a little smile, Ronan reached out for Rebecca's hand and started twirling her around, out on to the dance floor, then back into his arms. Johan tried to boogie his bulky frame between them, but was rebuffed as Ronan pulled Rebecca to him.

'He is like Johnny Travolta, no?' muttered Ingmar, who had sidled up alongside Katie at the bar. 'Care to join them?' he added unenthusiastically, and looked relieved when Katie shook her head. Ingmar was actually very fond of his partner, Siggi, and was growing increasingly weary of pretending to be a stud.

The night flew by. Ronan and Rebecca danced the macarena, the twist and the electric boogaloo. They moonwalked, they hand-jived, they bumped and they ground. Meanwhile, Katie and Suzy were chatted up by two blokes who claimed to be in *Coronation Street*, a Japanese businessman, an Irish dot-com guru and, right at the end of the evening, by Johan and Ingmar, neither of whom appeared to realize they had been here before.

'It is an excellent hotel for retrieving the airmiles,' Ingmar said.

Suzy swatted them all off like flies, with a cutting remark or a haughty turn of the shoulder. It didn't seem to deter them though, they just tried harder to win her attention, by buying her drinks or telling bad jokes. She watched them like a bored stepmother at the school nativity play. Katie found it hilarious.

'Do you have a boyfriend, Suzy?' she asked.

Suzy rolled her eyes. 'In a manner of speaking.'

'How do . . .?'

'I have a lover. He's married, has two daughters, lives in America.' She saw a flash of pity in Katie's eyes and continued firmly, 'Which is *just* the way I like it. I see him on my terms, have some fun and never have to worry about buying his dinner or ironing his shirts.'

'Women don't iron shirts any more,' Katie protested.

'Hunter's wife does. And good luck to her. But it's not for me.'

Katie didn't approve of going out with married men, but she liked Suzy's attitude. Enjoying all the good bits of a relationship without getting too attached. She could relate to that.

'No fighting in the Ikea car park on Sunday morning.'

'Exactly!' Suzy's eyes sparkled at the discovery of a kindred spirit. 'No dinners with other couples. No fighting over what to watch on telly.' Suddenly she remembered who she was talking to. 'Anyway. Enough of that. More champagne?'

At 3 a.m., the lights went up, revealing hordes of pale faces, red eyes and sticky bodies.

'So I guess we should find a cab,' Katie said. Her ears were ringing from the music.

Outside, there was a *Big Issue* seller, a glum-looking paparazzo and three minicab drivers leaning against beaten-up Cortinas.

'Don't get in their cars, they're death traps!' Rebecca shuddered. 'Come back to mine and we'll call one from there.'

They wandered back through the empty Mayfair streets. 'Don't sto-op moving,' Suzy sang, then checked herself. Where the hell had that come from?

Rebecca smiled indulgently. It had been a good night, she realized with a shock. In fact, she hadn't had so much fun in ages. Her mobile bleeped.

'Oh, text!' she gurgled. She surveyed the screen. 'Issfrom Tim.' She pursed her lips. 'Oh, I've got a lot of them.'

'What does he say?' Katie asked wearily.

'Let's see – well, this is the latest one. *Where fuck r u? Call me.*'

'Charming,' said Suzy. 'What time did he send that?'

'About ten minutes ago. Then there's: *Have gone home. C u around.* What time did he send that? Oooh, 1.47 a.m.' Nice one. And then there's . . .' She scrolled down. '*Bex am on yr doorstep. Why rn't you in?* Katie, you really did the trick tonight. I've driven him crazy.'

They had arrived at Dartmouth Mansions. A hint of embarrassment passed over Rebecca's pretty face.

'Er, guys . . . would you mind if I didn't give you a cup of tea? Only, I'm tired. You should easily find a cab at Marble Arch.'

'No problem,' said Ronan.

But Katie, empowered by dozens of glasses of free champagne, was having none of it.

'No way, Rebecca.'

'Sorry?'

'I said: "No." We're coming in. In fact, I think we might crash on your floor.'

'What?'

'You're going to call Tim, aren't you?'

'What?'

'You're going to call Tim as soon as you're alone.'

'No I'm not!' Rebecca was a terrible liar.

'Yes you are. If I leave you alone, you'll start worrying that you'll end up a lonely old maid and thinking you should just give him one more chance and that's what you'll do.'

'Way to go, girl!' Suzy swayed on her heels, then burped loudly. 'Oops!'

'How about if I text him?' Rebecca said to Katie. 'Just to say that I'm OK. Because he's probably worried about me. I did *say* I'd be in tonight.'

'No.' Katie grabbed Rebecca's wrist. 'Rebecca. I saw you in action tonight. And I finally realized. It doesn't matter how beautiful you are. You're so needy. If anyone even looks at you, you roll over and lie on your back, because you're so grateful for the attention. Well, you've got to stop doing that, even if it means me supervising you twenty-four hours a day.'

Rebecca sighed. She was too pissed to argue, but she was still going to give it a try. 'Well, you can't stay the night. It's far too uncomfortable sleeping on the floor.'

'There's a blow-up bed.'

'Well, I'm going back to mine,' Suzy said. Despite her unexpected befuddlement, she still knew that this was the moment to pounce. 'Maybe Ronan could help me find a taxi. In fact, we could share. I'm sure you're on my way.'

'Where do you live?' Ronan enquired politely.

'Primrose Hill,' Rebecca informed him. 'Far north of the river. Ronan lives south, Suzy.'

'So? We'll put the taxi on the *Seduce!* account. I need a man to make sure I get home safely.'

Ronan shrugged. 'OK.' He grinned at Katie apologetically. 'I guess I'll see you tomorrow.'

Katie gave him a huge, lascivious wink. 'Not too early, though.'

'Can we stop fannying around?' Rebecca snapped. 'I'm getting cold.'

Funny how you always get laid when you least expect it, Katie mused as she and Rebecca waited for the lift. Ronan had thought that tonight he would be cooking and serving dinner and still be home in time for the *Jonathan Ross Show.* She was excited for him. All right, Suzy already had a lover and she certainly wasn't interested in marriage and babies, but she had a good job and wore lovely clothes, which was more than you could say for most of the nightmares Ronan went out with.

She switched her mind back to the more urgent problem of Rebecca, who had headed straight to the answerphone and was listening to Tim's drunken messages.

'Now this is what I'm going to do, Rebecca. I am going to unplug your phones. I am going to confiscate your mobile. They are all going to spend the night in the same room as me, and in the morning I will take them home with me.'

'That's ridiculous. I can't live without a phone.'

'You can and you will. It's only going to be for forty-eight hours. A nice peaceful weekend. Then you'll be back at work. Where Tara or whoever's standing in for her can answer it for you.'

'No, no. But I *really* can't live without one. Suppose an urgent business call comes through? Suppose my mother tries to call? She's old and lonely.'

It was a cheap shot and Rebecca felt ashamed for trying it, but it worked. Almost.

'Oh, Rebecca, I'm so sorry,' Katie exclaimed.

'Yeah, well.' Rebecca shrugged.

'But listen, Rebecca, I will answer your mobile for you. Any urgent calls, I will make sure you get to hear about. I'll come round and deliver them to you in person.'

'No, silly, you don't need to do that. Call Johnny downstairs.'

'We'll talk about it in the morning,' said Katie. She plugged the blow-up bed's pump into the wall socket and watched it inflate.

19

Katie woke just after ten. She stared, puzzled, at the mobile phone, fax and two handsets that nestled on the pillow beside her. Then everything about last night came back to her.

Her clothes lay in a pile on the sofa. She picked up her top and almost gagged on the scent of stale fags, sweat, cooking smells and booze. Rebecca's bedroom door was still shut. Katie wondered if she dare take a shower, then decided that if she was to travel home on the underground without being arrested for vagrancy she really had no choice.

Ten minutes later, she emerged from the guest bathroom to find Rebecca huddled on the sofa, fragrant in blue and white striped pyjamas. At the sight of Katie, a furtive expression came over her face, like a teenage boy caught gawping at topless women on the beach.

'Hi!' she squawked loudly. 'Sleep well?'

'Um, OK,' said Katie. 'You?'

'Er, yes. Very well. Fantastic, actually. Best sleep in ages.' Why did Rebecca have one arm bent awkwardly behind her back? Perhaps she was doing her morning yoga.

'So you'll be going now?' Rebecca asked.

'Well, actually, I wouldn't mind a coffee before I head out.'

'A coffee? Oh, yeah. That would be great. I'll have it

black. Unless, there happens to be any soya milk in the fridge.'

What exactly is my job here, Katie wondered. Was she Rebecca's therapist or housekeeper, or a mixture of both?

Either way, she decided, it was time for her speech. She coughed a little nervously.

'So, Rebecca. Do you remember we spoke ages ago about how men were like dogs?'

'Mmm-hmmm,' said Rebecca, still bent in that peculiar position on the sofa.

Suddenly, Katie got it. 'Rebecca! What have you got behind your back?'

'Nothing.'

'For God's sake. Show me!'

Reluctantly, Rebecca stretched out her hand. There in her palm lay her Motorola.

'Rebecca, I am taking all your phones home with me! Did you really think I was going to forget?'

'I wasn't going to use it to call Tim! But I am expecting other calls.'

'We discussed this. I'll make sure they get to you.'

Rebecca scowled but handed over the phone. As she did, the sleeve of her dressing-gown slipped, to reveal her arm decorated with a number in blue biro.

'What is that?'

'Erm. Well. It's . . . Tara's number. In case I need her.'

'It's Tim's number, isn't it?'

'No!'

'It is! Rebecca, wash your arm!' Rebecca, rightly, looked astonished. 'Rebecca, come into the bathroom and wash your arm!' Katie marched into the bathroom. Meekly, Rebecca followed. Katie held out the Kiehl's soap and after a second Rebecca took it.

'So you don't know Tim's number off by heart?' Katie asked casually as she watched Rebecca scrubbing her arm.

'Of course not. You just programme numbers into your phone, don't you?' Rebecca glanced down at her arm in a last-ditch attempt at memorizing, but her only link to Tim was disappearing down the sink in a gush of soapy water.

'Well, I'm taking the phone away. All the phones. So you won't be able to contact him. It's for the best, Rebecca. Cold turkey. You can do so much better than Tim.'

Rebecca put the soap down. '*I can't!* God, Katie, it's all right for you. You're what — thirty or something? I'm thirty-six! Do you realize what that means? It means I'm basically forty. And soon I'll be fifty, and then I'll be . . . fucked.'

'No, it doesn't, it means you'll be at your peak! Think of Goldie Hawn. Meryl Streep. Susan Sarandon. Princess Anne!'

'Princess . . .?' Rebecca realized she was joking. She let out a snort of laughter. 'Whatever. I'd rather be Cameron Diaz.'

'No you wouldn't. There was a picture of her in *Heat* without her makeup on. Terrible acne. *And* she's single.' Katie placed a tentative hand on Rebecca's arm. 'Rebecca, you're always going on about being too high-maintenance. But I think you're not nearly high-maintenance enough. You're stunning and bright and you're wasting your time with Tim and Swedes in ugly suits. You could do so much better, I promise you. You've just got to learn to be a bit more picky.'

Rebecca said nothing.

Katie steered her back into the living room and sat down beside her. 'Now. *As* I was saying. About dogs. I've been doing my research and a lot of rules that apply to canines apply equally well to people.' She reached in her bag and pulled out a scrappy bit of paper. 'Would you like to hear some of them?'

'Oh, why not?' After all, there was bugger-all else to do today.

'OK. Well, for a start here's a list of dos and don'ts for dog trainers. I think some of them really apply to you and Tim.'

Rebecca listened.

Katie cleared her throat.

'OK. So, number one is *Don't fall for his cute act.*'

Rebecca thought back to the night of Jenny's dinner party. Tim flirting with her on the doorstep, flexing his tiny muscles. The way he pulled his face into daft expressions every time he arrived late, left early or told her he wouldn't be around this weekend. Daft expressions that told her she was an old misery guts intent on spoiling his fun.

'I always do that,' she admitted.

'We all do,' said Katie, who herself had been lost for a moment, thinking of Paul dressed up in her nightie, dancing around the flat to cheer her up, after turning up drunk on her doorstep at 5 a.m. She rallied. 'But no more. Be aware of the signs.'

'What's another rule?'

Katie consulted the list. 'OK. *Don't go to your dog to give affection.*'

'Oh no. Guilty.' Rebecca thought of herself snuggling up to Tim as he sat absorbed in *Match of the Day.* 'Whenever Tim put his arm around me I'd be so bloody grateful, I'd squeeze him back so hard, he'd say, "Ow, that hurts."'

'So in future, let him come to you,' said Katie.

'All right. What else?'

'Loads of things. But I think you should look at it yourself.' Katie handed over the scrappy piece of paper. 'There's something else we should talk about and that's *If this man was a dog, would I want him?* In other words, what were his previous owners like? Why did they get rid of him?'

Rebecca laughed. 'Tim was always pretty cagey about his previous owners. He probably killed them all.'

'Or he never had any,' Katie joked.

'More likely he's still sleeping with them all,' Rebecca said, suddenly bleak. 'What else do I need to think about?'

'Well . . . er . . . Does he bite?'

She was joking again, but Rebecca answered immediately, 'Yes, yes! He did bite me a couple of times. On my bum. It bloody hurt.'

'Did you tell him to stop?'

'Yeah, but he just laughed and did it again.'

How delightful. 'And we know he wasn't house-trained, judging by the way he left this place.' *Mind you, Rebecca needed some help in that department as well.* 'What was his place like?'

There was a pause and then Rebecca said: 'Actually, I don't know.'

Katie must have misunderstood. 'Sorry?'

'I've never been to his place.'

Katie tried to hide her surprise. 'How long have you been going out with him?'

'Three months.'

'Did you ever ask to go there?'

'Of course. But it was in Dulwich and my place is so central and . . . it always seemed to make more sense to crash here.'

'All the same . . .' Actually, Katie knew exactly where Rebecca was coming from. In all her time with Paul she had never met his parents, although he stayed with hers loads of times.

'I know. I know.' Rebecca looked at her hands. 'I kept thinking I should insist. But I thought that would be too high-maintenance.'

'It would have been normal.'

Rebecca sighed. 'You're right, I know. But Tim was always so slippery. Having hissy fits about what was the big deal and why did I want to tie him down? I was terrified to put any pressure on him in case I drove him away. I didn't think I could cope with that.'

Katie grinned. 'Maybe you *thought* you couldn't cope. But now you know if he was a dog, you wouldn't buy him.'

'Poor dog,' said Rebecca. 'Sitting in the petshop window. Nobody wanting him.'

'Oh, for God's sake. No one wants him because he's an evil, mangy mutt. Who *bites*.' Katie picked up her bag and deposited the phones in it. 'Anyway, I'm off. I'll return the phones after work on Monday. Maybe I could do some cleaning then as well.'

'That would be good.' Rebecca grabbed her handbag, reached in it for her purse and pulled out a bundle of notes. 'Here, Katie. I know I'm à pain in the arse. But thank you. I appreciate it.'

She shut the door. Katie walked down the corridor and pressed the button for the lift. Could this situation get any more mad? Then, just as the doors opened, she remembered something.

'Rebecca, Rebecca!' she yelled, banging on the red door. Rebecca opened it, looking surprised.

'Just one more thing.'

Katie darted across the room, to the desk in the corner. She bent over the laptop and removed the phone lead, then pulled the other end out of the wall socket.

'And I'll have this too,' she said, grabbing Rebecca's Palm Pilot.

She darted back along the corridor and into the waiting lift.

20

Ally Kilgour had led pretty much the perfect life, all her friends said so. The only daughter of adoring parents, with three older brothers, she had been one of the naughtiest girls at school, yet she still emerged with perfect exam results and a place at Manchester University. She read maths, got a first, and – after a brief spell in telesales – won a traineeship at HFBM and over ten years had worked her way up to her current position as vice-president. Along the way she had made dozens of friends, gone on a score of long-haul holidays and bought her cute little house in Camden (which had since quadrupled in value).

This Friday had marked another of Ally's triumphs, with a successful windup of a giant merger that she had been working on for months. She was looking forward to an evening celebrating at Rebecca's, but Jon, just back from a few days with his daughters in Cardiff, was having none of that. 'I've had the week from hell,' he'd told her over the phone. 'I'd like some quality time with you.'

So the pair of them went to the local Chinese, where Jon moaned about his dreadful trip to Cardiff, where he knew his ex-wife Bea was seeing someone new.

'The girls swear not, but I can tell something's going on. There's always been another man on the scene. Why else would she have left me?'

Oh, I can't imagine, Ally thought sarcastically, then stopped herself, shocked that she had allowed such a thought to enter her head.

Ally had been with Jon for six months. There had been only one other major boyfriend, Gareth, an architect, whom Ally met at university and who, everyone assumed, was her future husband. But then Ally discovered a text on his mobile from Joanne in his office thanking him for last night, and when she confronted him with this, he announced he was leaving her.

After an indecently short period, Gareth and Joanne were engaged and Ally was left as disoriented as a hill-walker without a map. For six months she cried about losing her boyfriend, and when she'd finished she started crying about having a baby, which was Ally's goal for her thirty-second year.

It didn't help that Ally's mother was always on her case, reminding her she was missing out on the greatest gift on God's earth and that she had four by the time she was Ally's age, and telling her to read a new report in today's papers warning 'career girls' that after thirty-five they had about as much chance of breeding as the giant pandas in London Zoo. Ally was getting desperate, and although she wasn't quite bursting into tears whenever she came across a Pampers advert, she would certainly quickly change channels.

But then she met Jon and everything was back on track again.

They were reunited six months ago, at the opening of a terrible art exhibition in Hoxton. She was standing in front of a canvas made up of scraps of patchwork, trying to work out what it was all about, when a shortish man with an aggressive expression pushed in front of her.

'Remember me?' he had snapped.

Ally hadn't.

'Queen's Park Ravers? The King George in White City. Must have been . . . ten years ago?'

'Jon Lyons!' Ally remembered. He had been the lead singer in the local pub band. Ally – who was twenty-four and new to London – had thought he was sex on legs. They had had sex four times, then he had dumped her for his lead guitarist, a rather ragged-looking blonde called Shelly. Ally had been quite upset at the time.

'So how are you, you old sex god?'

'Less of the old,' he preened. 'I'm well. I mean, I'm poor. I'm divorced. I've got two daughters I don't see enough of. Apart from that, I'm fine. And you?'

'I'm rich. I'm single. I have no children.' Usually, she hated to admit this last thing, but tonight it didn't feel so bad.

They had a drink two nights later and that weekend they had extraordinary, *Cosmo* cover-worthy sex. Ally had almost forgotten how important that was: she and Gareth had neglected that department for several years. A wiggle came back into her walk, and she stopped buying Temazepam over the Internet to help her sleep at night.

Two months later Jon had moved in. 'After all, there's no point my paying rent when I could be helping you with your mortgage,' he said, although they had never quite got around to arranging his payments.

But not long after, the doubts seriously started. Ally decided to whisk Jon away for a romantic weekend in a country house hotel, which he hated from the first night when the maître d' insisted he wore a tie in the restaurant. On Sunday morning, Ally had come out of the bathroom to find him methodically packing the coat hangers, tissues, teabags, coffee sachets, UHT milk cartons, complimentary rich tea biscuits and a face towel into his suitcase.

'What on earth are you doing?'

'Rip-off prices they charge, we might as well get our money's worth.'

'But I'm paying,' Ally pointed out, at which he exploded.

'Do you think I don't know that?'

For the first time, Ally felt a bell ringing at the back of her head. She ignored it, like she did the fire alarm at work, which frequently malfunctioned. Because Ally was the golden girl, whose life was following a plan, and Jon was an integral part of it. He would make a wonderful father. Even if he could be a bit grumpy with her, he was *great* with his daughters Siouxsie and Cheyenne and – let's face it – he hardly worked at all, which meant there would be no need to employ a nanny.

No, things couldn't be better, Ally told herself as they sat in the restaurant, and what was more, she was fairly sure tonight was a good night in her cycle.

All the same, it was hard to concentrate as Jon ranted on about the problems he was having finding funding for his short film.

'It's because they have no originality, no spark,' he moaned. 'They have no respect for mavericks, for artists. Bloody sheep.'

'Excuse me,' said Ally to the back of the sour-faced

waiter. 'Excuse me!' But he had disappeared into the kitchen. 'Where's our food?'

'They're bloody shite here,' Jon said automatically. 'So then, I found out they'd given the project to that public-school twat Cameron, probably because his daddy has something to do with the company. I mean, how fucking unjust is that?'

Ally ummed and aahed sympathetically, but her gaze was drawn to two chain-smoking young Sloanes at the next table.

'No, honestly,' the boy was saying, 'he sells the best skunk in town.' He had thick curly hair and vast eyes like Bambi. It was impossible to imagine him ever getting mad like Jon did.

'Would you fucking look at me!' Jon roared suddenly.

Ally was shaken. 'Sorry!' She tried to concentrate on her lover's woes. But she was too tired and she needed to eat, and, frankly, she had heard it all before. Without realizing it, slowly her eyes were drawn back to the chortling, Silk Cut-smoking Sloanes. The girl flicked her blonde hair back behind her ears.

'No! Did you rairly! God! What did Rory say? He must have been livid.'

'For Christ's sake!' Suddenly Jon was on his feet, storming out of the restaurant.

'Jon!' She jumped up and hurried after him. The Sloanes stopped talking and gaped.

'Hey! Where do you think you're going?' yelled the sour waiter. Well, at least they had his attention now.

'I'm following my boyfriend.'

'No you ain't. You got to pay first.'

'OK.' Ally fumbled in her purse and found a tenner. 'Here!'

'Oi! That don't cover it!'

'*What?* We only had two beers!'

'What about the food?'

'The food hasn't arrived yet. We've been waiting an hour and a half. That's why my boyfriend left.'

'It was just coming. You gotta pay for it!'

Furious, Ally grabbed two £20 notes from her purse and shoved them into his hand. 'But I'm never coming back here again. And I'm telling everyone in Camden you served fried rats.'

'Ooh, like I'm scared,' he minced.

Tears in her eyes, she hurried out into the street. Jon had disappeared. She clacked home, cursing the high heels she had put on to be sexy. He was waiting at the kitchen table, pretending to be immersed in the *Guardian*. Steam seemed to rise off him like a kettle.

'What was all that about?' Ally said pleasantly.

'You weren't listening to me. You were more interested in those posh wankers.'

'Oh, Jonny. I wasn't more interested in them. They were obnoxious and loud. I couldn't help it.'

He looked up pathetically. 'I'm a dullard. I must be. Why else did Bea leave me?'

'Oh, Jonny, you're not a dullard!' She crossed the kitchen and pushing the paper aside, plonked herself on his skinny knees. 'You're a wonderful, interesting bloke. I told you I was just exhausted. I'm sorry.'

He stared into her eyes. 'You won't do it again?'

'I won't do it again, Jonny. I love you. You're amazing.'

He still looked unconvinced. She made him a cup of tea and listened to him moan about something he had read in the *Guardian*, but eventually she had to give up and go to bed.

Even though tonight was a propitious night.

Lying naked between the sheets, she could hear some late-night news show rumbling on the telly. *We could have gone to Rebecca's dinner party*, Ally thought, imagining all her fabulous friends chattering away like Nancy Mitford and Noël Coward. Ally missed her friends. What with work and Jon there never seemed to be time for them now. Still, when she had a baby she would never leave the house again – apart from twelve-hour days at the office – so she might as well get into training for it now.

'Oh, fuck off, you twat!' Jon bellowed downstairs. 'Like you can tell a work of art from your arse.'

For a moment Ally felt irritation scour her veins like bleach. *Breathe deep, breathe deep*, she told herself. OK, Jon could be a little annoying – but no relationship was perfect.

And frankly, at her age, she was unlikely to do any better.

'Oh, you stupid cunt!' he roared.

Ally rolled over and fumbled in her bedside drawer for the last jar of Temazepam. She'd have to get her hands on some more soon.

Katie left Rebecca's, her phones and Palm Pilot safely in her bag, and walked to Marble Arch Tube. On the Central Line she thought of how she and Paul used to take the Tube into work in the morning. Just like today, Katie would be wearing last night's clothes and her hair would still be damp from the shower.

'It's all right, it's all right,' Paul would mutter soothingly into her ear as the carriage became increasingly packed. 'Loads of people will get off at Oxford Circus. It's all right.' Once he had muttered to himself, 'Soon I'll be out of this, thank God.' Katie pretended not to hear. These were still the days when the LA plan was officially a secret.

For the weeks that surrounded Paul's departure, Katie felt as if her heart had been gouged out by a knife. All his nights seemed taken up with farewell dinners with old friends, which he didn't invite her to, 'because you wouldn't know anyone, darling, and you'd be bored'.

Why the fuck hadn't she argued with him over that? Instead, she had simply gone home from work and lain on her bed for hours fully clothed. She couldn't eat, her throat was too tight. She couldn't sleep. She couldn't even cry. She just lay there like a zombie, listening to the roaring in her ears. When she did get up to go to the loo, she felt as if she was walking underwater.

Jess would knock on the door and ask if she wanted to watch *EastEnders* but Katie just shook her head.

'There are plenty more fish in the sea,' her cousin ventured. 'You'll meet someone else.'

'I don't *want* anyone else,' Katie would think. 'I just want Paul.' But she just nodded and tried to smile.

Every night between midnight and one, the bell would ring and Katie would let in a drunk but very affectionate Paul, who swore that he adored her, that she was going to have his babies, and that it didn't matter if he was going to LA because nothing could stand in the way of their love.

Katie didn't see how this could possibly be true, but she didn't say anything because she was just so happy to be sharing these moments with him.

The night before he left he took her out for dinner at Odette's in Regent's Park Road, where she pushed a fillet of sea bass around her plate and smoked heavily.

'Everything's going to be fine,' he assured her.

The following morning she accompanied him to Heathrow in a taxi. At Terminal 4, he cried and at last she did too.

'I love you,' he mouthed at the entrance to the departure gate. She went home and lay on her bed all day. That night he called her.

'I've just arrived and I'm so lonely. It's so *hot* and this motel is vile. God, I miss you, Katie.'

At work everyone was terribly nice to her and took her out to lunch a lot, and she managed to laugh at people's jokes and look as if she didn't have a care. The time difference made it harder: when she was in bed at night feeling lonely, he was at the office and up to his eyes and vice versa but Paul managed to ring her at least twice a day. 'I'm finding it so tough out here without you, Katie. Americans are so weird. If you order a drink with lunch they think you're an alcoholic and they all go to bed at nine.'

'Probably doing you the world of good,' Katie said as warmly as she could.

'It's not. How long is it going to be before you come over here?'

She could only manage a week's holiday, which was far too short. Paul, despite all his promises, made no effort to contribute to her ticket, although he was earning four times her salary.

So she flew out. They'd been apart for two months. She remembered the floaty dark red Ghost dress that she carried on to the plane and asked the hostess to hang up, so she would have something smart to change into at the end of that hellish twelve-hour flight. Standing in the dirty toilet, putting on her makeup. That tightening in her stomach as she imagined him waiting in the arrivals hall, nervous in new clothes, scanning the weary passengers pushing trolleys, perhaps . . . you never knew . . . holding a bunch of flowers.

She queued for an hour at immigration, collected her luggage, passed through customs. The sliding doors pulled back and he wasn't there.

Katie scanned the excited families juggling screaming babies, the bored limo drivers holding up signs. No Paul. The hope that had been bubbling up inside her evaporated and was replaced by a cold fear.

He turned up half an hour later, by which time Katie had bought a phonecard and rung his flat four times. She was sitting on her suitcase, studying her *Rough Guide to California*, steeling herself to check into a hotel.

'Baby, I'm so sorry. I fell asleep!' Fell asleep? When she had spent virtually the whole flight on full alert waiting for this moment?

It had been an OK trip, she supposed. California was beautiful, although it was colder than she had imagined it would be. Paul whisked her up the coast to a little B&B, where they went kayaking and saw a school of dolphins.

Once she got a bit weepy, when she heard Carole King singing 'Will You Still Love Me Tomorrow?' on the car radio but she blamed it on jetlag. After four days they returned to LA. Paul was needed back in the office, but he assured her she would find plenty of ways to occupy her days.

'Why couldn't you have taken the rest of the week off?' she asked him later.

'Why did you only stay a week?' he retorted.

Of course, they had no such conversation at the time. All Katie's agony and confusion just churned endlessly inside her. She went to the Guggenheim but, to her eternal regret, failed to go shopping – that was how depressed she was. At the end of the week, Paul took her back to the airport and put her on the flight home.

For nine of the twelve hours she cried hot, silent tears into her British Airways blanket. The Chinese man next to her glanced over sympathetically a couple of times, but said nothing. She clamped on her headphones and pretended *Congo: the Movie* was responsible for her display of emotion.

When she got home it was worse than ever before. She loved Paul more than anything, yet she knew now she could never make it work. Being in Paul's apartment in West Hollywood, she had felt no sense that she would ever live with him there. When she drove down Sunset, she simply couldn't imagine having a job here, finding friends. *And Paul never mentioned the possibility of her joining him.*

'I didn't think I could upset your life like that,' he said, when she pointed this out months later.

'You could have asked me anyway.'

The relationship dragged on. There were a lot more late-night or early-morning phone calls. Katie began to go out more. She saw a lot of her friend Barnaby, who had just been dumped by his lover Sean. They spent hours lying side by side on the sofa, drinking wine, listening to Elvis love songs and wallowing in their pain.

Barnaby knew a lot of people and he kept Katie busy with a round of parties. It wasn't officially over with Paul, but Katie forced herself to snog a couple of people and went out to dinner with a few good-looking men, who were clearly interested, and whose calls she never returned.

She walked through work like a ghost, occasionally brought to life when she overheard a producer saying something like: 'We'll send Paul on that story. We'd better organize a crew for him in Seattle.' Or picking up a schedule and finding out that Paul was *en route* to the Mexican jungle and would be incommunicado, except via satellite phone at £15 a minute, for the next ten days.

Summer arrived. Paul announced he was coming home for Giles Plimmer's wedding. Katie had grown to hate weddings. 'It'll never last,' she seethed, every time an announcement was made.

About four days before Paul arrived, she went out for lunch with Jeevan.

'Looking forward to seeing your man?' he asked.

'Of course,' she replied, stuffing a fistful of chips into her mouth.

'The wedding should be a laugh,' Jeevan continued. 'Paul'll be in his element, hobnobbing with Giles's media friends, probably slipping his business card in a few pockets. You never know, Katie, he might end up getting a job back in England. I'm not bitching, but he's such a networker. I wish I could be more like him. It drives me nuts the way he always gets away with that public school and Oxbridge line.'

'What do you mean: "Gets away with"?' asked Katie, confused.

'Well, you know, not having gone to Oxford. It's amazing he keeps it up, isn't it, all the "commemoration ball this" and "sub-fusc" that. I mean, I know Plimmer loves that kind of thing, but doesn't he ever get embarrassed?'

Something in Katie's expression made him stop. He put down his glass of wine. 'God, Katie. Didn't you know?'

'No,' Katie said. 'I had no idea.'

'Well, he did sort of go to Oxford,' Jeevan babbled. 'Just it was Oxford Poly. Did he never explain that to you? I'm sure he meant to.'

The incredulity in his eyes was unbearable. Thank God

Katie knew she could trust him not to blab it round the office.

'He definitely told me he went to Oxford University,' she said slowly. 'Jess was seeing a guy who'd been there and I said: "Oh, Paul went there too." And he said, "What college?" and Paul said: "Magdalen." And the guy asked if he knew a few people and Paul said the names sounded familiar, but no not really.'

'Katie,' said Jeevan, looking wildly over his shoulder for the waitress, 'I'm really sorry. I just assumed you must know. It's a standing joke that Paul's got this whole bullshit CV and Plimmer swallows it and people like me who really went to Oxford get left on the sidelines.'

'How could he have done it?' Katie asked after a moment's silence. 'How could he have lied to me? Did he think I would care where he went to university?'

'Of course not,' Jeevan assured her. He had mixed feelings about this conversation. He had always fancied Katie and thought Paul was an arse, but he would never have guessed the Oxford stuff would be news to her. Nor did he like seeing her so obviously shaken.

That night Paul rang.

'Paul. Where did you go to university?'

There was a pause. Then: 'Oxford.'

'Yes, I thought so. What college were you at?'

This time the pause was much longer. 'Magdalen.'

'But you weren't, Paul, were you?' And Paul started to cry.

'I meant to tell you. But it never seemed to be the right time.'

'But how could you possibly have thought I cared about things like that?'

'You didn't care. But other people did. And I thought you might blow my cover.'

Charming, Katie thought.

'Katie, I've always been straight with you. I swear. It was just this one little thing.'

But it wasn't. Paul had lied and lied and lied to her, to the point where she no longer knew if anything he said was true.

It was as if a lightbulb had gone on in her head. She couldn't take it any more. When Paul arrived in London, she told him it was over. He cried some more and said he had been going to ask her to marry him.

Katie didn't believe him.

And so, finally, it was officially over. Even though Katie had in practice been single for six months, the last thread of hope had gone, drifted off in the wind. Although every now and then Paul would still call her when he was drunk and beg her to take him back.

'OK,' she snapped once. 'I'll hand in my resignation tomorrow and get on a plane to LA. But we'll have to get married for me to have residency. Hello? Hello? Paul? The line's breaking up.'

He stopped calling after that.

And seventeen months later, she had met Crispin. Sometimes she thought about what a narrow escape she had had. Imagine if she had married Paul and gone to live thousands of miles from everyone who really mattered to her. And thank God, she hadn't done anything silly like give up on men. Because now she was in a mature relationship.

What she no longer believed in was all-consuming love. Anyone who gave themselves to another person was a fool. Life was too unfair: whatever you did for them, you could never tell what they were going to do to you. Love was a con, peddled by diamond merchants and film executives, and one you had to protect yourself from.

It was as Katie had always suspected. What really mattered was friendship. Her friends had got her through this. They were the most important thing in the world. They'd helped her and Katie was going to do everything possible to help them. She had made some stupid mistakes, but she was going to make damn sure no one else she cared for did the same.

22

Last night had been one of the most humiliating of Ronan's life. Suzy had been off her head, or so she kept telling him. 'I'm off my head,' she had gasped. 'Oooh.' The taxi rounded a corner very fast. 'Oh, Ronan. I feel dizzy, I'll have to lean on you.'

Back at her flat, she had suddenly become businesslike, paying off the taxi, not even assuming Ronan didn't want to stay with her. It irritated him, but he couldn't pretend he didn't want her. He focused all his energies on her gleaming black hair twisted in a knot behind her head. Ronan had a thing about hair. He wondered how it would feel brushing against his chest.

Her hall was small, cold and icy white. 'Take your shoes off,' Suzy commanded, bending down to unzip her soft leather boots. Quickly Ronan obeyed, unlacing his trainers. He stood up, Suzy grabbed his hand, and pulled him through the igloo-like living room into her equally stark bedroom.

Briskly, Suzy started undressing him. It was quite erotic in an ooh-matron sort of way. 'Mmm,' she said giving each of his buttocks a quick squeeze. 'Perfection.'

Ronan wasn't sure he liked being treated like a piece of fruit on a market stall, but Suzy was now pulling her dress over her head and standing before him in a black corset.

'What do you think?' she gasped.

'Lovely,' Ronan said truthfully.

And then they were wrestling on her bed, both enjoying the feel of their hot, naked bodies rubbing against each other, making rude slurping sounds. Suzy seemed determined to prove a point and busily crawled up and down Ronan's body rubbing her breasts against his chest and licking him everywhere, with particular attention being paid to the penis.

He couldn't really complain. He entered her and she gasped. He started moving as slowly as possible, terrified that any sudden movement would make him come.

But Suzy had other ideas. 'Fuck me,' she whispered hoarsely in his ear. 'Fuck me. Fuck meeeee!'

'What do you think I'm doing?' Ronan thought crossly. He moved a little faster, but it wasn't good enough for Suzy. She grabbed his bum and began pulling him in and out of her like a plumber trying to unblock a loo.

'Fuck. Me. Fuck. Me.'

Ronan obliged, his mind on Ann Widdecombe, Les Dawson, Kathy Bates. Oh God! It was no good. The Kathy had made him think of Catherine Zeta Jones!

'Uh! Awaagh! I'm . . .'

And it was over. Suzy was not pleased.

'Great. My first fuck of the month, and it lasts three seconds.' She lay on her back and gave Ronan a steely look. 'You haven't finished yet, you know.'

Ronan had never been great at cunnilingus. He hated the rancid taste, the bits of hair in his mouth, and he was never quite sure which bits to lick and which to nibble. Moreover, he was knackered. None the less, he was a gentleman and so set to as enthusiastically as he could.

For about five minutes, Suzy lay there in silence. Then . . .

'Christ! You are useless!' She sat bolt upright and pushed him aside. 'Don't worry. I'll do it myself.'

She reached past him, opened her bedside drawer and removed a huge pink vibrator.

Ronan did not live with two *Sex and the City* addicts for nothing.

'That's Rampant Rabbit.'

'Oh, congratulations.' Rolling flat on to her back, Suzy switched the object on. It started humming like a lawn-mower. Ronan stared in fascination.

'Do you mind? I'm trying to have an orgasm! So do you think you could wait next door until I've finished?'

Ronan was actually growing hard again, but he did as he was told. Shuffling into the bathroom, he found a pile of fluffy white towels. He wrapped one around him and wandered into the living room, where he sat on the edge of the sofa like a patient waiting for bad news. He didn't dare turn on the telly or pick up one of the magazines on the coffee table, instead he examined his fingernails and listened to the faint drilling sound coming from next door.

It only took five minutes. Suzy appeared at the door.

'I've finished,' she said. 'You can come back to bed now.'

They lay stiffly beside each other, at pains not to touch. Suzy was grinding her teeth. Ronan remembered how much cocaine she'd done. No wonder she'd been such a bitch. Oh well. The rhythmic sawing noise made him think of the sea, crashing on the beach near his parents' house in Sussex. His mind started to slip away: he was walking along the shingle, he was flying a kite, he was . . .

'Hey!' Suzy was shaking him violently.

'You're snoring,' she snapped. 'Roll on to your side.'

Ronan obeyed.

He was just losing consciousness for the second time, when Suzy switched on the light.

'Unbelievable,' she groaned. 'You are hogging all the duvet. No! No! Don't mind me. I'm just going to take a valium. Otherwise I won't get a wink.'

Ronan supposed he could have gone home, but he was really too exhausted. He listened to Suzy popping a pill out of a blister pack, taking a gulp of water.

'Should you do that after all the cocaine you've had?'

'Oh, fuck off.'

When he woke up at about 11 a.m., she was sleeping soundly, her face obscured by a Gucci eye mask.

He slipped out of bed, pulled on his clothes, considered leaving a note, then, deciding there was no point, sneaked out into the street.

It was a long, sweaty Tube ride home on the Northern Line. He showered, then poured himself a pint of orange juice and curled up in a towel in front of *CD: UK*.

He was just beginning to feel better when the door slammed.

'Hello!' It was Katie, lugging a huge bag. 'Good night?' she smirked.

'Not bad,' he said gruffly, avoiding eye contact.

'Come on,' giggled Katie, plonking herself down beside him. 'Dish! Did you shag her?'

'Yes.' Ronan's eyes remained fixed on the television.

'And?' Katie forgot Paul, carried away by this new excitement. It was always like this: that part of her memory was an uncomfortable place where she could never stay too long. Going back there, it was like picking a scab. When it came away, the wound looked as fresh as ever. Far better not to aggravate things, but to involve yourself in other people's lives.

'Go on, go on!' she urged her still coy flatmate.

'Well, it was all right. But I don't think I'll be seeing her again.'

'Ronan!' Katie was shocked but delighted. This was Ronan who fell hard for every girl he even had a slow dance with at the disco. Ronan telling her he had just had a one-night stand.

'You heartbreaker,' she giggled. Then she remembered. 'Though it shouldn't be too tricky to get out of. She does have a boyfriend.'

'Does she?' This was all he needed: some jock hammering his door down.

Just then 'Waltzing Matilda' started playing.

'Fuck! That's Rebecca's!' Katie turned her rucksack upside-down. A landline, various wires, a Psion and a mobile all fell on the floor. She grabbed the last.

One missed call.

Suzy.

Katie tried not to grin. Probably calling Rebecca to get Ronan's number. She wandered into the kitchen just as the phone rang again.

121.

It was naughty, but she had to listen. 'Becs, it's Suze. Just to say thanks for a fun night. Hope you haven't spoken to Tim. Sorry for borrowing your chef. He was a great lay. Not! Call me. Bye.'

Bloody hell. Thank God Katie hadn't answered that one. Poor Ronan! So that was where he had been going wrong all these years. Katie was debating deleting the message, when the phone rang again.

Tim.

Oh, bloody hell, what was she going to say to him? She let it ring, and a minute later voicemail called back.

'Becs, please answer the phone. I'm really sorry about last night. I got held up. I got to yours as quick as I could. Anyway, I really need to see you because you've got my Levis and my Fred Perry jumper and my West Ham shirt – and – I haven't got anything else to wear. So . . . could you call me back?'

The little shit. Katie stared at the phone in disgust. Then she had an idea. She pressed the call button.

'Becs?'

'Er, no, this is Rebecca's personal assistant.'

'What? Tara?'

'No, Tara is on honeymoon at the moment. I'm standing in. Um, Rebecca wanted me to tell you that if you wanted to collect your clothes, tomorrow morning would be convenient for her.'

'*Tomorrow morning?* What the fuck is all this? Why can't Rebecca speak to me herself? Is she frightened of me or something?'

'No. She's just busy this weekend. But she wanted to let you know tomorrow morning will be convenient. About eleven? Would that be OK? Goodbye, then.'

'Ronan,' she said, returning to the living room, 'are you

busy tomorrow morning? Because I think I may have another job for you. Assuming Rebecca agrees.'

And she picked up the phone again, to call Johnny the porter and ask if he could pass a message on to Rebecca.

23

And so the following morning, Rebecca, Katie and Ronan were in Rebecca's living room, giggling like children. The coffee table was covered with croissant crumbs and an empty cafetière sat on the floor. Rebecca was in her Agent Provocateur negligée. She wore just a tiny bit of makeup and her hair was tousled. Ronan wore nothing but a towel wrapped round his waist. A Tesco's bag sat on his knee. Only Katie, in cords and a jumper, was decent.

'Turn the music up,' Rebecca commanded, gesturing at the stereo.

Ronan grabbed the remote. Moorcheeba boomed through the room. Rebecca glanced at her watch. 'He's late. For a bloody change.'

'He'll be here soon,' Katie soothed her. She picked up the *Daily Mail*. 'Do you want your horoscope?'

'No, thanks, there isn't time.'

Ronan was rifling through the plastic bag. 'Christ, look at this!' he yelped. He held up a claret and blue football shirt. 'You never told me he was a West Ham supporter.'

'Is West Ham bad?' Rebecca asked.

Ronan was about to explain just *how* bad, but Rebecca interrupted him.

'Katie, do you have to rush off after this?'

'No. Do you want me to do some cleaning?'

Rebecca looked uncomfortable. 'Well, actually there was something else I'd like to talk to you about.'

Before she could say more, the doorbell rang. Everyone jumped to their feet.

'OK,' said Katie. 'Count to ten, then action.'

'Ten, nine, eight,' they all chanted. It rang again. 'Go on,' said Rebecca to Ronan.

Ronan ambled over to the door. His shoulder muscles were rippling. God, he was sexy, Katie thought happily. How could that cow Suzy not have appreciated him?

'Yeah,' he drawled into the entryphone.

'Rebecca?' squawked a male voice.

'Uh,' said Ronan sleepily. 'Um. Rebecca's asleep right now.'

'Oh? Well, can you wake her up?'

'She's pretty out of it.'

'But we had an *appointment*.'

'Did you? Oh. Well, I'm sure I can help. Come up.' Ronan buzzed Tim in, while Rebecca and Katie bent double with silent giggles.

'OK,' said Katie. 'Into the bedroom, Rebecca. I'm going to hide in the spare room.'

The lift took about a minute. Then the buzz of the front door.

Ronan walked slowly to it and opened it, scratching his head and yawning.

On the threshold, Tim looked put out.

'Er, hello. So is – um – Rebecca here?'

Ronan yanked at the towel around his waist. 'Sorry, mate, I told you, she's asleep.'

'She knew I was coming round.'

'Yeah,' Ronan grinned. 'But she's a little bit tired now. Doesn't matter. I've got what you came for.'

He ambled into the centre of the room, giving Tim a perfect view of his broad, brown smooth back, the result of hundreds of unemployed hours spent lying in the park. 'It's this, isn't it?' he said, holding up the Tesco's bag.

Tim snatched it. 'Thanks.'

From the bedroom came Rebecca's voice, lazy and sated. 'Honey, what's going on? Come here.'

'Just a minute,' shouted Ronan. He smiled at Tim, his long lashes fluttering on his cheeks. 'So, mate. I'll be seeing you then.'

Tim made for the door as if the floor was on fire. 'Thanks,' he stuttered again. His ferrety face was beetroot. 'Er, see ya. Bye.' And he was gone.

As the door slammed, the women emerged from the two bedrooms, hooting and applauding.

'Genius!' said Katie. 'Ronan – why aren't you in Hollywood?'

'He never got to see me looking shagged out,' Rebecca moaned.

'It doesn't matter,' Katie assured her. 'He was still completely freaked.'

Rebecca kissed her, and then a very pleased Ronan on the cheek. 'Thank you,' she said, falling back on the sofa. 'It was the sweetest revenge.'

'There's just one more thing we have to do now,' Katie said. 'Hand me your phone.'

Rebecca picked up her mobile from the table. Deftly, Katie scrolled through her address book until she came to *Tim*.

'I'd like you to delete this,' she said.

Giggling, Rebecca grabbed it. 'Delete?' she read in a Stephen Hawking voice. Then she switched to her own Antipodean twang. 'Yes, please!' And she pressed the button.

'And now I want you to go through your inbox and delete all his texts,' Katie said. 'Wipe him from your life.'

Still chortling, Rebecca did just that.

'And his email address. And all the details in your Psion. They all have to go.'

Rebecca clapped her hands as she complied. 'This is fabulous.'

'So,' said Katie, when Armageddon was complete. 'You were going to say something?'

She knew what was coming. The love training had served its purpose and Rebecca really needed a proper cleaner, preferably a Filipina. She would be out on her arse.

'Oh yes,' said Rebecca. 'Sit down and I'll tell you.'

Katie sat.

'Listen,' Rebecca began. 'I was alone yesterday, with no phone, so I did some thinking – for a change. I realized that you've really helped me with Tim, long before today even. But . . .'

Here it comes.

'But your work's far from over. I still need you to keep an eye on me. To stop me behaving like an idiot that prostrates herself in front of every man and is pathetically grateful for their attention. I need you to teach me to be the leader of the pack.'

Ronan, now dressed in his usual Gap-ware, stared fixedly

out of the window. He always found women talking so personally embarrassing. Unless they were Katie and Jess, of course, but then he didn't think of them as women.

'And . . .' Rebecca said. 'It's not just me I'd like you to keep an eye on. You see, I've been thinking about my girlfriends' love lives – and they're all in a total mess. My friend Ally has a vile boyfriend but she doesn't seem to think she can do any better. Jenny, who should be ecstatic about her man, slags him off at every opportunity. And Suzy only goes for secret trysts with ancient captains of industry that none of us ever get to meet, spiced up with shags with young stud muffins.' She giggled. 'Oh, sorry, Ronan.'

Ronan shrugged and smiled, mortified. He was sure Rebecca knew the shaming truth about his uselessness in bed. Yesterday afternoon, he had sneaked out and bought a copy of *Our Bodies Ourselves*, which he kept hidden under a floorboard and studied during the day when he was positive both the girls were out. Whatever happened, he would learn to love oral sex.

Oblivious to his red face, Rebecca continued: 'What I'm saying is – my friends are far from alone. There are millions of women out there who need their love lives put in order. And this idea of treating your man like a dog is genius. So I think Greenhall and Graham should launch you as a professional love trainer. I can get you all the press coverage you need.'

Katie and Ronan looked at each other and tried not to laugh.

'I'm not sure I can see this working,' Ronan said carefully.

'Why not? People have personal trainers, don't they, to

make sure their bodies are in top shape? They have people who sort out their tax and arrange their flowers and tell them what colours to wear. Why the hell shouldn't they have a love trainer?'

Katie shrugged. 'I still don't see what my role would be. Wouldn't I just be another Dear Deirdre-type person?'

'With a photo casebook!' Ronan interjected. Now he knew what he was talking about.

Rebecca shook her head emphatically. 'No! Deirdre deals with all sorts of problems from where to get your wedding dress to . . . incest! You are love life only – but you're not just a column, you're hands on. You drag people off to the Met Bar and make them enjoy themselves, rather than sitting in and moping by the phone. You delete numbers from their mobiles. You teach them to be the leader of the pack! You tell them what their friends are secretly thinking but daren't tell them . . . God, I'd love it if someone told Ally to leave that louse Jon.'

'Katie's good at that,' Ronan agreed earnestly. 'She can be quite firm.'

Rebecca's imagination was spinning away. 'There could be a private practice, a TV show, a column, a slot on *Breakfast Today*, a book . . .'

'A range of Katie-inspired accessories,' said Ronan.

'I'm not joking! You could be like . . . the Jamie Oliver of people's love lives!'

'But what's in it for you, Rebecca?' Katie just didn't understand.

'My cut, of course. Fifteen per cent is our normal terms.'

'But who on earth would want to watch me on TV? *You* should do it, Rebecca.'

'No, that's where you're wrong. For a start I'd give shite advice and get sued, but more importantly, I'm too glamorous. People wouldn't believe a word of my advice. They'd be like "As if she's ever had trouble finding a boyfriend!"' Rebecca held up her hand to silence them. 'Which we *know* is not the case, but that is the way the public's mind works. Katie, on the other hand, is very ordinary-looking. Not unattractive, but certainly not threatening. But she has a gorgeous boyfriend, so her theories must work.'

'How do you know he's gorgeous?'

'Ronan told me. When we were dancing on Friday night.' Ronan nodded smugly.

'Look, I know it's a lot to take on board, but I think we should give it a go. You're a cleaner – which, incidentally, the press will *love*. What have you got to lose?'

'My dignity?'

'Oh, silly, what dignity? It's got to be a step forward for you. You could become very famous.'

'Jess is going to be so jealous,' Ronan muttered.

'Anyway,' said Rebecca, who had now pulled on her tracksuit top and was marching up and down the room in excitement. 'This is how I think we do it. I have a word with Suzy and we see if she likes it. Which she will. We organize a few case studies for you to sort out, Suzy runs a feature and lo! The whole of London will be talking about love trainer.'

So to humour Rebecca, Katie agreed that talking to Suzy couldn't hurt. Nothing would seriously come of it. The whole idea was utterly mad.

'Waltzing Matilda' began. Rebecca peered at her screen.

'Number withheld. It's probably Tim trying to sneak through.' She handed the phone to Katie. 'You answer it.'

'Hello?' said Katie. She thought she sounded most professional.

'Hello? Is this Rebecca?' A man. Sounded like Benny from Abba.

'No, it's her personal assistant. Can I help?'

'Ja! Probably! This is Johan Gustafson. We met the other night at the Met Bar. I am calling Rebecca because I am taking her out for dinner tomorrow. I haff booked a table at Claridge's for eight.'

'Oh,' said Katie, not even looking at Rebecca. 'I'm terribly sorry, but Rebecca won't be able to make it.'

'But why not?'

'There's been a change of plan.' Katie cast her mind about desperately. Years of answering the phone for Jess had taught her a few good lines. 'I'm afraid Rebecca has got back with her husband. She's having dinner with him tomorrow.'

'Who is it?' Rebecca was mouthing wildly. Katie ignored her.

'Rebecca is married? But I didn't know! She has misled me.'

Well, you're married too, Johan, Katie wanted to say. 'She and her husband were going through a rough patch,' she told him sweetly. 'But now they've made things up. So there's no point ever calling here again. Goodbye.'

She turned to Rebecca. 'That was Johan. From Friday night.'

Rebecca clapped her hand to her mouth. 'I'd forgotten all about him!'

They got up to leave. 'There's just one more thing, guys,' Rebecca said.

They waited.

'I think the love training is going to keep you kind of busy, Katie. And . . . to be honest, you're not the world's greatest cleaner.'

Katie knew it.

'So, Ronan, I was wondering if you could take over? I mean, say if you think it's beneath you, but I saw how beautifully you tidied up the kitchen on Friday night. And it looks to me like you could do with a proper job.'

24

Suzy took the call from Rebecca in her office and was instantly converted. A love trainer. It was the kind of thing her cretinous readers would adore – especially with a doggie theme attached. At the moment they were getting their guidance from Lavinia, the *Seduce!* astrologer: real name Elspeth Silver, whose other job was as cookery editor on *Handbook* magazine. But there was no way Suzy was going to tell Rebecca straight off. You had to play hard to get, as she was sure the love trainer would agree.

She put on her best bored tone.

'I have to say, I like the idea of men as hunter-gatherers, but isn't it just a bit of a gimmick? I mean, Becky, at the moment all Katie's actually achieved is persuading you to dump a complete arsehole, which is what we've all been praying you'd do for months.'

Rebecca was offended. 'You never told me you felt that way.'

'What would have been the point? You wouldn't have listened and you'd have hated us.'

'Well, that is the whole point of Katie,' Rebecca said. 'She tells you what your friends are secretly thinking.'

'So what would she tell me, Rebecca?' Suzy teased.

Rebecca was cool. 'How should I know? You'd have to ask her.' *She'd ask, does your boyfriend really exist, or have you invented him?*

'Give me an example of one of her rules,' Suzy challenged.

'Actually,' Rebecca said smugly, 'I have a list here. I can email it to you.'

A couple of seconds later, Suzy heard a ping on her screen. She opened the file, scanned it and chuckled appreciatively.

'I like this one. *Be firm. Ignore the dog when it's playing up, then later when it's being good, reward it.* I've always used that tactic. Hunter's got this really irritating habit of trying to wind me up by showing me photos of Justine and the girls. He hopes I'll beg him to leave them, but I just glance at them and yawn.'

'And how do you reward him?' Rebecca was fascinated. This was the most Suzy had *ever* revealed about Hunter.

'How do you think?' Time to change the subject. 'Rebecca, I'm going to think about this. I'm going to need to see Katie in action before I offer her a proper job. Perhaps if she finds you a boyfriend, I'll consider it.'

'Fair enough.' Rebecca put a smile into her voice, but she was scowling as much as Dr Lumet the Botox man would allow her. *For fuck's sake*, she thought as she put down the phone. It was bad enough being a spinster, but now her whole career rested on finding a man.

Yesterday, she'd been feeling brave about life but today was different. She'd discovered another grey hair and there were thread veins in her cheeks. She decided to ring her mother. 'I'm going to be one of those old women you see tottering around the supermarket mumbling to themselves,' she wailed down the phone to Sydney. 'My house will smell funny and I'll have dozens of godchildren and the highlight of my week will be the church jumble sale.'

'I don't see why,' said Laurel Greenhall. 'I'm a spinster and I'm nothing like that.'

'You're not a spinster, Mum! You were married and you have a child.'

'Married for all of five minutes before your dad buggered off and left me, and then as soon as you were eighteen you did the same.' She sounded perfectly cheery, but Rebecca felt the usual prong of guilt in her stomach.

'I visit as often as I can,' she defended herself. 'It's not like I'm the one who has a problem getting on planes.'

'It's not my fault I have a phobia.'

They were not going there again. 'Anyway, Mum, what am I going to do? I'd just resigned myself to spinsterhood, but Suzy says I have to find a man or the love trainer's no go.'

'What about that nice Ben?' Laurel asked.

'Oh, Mum! I don't want to go through that again. We're just friends, all right?' To her relief, her other line started bleeping. 'I have to go, Ma. Call you later.'

'Look forward to it, sweetie,' said Laurel, but Rebecca was already talking to Katie.

'So you have to find me a man or the deal's off,' Rebecca told her.

'That's ridiculous,' Katie said.

'Why?' Rebecca was constantly surprised by this new firmness.

'Because you're still on the rebound from Tim. I think it's too early for you to find someone new. You need to get to know yourself a little better. Have some adventures.' She seized around for some examples. 'Hunt down Osama

Bin Laden. Learn to be a snake charmer. You can't tell me that from now on the highlight of your life is going to be Dirty Den returning to *EastEnders*.'

Rebecca was thinking hard. 'I'd like to cycle across Costa Rica,' she said, to Katie's amazement. 'One of my clients did it a few years ago for charity. He said it was amazing.'

'Then cycle across Costa Rica.'

'Those trips take months though. What about work? I can't just shoot off and leave it all to Ben.'

'Can't you?'

'Well, maybe I can. But what about ... my life? I'm thirty-six, Katie, I don't have time to waste. I should be in London, going to dinner parties and gallery openings and meeting men.'

'Rebecca, as far as I can see, your whole life has been about meeting men. You're putting so many things on hold because you think they'll only be worth doing with a man around.'

Rebecca cringed. Sometimes she felt Katie could see right inside her. She sighed and leaned back in her chair.

'You're right as bloody usual. I'll go online and find out about sponsored cycle rides in hot, mountainous, Third World countries.' Her eye fell on her desk diary. 'But in the meantime, I'm going to explore one more man-meeting opportunity. Big party next week. It's for a historian called John Hilton, he's just written a new biography of Napoleon. Fascinating, apparently.'

'Oh, Crispin is reading that,' Katie said. Crispin always liked to be ahead of the game and was a member of a club that delivered must-reads before they hit the bookshops.

'Is he, indeed?' said Rebecca curiously. One of these

days she'd love to meet the good-looking, fantastically erudite Crispin. 'Well, Crispin will be very jealous when he hears that I was going to ask if you wanted to come to the party too. Lots of publishing and newspaper people will be there and I think it's time to start introducing you to them as the love trainer.'

Katie felt a hum of excitement. Perhaps Rebecca would introduce her to Salman Rushdie and . . . P. D. James! She started thinking what she would wear.

Rebecca continued: 'And you can help me too. These are the kinds of parties where I always get pissed and end up going home with the waiter.'

'Exactly like Suzy and Ronan.' They both chuckled.

'Anyway,' Rebecca continued, 'you should definitely start thinking of yourself as a love trainer now. I'll pay you for every session with me, so don't worry about that. I'm going to get some cards printed for you and talk to TV and books people. And you should start spreading the word around. Telling your friends who are movers and shakers.'

'OK,' Katie said, rolling her eyes at the idea of her friends moving and shaking.

She put the phone down, confused. Personally, she would love to cycle across Costa Rica, and tend to orang-utans in Borneo, and bungee-jump off a bridge in New Zealand. Maybe she ought to look into buying one of those round-the-world tickets. But she couldn't possibly think of leaving. What would Crispin say? She'd asked him once to take a year off so they could backpack round the world together but he'd just laughed as if she'd told some hilarious joke and didn't even reply.

Anyway, it wasn't just Crispin she had to think of now. She had Rebecca – and a possible new career as a love trainer – to consider.

Was all this what she actually wanted? Katie wasn't sure. Would anyone really take her, Katie Wallace, seriously? It seemed so unlikely. But then the alternative was to go back to cleaning and keep looking for jobs that involved water coolers and pension schemes and Christmas parties.

It was a no-brainer. She was going to have to give the love training a go. Katie began to feel a warm, tickly sensation in her stomach. She had so much good advice to give, which was wasted on her immediate circle of friends. Perhaps she really could help people. And after all, she had nothing to lose.

25

On Wednesday night, Hunter was in town, so Suzy cancelled a night out with Freddie, and caught a taxi straight from work to Clarkson's Hotel to have brisk, no-nonsense sex with her forty-eight-year-old lover.

'God, that was great,' Hunter breathed afterwards. He sat up and rubbed his light blue eyes. He might be getting on, but his body was still lean and his grey hair looked distinguished rather than sad. Suzy watched him admiringly as he leaned over to the bedside table and consulted his Rolex. 'It's only eight. What would you like to do now?'

Watch TV, Suzy thought, but that really wasn't on. One of the few obligations of a mistress was always to be bright and sparky and game for anything. Suddenly, one of Katie's rules flashed into her head.

There is nothing democratic about your relationship with your dog. You are leader of the pack.

Shit. Perhaps I'm going soft. But one had to make *some* effort. Most of the time, let's face it, Hunter was eating out of her tiny, manicured hands.

'We could go clubbing,' she teased. 'The Ministry of Sound does a handbag house night on Wednesdays. But it won't really get going until about two.'

Hunter stuck out his tongue. Suzy loved to rub in the age difference. 'I was thinking more in terms of getting some dinner,' he drawled. 'Tell you what, why don't you phone down to the restaurant and ask for a table in fifteen minutes.' He rolled off the bed and padded towards the bathroom.

Suzy didn't really want dinner in the restaurant: too many rich sauces and everything smeared in butter. Still, she could always order a salad. Suzy enjoyed dinners with Hunter. They had no friends in common, so instead of gossiping they actually had to talk about *issues*: world affairs, the arts, the stock market. Hunter was incredibly well informed and all his travelling meant he had always seen the latest movies on the plane. Suzy found it quite refreshing. She loved her friends, but sometimes she did find this incessant talk about who was sexier, Justin Timberlake or Robbie Williams, a bit tiresome. This was the stuff her magazine was full of, but the magazine's readers were aged fourteen to twenty-six. Suzy's friends were all in their thirties, for God's sake, but nobody seemed to have told them.

She picked up the phone and dialled the restaurant.

'Oh, Miss-us Knipper,' breathed the maître d', who knew damn well Suzy was no one of the sort. 'For you I always have a table, you know thees. *But* . . . tonight there is a little problem. A large party from Japan. I tell you what I do, I call back in five minutes with a solution.'

'No problem,' said Suzy, far more pleasant than usual, and hung up. She got out of bed and pulled on her underwear, followed by her jumper and little black skirt. Quite Parisian schoolgirl, today's look, she thought, twirling admiringly in front of the mirror. Hunter had loved it. She bent over to retrieve her stockings and suspender belt. *So* ridiculous, but if that was what made him happy . . .

The phone rang. Must be the restaurant. Suzy ran over to the desk and picked it up.

At the same time, Hunter grabbed it in the bathroom.

'Hello?' they said simultaneously.

'Hunty?' said a woman's voice. It was soft and low and pretty.

Shit! Justine! Immediately Suzy hung up.

'You didn't hear another voice,' Hunter was saying through the bathroom door. 'No, honey. You're imagining it . . . honey, honey! . . . It's all in your head. Are you going crazy or something? . . . Honey. I'm taking a client out to dinner now. I'll have to call you later. I haven't got time for this . . . Honey?'

Suzy sat in the flowery upholstered armchair. Her legs felt like putty. How could she have been so bloody stupid? Eventually, she heard Hunter slam down the extension. He opened the bathroom door.

'I'm sorry,' she said, looking him straight in the eye. 'I'm an idiot. Did you manage to convince her?'

Hunter shook his head. He looked oddly calm. 'She's really mad. She's been suspecting something for a while and now she thinks she has her proof. She says she's catching a plane out tonight. Crisis talks tomorrow.'

'Oh fuck. I don't know what to say.'

But Hunter still seemed unmoved. 'Well, it was going to come out sometime,' he said, sitting on the desk beside her and stroking her raven hair. 'Just a pity she had to find out this way.'

Suzy looked up at him, confused. 'Why was it going to

come out sometime? Did she have a team of private detectives on me?' Suzy did occasionally worry about this and tried not to be seen out too often with Hunter in public.

Hunter leaned over and tilted her chin, so she was looking into his eyes. 'No, baby. But sooner or later, I was going to have to tell her. I want us to be together properly, not going about things in this hole-and-corner way.'

There was a buzzing in Suzy's ears. 'You want us . . . to be together?'

'Well, don't look so surprised, baby. You know how I feel about you. This was inevitable. It's destiny.'

What a load of crap, Suzy thought. *There was no such thing as destiny.* 'But . . . what about your daughters?' she bleated.

'Hell, they're eighteen and seventeen. Old enough to look after themselves. Old enough to know that their parents haven't been happy for years. And now you can meet them, baby. Isn't that great?'

Suzy had never been so shocked. *Meet Hunter's daughters. A pair of airhead mall rats. She'd rather wear court shoes and shop at Costco.*

'But Hunter,' she simpered. 'I'm not sure I can do this. I'm a Catholic, you know. I believe families should stay together.'

'I didn't know you were a Catholic,' Hunter said.

I'm not. 'Oh yes,' she nodded.

'Well, don't worry, baby. There's always a way round these things. And these days divorcees can get remarried in a church. You'll still have your white dress and your bridesmaids.'

'But . . .'

'Baby. Justine and I didn't love each other any more. You had nothing to do with that. But you are going to make me very, very happy. God, I can't wait to show you Philly.'

Suzy felt as if she had just stepped over the edge of the Grand Canyon. 'You're not expecting me to come and live in Philadelphia?'

He grinned. 'Well, of course. But we'll travel all the time.'

And what about my job? What about my friends? What about my life in London? Everyone knows American telly is crap. And where would I buy drugs?

Suzy had to put a stop to this. But then the phone rang again.

'Hello?' said Hunter nervously, then relaxed. 'Ah, thank you, John-Paul. We'll be down in five minutes. And could you put some of your best champagne on ice? My . . . wife and I have something to celebrate.'

About the same time eight miles south of Hunter's hotel, Jenny was preparing a pasta supper and listening to her favourite, Frank Floyd's Sunday show on Radio 2. Jenny could never decide if Radio 2 was now acceptable in an ironic sort of way or if it was still irredeemably uncool. She suspected the latter. But all the same, Frank was very funny teasing his guest Dolly Parton about her exploding breast implants.

Gordon sat at the kitchen table reading the *Sunday Times*, his hand stuck absently down the front of his underpants. Jenny hated this habit almost as much as the way he laughed uproariously whenever he farted. But today she decided to say nothing. At least he seemed happy now. Earlier, he had been incredibly tense and distracted. Probably something to do with Arsenal, but it was still completely out of character. Normally Jenny was the moody one: sighing loudly and dramatically until – about three hours later – Gordon got the hint.

With most of her boyfriends, Jenny had enjoyed plenty of scenes. She would slam doors and run out crying into the street. They would run after her, grab her and stop her struggling with a passionate kiss. But with Gordy the only time she had run out of his house, she had spent half an hour on the bench at the end of the street, nursing an expression of tearful devastation and haughtily ignoring the local skateboard posse who kept whizzing past her. Still Gordy hadn't come and eventually, she had had to put her prepared face away. Back home, he was watching *Match of the Day*.

'You all right?' he'd said. 'I called you, but you left your phone behind.' He pointed to her mobile, recharging on top of the bookcase. Then he held out his arms to her. 'Come and give me a kiss,' he said. 'Sorry if I upset you.'

Jenny hadn't tried that one again.

Tonight, however, she had no idea what was on Gordy's mind and when she asked he just sighed and said, 'Nothing.' Oh well, she would just carry on enjoying the radio.

'Oh!' cried Dolly. 'I do declare, Frank, yew are too much.'

'Well, here's one of your classic tunes, Dolly,' Frank was saying. 'But just before we play it, I have a message here from Gordon Finch in Balham to Jenny. It says "Jen. It's been four years this Wednesday. I know you want us to get married, so how about it?"'

'Oh mah Lord!' cried Dolly. 'That is sooooo sweet.'

The strains of 'I Will Always Love You' filled the kitchen. Jenny burst into tears.

Gordon stood up and shyly held out his arms to her.

'So what do you think, porker?'

A thousand responses rushed through Jenny's brain. She was being proposed to. This was what it felt like! She was moved, yet at the same time she felt oddly detached. It was such a pity they were in Balham, she thought, not on top of the Eiffel Tower or watching the sun set over the Orinoco River. Then again, a man wanted to spend the rest of his life with her. But it was only Gordy. Could Jenny not have done a little better for herself? Wasn't there still time?

She looked at Gordy, so unusually shy, so hopeful.

But before she could say anything, the phone started ringing. It turned out *everyone* listened to Radio 2.

26

The following Tuesday, a very excited Katie scoured Jess's wardrobe for a suitable outfit for John Hilton's party.

'You're so lucky,' Jess whined continually. Jess was having a bad time at the moment. First she had been pissed off that the others had gone to the Met Bar without her, and now Ronan had snaffled the job she had been eyeballing for months. 'Why can't I bloody come?'

'When the love training is up and running, I'll be invited to these things in my own right. And you can come to all of them with me.'

Katie wasn't really concentrating, she was trying to work out what to wear. In the end she settled for a fitted white shirt from Jane Norman and a slim black pencil skirt. No tights and some of Jess's black heels. It was – almost – the kind of thing Suzy would wear. According to Rebecca, Suzy was being very quiet at the moment, with no word on the love training – or anything else.

'Very Audrey Hepburn,' Jess said delightedly.

The party was from six until nine. 'It's at the Foreign Press Association off Pall Mall,' Rebecca had told her. 'Horrible, stuffy room, nasty sausages on sticks and warm white wine. I've put your name on the guest list. I'll see you there at seven.'

Katie left home punctually at 6.30 p.m., but, thanks to a signalling failure at Embankment and getting completely lost around Trafalgar Square, she didn't find the stern-looking building until 7.45. She was covered in a fine film of sweat. She *hated* being late.

The room was full of groups of rather shabby-looking people, laughing loudly and talking about reviews in the *Spectator*. Katie couldn't see Rebecca anywhere. She pushed through the crowd, a fixed smile on her face, trying to catch someone's eye.

God, it was embarrassing. She felt about seven years old. *Just keep walking,* she told herself. *She's got to be here somewhere. Pretend you've seen someone you know.* She jerked her head and with a little wave mouthed 'hello' in the direction of the door. No one even noticed.

To her relief, she spotted a table covered in wine glasses. Remembering what Rebecca had said about the white, Katie grabbed some red. It tasted like insecticide, but one gulp made her feel better. She surveyed the buffet. Some dusty-looking sausage rolls, a few curling egg sandwiches and some crisps. Unpromising, but Katie was starving. She took a paper plate and piled it high. She looked like a pig, but who cared? Nobody knew her.

'Oh, thanks,' said a man, grabbing a handful of Twiglets from her plate. Katie spun round.

'Excuse me?'

He was tall, with spiky brown hair and a freckled face, in a blue shirt and baggy blue trousers. He smiled at her. 'You couldn't get me a glass of red, could you?'

Was this some kind of weird pass? 'Sorry,' said Katie witheringly. 'I'm looking for my friend.'

She squeezed past him. Ah, there was Rebecca standing by an open window and talking to a tall man with cropped blond hair. She held a glass of wine in one hand and with the other she was gesturing furiously. As Katie got nearer, she threw back her head and laughed very loudly. The man, meanwhile, had his back to the wall and a panicked expression on his face. The more Rebecca talked, the more nervous he looked. Oh God, Katie thought. Rebecca was on the pull. An air of desperation hung over her like Dior's Poison.

Time to intervene. 'Rebecca, hi!' she exclaimed, inserting herself between the two bodies. 'So sorry I'm late. I did call you. Did you get my message?'

Rebecca looked less than pleased. 'Oh, hi,' she said. 'Yeah, I got the message. No problem.'

'Nice to meet you,' Katie said, holding out her hand and smiling at the man. 'I'm Katie Wallace. And you are?'

'Duff Mitchell,' said the man, crushing Katie's hand. He had a nasal South African accent. 'Very nice to meet you, Katie. So are you an author?'

'Yes, she is,' said Rebecca. Her voice was slightly slurred and she had the predatory light in her eyes that Katie had seen with Johan. She clearly wanted Katie to disappear back into the crowd. But this was not going to happen.

'Oh, my glass is empty,' Katie trilled. 'Would you mind awfully getting me another one, Duff?'

'No probs,' said Duff, spraying Katie with wine-coloured spittle in his excitement at being granted a get-out clause. 'Rebecca?' he added politely. 'Another glass of white?'

'Yes, *please*.'

Duff scurried off towards the bar.

Katie turned to Rebecca. 'What are you doing?' she hissed.

'Just talking,' said Rebecca defensively. 'Duff's very nice. He works for Flyby publishers. He could publish your book.'

'You were flirting with him,' Katie hissed.

'I was not!' But Katie stared her out. 'OK, I was a little. But he's a real sweetie. He hasn't been living in London that long. I think he could do with some friends.'

'When did he arrive in London? Last week?' Rebecca didn't answer. Katie looked around the room. 'Come on, we're going to find someone else to talk to.'

'But we can't do that! Duff's gone to get the drinks. It's *rude*.'

'Do you seriously think he's coming back?' She gestured to Duff on the other side of the room talking happily to a young man in combats.

Rebecca scowled. 'Rebecca! I am your *love trainer*! You have got to stop flinging yourself at every man who smiles at you. I thought you were embracing spinsterhood.'

'I am! But I'm not a bloody nun. I'm not going out hunting guys down, but if I meet a nice one you can't expect me to ignore him. I'm nearly fifty, Katie.'

Katie sighed. She knew she was being a bit too harsh. 'OK, you can talk to him again. But you've got to play it cool this time. Do what I tell you. And that means for starters, we go and find someone else to talk to, rather than stalking the poor man.'

'OK, OK,' Rebecca huffed. She peered around the room. 'Let's go and talk to Jeremy. We should get you on his show.'

It was Jeremy Jackson. Katie knew he was the presenter of *Breakfast Today*, not because she had ever watched it (it

was on far too early for her) but because not ...
when the papers didn't carry some story abou...
ex-wife, his poor abandoned children in Don...
hatred of his co-presenter Imogen Watts and h...
new girlfriend, now pregnant with their baby.

'Shouldn't he be in bed?' she asked Rebecca. 'Doesn't he have to get up at 3 a.m. or something?'

'Oh no, he's on a three-month sabbatical to write his bloody book,' Rebecca replied. 'Bloody lazy bastard. All he has to do is babble into a tape-recorder for three hours a day and then the ghostwriter has the nightmare of turning it into something readable. But the way he bangs on about it, you'd think he'd been redesigning the Sistine Chapel.'

Her face changed as they approached Jeremy, who was in intense conversation with a pretty blonde girl who looked about nineteen and was most certainly not the lovely new pregnant girlfriend as featured a fortnight ago in *Hello!*

'Jez!' Rebecca screeched, leaning forward for a kiss. 'How's it going?'

The blonde seized her get-out clause. 'Well, nice meeting you,' she squawked, backing away.

'Hey!' Jeremy yelled after her. 'Don't forget to call me.'

'Jeremy, I'd like you to meet my new client, Katie,' said Rebecca with a winning smile. 'She's a love trainer. I think she'd be brilliant for the show.'

'Hi,' said Jeremy, holding out a limp hand and looking over Katie's left shoulder for someone prettier.

'How's it all going?' Rebecca asked brightly.

'It's hell,' Jeremy groaned. 'I'm really stuck on chapter

ght right now, Rebecca. I don't know how much I should reveal about the divorce settlement – I'm terrified if I say too much Debbie's solicitors will be down on me again.'

He droned on while Rebecca hmmmed and looked concerned, the flirty figure of a few moments earlier entirely banished. Someone tapped Katie's elbow. She looked round. It was Duff, holding three glasses of wine precariously between his splayed fingers.

'Where did you get to?' he asked. His tone was light, but he looked a little hurt. Oh well, so he *had* come back.

'Sorry,' said Katie insincerely. 'Rebecca was whisked away by an old friend.' She indicated Rebecca and Jeremy, locked in earnest conversation.

'Thanks,' said Rebecca abruptly, taking the glass from Duff without even looking at him.

This was excellent: Rebecca on a manhunt was overloud and in-your-face. Rebecca in work mode was uninterested to the point of rudeness. Duff looked confused. Perfect. *You set the agenda,* Katie thought. *The dog does what you tell him to.*

She looked at Duff contemplatively. Pity about the stupid name. But in other respects he seemed OK.

'So what's this book you're writing for Rebecca?' Duff asked her.

Katie found she didn't want to talk about it. 'Oh, you know . . . just a silly sort of self-help book. Nothing to get excited about.'

'Oh, I don't know,' Duff said. 'Self-help books are where it's at these days. We sell millions of them. Lot of clueless people out there, needing guidance.'

'Really?' Katie was cheered.

'Sure. What are your qualifications? Are you a counsellor or something? Do you have a degree in psychology?'

'Never mind all that,' said Rebecca, intervening suddenly. 'Katie has a fascinating life story, which you will learn all about in due course, when her proposal is ready.' She turned back to Jeremy.

'Well, that was telling me,' Duff laughed. 'I've never met Rebecca before. She seems great. Really feisty.'

'Oh, she's incredible,' Katie gushed. She glanced at Rebecca. This was very promising. Rebecca mustn't be allowed to blow it. It was time she had a few words.

A middle-aged, bosomy woman in a flowing white kaftan barged between them. 'Aargh! Duff! My favourite boy!' she yelled, kissing him fulsomely. As she squawked about how long it had been, Katie turned round and tapped Rebecca on the shoulder.

'So do you think I should reveal the details of that affair?' Jeremy was asking.

'What?' Rebecca snapped.

'I just need a quick word,' Katie said, rolling her eyes in Duff's direction.

Rebecca didn't blink. 'Jezzie, darling, it's all going to be fine,' she said firmly. 'Sleep on it and give me a call in the morning. But I know we've got a *Sunday Times* bestseller on our hands here.' She kissed him firmly on both cheeks. 'Talk in the morning, baby.'

Jez dived back into the party in search of the nineteen-year-old.

'OK,' whispered Katie, like a KGB agent imparting vital information. 'Duff does seem interested. So now you have to make it work. Talk to him. About books or travel or politics. All personal questions are banned.'

'But that's *rude!*' Rebecca gasped.

'Rebecca, what's with the rude fixation? You'd be rude to a publisher who was screwing over one of your clients, wouldn't you? We are in business here. The business of finding you a man.'

'Yes, but if I was talking to some bastard publisher and I wanted to soften him up I'd ask him all about his favourite football team and his ugly children and where he went on his holidays.'

'Fine. But this is different. I swear. Don't ask personal questions and the man will have to work to get your attention.'

Rebecca nodded obediently. 'OK, I'll try it.'

'And if he asks a personal question, tell him as little as possible. Be mysterious. Most importantly, keep the whole thing brief. No matter how well it's going, after ten minutes you must walk away. Leave him wanting more.'

'OK.' Rebecca looked so serious. Katie felt a sudden wave of affection for her.

'So go ahead, and remember: if it doesn't work out it wasn't meant to be.'

Duff was laughing away with kaftan lady but as they glanced over at him, he looked up and smiled.

'Do you know her?' Katie asked.

'Unfortunately, yes,' said Rebecca. 'Dorothy Holmes. Books PR supremo. Loathsome bitch. She's the person I was thinking of getting to do your PR once we've got you launched. Distract her, Katie. Then I get to talk to Duff.'

They moved over. 'Dorothy!' yelled Rebecca, and there

was another noisy round of airkissing before Katie was introduced. 'She's my hottest property,' Rebecca announced.

'Really?' Dorothy gave a tight smile.

'I love your kaftan,' Katie said hastily. 'Is it from India?'

Dorothy yawned faintly. 'Sri Lanka actually.'

Katie laughed nervously, although it wasn't funny at all. She was straining her ears to pick up on Rebecca's conversation.

'So next year I'm off to Costa Rica,' she was saying. 'It's the most biodiverse nation on earth.'

It sounded promising. Katie glanced back at Dorothy, who was waving enthusiastically at someone on the other side of the room.

'Excuse me,' she said and hurried off.

So now Katie was left alone again, feeling like a tool. She glanced at her watch: seven more minutes and she would drag Rebecca away. How to fill the time until then? The loo. Perfect. It took her one minute to fight her way to the ladies, another two minutes to queue, two more in the cubicle and one washing her hands.

Three minutes until she intervened, she calculated, as she stepped back into the party. The room was emptying, making her status as a saddo increasingly obvious. Never mind: she would walk intently towards the bar, get a drink, and then she and Rebecca would leave.

'Hi,' said a voice behind her. She looked round. It was the freckle man. Trying his luck again.

'Hello,' said Katie in her nastiest voice.

'How about a top-up?' He held out his glass.

'What is this?' Katie said. 'Get your own wine.'

He looked at her as if he had been hit. 'You're a terrible waitress,' he snapped back.

'What? I'm . . .' Katie looked down at the white shirt and black skirt and it clicked. He thought she was a waitress. So much for bloody Audrey Hepburn.

'Wait,' she cried as he walked away. For some reason it was important Katie explained the mistake. He didn't hear her. Instead, he walked up to Rebecca and gave her an affectionate peck on the cheek. Katie watched her introduce him to Duff. They had an easy body language. Clearly they had known each other for years.

Katie hovered on the sidelines, too embarrassed to approach. It wasn't as if she had to break Rebecca and Duff up now, this guy had done it for her.

'Katie!' Rebecca yelled, beckoning her over imperiously.

Katie sidled over. She didn't want to catch the man's eye.

'Katie,' Rebecca gushed. 'I want to introduce you to Ben. Ben Graham. My partner. Business, that is. Ben, this is Katie. You know, the one I told you about?' She nudged him gently and glanced at Duff, but he was waving at someone on the other side of the room. '*The love trainer*,' she mouthed.

Ben looked bemused, then he burst out laughing.

'Ah, ha, ha, ha! You're the love trainer! I thought you were a waitress!'

'I know,' Katie said. She could feel her skin turn as red as the gut-rot in her hand.

'I kept asking her for glasses of wine,' he explained to Rebecca.

'An understandable mistake,' Rebecca said, examining

Katie's outfit. 'Katie, just because you're working, you don't have to wear a uniform.'

'What's going on?' grinned Duff, returning to the conversation.

Ben was still laughing, in fact tears were pouring down his cheeks. *It's not that funny*, Katie thought, embarrassed.

'Sorry!' he gasped. 'But you were so rude to me.' He reached out and brushed her hand. 'Let me get you a glass of wine and make it up to you.'

As he touched her, Katie – to her shock – felt a jolt run right through her, like she'd missed a step in the dark. Only it didn't feel bad – it felt good.

Oh my God, she thought. *I fancy him.*

Their eyes met. *And he fancies me too.*

'Some wine?' he asked politely. 'I am so sorry.'

Suddenly Katie just wanted to get out of there. She tried to remember what Crispin had said he was doing tonight. It would be good to see him.

'No thanks,' she stammered. 'We have to go.' Gently, she tapped Rebecca on the arm. To Katie's relief, she got the hint.

'Lovely to meet you, Duff. But I've got to be off.' Rebecca gave him a brief, businesslike handshake and turned on her heel. Katie followed her.

'Where are you going?' Ben shouted after them. Rebecca glanced round and gave him an airy wave.

'Home, darling.'

'Ben won't believe it,' she giggled to Katie as they trotted down the steps. 'Normally I'm always the last to leave the party and I always want to go on somewhere else. I'm learning. Aren't I?'

'You are,' said Katie fondly. She was proud of her pupil, but furious with herself. *That's what comes of drinking crap wine*, she told herself, but she knew it was more than that.

27

'So what now?' asked Suzy. It was Wednesday evening and she and Jenny were lying in her health club's sauna. Suzy had been having a one-on-one yoga class: she never joined in with the hoi polloi.

Jenny was panting too hard to answer. She had just come out of a horrible step class. Now the engagement had been announced she had six months to lose three stone – well, maybe just one would do – and she had embarked on a new exercise regime and diet. She grabbed a chunk of fat on her thigh. Forget about pinching an inch, there was at least a mile here. God, she was disgusting.

'Jenny?'

'Oh, sorry.' Jenny sat up and wiped some sweat from her face. 'Well, Mum's insisted we put the announcement in *The Times* and the *Telegraph*. And we're going to have an engagement party. July twenty-first. You'll be there, won't you? And Hunter too, of course.'

'Wouldn't miss it for the world,' Suzy promised. She had no intention of bringing Hunter, but Jenny must know that.

'And we have to settle on a date and book a venue.' Suzy brightened slightly. 'And I have to choose my dress.'

'Just so long as you're not expecting me to be a bridesmaid.'

'Actually, I have a tartan meringue with matching cloche hat sitting in my wardrobe just waiting for you.'

They giggled. 'So did you say yes immediately?' Suzy asked. She too had been listening to Frank Floyd that night but she would rather die than admit it. Hunter had returned to Philadelphia for crisis talks with Justine, which had ended in her throwing him out and saying she'd screw him for every cent he had.

'What choice did I have? The show's producer called and asked what my answer was. Dolly was dying to know. I could hardly say I was thinking about it.'

'Clever Gordon. He knew that way he couldn't lose.'

'Well, I would probably have said yes anyway.'

'*Probably*?' Suzy sat up, surprised.

'I mean definitely,' Jenny said, sitting up and splashing more water on the coals. 'Well, no, I mean probably. I mean, I don't know, Suze. I adore Gordy, but I just don't know if I want to marry him.'

'It's a huge commitment,' Suzy said. She tried to keep her tone neutral. Personally, she had never understood why anyone fell for the marriage fantasy. All that expense when it was inevitably going to end in tears. She blamed pop music and magazines like her own.

'I don't know, Suze,' Jenny continued. 'Gordy's gorgeous. It's just . . . it's just I guess I never thought that my destiny was an IT consultant from Shropshire.' She wiggled uncomfortably on her towel. 'It means that unless we win the lottery I will never live anywhere nicer than Balham, that I won't be able to send my children to private schools, that I'll never be able to afford to fly business class or get a haircut from Nicky Clarke. I'm going to spend the rest of my life eating takeaways from the Bengal Lancer, or splashing out on an evening at the Peking Duck.'

She felt a cow for saying it, but she was desperate to confess. And surely Suzy would understand. After all, she only went out with rich men.

But Suzy looked outraged. 'Jenny, what are you saying? That you should dump Gordy and hold out for Prince Albert of Monaco?'

'Actually, I was hoping for Prince Andrew now he's back on the market.' Jenny giggled. She paused. 'Look, I'm just saying it's hard to accept that this is going to be my life. And besides . . .'

'Besides?'

'I think I've . . .'

'You think you've what?'

'I think I've . . . met someone else.'

Suzy gasped. 'Jenny! Who?'

Jenny took a swig of water. 'His name's Fabrice. He works in our Paris office. He was over here a couple of weeks ago and we had lunch. And I just felt something . . .'

Suzy sighed. Jenny was the queen of crushes. If Suzy had a pound for every conversation they had had along these lines, she would have retired about five years ago to her dream villa in the South of France.

'Jen, just because you fancy someone doesn't mean you shouldn't marry Gordon.'

'This wasn't just fancying someone. There was a connection there. The way we looked at each other. We just had so much to say to each other. I know it sounds silly, but I really thought he could be the One.'

Suzy snorted. She was always commissioning articles

entitled 'How Do You Know He's the One?' As far as she was concerned it was all bollocks. Love was a temporary state of insanity, and if you were needy enough to want a life partner you should forget endless passion and look for someone you could jostle along with.

She thought of Katie, the love trainer. Wasn't that her philosophy? Suzy grinned. The girl was like her mini-me, even if she did have a long-term boyfriend. Although there was no doubt Katie was softer than Suzy was. She'd watched her fussing round Rebecca the other night and there had been genuine anxiety in her eyes. Suzy, on the other hand, had only felt irritation at her friend's gullibility. Still, Katie was very young. She'd learn.

Jenny was still talking. 'That was two weeks ago and since then we've been emailing like crazy. The last one said: "I can't wait for my next trip to London." What do you think that means? Do you think he likes me?'

The only way to deal with such nonsense was to ignore it. Suzy stood up and wrapped herself in a fluffy white towel. 'I'm going to have a shower.'

Jenny followed her out of the sauna. They hung up their towels and took their places in neighbouring cubicles.

'Anyway,' she yelled over the pounding water, 'I've got a meeting in Brussels in two weeks, but I was wondering if I could catch the train from there to Paris. It's only a couple of hours, I think.'

'Does he know you're engaged?' Suzy yelled back.

'Well, I wasn't when I met him.'

'Yes, but you'd been with Gordy four years. Does he know you have a live-in partner?'

Jenny said nothing.

268

'Jenny?'

'Oh, sorry. I had shampoo in my eyes. No. No, he doesn't. It didn't seem relevant. We didn't talk about our private lives. We were talking about . . . books and films and places we'd been to. He's really well travelled. He said he'd love to show me Rio.'

'Oh, please!' Suzy turned off the shower and reached over the cubicle door for her robe.

'So do you think I should go to Paris?' Jenny said, following her.

Suzy had disappeared into one of the changing cubicles. She shouted over the door.

'Jenny, I think before you do absolutely anything, you need to work out what's going on with Gordy. If you seriously think that Fabrice is the One, then why are you marrying someone else?'

Jenny looked at the carpet like a sulky teenager.

Suzy softened. After all, Gordy was sane and loyal, but he was a bit boring. And this Fabrice did sound rather sexy. Maybe Jenny was right not to be settling for second-best. Either way, Suzy had just worked out how she could turn all this to her advantage.

'Listen,' she said, emerging fully dressed from the cubicle. 'I'm working on a secret project for the magazine right now involving a client of Rebecca's called the love trainer, who analyses relationships. Why don't you get her to check you and Gordy out? It can't hurt!'

'Doesn't she cost a fortune?' Jenny asked suspiciously. But she was already tempted. Jenny loved that kind of stuff. In her time she had had her aura read, her colours done and her handwriting analysed. A report had come back on the last saying the analyst was almost certain this specimen came from a prison warder. Jenny had never told anyone that.

'Don't worry,' said Suzy. 'I'll blag you a freebie.' Apart from her mortgage, Suzy paid for virtually nothing. Clothes, haircuts, holidays, even cars were all lavished upon her by companies desperate for free publicity. She couldn't remember the last time she had actually had to purchase a bottle of shampoo or bought a ticket for the cinema. Jenny was deeply envious, even though she received plenty of the cast-offs.

'But we can't go and see a love trainer! It would be like . . . couples counselling. Only sad people do that.'

'I don't think the love trainer quite works like that. It's more informal. More hands on. She observes you in your own environment and then advises you. Gordon need never know.'

Jenny laughed. 'I know Gordon's a bit of an idiot, but even he might notice some woman in a white coat with a clipboard wandering around the house taking notes.'

'It's more subtle than that. Katie usually pretends to be staff.'

Jenny hooted. 'Staff? Does she usually work at the palace? Telling Camilla to hold on in there and one day she'll be queen?'

'No. No . . . she's more like a cleaning lady.'

'But I've already got a cleaning lady. I'm not getting rid of Vincentia. Anyway, she comes when we're at work.'

Suzy thought. 'OK. What about if she was a waitress?'

'What, at the Bengal Lancer? How would she do it?

Analysing our relationship by the number of poppadoms we order?'

'No!' Suzy started combing her damp hair. 'At your engagement party. She could pour drinks. Serve the canapés.'

Jenny, who had been sitting on a bench waiting for her, stood up.

'OK,' she said. 'It's got to be worth a go.'

'But until then no more flirting with Fabrice.'

'Not even an email?'

'Not even an email. Let Katie check out you and Gordy and give you some sound advice.'

Jenny pouted, then smiled.

'It's a deal,' she said.

Suzy thought it better not to tell Jenny that Katie believed in treating men like dogs. Put like that, it sounded rather brutal. In the cab on the way home, she realized Jenny hadn't asked her a single question about Hunter. Pity, really. Suzy would have liked to talk to someone about her current dilemma. But she simply had no idea how to start such a conversation. After keeping herself to herself for so long, her friends would probably have her committed.

28

All day after John Hilton's party Rebecca tried to put Duff out of her mind. She had a busy afternoon negotiating a complicated contract. Every time her email pinged, she jumped, but it was always just bloody work. 'Any calls?' she casually asked Tara every time she returned from the loo (drinking eight pints of water a day meant you went a lot).

At about three, unable to stand it any longer, she flicked through her Rolodex and found the number of Flyby, the publisher where Duff worked.

'Duff Mitchell,' she muttered into the handset. She was terrified Ben would walk in and hear her.

'Who?' barked the operator.

'Duff . . . Mitchell.'

A phone rang. 'Duff Mitchell's office,' trilled a voice.

Rebecca hung up. Oh, very good, very mature. Where had that got her? Precisely nowhere, except she now knew Duff was important enough to have a secretary. He was probably sleeping with her. It took her back to being thirteen, when she and her best friend Liza Moore had spent hours after school calling boys they fancied, then hanging up when they picked up the phone. Liza, she had heard, was married with three children now and Rebecca had advanced not one jot.

At that moment, her phone beeped. Rebecca snatched it.

It won't be him, she told herself firmly. But she didn't recognize the number. She opened the message and squealed.

Hope u got home safe last night, she read. *Dinner sometime? Duff.*

Once, she would have been straight on the phone to one of the girls. Now it was Katie.

'So what do you think?'

Katie wasn't sure. She disapproved of texting. Too detached, yet at the same time too pushy – that little envelope icon demanding attention. And the 'Duff' without a surname was a little too familiar – although in fairness, it was unlikely that Rebecca would know two Duffs. And it hardly made him a wife-beater.

'What shall I reply?' Rebecca asked.

'Nothing for now,' Katie instructed. 'Leave it twenty-four hours.'

'That's . . .'

'Rude? No, Rebecca, it's not. He isn't one of your closest friends, he isn't family, he isn't a work contact.'

'Well, he is sort of,' Rebecca retorted. Her face fell. 'He probably only wants to talk about work.'

'No, then he would have asked you out for lunch.'

'True! So tomorrow I can reply? And what do I say?'

'Oh . . . say: *Dinner sometime great. Free week on Weds. Any good? All best, Rebecca Greenhall.*'

'Next Wednesday? That's ridiculous. He'll have forgotten what I look like.' Rebecca looked down at her diary. 'Anyway, I'm busy that night.'

'Rebecca, you know I didn't mean literally that night.

273

I'm just saying leave it a week. You have to show him who's boss.'

'But . . .' Rebecca knew she was beaten. OK. I can do Tuesday that week. Is that too soon?'

'It's fine. But don't let him know that until tomorrow.'

'Fine. Fine.' Rebecca had every intention of texting him as soon as she got home. After all, what difference could a few hours make? 'We'll speak tomorrow. Bye.'

Ten minutes later, she looked up. Katie was standing outside her glass box.

'What are you doing here?' she asked as the love trainer opened the door.

'I was buying a birthday present in Selfridges. But I thought I should drop in.'

'What for?' Rebecca felt a flutter of alarm.

'To collect your mobile.'

'What? Oh no, Katie. Not that again. I need it for work.'

'I'll make sure you get any important messages.'

Rebecca pouted. 'I can still call Duff in the office.'

'Of course you can. You can go round there if you like and tell him you love him and want to have his babies. Confiscating the mobile is just a reminder that you'd be better off keeping silent.'

For a moment Rebecca thought Katie was going to make a grab for the phone. Reluctantly, she handed it over.

If Katie hadn't been her client who was going to make her a lot of money, Rebecca would probably hate her, she thought. She could be so stern. But then she had been so pleased when Duff got in touch. When you thought about it, it was weird the way Katie's approach to love was so clinical, when she clearly took so much pleasure from other people's romances. Wasn't falling in love all about letting go?

Clearly not, Rebecca told herself, otherwise she'd have found a man decades ago. Katie obviously knew what she was doing.

'I'll return it tomorrow,' Katie said. 'Don't worry. Everything will work out just fine.'

Precisely twenty-four hours later Katie turned up at the office with the phone. Rebecca punched in a reply to Duff and showed it to Katie for approval. She pressed Send. Five minutes later, it rang.

'Hello,' Rebecca said fiercely, assuming it was something work-related. 'Oh! Hello! Yes. How are you? Just a minute.'

Katie was standing up. Rebecca gestured at her to sit again.

'It's Duff,' she mouthed. 'What do I say?'

Despite herself, Katie clapped her hands in excitement. 'Say how nice to hear from him. Ask if next Tuesday suits him and where he'd like to go. And then hang up. No chat. Leave him wanting more.'

'OK.' Rebecca returned to the phone. 'Sorry about that – I was on the other line.' She listened. 'Good. Good . . . OK . . . About seven-thirty should be good for me . . . No, I'll call if there's a change of plan . . . OK, see you then. Bye!'

She hung up. 'Was that good?'

'It was brilliant,' Katie said proudly. 'Now he'll be freaked out. He has no idea if this dinner's business or pleasure.'

Rebecca laughed. 'I'm so happy. Normally I'd have

spent hours on the phone, trying to make him like me. I feel so . . . empowered.'

She frowned. 'Now, what do you think I should wear?'

29

Suzy waited a day before calling Rebecca to say she thought Katie's trial run should be with Jenny and Gordon.

Rebecca wasn't sure.

'Jenny is the luckiest woman in the world,' she objected. 'How can Katie possibly help her?'

Suzy yawned. 'You know Jenny. She just wants reassurance. To hear that she's made the perfect choice. That she'll have the perfect life.'

Rebecca relaxed. That shouldn't be too difficult. She had always seen Katie as a kind of Terminator figure telling women who loved too much to dump the bastard. But there was no reason why she shouldn't perform another role: telling women who were just so damn fussy they didn't know that they were born.

'OK, OK, I'll set Katie on to her. It can't do any harm.'

As soon as she put down the phone she forgot the conversation entirely. There were other things to worry about: like tonight's dinner with Duff. *Or more likely tonight's duff dinner*, she told herself, determined not to get her hopes up.

Bizarrely, Duff had announced he would pick her up from the flat at 7.30 p.m. Nobody had ever done such a thing for Rebecca. She felt like Sandy in *Grease* waiting for Danny to take her to the drive-in. Only instead of the anxious father warning him to take care of his daughter or pay the price, she had Katie telling her exactly what to do.

'Wear trousers, not a skirt, you don't want to look like you've made too much of an effort,' she instructed, lolling on Rebecca's bed. Reluctantly, Rebecca took off her new pencil skirt and replaced it with some black bootlegs.

'They're actually sexier,' Katie pronounced. 'Because you're not so obvious now.' She glanced around the room. It looked different: the curtains had been cleaned, all the clutter that used to cover the bedside table had been magicked away, and the nasty gilt mirror that used to sit above it had been replaced by a nice one with a beechwood frame.

'This room looks much bigger now,' she said admiringly. 'When did you get round to rearranging the furniture?'

'Oh, Ronan did all that. He said once he'd got the cleaning under control, he had time to do a little bit of tweaking. It's great, isn't it? He should host one of those home-decoration shows.'

'He should, shouldn't he? Maybe you could find him something.' Her tone was flippant, but Katie meant it.

'I probably should. But then I'd lose him as a cleaner. And that would be a *disaster*. I mean, losing you was quite different. I don't really think cleaning was your forte, Katie.'

She was probably right, but Katie still felt a little hurt.

Katie left the flat and waited in the little coffee shop across the road. It was 7.15. At 7.20 a taxi drew up outside the block and sat there, engine purring. Katie's heart clutched in excitement. Duff was early. Excellent sign. The taxi continued to wait. Katie watched through the steamy window over her can of Diet Coke, feeling like one of the lady detectives she loved to read about. Sure enough, at 7.29 Duff got out of the taxi and walked up to Rebecca's door. He rang on the bell and waited on the front steps, twisting his hands nervously in front of him.

Five minutes later, Rebecca appeared, looking glorious. She glanced across the road, saw Katie and gave just the faintest hint of a smile. Then she got into the cab and it drove off.

In the back of the taxi, Rebecca smiled demurely. 'So where are we going?' she asked. The meter already read £35, although no doubt Duff would claim the fare on expenses.

'Well, I thought we'd try this really cool place that I've found. It's in the West End.'

The West End? This was excellent. Perhaps he was taking her to L'Escargot? Joe Allen's could be nice. Or Sheeky's. The taxi carried them down Park Lane and into Hyde Park Corner, then shot off down Piccadilly. Maybe they were going to L'Oranger? Or that cool new place in Chinatown? Rebecca grinned. It was wonderful to be made to feel so special.

They went half-way round Piccadilly Circus and stopped just before Leicester Square. 'Well, here we are!' said Duff, gesturing to a flashing neon sign across the road.

Rebecca was sure she had misunderstood. 'That's . . . TGI Friday's.'

'That's right,' Duff nodded cheerfully. 'Do you know it?'

'Well,' Rebecca said faintly. 'Only by reputation . . .'

'Well, are you in for a treat,' he said, ushering her through the door. 'They do great cocktails.' He turned, smiling, to the girl at the desk. 'I've booked!'

Rebecca looked around at the pile of plastic menus and the tables packed with gangs of giggling women on their monthly night out and depressed-looking German tourists. *Don't be high-maintenance*, she told herself sternly. 'It looks great,' she burbled.

'I came here for the first time about a month ago,' Duff informed her excitedly. 'We don't have TGIs in South Africa, you know?'

'Don't you? We do in Australia.' Rebecca felt quite faint.

'Is that so?' Duff marvelled. 'Of course, it's a pity it's only Tuesday.' He snorted at his enormous wit. 'Because . . . it's TGI Friday's!'

A waitress with lank hair and acne showed them to a dark corner table, directly beneath the air-conditioning vent and a speaker blaring Bryan Adams.

'I'm going to have a Slow Comfortable Screw Against the Wall,' Duff sniggered.

'A Long Island Iced Tea,' said Rebecca. Someone had once told her that was the strongest cocktail in existence. She was going to need as much alcohol in her bloodstream as possible, if she was going to get through the evening.

Duff waved away the menus.

'It's got to be burgers, hasn't it? Well done, please.'

'Actually . . .' said Rebecca. She hadn't eaten a burger in ten years. But the waitress had already gone.

As they waited for their food, Duff talked non-stop about his passion for surfing. 'Point break . . . swell . . . longboards . . . leashes . . . wetsuits.' It was as if he'd just been released from solitary confinement. Rebecca watched his Adam's apple bobbing up and down in his scrawny throat like a bucket in a well. *How did I get here?* she wondered. *He seemed so nice at the party.*

'I guess you like surfing too?' he said after about half an hour. 'Being Australian and all that.'

'Well, we didn't live anywhere near the beach . . .' Rebecca began.

He looked shocked. 'Didn't you? I can't see the point of living in a city like Sydney if you don't use its amenities.'

'Well, it wasn't up to me. It was my mum's choice. And we didn't have much money. Beach-side properties are expensive.'

Duff looked unconvinced. 'So, living in England, you must miss the surf,' Rebecca said quickly. She didn't know why she was being so polite.

'I do. I bloody hate living here. The dirt, the expense, the workaholism. Everybody's so obsessed with status here. What do you do? How much do you earn? Can't they see there's more to life than that?'

'So why did you leave South Africa?'

'Well, there are so many more opportunities here. I mean, why did you leave Australia?'

'I . . .'

'But you're obviously doing well. You must be making a lot of money if you don't mind me saying so.'

I *do*, Rebecca wanted to yell, but at that point the food arrived. And then Duff was off again, sprinkling bits of burger all round the table in his haste to tell her about shin hairs, dings, paddleboards and flat spells. *I certainly know all about those*, Rebecca thought dully.

At 10.30, after Rebecca had declined dessert and coffee, he asked for the bill.

'Here,' said Rebecca, reaching for her bag. 'Let me.'

Duff looked confused, then pleased.

'Well, that's very kind of you,' he said.

'So . . .' he added as they waited for her card to go through the machine. 'Do you fancy a drink somewhere else?'

Rebecca could think of nothing she would like less.

'Why not?' she said.

Because after all maybe she was being too hard on Duff? It wasn't his fault he was a South African hick. She was nearly fifty, she couldn't afford to be so picky. He really wasn't bad looking. And he obviously liked her. No, she would give him one more chance.

But just as they stepped out on to the street, thronging with beggars, crack dealers and boisterous French teenagers, Rebecca's mobile rang.

She knew who it would be. 'Are you still with him?' Katie asked.

'Oh God! I'll be with you straight away!'

'Sorry?' Katie obviously hadn't expected Rebecca to be quite so enthusiastic.

'Which hospital is it? St Marvin's. I'll get a cab. See you in ten minutes. Be brave!'

She hung up. 'I'm really sorry, but my friend has just gone into labour. I have to join her.'

'Really?' Duff frowned. 'Where's her husband?'

'Oh, she hasn't got one. She's a lesbian. Used a turkey baster. Anyway, nice to see you again.' Rebecca really didn't want to kiss him. She held out her hand. He grabbed it and pulled her towards him.

'Goodnight,' he said with a slobbery kiss on the cheek.

'Taxi!' she yelled, jumping on to the road and waving her arms up and down like a castaway trying to attract a rescue plane.

'I'd give you a lift,' she said, climbing into the cab. 'But it's totally out of your way.'

'Oh God, I feel really bad,' Rebecca said. It was the following evening at her flat and she and Katie were having a debrief. 'Perhaps I was too hard on him. He wasn't that bad. We could have been friends.'

'You've got enough friends,' Katie said. 'You don't need any more.'

'Dating is a nightmare,' Rebecca said disconsolately. 'Who invented it? In the old days I used to just snog someone at a party and the next morning we'd be a couple. There was none of this going out to dinner and asking polite questions crap.'

'It's an American import. Like Starbucks and Buffy.'

'I *love* Buffy,' Rebecca said. Suddenly she looked even more downcast. '*Why* am I having to do all this? I should have just married my first boyfriend from school.'

'Well, at least you learned something last night. You acted a bit bored, you left early, and today Duff's been bombarding you with texts. He sent you flowers. It never fails.'

'Yes, but that's because I genuinely wasn't interested. You can't fake these things. It never works.'

She had a point. 'All the same,' Katie said, 'perhaps this

isn't such a bad idea. Going on dates with dorks. You can practise your new, cool stance on a few of them and then when you've got it perfect, we can send you out with someone you actually like.'

'*If* I ever get asked out again,' Rebecca retorted. 'Which is unlikely, because . . .'

'You're nearly fifty. I know. But even fifty-year-olds go on dates. *Cher* goes on dates, I was reading about it in *OK!* And if there are men out there brave enough to ask Cher out, they're brave enough to ask you out.'

'Maybe there'll be someone nice at Jenny and Gordon's party,' Rebecca said.

'Maybe. Maybe not. Either way, I'll be there to help you.' Katie leaned forward and patted her on the arm. 'You just have to have faith.'

30

Since the crisis summit with Justine, Hunter and Suzy's lives had changed unimaginably. He had confessed everything, she had consulted lawyers and they had both told the girls – who were inconsolable.

Hunter had decided social life in Philadelphia would be impossible after a divorce, so he had put in with his employers Peterson O'Brien for a transfer to the London office. In the meantime, he was alternating between one week in Philadelphia and one in London, where he announced he would henceforth be staying with Suzy.

'Hotels are so depressing,' he told her. 'I'm having to live in one in Philly now, so at least when I'm in London I can shack up in your cosy pad.'

If that's OK with you, Suzy fumed. But after so many years at the bank, Hunter only knew how to issue orders, not requests. It simply didn't occur to him that Suzy wouldn't be thrilled to spend every night with him.

In their eighteen months together Hunter had never actually been to Suzy's. The first time he walked across the threshold he was taken aback.

'But it's so . . . small,' he managed eventually.

'Property in London is expensive,' Suzy explained, pissed off. She had wanted him to congratulate her on the white leather sofa from Ligne Roset, the real Basquiat on the wall. 'It's in Primrose Hill, that's what counts.'

Still, Hunter seemed a bit dazed. 'I thought you were doing better for yourself,' he murmured.

He had been equally bemused to learn there was only one bathroom, no garden, the kitchen was the size of a seat in First Class and Suzy's mattress was old and lumpy. There was no room in her packed wardrobe for his four identical Savile Row suits and Anna, the Polish cleaner, refused point-blank to iron his shirts.

'*I say no ironing!*' her note read. '*Try to take me for a fool again, I quit.*'

After a tense stand-off, Suzy had agreed to do them. So far, she had only scorched one. Her iron wasn't very good, she seemed to remember nicking it from her gran, way back when she was still at university. She would have to get Gemma to blag her a new one. They'd say they were doing a feature. Household gadgets: the new cool.

At least she had cable, she thought now, walking in the door after work. Her dynamic banker lover was slumped on the sofa, holding a bottle of beer and gaping at the motorbike racing on Sky Sports like an inmate of an old folks' home.

'Hi, baby,' he said, without even looking round.

Suzy had always known Hunter was into bikes, she had even found it quite cool. But now that there were back issues of *Suzuki* magazine all over the coffee table and a constant sound of revving engines emanating from the telly, she was less impressed.

'I'm starving,' she said. 'Shall I order something in?'

Now she had Hunter's attention. 'Couldn't you cook something?'

Suzy tried to hide her irritation. 'Well, I could, *darling.*'

She put as much emphasis as possible on the last word. 'But I very much doubt there's any food in the house, unless you went to the supermarket on the way home.'

'It's still open now, isn't it?' Hunter said.

How on earth did he know so much about British shopping hours? 'It *is*, but it's a half-hour round trip. I could have popped in on the way home, but I thought it would be fun if I ordered in.'

'You could drive there now.'

God, how American! 'I'm not wasting all that petrol to pick up a Sainsbury's ready meal, when I can pay a delivery man to bring something much tastier to the door.'

Hunter picked up the remote and turned down the volume. 'Suzy,' he said in the voice he reserved for incompetent secretaries, 'I am sick and tired of delivery pizzas and delivery Indians.'

'We had delivery Japanese last night.'

'It's not the type of food I have a problem with. It's just takeaways – they're fine every once in a while, but it's nicer to have a proper home-cooked meal. Steak and potatoes. Sweetcorn. And a dessert.'

'Well, if that's what you want, we could always go to McDonalds,' she snapped. In the past, Suzy had always remained a model of calm and control. But in the past Hunter had never criticized her housekeeping skills.

'I just told you! I don't want to eat in a restaurant. I spend most of my life in restaurants. When I'm home I want to stay home and not eat processed muck.' He softened slightly. 'I'm sorry, baby, but that's what I'm used to.'

He regretted it as soon as he said it. Suzy's face was white.

'You mean that's what Justine did for you every night. Well, good for her, Hunter! She has a part-time job at the university. I am in the office from eight until eight almost every night. As are you! If you feel like cooking a nice home-cooked meal when you get home, you're welcome. But don't put any more pressure on me.' She spun round and stormed into the bedroom.

Hunter was immediately distraught. He didn't know why he'd said that. He adored Suzy precisely because she wasn't Justine, because she talked about more than the tie-backs for the new curtains and who had brought muffins to the coffee morning.

He followed her. Suzy was curled up on the duvet, flicking through *Tatler*.

'Losers,' she muttered without even catching his eye. 'All these ideas we covered at least a year ago.'

He sat down beside her. 'How was your day, honey?'

She brightened up immediately. 'Oh, fine. We've confirmed Banella Brookham for our Christmas cover, which is excellent. Rebecca was giving me a bit of grief about putting a love trainer on Jenny and Gordon, but I soon saw her off.'

'A what trainer?' This sounded exciting. Hunter ran his hand down Suzy's back. 'Is that a sex thing?'

Suzy rolled over and hauled herself off the bed. 'Typical man,' she sighed. 'No, it's not a sex thing. It's about relationships. Jenny's got all these stupid doubts about marrying Gordon, so this woman is going to check them out and tell her if she's doing the right thing.'

'Jenny? Gordon? Are these characters in a soap, honey?'

Suzy raised her eyes to the ceiling. 'Er, no! They're friends of mine.' She stopped herself. Not a road to go down.

Too late. 'I'd love to start getting to know some of these friends, baby.'

'And soon you will.' She leaned forward and kissed him on the cheek. 'Now, how about I dial out for a nice Chinese and while we're waiting for it, I give you a little treat.'

Hunter smiled. But as her hands fiddled with his belt, his mind went back to the love trainer. He wondered who he or she was. Could they have helped him and Justine?

He looked down at Suzy's shiny black head bobbing rhythmically up and down, and groaned. Once he had met this woman he was lost. No shrink, guru or therapist in the world could have kept his marriage in place. And soon he would be the husband of Mrs Hunter Knipper the Second.

He shut his eyes and placed his hands gently on her head.

31

It was 21 July, the night of Jenny's engagement party, and the weather was perfect: hot and cloudless. Jenny took the afternoon off work and she and Gordon rushed round their tiny garden setting up trestle-tables, struggling with deck-chairs and stringing fairy lights through the bushes.

At 5 p.m. the doorbell rang and there was Rebecca, looking devastating in a backless, black, lacy dress.

'Colette Dinnigan,' Jenny shrieked approvingly, only then noticing the two dark girls flanking her friend like bodyguards.

There had been a bit of a tussle about who was going to work at the party. Obviously, the other waiter had to be a friend of Katie's, so he or she could do most of the legwork while she observed Jenny and Gordon. The obvious choice was Ronan, but he refused. He wouldn't give a reason, but everyone knew it was because Suzy would be there.

So Katie had suggested Jess, an idea which had gone down with Rebecca about as well as the Ebola virus.

'How do I know she won't nick all Jenny's jewellery? No, sorry, Katie. Your friend is a thief.'

'She only stole an invitation. Please, Rebecca. She really needs the work.'

Rebecca sighed. 'Oh, all bloody right then.'

Jess had been having a bad time lately. She'd been up

for three adverts but failed to get any of them. At the moment she had been waiting for three weeks to find out if she'd made it to the second audition to play a boot-faced teacher in a BBC children's drama. Katie desperately wanted her to have a slice of their fun.

'This is Katie,' Rebecca said, and the girl with the frizzy hair stepped forward and shook her hand.

'Nice to meet you.'

'Nice to meet you,' Jenny replied, flushing bright pink. 'So – er – do we need to have a chat before we get started?'

'Oh no,' said Katie. 'The chat comes afterwards. Just point out who your fiancé is and I'll do the rest.'

She couldn't confess that Rebecca had told her about Gordon and Jenny *ad nauseam*, and that although Katie suspected Rebecca was biased, she did think Gordon sounded like a lovely bloke.

'Go and have your bath, Jenny, go!' Rebecca waved a hand dismissively. 'We'll get set up down here.'

The door slammed. A man with floppy, blond hair staggered into the room, carrying three crates of beer. There were sweat stains under his arms. He looked around in bemusement.

'Gordy!'

'Rebecca!' He gave her a big kiss. 'Bit early, aren't you?'

'Just thought I'd give you guys a hand.'

'Ah,' said Gordon. 'That's really sweet.' He turned to Katie. 'Hello! I'm the host. And you must be one of the waitresses.'

For some reason, Katie remembered that night at the book launch and Ben. She flushed slightly.

'Hi,' Jess said, pushing past her. 'Yes, I'm Jessica and this is Katie.' She put on a silly American accent. 'We're your waitresses for tonight.' Rebecca looked at her with dislike.

Gordon stared at her. 'Hey, don't I know you from somewhere?'

'Er, possibly,' Jess said cautiously. She got asked this all the time. Usually people recognized her from a nappy advert where she played a harassed yet jolly young mum.

Gordon snapped his fingers. 'I know! You were the girlfriend in *Marvin's Millions*!'

Jess looked at him suspiciously. *Marvin's Millions* was a British film she had made five years ago. It was the story of a boy who worked in an abattoir in Toxteth and by night played banjo in the local pub. It starred Ricky Tomlinson and Kathy Burke, Jess had a small but important part as Rhys Ifans's girlfriend and everyone had thought it was going to be her big break. But the critics panned it and afterwards she didn't work for a year.

'I knew I'd seen you before! I love that film! I've got it on DVD. Come and look!'

Jess had to follow him into the living room and admire the glossy case decorated with quotes. 'Extraordinary', the *Independent*; 'Remarkable', *The Times*. The full sentences had been 'It's extraordinary that lottery money could be given to something as bad as this', and 'What is remarkable is that this film ever got the green light in the first place.' Jess had given her copy to Oxfam.

'Oh, I thought it was hilarious,' Gordon said. 'It's so cool to meet you. Why on earth are you waitressing? You should be on your way to the bloody Oscars ceremony.'

Jess glowed. What a lovely man. She would tell Katie so at the first opportunity.

Rebecca stuck her head around the door. 'Come on, guys. Work to do.'

By 7 p.m. the canapés were set out on trays. Beer cans floated in the kitchen sink and an army of champagne flutes were lined up on the table.

The party had officially started, meaning they had at least another clear hour before any guests arrived. So when the doorbell rang at 7.03 p.m. everyone was a bit confused.

'Is the music too loud?' Jenny asked. 'Maybe it's next door, complaining already.'

Rebecca was in the hall, peering through the spyhole.

'It's Ally and Jon!' she yelled.

'Shit!' Jenny squeaked. 'Look after them. I've got to get changed.' She darted up the stairs, pulling the turban off her hair.

Loud mwah-mwahing emanated from the hall. Rebecca came back in with a tall, dark woman in a microscopic denim skirt.

'Ally!' cried Gordon, embracing her. He turned to the man, who trailed behind her, looking morose in faded jeans and an Empire State Building T-shirt. 'Jon! How are you, mate? Did you watch the footie last night? Wasn't it a shocker?'

'Actually, I'm not into football.'

'Oh. So what is your sport?'

'I don't have much time for sport. I prefer to *do* something with my life, rather than watch it from the sofa.'

Katie pretended to busy herself pouring out glasses of

champagne, but really she was listening, astonished. Who was this horrible man?

Jenny burst into the kitchen in a low-cut orange dress. She looked very pretty, but a little green in the face.

'Ally! Jon!' If Brad and Jennifer had just walked in she couldn't have sounded more delighted.

'Babes, why have you gone that colour?' asked Gordy.

'What colour?' Jenny ran to the mirror and studied herself. 'Oh, my God! I must . . . be allergic to my shampoo or something. Excuse me a minute.'

She rushed out of the room again. 'It's her Boots anti-redness cream,' Rebecca giggled quietly to Katie. 'It always makes her go green but she'll never admit she's been using it.'

'What's with him?' Katie muttered, nodding at Jon, who was now standing next to Ally, his hand proprietorially on her bum.

'Oh, God, that's horrible Jon, the world's rudest man. We all hate him. But she's lovely – she's Ally, my oldest friend in London.'

'She could do better than that,' Katie said indignantly.

'Of course she could, but how can we tell her?' Rebecca paused for a moment. 'Or maybe *you* could?'

'I can't just randomly tell her her boyfriend's a plonker.'

'No, but . . .' Rebecca smiled. 'Well, just keep an eye on them. It could come in useful some day.'

The party was a screaming success. By 9 p.m. the garden was packed with lanky women and gay men all shrieking at one another's jokes and dancing increasingly energetically to Ibiza's latest sounds. Grumpy Mrs Ellison from next door stuck her head out of the window and yelled for them to turn it down, so Gordon was inveigled into persuading her to join them and after four glasses of champagne she was dancing animatedly with a quantity surveyor called Karl.

Jess and Katie were run off their feet. It was almost impossible for Katie to keep a close eye on her target. She couldn't keep refilling Jenny and Gordon's glasses, they were quite pissed enough as it was, flitting from group to group, accepting congratulations.

She'd go and check out Ally, she decided. She could see her at the far end of the garden talking and laughing with a tall, glamorous man with long, glossy black hair. Jon was standing moodily beside her, running his finger round and round the rim of his glass. He looked like a little boy being dragged round Tesco's by his mother. Any minute now he would start wailing for a Big Mac and the toilet.

'How fascinating, Guy,' Ally was saying. She turned absently to Katie. 'Oh yes, thanks, I'd love a top-up. Everyone else I know loved that exhibition. What didn't you like about it?'

'I just thought it was pretentious wank,' said Guy cheerfully and Ally laughed uproariously. He turned to Jon. 'What about you? Do you like Hervé Flaubertin?'

'He's my idol,' Jon snarled, so viciously Guy took a step back.

Bad dog, Katie thought automatically.

'Well . . . nice talking to you,' said Guy, head pivoting as he searched for someone to rescue him. 'I must just . . .' And he darted off.

'Can we go soon?' Jon whined, tugging at Ally's sleeve.

Ally looked at her watch. 'Not yet, darling. It's only nine. Jenny would be hurt. Give it another half hour. Come on, I'll introduce you to some fun people.'

Katie moved on to Jenny, who was standing in a small group under a rose bush.

'So where's the ring?' a tall woman with dark circles under her eyes was asking.

Jenny grimaced. 'Actually, Isabelle, I haven't got one. Yet. Gordy said that whatever he chose I'd send right back, so it's better if we choose it together.'

'Oh, but there are ways round that! When Lawrence proposed to me he bought it six months in advance and showed it to all my girlfriends to be sure I'd like it. Then he took me away for the weekend and hid it in a little bowl of strawberries.' Lawrence, who was impossibly tall, with bad teeth, grinned sheepishly.

'Lucky you didn't swallow it,' said a sharp little voice. It was Suzy, who had just joined the group.

For a moment Isabelle looked nonplussed, then she decided she had better laugh. 'Ah, ha, ha, Suze. Of course I didn't swallow.'

'She never does,' Lawrence bellowed. 'Oh sorry, darling. Only joking.'

'Too much information,' Suzy said drily. She was wearing a knee-length ball dress, far more suitable for an evening at the Paris Opera than a South London garden. She turned to Jenny. 'And what did Gordy get you for your birthday?' As she spoke, she turned and gave Katie, still hovering with the champagne bottle, a barely perceptible wink.

'Oh, when was your birthday?' Isabelle shrilled.

'Last month. He still hasn't got me anything actually.'

'Lawrence took me to New York for mine.'

Useless idiot, Katie thought. Crispin always remembered her birthday. For the last one he had given her a beautiful Chinese jacket that he had ordered specially. Paul, on the other hand, had always forgotten. Birthdays, anniversaries and Valentine's Day had always involved him sneaking off to the garage for a box of chocolates and a wilting bunch of flowers.

'And what about the honeymoon?' Isabelle continued.

'Well, I quite fancy the Maldives. But Gordy says not over his dead body.'

'He's right,' said a good-looking man in a sheepskin jerkin, who had just joined the group. 'So common. All those Essex people getting skin cancer. I think you should go to Bournemouth.'

'Oh, shut up, Freddie,' Suzy said, stifling a yawn. Just then her phone rang. Katie watched her glance at the number and make a face as if she had just found a hairball in her risotto.

'Hi, Hunter,' she said wearily. 'Yes, I'll be there in half an hour . . . Actually, make it an hour . . . I told you, I'm at my friend's engagement party . . . No, I'll be there at ten-thirty . . . Well, there must be something in the fridge . . . OK . . . Sorry . . . Yes, see you. Bye.'

She snapped her phone shut. Everyone was listening, gripped.

'Oh, darling,' said Freddie, breaking the silence. 'Stop it at once. Nobody believes in your mystery man. You just invented him, so you don't have to admit you're a sad loser with no boyfriend.'

'God, I wish,' Suzy sighed. 'If that were the case I

wouldn't have to rush home early, because Hunter's *lonely*.'
Her voice dripped with scorn.

'You should have brought him!' Freddie cried. 'The
more the merrier.'

'Oh, I don't think it would have been his kind of thing.'
Suzy could hardly articulate her feeling that the thought
of Hunter hanging around her, wanting to be introduced
to her friends, made her feel a bit queasy. Hunter was
gorgeous, but he wasn't exactly *cool*. In business mode,
which was how Suzy had used to see him, he wore hand-
made brogues and Gieves and Hawkes, shirts – hardly
fashionable, but very distinguished. But off duty, as she
was now discovering, he favoured a Snoopy T-shirt and
revolting, battered trainers that looked like they had come
from Dalston market.

Most importantly, Hunter's presence would seriously
inhibit Suzy's consumption of snow. And a party without
coke was like toast without Marmite. Unthinkable. Talking
of which . . .

'Fancy showing me where the loo is?' she asked Freddie
meaningfully.

'But you know where . . .' Suzy pulled a face at him. 'Of
course,' said Freddie, clearly a bit slow on the uptake. 'Love
to.'

Katie watched them scuttle off.

'Hello,' said a voice behind her left ear.

She turned round. Tufty hair, a snowstorm of freckles
and a sideways smile. Ben.

Normally Katie would have pretended not to remember
him, but he *was* Rebecca's business partner.

'Hello.' She sounded rather nervous.

'Still wearing the waitress outfit,' Ben said. 'You look like a domino.'

'Actually, tonight I *am* a waitress,' Katie said. Her voice sounded stilted and odd.

He laughed. 'OK,' he said. 'I'll have the egg mayonnaise on rye, but could you hold the egg and the mayo. And I'd like the bread white. Hovis, if at all possible.'

'No, I *am* a waitress. I'm . . . helping Jenny out.'

'Helping Jenny out? I thought you were Rebecca's hottest client. She can't be doing very well with you.'

Katie couldn't work out if he was joking. She decided to ignore him. She held out the bottle. 'Champagne?'

'I thought you'd never ask.'

'Ben!' It was Gordon, by now completely legless.

'Gord! Congratulations.' The men hugged awkwardly.

Gordon grinned. 'Thanks, man. It's cool, isn't it?'

'Have you met Katie?' Ben asked. 'She's Rebecca's latest protégée.'

Gordon looked confused. 'I thought you were a waitress.'

'I am,' said Katie. She shot Ben a warning look. 'You're thinking of the other waitress,' she said. 'Jessica Harrison. She's an actress.'

'Oh yeah!' said Gordon, his face brightening. 'She's wicked. She was in *Marvin's Millions*. Fucking great film. Have you seen it?'

'I have actually,' said Ben. He looked amused.

'So is she one of your clients?' Gordon asked. 'Because she should be.'

'We're certainly having a look at her,' Ben said.

Ally tapped Gordon on the shoulder. Her mouth was set in a thin line like a hyphen. Jon stood behind her.

'Al!' Gordon bellowed, turning round. 'Do you fancy a spliff?'

'No. We've got to go. Jon's got an early start.'

'Oh, come on! It's only eleven. How about a beer?'

'No. Jon's tired.' She kissed Gordon on the cheek. 'Thanks for a great party.'

'See ya,' Jon mumbled, refusing to make eye contact.

Ben leaned over to Katie. 'Charles Darwin got it wrong about evolution,' he whispered. 'Otherwise how could that man exist?' Katie giggled, then wished she hadn't.

'Ben!' It was Rebecca, slightly pissed. Earlier, Katie had watched her dancing with a small man with curly, cropped red hair. She looked happy and very free.

'Becs.' They kissed affectionately. What was the deal between these two anyway, Katie wondered. Had they always just been friends?

'So you've found Katie?' Rebecca said. 'I hope you didn't blow her cover.'

'Cover?' Ben grinned. 'So you're working tonight. How very Mata Hari. And who are you investigating? A Rottweiler? Or a poodle?'

'She can't tell you that,' Rebecca slurred. 'She's bound by her professional code.'

'Ooh! Get you! Come on, Katie, who is it?'

'Who's what?' said Jenny, bounding over, sweating slightly from the dancing.

'Nothing,' Rebecca said firmly. She plucked at the straps of Jenny's dress. 'Jen, you've got to tighten these. Your left nipple is showing.'

300

'Oh God!' said Jenny, looking down in horror. 'Did everyone see?'

'Doesn't matter if they did,' Rebecca said fondly.

The red-haired man appeared beside her, clutching two glasses. 'Here's your drink, Rebecca,' he said eagerly.

'Oh thanks, Simon,' Rebecca said absently. She grabbed Jenny's hand. 'C'mon, let's go and dance.'

Simon stood there at a loss. Neither Katie nor Ben felt inclined to rescue him. After a moment, he mumbled something to himself and moved off.

They were alone again.

'It's Gordon and Jenny, isn't it?' Ben said. 'You're checking out their relationship.'

'I can't say,' said Katie. She wished she didn't sound so schoolmarmish.

'Oh, come on, it's obvious. Why else would you be here?'

Katie said nothing. Ben looked at her. She could feel his eyes on her, like needles.

'Gordy's a lovely guy,' he warned. 'And he adores Jenny. Please don't mess with them.'

'I'm not messing with them,' Katie protested. 'Jenny just wants some advice and I'm going to give it to her. She doesn't have to do anything I say.'

'Jenny's pretty gullible. She'll do anything you tell her.'

Katie flared. 'Don't talk about Jenny like she's a child. She's quite old enough to know her own mind. And don't tell me how to do my job.'

Ben laughed. 'Job? You don't have a job. You've just invented some neat theory about how men are like dogs and just need to be trained to fall in love. It's bollocks.'

Katie flinched. She hated the way Ben was looking at her. It was as if he knew she was a fraud. Which she wasn't at all. Was she?

Time to hit back.

'I don't train people to fall in love,' she snapped. 'I train them to fall out of it. More champagne?'

Automatically, Ben held out his glass. She filled it right to the brim, then turned and walked away.

32

The party was a huge success, the proof being that the police called twice and eventually shut it down at 3 a.m.

'I still know how to do it,' Jenny crowed drunkenly. She paid Jess and Katie, who were stacking the hire glasses into their cardboard containers, and told them to go home.

'You've done wonders,' she crooned, adding in a horrible stage whisper to Katie, 'and I'll see you tomorrow.'

Rebecca had already pronounced that the debrief would take place at five the following afternoon at Greenhall and Graham.

'Obviously you can't go to Jenny's,' she said. 'And – no offence, Katie – your flat is too grotty.'

None was taken. For a start it was true, and anyway Katie was beginning to understand that the less people knew about her background, the better. The love trainer had to be wise and all-knowing and a bit mysterious. *Then* people like Ben would no longer question her.

Katie was thinking this as she lay in bed the following morning, listening to the roar of traffic outside on the Old Kent Road. She had woken annoyingly early. Ben's words from last night trampled round her head like a herd of cattle. *Why* had he been so hostile to her, she thought. What had she ever done to him? And why did she mind so much?

You mind because you fancy him, said a little voice. *In fact you want to fuck his brains out.*

But he has freckles, she thought. *So? Paul had a fat arse and you just couldn't get enough of him.* She remembered his hand touching hers at the book launch. It had been like an electric shock. Bad. No, good. No, bad. She didn't know.

Katie pulled the duvet over her head. No wonder she felt so awkward around Ben, when something about him reminded her of Paul. Not that they were physically similar in any way – it was all to do with the way Katie wanted to reach out and touch his skin. She could remember the feel of his hand against hers: warm and dry.

And no doubt Ben, like Paul, was a double-dealing bastard.

There's no shame in feeling this way, she told herself firmly. *It's all chemical. Your chromosomes reacting with his. Producing something called lust. It's like being hungry or cold. It doesn't mean anything. You don't have to do anything about it.*

Feeling a bit better, she tried to go back to sleep. But when that didn't work, she got up and took a long bath. She spent most of the day thinking about Jenny and Gordon, but she also spent an unusually long amount of time in front of the mirror, testing different outfits, applying makeup and sleeking her hair.

'I have to look professional, don't I?' she told her reflection.

As soon as she entered Greenhall and Graham, her eyes swivelled over to the left-hand corner and Ben's glass box. It was dark. No one home.

And what a prat you are, she told herself. She giggled and suddenly felt better.

'Katie,' exclaimed Rebecca, coming to the door of her own cubicle. Jenny, who was standing behind her, looking a little pale, waved. 'You look terribly happy.'

'It's a lovely day,' Katie said vaguely, gesturing through the window at the perfect summer sky.

'Well, I have exciting news,' Rebecca said. 'Simon texted me! Asked me out to dinner. I think I've got my mojo back.'

'Simon?'

'You know, Simon! The short ginger from last night.'

Katie beamed. 'Well *done*! And how have you responded?'

'I haven't of course. I'll wait three days, then I'll give him an answer.'

'She's a model pupil,' Jenny grinned. There was a sudden pause as they all remembered what Katie was there for.

'I'll leave you two alone,' Rebecca said, picking up a pile of papers. 'I'll be in Ben's office if you need me.'

Katie and Jenny were left alone. They smiled at each other.

'Great sandals,' said Katie, nodding at Jenny's feet.

'Oh, thank you! £27.99. Dolcis.'

Silence fell. OK. It was time to get down to business. 'Right, Jenny, I'm going to ask you a few questions. They may sound a bit silly. But be patient with me. Why don't you sit over there?' She gestured towards Rebecca's chair.

'All right.' Jenny sat down keenly.

Katie swallowed and sat also. 'Right then,' she said, glancing at the piece of paper in her hand. 'If Gordon was a dog, what kind of dog would he be?'

Jenny *loved* this kind of question. She wiggled happily in her chair.

'Ooh, I don't know! Yes, yes, I do. He'd be a labrador puppy, like in the Andrex ads. Cute but a bit hopeless.'

That made sense. 'So basically Gordon needs house-training?'

'Well, no. Not really. Gordy's actually pretty good around the house. Better than me, probably. I suppose what I'd like him to be is a bit more sensitive. To know when I'm pissed off with him.'

Katie's ears pricked up. 'So you don't tell him when you're pissed off?'

'Of course. I scream. I shout. But I hate that.'

'But there seems to be no other way of getting through?'

'Exactly. If I sit there and fume, then he simply doesn't notice. He just goes on doing his work, or watching telly or reading the paper.'

'OK,' said Katie. She loved it when all the pieces started falling into place. 'I'm going to explain a few things to you.' And she gave her spiel about how dogs didn't believe in democracy and how every pack could only have one leader.

'So shouting at Gordy really isn't a good idea,' she concluded. 'Only weak dog owners shout. You should be able to get your own way by talking quietly to him. It's all about respect.'

'But I've tried keeping quiet. He just doesn't get the message.'

'He doesn't get the message because you sulk. And sulking means nothing to dogs. They don't think like us.'

'Gordy's *not* a dog.' Jenny felt duty-bound to point this out.

'I know, I know. But it helps to think of him that way. As a totally alien creature who lives by different rules. Dogs and men don't have the same logic as us. If we sulk, they just don't get it. They don't associate our bad mood with what they've done wrong. If you want to teach Gordy how to behave, you have to tell him off at the time. Otherwise, he'll just think you're a grumpy old cow.'

'I probably am,' Jenny sighed.

'No, you're just not dealing with him in the right way. But it's easily fixed.'

'Is it?' Jenny asked. 'I don't know.'

Katie looked at her. 'Jenny, do you want to fix things?'

'I think so.' But she looked doubtful.

'Tell me a bit more about you and Gordy. How did you meet?'

And the whole story came out. Jenny told Katie how she had met Gordon four years ago, when – if she was honest – she was still a little bit on the rebound from Mark, who had left her for his personal trainer, Toby. How Gordon had been so patient with her, taking her out for dozens of dinners before she decided to kiss him. How he had been surprisingly good in bed. How he made her chicken soup when she had flu and went to the all-night chemist to buy her thrush cream. But then how just a year into the relationship Jenny had had a drink with a former colleague and that night dreamed she was doing the filthiest things to him. How she had started phoning his home number and hanging up.

How eventually her obsession had died down, but six months later, when Gordon was away in Shropshire, she had gone to a party and bumped into Martin, another old mate from college, in town for the weekend from Edinburgh where he now lived. They talked all night. At about one in the morning they kissed. Jenny had left in a fluster, but not before he had given her his email address.

A series of flirty emails were exchanged and next time he came to London he called her. Jenny had made some excuse to Gordon and slipped out to meet him in a bar. Almost instantly, she went off him when he insisted on drinking girlie purple cocktails. Still, they had got very drunk and held hands across the table, and eventually, at kicking-out time, they had wandered down a side street and had a rather ineffectual snog in an alleyway. Finally, he stroked her face.

'You're not really into this,' he told her softly. 'Go home to your boyfriend.'

Mortified, Jenny crept home to find Gordon sleeping. She threw up in the loo, a combination of relief and drinking too much on an empty stomach. Then she lay awake for hours, her head clattering with remorse. How could she have been so stupid to risk what they had? Thank God she had got away with it.

But then, eight months later, she found herself snogging a guy she met in a nightclub. Suzy had seen it all and been unamused. And now, of course, there was Fabrice in Paris. Not that anything had happened there yet, but she was thinking about him all the time, doing little quizzes crossing off the letters shared by both their names to work out if their relationship would end in love, marriage, hatred or adoration.

Excitingly, it was always adoration – although Jenny

didn't know Fabrice's middle name. She wasn't sure if that made a difference.

'They're only snogs,' she said now to Katie. 'I'd never go any further than that.'

Katie said nothing.

'So what do you think?'

Katie was thinking fast. Jenny didn't deserve Gordon, that much was clear. She'd been messing around behind his back, just like Paul had messed around behind hers. It was only fair to set him free – just as she wished Paul had done with her.

She breathed deeply. 'Jenny, I think you have to leave Gordon. You obviously don't love him. You're constantly scouting for another relationship. If you do marry him, are the secret snogs really going to stop? I think you need some time on your own to decide what you want out of life.'

Jenny looked aghast. 'But I can't leave Gordy! Where would I live? Anyway, he'd die of heartbreak.'

'No he won't. No one has ever died of heartbreak. He'll be very sad for a while and then he'll get over it. Harsh, but true.'

Jenny chewed her lip, thinking.

'And do you think I should go to Paris and see Fabrice?' she asked.

'Jenny, I think that says it all. Your first concern is Fabrice, not Gordon.'

'And?' Jenny couldn't help herself.

'And no, you shouldn't go to Paris. Men are not the answer to your problems. You have to learn to like yourself, be happy in your own company, before you're ready to have a relationship with someone else.'

'Mmmm.' Jenny studied her orange toenails.

Katie picked up her pen. She knew what was going to happen.

Confiscate passport, she wrote on the pad in front of her.

'So what do you think, Jenny? Are you brave enough to leave Gordon?'

'I don't know. I think so.' Her face fell. 'But do I have to do it tonight?'

Katie wasn't that tough. 'Of course not. But soon. In the next couple of weeks. Before the wedding plans take off. Before things get out of control.'

She looked up and saw Rebecca walking across the office. She waved and smiled. Katie ignored her. Rebecca would be furious if she knew what she had just said, but that wasn't her problem. She had a professional duty to give correct advice.

Jenny stood up. She was pale, but her mouth was set in a determined line. 'Thanks for your time, Katie. I really appreciate it.'

'You're welcome.'

'You're very wise,' Jenny said admiringly. 'Are you married?' She had searched for a ring but seen nothing.

'No. No. But I have a . . . partner.' Katie *despised* that word: it made her sound like a solicitor.

'That must be a wonderful relationship.' Jenny picked up her bag. 'Well? Do I call you, or do you call me?'

'I'll call you tomorrow and see how you're doing.'

'Would you? Thanks.'

She got up to leave. Katie followed. That had been her first proper love-training session. She should feel ebullient – instead she felt strangely flat, like day-old champagne.

33

Suzanne couldn't believe what she was hearing.

'She told you to leave Gordy? Actually walk out on him?'

'Yes,' Jenny giggled. She was in her bedroom, with the door locked. Downstairs, her fiancé was snoring in front of the telly, his mouth slightly open, two days' beard growth on his chin.

Looking around their house, she had felt a little pang. They had done a lot of work on it over the years, sanding the floors, decking the garden, repainting every room, ripping out and replacing the bathrooms. What a shame to have to leave it all behind.

But at the same time breaking off an engagement was rather romantic. It made her feel like Julia Roberts.

'So she really does mean business,' Suzy mused. She was impressed. Even though she had seen Katie deal with Rebecca, she hadn't thought she would be so uncompromising with cuddly old Gordon. She must be much tougher than she looked.

'Who are you talking to?' Hunter asked. He had ambled into the bedroom and – oh my God! – was about to climb on the duvet beside her.

'Shoes off, shoes off,' Suzy squawked. One eye on Hunter, she continued, 'So, Jen, when are you actually going to do the dirty deed?'

'Well, not tonight. But by the end of the week, definitely.'

'And is Katie going to keep you to that?'

'Oh yes. I tell you, Suzy, she's fierce. She's like Karim at the gym and that woman who used to run my class at Weight Watchers put together. No slack allowed.'

They said goodbye, having both forgotten that Jenny's trips to the gym and to Weight Watchers never lasted more than a few days.

'So how's it going with the love trainer?' Hunter asked.

Suzy's eyes narrowed. 'Very well, it seems. I think I'm going to call her in the morning.'

'What did you say her name was, honey?'

'Katie Wallace.'

When Suzy was in the bathroom, applying her layers of night cream, Hunter opened her bag and removed her Palm Pilot.

He would call this Katie Wallace as soon as he got to the office.

Katie was woken at nine by her phone ringing. Naked, she dashed across the room and pulled it from her bag. *Number withheld.*

'Hello,' she grunted. First thing in the morning she always sounded like a forty-a-dayer.

'Did I wake you?' asked an amused female voice.

'Oh no! I've been awake for hours!'

'Of course you have.'

'Er, who is this?'

'Oh, sorry. Didn't I say? It's Suzanne Bell here at *Seduce!*'

Katie felt a thud of excitement mixed with terror. 'Hi!'

'I'm calling because I'm impressed with what you told

Jenny. Not many people would have the guts to give advice like that.'

'Oh, thanks.' Katie's brain was fully in gear now. 'But actually, Jenny shouldn't have told you what I said. My advice is confidential.'

Suzy laughed. 'That's up to Jenny, isn't it?' Katie said nothing. She had just realized that the blinds were up, allowing Vijay Panashatiyam in the sweatshop opposite an excellent view of her naked body. She dropped on to all fours and started crawling towards the window.

'Anyway, she's taken your advice to heart,' Suzanne continued.

'She's really going to do it?' Having pulled down the blinds, Katie settled back on her bed.

'So it seems. But to get to the point, I'm impressed with what you did for Rebecca too. Helped her get rid of that awful Tim and stopped her from falling in love with that dreadful-sounding — what's his name? — Duff. So I'd like to offer you a column for six months. *The Love Trainer.* Subtitle: how to treat your man like a dog. We'll find a couple with problems each month and you can solve them.'

'But where will we find them?' Katie panicked.

'Oh, don't worry, that's up to the *Seduce!* team. I'm going to get someone on the case this morning. I want to move with this quickly, so hopefully we can run the first piece in the . . .' There was a pause as Suzy inspected her desk calendar. 'Actually, we've got a hole in the November issue. That comes out at mid-October, so I'd need the copy in two weeks at the absolute latest.'

Katie was confused. 'By the end of September for November?'

'Get Rebecca to explain it to you. I need to call her to discuss your fee. It won't be enough for you to live on, but I'd have thought the exposure would soon bring you loads of other work.'

'Thank you, Suzanne,' Katie squeaked.

'It's my pleasure. Now, someone will be in touch in the next couple of days with the case study we want you to analyse. In the meantime, we're going to need to get your picture taken. Preferably by the end of the week. I'll have Gemma, my assistant, call you.'

'Thanks,' Katie said again. She felt as if she had climbed on to a ferris wheel. She could hardly take it all in.

'Well, thank you for talking some sense into my friends. If I could only get you to sort out Ally we'd have a hat trick.'

No sooner had Katie hung up than the phone rang again.

'Hello?' She was sure it would be Suzy, telling her she'd changed her mind.

'Is that Miss Katie Wallace?' said a squeaky, female American voice.

'Yes.'

'Just one minute, Ms Wallace. Putting you through to Mr Hunter Knipper.'

'Mr . . .?' But now a man had come on. American too. Deep voice. Sounded kind.

'Is that Katie?'

'It is.'

'Katie,' he said. 'What I'm calling about is strictly confidential. I am Suzanne Bell's boyfriend. And I need your help.'

34

Jenny meant to leave Gordon, but along with doing her bikini line or painting her toenails, it never seemed to be her top priority. The Saturday night after she met Katie, they went ten-pin bowling with a group of friends and had a great laugh. *If I left Gordy, most of these people would hate me,* she thought with a pang. *I'd never see them again.*

The following weekend he had rented a cottage in Norfolk for them and two other couples. They went sailing, walked along the sand dunes and had a huge roast dinner and many pints in the local pub.

Once or twice Gordy infuriated her – by leaving their bathroom window open, so it was freezing when she went up to bed, and by making a joke about her fondness for white wine in front of all their friends. Once she would have sulked or raged, but not now.

'Please don't do that, Gordy,' she said quietly but firmly on both occasions. 'It really annoys/upsets me.'

'God, sorry!' Gordon exclaimed, looking genuinely contrite. 'I didn't know.'

So maybe Katie was right. Maybe all that was needed was a firm hand. Certainly, Gordy seemed unusually attentive. And on the drive home, he pulled out his trump card.

'Next week we're going to go to Hatton Garden and choose your ring. It's going to be the most beautiful one you've ever seen.'

Obviously, this was the moment to say she was having doubts, but Jenny was exhausted after all that fresh air. She couldn't handle a fight, she'd do it in the morning.

Naturally, both Katie and Suzy were monitoring the situation very carefully. 'I'm going to do it,' Jenny told them both. 'I'm just waiting for some time alone. You know what Gordon's like. We're always surrounded by people.'

She could tell Katie wasn't impressed. 'I'm giving you one week,' she said. 'If you haven't done it by Friday, then you're going to marry Gordon and stay with him for the rest of your life.'

'Can't we make it Sunday?' Jenny pleaded. 'It's so hard to find a moment alone.'

So on Wednesday they went to Hatton Garden and chose a beautiful diamond solitaire. None of the rings on display had price tags and Jenny tried not to peek. But later, she dug around in Gordy's sock drawer and found the receipt. It was so expensive, she felt faint. Still, he could always take it back. Engagements must get broken off all the time.

It would have helped if she had heard from Fabrice, but he was being strangely silent. Maybe he was away on business. She knew what Katie had said about how other men shouldn't even come into it, but Katie hadn't seen the chemistry between them. Knowing he was there would give her the courage she needed.

All week she jumped whenever her email pinged, but it was always just something to do with work, or occasionally Gordy with some funny snippet from the paper, or a bad round-robin joke. Jenny felt like a chainsaw was sawing at her nerves.

Finally, on Friday at 5 p.m., the message she was waiting for popped up on her screen.

Pretty Jenny, I've been thinking of you all week. Paris is so beautiful at this time of year, just like you. When are you going to make the trip to see me?

Her heart twanged. Instantly she hit reply.

How about next weekend?

She waited a few minutes for his answer, but none came. Oh well, they were an hour ahead in Paris. He'd probably left for the weekend. She knew what she had to do. With a few clicks of the mouse, she was on the Eurostar website booking a ticket to leave London Friday night, return Sunday. Bloody hell, it was expensive, but how could she put a price on her future happiness?

Should she book a hotel? Probably. It would be a bit forward to expect Fabrice to put her up. But what a waste of money if she didn't use it. Fuck it. In the unlikely event of needing a place to stay, she'd find something when she got there.

She supposed she should tell Gordy tonight. But they were going out to dinner with Lawrence and Isabelle. Tomorrow would be better. For once they had few plans this weekend, which meant they would have two days to sort everything out.

She printed out the Eurostar booking, followed by Fabrice's email. The next few days were going to be tough. Reading it would give her the strength to do what she had to do.

*

As well as keeping an eye on Jenny's situation, Suzy felt she had quite enough problems of her own.

'So where are you going tonight?' Hunter asked plaintively. As usual the sports rumbled on in the background.

'I'm having dinner with Freddie,' Suzy said, adding a touch more eyebrow pencil. She hated putting on her makeup in front of Hunter, but the mirrors in the bathroom and the bedroom simply weren't good enough.

'And who's Freddie?'

'He's an old mate. Works for a film company.'

'So when can I meet him? I'd love to.'

He's gay and you've probably never met a gay man, you'd wear a suit and Freddie would laugh at you, Freddie and I won't be able to do a couple of lines and cackle a lot at each other's jokes.

'Darling, I don't get to see Fred very often and I'd just like a bit of quality time with him. *Plus* it's kind of a work dinner. And you know how important my work is. Bringing my . . . other half along wouldn't look professional. You will get to meet him. You'll get to meet all my friends, I promise.'

'When?'

God, this was worse than having a baby. Or a dog, come to that. *My dog howls whenever I leave it on its own. What's the answer, love trainer?* 'Soon. I promise.'

'Why don't we . . .' He looked around the tiny room. 'Take them all out to dinner or something.'

'Hunts, we don't need to do that. They have plenty of money of their own.'

'I know, but I'd like to make a gesture. These people are going to be important to me. Just like my girls will be to you.'

Suzy smiled weakly. Her cab honked outside. 'I've got to run,' she said. Suddenly, she felt a flicker of guilt. 'What are you going to do, sweetie?'

Hunter smirked. 'Actually, I'm going out.'

Going out. Suzy failed to hide her surprise. 'Oh?'

'I'll probably be back before you, though.' *Don't tell her where you're going, don't even make something up,* Katie had said. He wouldn't.

She couldn't resist. 'So where are you going?'

'Just to meet a friend.'

The taxi hooted again.

'Well . . . how nice. See you later then, darling.' She gave him a kiss on the mouth and then she was out the door.

In the back of the cab, she fumed. *But you're going out, why shouldn't he? But she was a very important magazine editor and he didn't know a soul in London. Well, perhaps he wants to get to know some people.*

Suzy started to feel a little bit bad. Perhaps it wasn't nice to leave Hunter home alone night after night. You wouldn't do it to a dog.

'But I would never have a dog,' she said aloud.

'Pardon?' said the driver.

Perhaps Hunter had had enough. Perhaps he had got the message. Perhaps soon he'd be back in Philadelphia and Suzy would get her home and her life back.

Why didn't this make her feel as good as it should?

'You were right,' Hunter told Katie. 'She was needled, I could see it.' He lifted his champagne glass to her in a toast. 'I can see why she rates you, love trainer.'

319

'Well she doesn't yet,' said Katie. 'They're still looking for a case study for my first column.'

'Maybe they should suggest me?' Hunter laughed. He felt a bit drunk. They were sitting in the Blue Bar of the Berkeley Hotel, surrounded by skinny girls in summer dresses and bankers in suits. It was a relief to be out of that tiny, white flat, away from the television, talking to another human being who wasn't work and wasn't Suzy.

'I love her so much,' he told Katie after his next glass. 'And I thought she loved me. But . . . I don't know . . . she just seems unsettled by my presence. We don't seem to have fun any more.'

'Well, you did move in rather suddenly,' Katie said gently.

'I guess so. But Justine found out rather suddenly. And it was what we'd always wanted.'

'Did you actually ever ask Suzy that?'

Hunter blinked, hurt. 'Of course I did!' He frowned. 'Well, maybe I didn't, not in so many words. But when you have a connection like ours, obviously you're going to want to be together all the time. It's what all women want, right?'

He watched a cloud of annoyance scud over Katie's face. 'Well, actually, Hunter, no. Not *all* women.'

He was surprised at her tone. The love trainer was obviously a feminist. In fact, all the English women he met seemed to be bra-burners, with no obvious interest in domesticity, let alone marriage.

But you either put up or shut up. Hunter had been around long enough to know that. Smiling, he put up his hands. 'OK, OK. Sorry! That's obviously where I've been going wrong. Thinking Suzanne is like other women, when in fact she's unique.'

'She's certainly that,' Katie said.

'OK,' said Hunter, waving to the waiter. 'Well, how about I buy you another drink and you tell me how I can understand her.'

'Understanding her's one thing,' Katie grinned. 'But then you've got to train her. I'll have a Cosmopolitan, please.'

35

Simon, the short ginger, called Rebecca on Tuesday to confirm their date. 'I hope you like sushi?' he'd said. 'Because I thought we'd go to Nobu.'

Did Rebecca like sushi? Did the Pope shit in the woods? Simon might only come up to her elbow, but he had plenty of other qualities – not least perfect taste in restaurants. As she walked down Park Lane, she made a list of his attributes:

Pros	Cons
– *Rich (he was something in the City. She'd need to check with Ally exactly what. Rebecca never understood what other people did for a living and if you didn't ask them to elucidate in the first five minutes, it was too late for ever).*	– *Short* – *Why wasn't he married?*
– *Had flat in Notting Hill*	
– *Was thirty-nine*	
– *Wasn't married*	
– *No kids*	
– *Wasn't South African*	
– *His father was a vicar, which*	

meant he believed in fidelity
and family values
— Had been to Australia and
liked it

By the time she arrived at Nobu, she was thoroughly over-excited. They'd date for a year, then get married. She'd get pregnant on their honeymoon and their first child would be a boy, called Ned. They'd sell both their properties and buy a large house in Little Venice, next door to the guy from *Riverdance*.

Simon was waiting at a corner table. He stood up when he saw her and kissed her on both cheeks.

'You look beautiful,' he said.

It was 8 p.m. and Nobu was buzzing. Rebecca spotted Sven Goran-Eriksson and Pamela Anderson – although not together. At the table next to them, a beautifully made-up woman with a helmet of blonde hair was sitting with a young black woman in a silver chainmail dress.

'I'm so sorry you are having to spend your birthday alone in London,' said the blonde. She had a faint French accent. 'But I have a leetle present for you anyway.' She handed over a huge gift-wrapped box. The girl opened it. It was brimming with Christian Dior products. A skewer of jealousy kebabed Rebecca's heart.

'Oh my Gawd!' the girl screamed. She had a New York accent, like someone scraping ice off a car windscreen. 'I love Dee-awr! Oh, excuse me.' She grabbed her throbbing phone. 'Hello? Hello, darling. Yes! Where are you? In Ibiza? Oh, that is SO COOL! Hang on, I have my call waiting. Darling? Where are you? In Greece. Oh my

Gawd. And I'm in Nobu. No, not Nobu Tribeca. Nobu London.'

Rebecca caught Simon's eye. They both tried not to giggle.

It was hard to talk much over dinner because Mrs France and Miss Noo Yawk engaged all their attention, like a cabaret.

The women had summoned over the maître d' to tell him how much they loved Nobu.

'Nobu Paris is fantastic of course,' the black woman was saying. 'And Tokyo is to die for. But my favourite is London.'

'That's great,' said the maître d'. He looked as if he was about to cry.

'Vegas Nobu is incredibly amusing too,' chipped in the French woman.

'Of course I always have the cod with black bean miso,' the black woman was bellowing. Her mobile rang. 'George! Ciao! How's Dubai?'

'Oh God,' whispered Simon. 'This is just McDonald's for Eurotrash. Wherever you go, the same décor, the same menu. The customers don't even have to look at it.'

They managed to talk a little. About Simon's childhood in the country. About a film they had both seen. Publishing gossip. Simon had seen Rebecca's photo in this week's *Bookseller* at a piss-boring function.

'It didn't do you justice,' he said, smiling fondly. 'I'd like to take your picture. I'm quite good at photography.'

When? Rebecca once would have asked, whipping out her diary. But now she just smiled vaguely and muttered something neutral.

'They really should open a Nobu Monte Carlo,' they were saying next door.

Rebecca was enjoying herself. Simon was funny and clever. He obviously had some cash. All the ticks were going in the right boxes. Normally, she would have slept with him. To be honest, she would have slept with anyone who took her to Nobu. But tonight would be different. She would be going home alone.

'Here,' said Rebecca, when the bill came. 'Let me.'

Simon looked surprised, but pleased. 'No, no,' he said. 'This is on me.'

'So . . .' he added as they waited for his card to go through the machine. 'Do you fancy a nightcap?'

'Well, just a quick one,' she said. And she meant it.

So they entered the Met Bar, scene of Rebecca's old flirtations with Johan. What a coked-up fool she had been that night. But everything was different now. It was karma to return here, her chance to put things right.

'It's such a meat market here,' Simon said. 'But I find it amusing.'

Rebecca had a Brandy Alexander and he had an Irish coffee.

'So, Rebecca,' said Simon. He took a deep breath. 'I hope you don't mind me saying this . . .'

He's going to tell me I have seaweed between my teeth, she thought.

'But I think you're a really, really attractive woman and I was wondering if you had a boyfriend.'

Rebecca stared at him. Had he confused her with someone else? There was a model at the table next door sipping a glass of neat vodka. Perhaps the question had been meant for her?

'No, I don't,' she said.

Just then her handbag started vibrating.

'Excuse me,' she said, taking out her phone.

She knew who it would be. 'Are you still with him?' Katie asked.

'Mmm-hmm.' She said it in the most seductive way she knew. Simon looked away politely, but a flash of jealousy crossed his features.

'Well, you have ten more minutes,' Katie said. 'And then you have to leave. When you get home, call me. From the landline, so I know that's where you are.'

'Mmm-hmm. See you. Bye.'

'Sorry about that,' she told Simon. Once Rebecca would have added: 'That was my friend Ally/business partner Ben/PA/mum' to make the man feel better. But things were different now.

She finished off her drink. 'I have to go.'

'Really?' said Simon. He looked upset.

They stood on the pavement, waiting for the doorman to find a cab. 'I really enjoyed myself tonight,' Simon said.

She said nothing.

'But, Rebecca, I don't want to hassle you. You must get guys bothering you all the time. So we'll leave it like this. You call me if you want to see me again. If I don't hear from you, I'll leave you alone.'

'OK,' said Rebecca, confused. A taxi pulled up and she climbed in.

'Thanks for a lovely evening,' she said through the window. She hadn't even kissed him goodbye.

'No,' said Simon. 'Thank *you*.' The taxi pulled out. She glanced over her shoulder and watched him, standing alone and keen, on the pavement. If she'd thrown him a ball, there was no doubt he'd have run to catch it.

36

When Jenny got home from work on Friday, her Eurostar booking in her handbag, Gordon was waiting on the front step with two packed bags.

'Maybe he's leaving me,' she thought, confused. But then she realized something quite different was going on.

'Babe, I was getting worried,' Gordon called. 'I was just about to try your mobile. We've got to get to the airport.'

'The airport?'

'Yes. We're going to Berlin for the weekend. My surprise. The taxi should be here any minute.'

Jenny dropped her bag on the ground and screamed.

'Berlin! Oh my God, Gordy! I've always wanted to go there.' She pulled his face towards her and gave him a huge kiss on the mouth.

'Thought you'd be pleased,' he muttered, looking shy and proud.

Two hours later they were in the departure lounge and by midnight they were in Berlin.

'Are you sure you won't get bored?' Jenny asked as their taxi carried them to their hotel, just off the main shopping street. She was deeply touched. She loved old European cities but Gordy preferred climbing a mountain or rowing down a river.

'Nah. You can go to the galleries and I'll look at the war memorabilia. I'll be in heaven.'

The hotel was nothing special; their room a tiny box with a view over a housing estate. But Jenny didn't care.

'Honey bear,' she whispered to Gordon as she slipped into the queen-sized bed beside him. It was an endearment she hadn't used for some time.

'My porker,' he replied, rolling on top of her and slowly licking her nipples.

Jenny had intended to get up early to go to the shops, but they ended up having sex half the night and in the morning they had a long lie-in. Then they took a bus all round the city past the bombed-out cathedral, under the Brandenburg Gate, down Unter den Linden and past Checkpoint Charlie. In the afternoon, Jenny went shopping, while Gordy watched football on Eurosport. And that night they had a wonderful dinner of lamb and potatoes in a very smart restaurant just beside the Gate.

'So much meat! I don't understand how German girls stay so gorgeous and skinny,' Jenny exclaimed.

'But none of them are half as gorgeous as you.'

'Oi! What about half as skinny!' She jabbed him with her fork but she was pleased. Usually when she fished for compliments she couldn't even hook a tiddler.

That night was full of more hot and dirty sex. At dawn, Jenny lay awake. She held up her left hand to admire her diamond and laid her right hand on Gordon's bare bottom.

I've been a complete idiot, she thought. *Fantasizing about some Frenchman I barely know. I'm going to marry the nicest man in the world.* The bubble of happiness, which had been missing for so long, started travelling up her throat. Tears pricked at her eyes.

God, I've had a narrow escape. She suddenly remembered the love trainer. *And as for that Katie she doesn't know Jack.* On Monday, she would ring Suzy and report her change of heart. And then she would get straight down to organizing the wedding. She couldn't decide if she wanted it in a church or not. Perhaps somewhere like a canal boat would be more romantic. God, it was going to be fun. Jenny liked nothing more than a good party.

She drifted off to sleep and woke three hours later to find Gordon standing over her.

'Hi, sexy,' she muttered.

'Jenny,' he said, and his voice sounded very strange. 'What the hell is this?'

He waved a piece of paper at her. For a moment she had no idea what it could be. Then, with a sickening jolt, it came to her. Fabrice's email. It seemed like a lifetime ago she had slipped it in her bag.

'Gordy, sweetheart. It's not what it seems.'

'And how does it seem?' His voice was metallic. He looked as if he had been physically assaulted.

'It – he – he's just a guy in our Paris office. We flirt together. But it's a joke. It doesn't mean anything.'

'It doesn't mean anything? So why do you have a Eurostar return ticket for Friday night?'

'I . . . It's a business meeting!'

'A business meeting! Over the weekend?'

Attack was the best form of defence. 'Why were you looking in my bag?'

'You had our tickets. I wanted to check what time we were leaving tonight.'

Damn. She remembered him giving her the tickets and

passports at Heathrow. 'Here you are, monitor,' he'd said with a mock salute. She always looked after their documents when they went on holiday. At the time, she had thought she must hide the Paris stuff, but by the time they got to Berlin she was so excited she forgot all about it.

'So who is Fabrice?'

'I told you . . . he's a colleague.'

'So you're fucking a colleague.' Suddenly Gordy started to cry, slumped on the edge of the bed, his face in his hands. 'Jenny, you're the love of my life. We got engaged a month ago. We bought a ring last week. And all this time you've been shagging some French guy. How long's it been going on?'

'Gordy, we're not shagging! It was just a flirtation. And I was going to Paris to . . . to look at wedding dresses. That's why I didn't want to tell you.'

Every lie she told dug her deeper in. His expression was battling between hopefulness and anger. Anger won.

'I thought I knew you. But I knew nothing at all.'

'Gordy! It's a misunderstanding.'

'Yes, it is. Our whole relationship. The past four years. A misunderstanding. God, Jenny, I loved you.' He was fully dressed, she noticed.

'I love you,' she cried.

'Oh, stop lying.' He stood up. 'Well, I have my ticket now. And my passport. I'm going to go to the airport now and catch the first flight home. But you might as well stay. Enjoy Berlin. It's only a few hours on the train from Paris.'

He picked up his bag and walked out of the room.

'Gordy! Gordy!' Jenny grabbed a sheet from the bed and, wrapping it round her, stumbled out into the corridor like a clumsy ghost, just in time to see him step into an open lift.

'Gordy!' Jenny ran after him, but the doors closed. He didn't even look round.

Jenny stood still, gulping back tears. From down the corridor she heard a bang. She whirled round to see the bedroom door slammed shut behind her.

37

It was a beautiful London Sunday and Suzy and Hunter decided to make the most of it. Up late, then down to Regent's Park Road, the trendiest street in London, for breakfast at a pavement café.

'I'm sure that's Kate Moss,' Suzy hissed, kicking her boyfriend and nodding at a woman in a headscarf and dark glasses, laughing with her friends. A Weimaraner with a sleek, silver head snoozed at her feet.

Hunter looked up from *Sunday Business*. 'Uh? Yeah.' Hunter probably didn't know who Kate Moss was, Suzy thought. But maybe Kate Moss recognized Suzy? They had shaken hands a couple of times at parties, and she featured virtually every month in the magazine. But what would Kate think of her sitting here with this old man? Perhaps she would think he was Suzy's father. Would that make it better or worse? Suzy looked again at Kate's beautiful dog, then back at Hunter. Kate had a pedigree, hers was definitely a mongrel – albeit a very nice and rich mongrel.

Suzy pulled her peaked cap a little further down over her eyes and her scarf over her face.

'Shall we get the bill?' she asked.

Hunter blinked at her. 'I was planning on a refill, baby.'

'OK.' She buried her face in the *News of the World* and

when Kate – who might have been someone else – walked past, she leaned over and pretended to be looking for something in her bag.

'Are you OK?' Hunter asked.

'Fine!'

After breakfast, they walked up Primrose Hill to the Heath. At times like these Suzy loved being with Hunter. With him London looked new again. Where she saw pollution and potential muggers, he saw a hazy blue sky and teenage boys having a laugh. They walked past the Ladies' Pond, up past Kenwood, holding hands and laughing like annoying people in an advert for engagement rings.

'Hi, Suzy,' said a male voice behind them.

She swung round. Oh my God. It was Joachim, her dealer. Immediately she dropped Hunter's hand.

'How's it going?' Joachim said, coming over and kissing her on both cheeks. He had two blackened front teeth and a hollow face. He looked dodgy: he *was* dodgy. Suzy lived in fear of him being arrested and shopping all his up-market clients to the police, but he sold way the best charlie in North London and at very reasonable prices too.

'Fine,' she squeaked breathily. 'Just fine. You?'

'Cool,' he said, eyes travelling over to Hunter in his North Face anorak and hideous trainers. 'Hello. I'm Jo. And you are?'

'I'm Suzy's boyfriend, Hunter.' Suzy cringed. What would Joachim think? But more to the point, she realized surprised, she was worrying about what Hunter would make of her grungy friends.

The men shook hands and to Suzy's irritation started

to chat: about the good weather, about – for God's sake – motorbike racing. She shifted from foot to foot.

'So whadda you do, Jo?' Hunter asked with the inevitability of night following day.

'Hunter,' she snapped. 'I really think it's time we were on our way.'

She caught Jo's eye. Amused, knowing. He'd tell everyone that he'd just met Suzy out walking with some granddad type.

'Yeah, I mustn't keep you,' he drawled. He stuck out his rather dirty hand again. 'Nice to meet you, Hunter.'

'Come round for dinner sometime,' Hunter said.

'I'd love to. See you, Suze.'

'See you,' she murmured, yanking sharply at Hunter's arm.

They walked on, side by side, no longer talking or touching.

'He was nice,' Hunter said reflectively. 'I'd love to meet more of your friends, Suzanne.'

She glanced at him suspiciously. Was he taking the piss?

'Good,' she said a little shortly. How long was she going to be able to keep this up for? How long until she had to break the news to Hunter that Philadelphia and a reunion with Justine beckoned? Although she would miss days like these.

'So what are you doing tonight, baby?'

Suzy shrugged. 'Watching TV. *24*'s on.'

'That's a pity.'

'Why?' Suzy asked.

'Well, I'd arranged to have dinner with my friend Maxine. She's a model agent I got to know through my advertising contacts. I'd booked a table at Sketch. But I know how much you love *24*, baby.'

'I could always video it.' Model agent? Suzy didn't like the sound of this at all. She was probably really *tall*. And blonde. Which, in fact, was what Justine looked like. For the first time, at the thought of Justine, Suzy felt a prickle of envy like heat rash.

'You could video it, but I dunno, honey. Maybe it's better you don't come along. It's just ... Maxine's kinda young and she's having boyfriend problems. I think she'd like to confide in me a little. Having a stranger there might ... intimidate her.'

I bet it might. Intimidate her from getting hold of your wallet.

'Fine,' Suzy said shortly. 'I understand. You go. Don't worry about me. It was just ... I was looking forward to an evening in together.'

Hunter smiled at her gently. 'Sure, honey, I know. But this is *work*. Well, kind of. And you know how important that is to me.'

Suzy knew she had heard this excuse before, she just couldn't quite remember where. 'Sure,' she said. 'Work first. I understand.' She wished she didn't sound so bitter.

In Berlin, Jenny was standing wrapped in a sheet in the strip-lit corridor. She accosted a young Japanese couple pulling vast wheelie bags down the corridor and asked them to send someone up to open the door, but they spoke no English and simply giggled, hiding their faces behind their hands. She turned to a German woman emerging from her room.

'I shall tell reception,' she agreed unenthusiastically. 'But what a stupid thing to do.'

After a tut-tutting, cross-eyed receptionist had let her back in, she tried to call Gordy a dozen times on his mobile, but it was switched off. She got dressed. She might as well go to the airport too. The flight was booked for seven, but there was bound to be an earlier one.

'So you are one hour late, checking out,' said the cross-eyed receptionist. 'That will mean you must pay a half-day late-occupancy fee.'

'What do you mean I'm late checking out? It's noon.'

'It is 1 p.m., madame. And these are the rules.'

It took a few seconds before Jenny remembered her watch was still set on English time. When she wanted to know Berlin time she asked Gordy. They'd always done it like that on holiday.

She paid the extra £45 and caught a taxi to the airport. There, she discovered there was no free flight until seven.

'Nothing! So I have to wait five hours?'

'You can go back into the city,' said the woman at the BA desk. 'Alternatively, there is much good shopping at the airport.'

It wasn't worth going back into town, so she spent the next five hours sitting on a hard metal bench, reading a ridiculously expensive copy of today's *Sunday Times*. It was a foreign edition, so there wasn't even a colour mag or a Style section. Jenny found herself reading and re-reading an article about the pros and cons of the euro, without taking in a word. Every ten minutes she called Gordon, but his phone went straight to voicemail.

The flight was delayed two hours. She didn't get to Heathrow until nine. Gordon didn't answer until she was on the Heathrow Express.

'What do you want?' His tone would have made a polar bear shiver.

'I just want to tell you that I'm on my way. That we're going to talk.'

'No, we're not.'

'No, Gordy! Please don't be like this. Nothing's happened. You have to let me explain.'

'I don't think so. And please don't think of coming home tonight. I've had the locks changed. You won't be able to get in.'

'You've done what?'

'I don't want you sleeping in my house.'

'It's our house!'

'Not any more.'

'But what about all my things?'

'I've been packing them. I'll leave them in the shed tomorrow morning. I haven't changed that lock. You can come and collect them when I'm out.'

'But Gordy . . .'

'Come and collect them in the morning,' he repeated. And he hung up.

The train was pulling into Paddington. Trying hard to fight back the tears, Jenny called Suzy.

'It's me. I'm coming over.'

Suzy had just waved Hunter out the door and – rather disconcertedly – settled down to watch *24*.

'So you did it? You left Gordy?'

338

'No,' Jenny said. 'I didn't leave Gordy.' To her humiliation, she started to sob. The businessman in the next seat looked away. 'Oh God, Suzy. He left me.'

38

Hunter didn't get home until eleven. Jenny – who had been there an hour – was in the bath, sobbing loudly and preventing Suzy from using the loo.

Amazingly, Hunter seemed delighted to have a house guest.

'Sounds like she's been a naughty girl,' he chortled when Suzy explained. 'But then, who am I to judge?'

'Our relationship is *completely* different,' Suzy sniffed.

'Well, it'll be great to meet her,' Hunter said, going to the fridge to fetch some mineral water. 'I was wondering when you were going to get round to introducing me to your friends.'

'She won't be on good form,' Suzy warned. 'Expect a lot of tears. And to never see the inside of the bathroom again.'

Hunter laughed. 'Baby, the sooner my divorce comes through and we move into a mansion in Hampstead the better. Then you can have *all* your unhappy friends to stay.'

Who would have thought it? Suzy had always admired Hunter's looks, his status and . . . to be honest . . . his money. She had never, ever guessed that he could be so *nice*.

Annoyingly, it seemed she wasn't the only one who thought so.

'So how was Sketch?' she asked, trying to sound uninterested. Hunter had worn his best Paul Smith suit – the one

Suzy loved. He had left whistling at seven and had only *just* got back – at eleven. On a school night! Again, the jealousy ground in her stomach like broken glass.

'Oh, OK,' he said airily. 'Pretentious. Decent enough food, I guess – as it should be at that price.'

'And your . . . friend?'

Hunter pulled a face. 'Frankly, she's kinda dull. I mean, she's twenty-six, she doesn't have a lot to say for herself exactly. I kind of get the idea she's looking for a rich husband.'

'And will she find one?' Tone light.

'Not if she's so obvious about it.' Tone joking. He bent over and kissed Suzy on the forehead. An uncley kiss. She was still a bit unsure.

'So tell me about Jenny?' he said, pulling off his jacket.

Suzy's spirits sank still further as she remembered the last time she had gone on holiday with Jenny. Clothes all over their hotel-room floor, tea bags from the complimentary selection in the bathroom sink, leaflets from the tourist information office scattered all over the desk. She had vowed never to repeat the experience. And now Jenny was going to be living in her *home*. It was bad enough having a man there permanently, although to his credit Hunter wasn't *too* bad. Justine had trained him well.

God, she just hoped that Jenny didn't put him off her.

'She can be a little untidy . . .' she warned. But before she could fully prepare him, the bathroom door opened and a red-faced Jenny, dressed in Suzy's tiny bathrobe, emerged. Throwing back her shoulders, Suzy prepared herself to let the two sides of her life meet.

*

Katie was shocked.

'He found a Eurostar ticket!'

'He did indeed,' said Suzy grimly. She was shattered. Jenny had kept her up half the night repeating her sad story. Her bawling had woken Hunter up. He had been very good about it.

'But that is *precisely* what I told her not to do! What an idiot!'

'I told her the same,' Suzy said. 'But she never listens.'

Then why the hell did she want to consult the love trainer, Katie wondered. It was the same every time. All those hours at school and college spent counselling weeping girlfriends, who thanked you and then went off and did exactly the opposite of what you told them. What was the point?

'Well, I guess the end result is the same,' Suzy said. 'They've split up. Which is what you suggested.'

'Yes, but not like this. Poor Gordon, he seemed like such a sweetheart. He must be devastated.'

'Look, Katie, don't take it badly. Jenny is a sweetheart, but she's always taken Gordon for granted. This will have given her a wake-up call. Taught her not to be so careless with the next one.'

'I suppose.' But Katie still felt awful. *I've broken up a couple. An* engaged *couple.* But no, she hadn't done anything – it was Jenny who had bought the train ticket, expressly disobeying orders. A thought occurred to her. 'She's not still going to Paris, is she?'

'Well, she says not. But I have my suspicions.'

'Right. Well, at least we can do something to salvage the situation.'

'We?'

'Yes, you. I need you to help me.' And Suzy laughed as Katie told her what needed to be done.

Rebecca was devastated. 'He's kicked her out,' she said uncomprehendingly to Katie. 'And they were so in love.'

'I know. It's very sad.'

Rebecca shook her head. They were sitting in her office. 'Men. I honestly don't understand them, Katie. They can turn on you just like that.' She clicked her fingers.

'Women do it as well.'

'Not often. Women are great. Men are tossers.' She shook her head sadly. 'I wish I was a lesbian.'

'I know what you mean,' Katie smiled.

'I'd pay to watch you together,' said a voice at the door. It was Ben.

Katie felt like a cricket ball had thumped her in the chest. Her hands flew to her hair to check it was smooth.

'You're disgusting,' said Rebecca.

'So what's new?' He turned to Katie. 'Hello,' he said. He didn't sound terribly friendly.

'Hello.'

'Nice work with Jenny and Gordon,' he said mildly.

'That is so totally unfair,' Rebecca protested. 'Katie had nothing to do with Jenny and Gordon. Gordon kicked Jenny out. There was nothing Katie could do about it.'

Ben snorted. 'She could have seen it coming.'

Did Ben always talk about people as if they weren't there? 'I'm a love trainer, not a clairvoyant,' Katie said acidly. *Did I get it wrong?* she asked herself. But Jenny had been going to go off with Fabrice, whatever happened. And if she had dumped Gordon first, like Katie suggested, then he would have been spared the shock of finding that ticket.

'Sorry,' Ben chuckled. He had a nice dimple in his left cheek, Katie noticed. 'You're right. I'm sure you had nothing to do with Jenny and Gordon splitting up. But it *was* a bit of a coincidence: you at the party, checking them out, and a couple of weeks later it's all over.'

Katie shrugged.

He turned to Rebecca. 'Love trainer. It's such a hilarious title. And hopefully it'll make us millions, Rebecca.'

'It'll make *me* millions. It won't make you a penny.'

He laughed. *I like the way his nose crinkles up*, Katie thought. She almost slapped herself.

'So, when you're finished we need to talk about the Mergassey deal,' he was saying to Rebecca.

'Shall we do it over lunch?' Rebecca suggested. 'I've just been blown out.'

'Excellent idea.' He grinned. 'Tevere's at one?'

'Perfect. Ask Tara to book it.'

'See you later. See you, Katie.'

'Sorry about that,' said Rebecca as he shut the door. 'Ben can be so rude sometimes, but really he's a pussy cat.'

Katie had to know. 'Rebecca, I hope you don't mind me asking. But . . . what's the deal with you two?'

Rebecca rolled her eyes. 'Katie, I'm surprised at you.' She pretended to consult her diary. 'You're only the . . . let me see . . . nine-millionth person this week to have asked that question.'

'Sorry. But you know *why* people ask.'

'Yeah, I do,' Rebecca conceded. 'But there's nothing going on between me and Ben. When we met we were both with other people. We became business partners. The other people disappeared along the way, but by then sex was out of the question.'

So they had fancied each other, the timing had just been all wrong. 'And now?'

'God, Katie, I can't believe you're pursuing this. Ben and I are not interested in each other. And even if I ever had been, until just a few months ago he had a long-term girlfriend and I don't fancy muscling in on the rebound. Anyway, I'm going out with Simon tonight. Second date.'

'Oh, my God!' cried Katie, instantly distracted. 'Where's he taking you?'

'The Boxwood Café. I'm really excited, I've been longing to go there for ages.'

'Well, you know how to behave.'

'Of course. I'll be home alone at midnight. Do you want to call and check?'

'No,' said Katie. 'This time I'm going to trust you.'

39

Rebecca had waited ten days to call Simon. When she did, he sounded as if he had just won the lottery.

'God, I never thought I'd hear from you again. This is *so* great! I'll book a table.'

Talk about keen. Remembering this, as the cab carried her from the office (no time to go home and change) to the restaurant, Rebecca couldn't help wondering if Simon was a bit wet.

Still . . . the Boxwood Café. God knows how he had wangled a table.

She took a taxi to the restaurant just off Hyde Park Corner, left her coat at reception and – slowly, so as not to trip in her heels – descended the wide staircase into the dun-coloured room. She could see Simon sitting at a corner table, glancing tetchily at his watch. He spotted her and jumped up.

'I adore this kind of food,' she exclaimed, sitting down and studying the menu. 'Good, brunchy American stuff. I think I'll go for a lovely Caesar salad.'

'That's what I was going to have!' he gasped. He looked at her meaningfully. 'You know, Rebecca, we really have so much in common.'

It was a lovely dinner, but not as good as that first one at Nobu. They talked and laughed, or rather Simon laughed at nearly everything she said, whether it was funny or not.

The conversation turned to politics.

'The education in this country's a mess,' Rebecca exclaimed. 'You should see some of the idiots who come to me looking for jobs. They're totally illiterate.'

'So you'd educate your children privately, would you?' Simon asked eagerly.

'Well, yes, assuming I could afford it.' *And I ever have any*, she thought, but declined to say the obvious.

'I think it's so important to be in agreement on these things,' he said, sitting back happily.

They moved on to the topic of birthdays. 'Mine's coming up soon,' Rebecca sighed.

'We'll have to do something nice,' Simon said.

Why didn't her heart sing?

All the same, they were still there at midnight, the last people in the restaurant.

'Please let me get this,' Rebecca argued when the bill arrived.

'No,' said Simon. 'I absolutely insist.'

The waiter took away his credit card. Simon leaned forward.

'So listen, what are you doing this weekend?'

'I'm not sure,' she said, and then astonished herself by saying, 'I think I might be going to Amsterdam.'

'Amsterdam! Cool! I've always wanted to go there. How come?'

'There's a client there I have to meet.' Where were these lies coming from? She was vaguely thinking of going to

Amsterdam soon for some business, but this weekend she had intended to relive her youth and go clubbing with Freddie.

There was a two-second pause. Simon was clearly waiting for her to say, 'Would you like to come too?' She smiled at him vaguely.

'Well, when will you know for sure?' he asked.

'I don't know, maybe tomorrow.'

'It's just that I'd said I'd play football. But I could cancel. It depends on what you're doing.'

He bent down to sign his card slip. Rebecca stared at him. What was this? The man was acting as if they'd been married for years, when they hadn't even slept together. She really didn't like it.

He helped her on with her coat and insisted on carrying her heavy bag. If he had been holding it in his mouth and humbly wagging his tail, the resemblance to a hound would have been complete.

I've done it, Rebecca thought. *I'm leader of the pack.*

They stood out on the pavement, searching for a cab. This was it. This was the moment when they agreed to share, she suggested he came up for a coffee, and the whole story started again.

Rebecca glanced sideways at Simon. OK, he was a bit short, but he also had a straight Roman nose and a nice, firm body. He was clever and rich and amusing. But something was missing.

I don't fancy him, Rebecca realized. *I just fancy the idea of him.*

She had done it a dozen times before. Met a man and flirted with him. It was what she was programmed to do.

They had dinner and she flirted with him some more. Then she took him home and slept with him. And the following morning they were a couple – for anything between three months to three years.

They should have been one-night stands. Well, maybe not all of them, but most of them. Rebecca had gone with them all because she had been grateful for their attention, amazed anyone could want her.

She still didn't believe anyone would really love her, but she knew one thing: she couldn't waste any more time settling for second-best.

'Taxi!' she yelled. Immediately, one screeched to a halt.

'You get this,' she said.

'No, no. You're the lady. It's yours.'

He was expecting her to offer him a ride. But instead she said, 'Well, if you don't mind. Oh look, there's another one. Quick! Grab it.'

Bemused, Simon did as he was told.

'Listen,' he said as she climbed into her taxi. 'I don't want to bother you. You call me.'

'Great!' she squeaked. As an afterthought, she stuck her head out of the window. 'Thanks for a lovely evening.'

She didn't have the guts to say she never wanted to see him again. He'd figure it out soon enough.

Just then her mobile beeped. She pulled it out of her bag. Text. From Simon.

X, it said.

Rebecca felt slightly queasy. Hastily, she deleted it, turned the phone off and stuffed it back in her bag.

40

That same evening, Ally and Jenny were sitting in a gastro-pub in Camden, eating organic sausages.

'He won't return my calls, he's changed the locks. I've blown it, Al, totally blown it.'

'Jenny, he's just upset. Give it time, he'll calm down.' Ally wasn't really listening. Her period was two days late.

'He won't,' Jenny said bleakly. 'It's all over.' She had wangled a week off work by telling them her grandmother had died. She had spent most of it crying on Suzy's futon and redialling Gordy's mobile. It was always switched off.

Ally still didn't fully understand what had happened. 'Jen, this is a horrible question, but . . . was he having an affair?'

Jenny almost laughed. 'Gordy? No! No. But . . . he thought I was.'

'He thought *you* were? Has he gone crazy?'

'Well, the thing is . . . I sort of was.'

Ally took a deep breath. She loved Jenny, but she had always feared this might happen one day.

'What does sort of mean, Jen?'

Jenny told her an abbreviated version of the story. Ally hadn't known about the Frenchman. But every other detail sounded familiar, right down to the Eurostar booking.

'But you won't be going to Paris now?'

'Of course I will! What do I have to lose?'

'But you want Gordy back, don't you?'

'Of course I do. But he's made it plain. He's not having any of it.'

'Jenny,' said Ally. 'You can't give up so easily. You've got to fight for your man.'

'Do you think so?' Jenny snuffled.

'Jen! I *know* so.'

'The love trainer said I shouldn't go.'

'Sorry?'

'The love trainer. You know, Rebecca's new client?'

'No.' Ally looked unperturbed, but in her mind she was back in the playground, being passed over for the rounders team. Why did her friends never tell her anything any more?

'Haven't you heard of her?' Jenny's eyes grew rounder. 'She's going to be *huge*.'

She told Ally all about Katie. Ally listened, initially sceptically, but as she heard what advice she had given Jenny, her attitude changed.

'Sounds like she knows her stuff, Jen. I mean, maybe it was harsh telling you to dump Gordy, but you were planning to be unfaithful. You should listen to her about Paris.'

Jenny grimaced. 'Whatever. Gordy's left me now. I'm a free woman. I need cheering up.'

Ally wiggled in her seat. 'Um. You don't have her number, do you?'

The joy of Jenny was she was so totally self-absorbed, she never got it. 'Sure,' she said, pulling out her phone and scrolling down the numbers.

'Because it could be interesting business for the bank.

To . . . get a love trainer on board. There's a lot of interest in these self-help people.'

'Mmmm.' Jenny wasn't even listening, her mind on what she'd wear to Paris. 'Here it is.' She read out Katie's number. Ally scribbled it down.

Suddenly Jenny squeaked. 'Oh hello, Jon. How are you?'

Ally turned round. Jon was standing there, face white, hands clenched.

'Sweetheart. What are you doing here?' she asked, confused.

'I've been waiting for you,' he said. His voice was calm. 'I didn't know where you were.'

Her tone was equally level and low. 'I told you I was meeting Jenny.'

'Yes, but it's late. I was worried.'

Ally glanced at her watch. It was 10.30. 'Well, no need to come all the way down here. You could have rung.'

'I *did* ring!' he yelled. 'You didn't bloody answer.'

Hands shaking, Ally reached into her bag. There was her mobile. *Five missed calls.*

'I'm sorry, sweetheart, I didn't hear. It's noisy in here.'

Jenny's mouth was hanging open.

'We were just getting the bill, weren't we, Jen?'

'Well . . .'

'*Weren't* we?' said Ally, signalling to the waiter. She thought she would die of humiliation. She nodded to Jon. 'Why don't you have a glass of wine with us while we're waiting?'

'No,' he said. He turned round and pushed through the crowd of happy drinkers, out into the night.

'Oh, my God,' said Ally. 'I'm so sorry about that.'

But Jenny was staring at her admiringly. 'That's *so* romantic,' she said softly. 'Gordy would never come and find me like that. Jon must really love you.'

They paid the bill and left. Ally tried to hide her fury as she kissed Jenny goodbye, but her cheeks were burning, her heart banging like a tribe of drummers. She hurried home. Her mouth felt like sawdust and her body as if it did not belong to her but was floating apart.

How could he do that to me? Is he insane? What am I doing with him?

He was sitting in front of *News 24* as if nothing had happened.

'What was that about?' she asked coolly. 'Why did you have to embarrass me in front of my friend?'

'You were late,' he replied, equally pleasantly. 'I didn't know where you were.'

'I wasn't late! Since when do I have to be home by ten?'

His pudgy face twisted. 'Ally! I didn't know where you were.'

'Did you have to talk to me like that in front of my friend?'

'Well, you're talking about me. Behind my back.'

'I don't say anything,' Ally cried. It was true. She never told her friends the truth about life with Jon. It would be too humiliating.

'Yeah, right.' He folded his arms and turned back to the TV.

'I didn't!'

There was silence. John Simpson, up a mountainside surrounded by goats, droned on. Ally decided to change tactics.

'So poor old Jenny. Gordy's chucked her out, she doesn't know what to do.'

'Serves her right,' Jon muttered into the goatee he had recently started growing.

'*What?*'

'I said: serves her right. Jenny's always been a flirt. Gordon probably got sick of it.'

'How can you say that? What's wrong with flirting? Jenny just likes to have fun.'

'Bea was a flirt,' he said bitterly. He turned up the volume.

Dislike flooded Ally's veins like poison. She was sick of Jon, sick of his bile, sick of his possessiveness and his temper tantrums. But what was she going to do? She wanted a baby and she wanted one soon. She didn't have *time* to look for anyone else. And Jon was a great father. *And* he'd take charge of the child care.

She felt trapped and breathless. She could almost feel the bars of her cage, crushing in on her.

'I'm going to bed,' she said softly.

Jon turned round, his face softer, his eyes panicked.

'Are you angry with me?'

'Yes, I am.'

He stood up and pulled her to him. 'Oh, baby, don't be angry. It's only because I love you, I get like this. Isn't it? Only because I love you. It's a good thing, really. Isn't it?'

He kissed her hair and stroked her back. She was too tired to argue any more.

'I'm going to bed,' she repeated.

In the bathroom, she locked the door and sat on the

loo, her head in her hands. Then, as she reached for some paper, she noticed.

She had her period.

She glanced at her watch. 11.08. Was it too late to call the love trainer?

Fuck it, if she didn't want to take the call she'd leave a message.

Running the bath taps to drown herself out, she dialled the number.

'Er, hello? Is that Katie?'

41

'Who was that?' Crispin asked.

Katie thought fast. They had been lying on Crispin's sofa, watching a DVD of *The Battle for Algiers*. The title hadn't appealed to her at all, but she had to admit it hadn't been too bad.

'Just a friend of Rebecca's. She's starting up a new company and she needs staff. So – as you heard – I suggested we meet.'

'What kind of company?'

'Well . . . she didn't really say. She'll explain when we meet.'

'Sounds good,' he said vaguely, eyes on the 'extra features' menu. He turned and smiled. 'It's about time you got a proper job.'

Katie felt dizzy. She kept meaning to tell Crispin about the love training, but something kept putting her off. She knew he'd think it was a ridiculous job, and she couldn't face his mockery. But whatever she did, he was going to know all about it as soon as the November issue of *Seduce!* hit the shops. Katie was under no illusion Crispin wouldn't find out – a secretary in his chambers would tell him, or a mate's girlfriend. So she had to break it to him soon.

But not tonight. She was tired, she didn't want a fight. Her relationship with Crispin had stayed so easy for so long. She didn't want anything to change.

She'd break the news in the next week or so.

'Do you think I did a bad thing?' As usual, Rebecca was filled with remorse, convinced her punishment for rejecting Simon would be a crop of hairs on her chin and a compulsion to wear flesh-coloured pop sox.

'No, Rebecca, you didn't do a bad thing,' Katie said wearily. 'You realized you didn't fancy him.'

'But that's so superficial. Maybe physical attraction would have grown.'

'I doubt it. Rebecca, this is great! In the old days you'd have rather gone out with someone you didn't fancy than have nobody. You've changed.'

Rebecca looked up and smiled. 'Do you think so?'

'Definitely.' Katie felt the thrill of achievement. She might have failed with Jenny, but at least here she was getting somewhere.

'But I'll still end up organizing jumble sales and having three million godchildren.'

'Better than having to have sex with someone you don't fancy every night for the rest of your life. And I'm not so sure about the godchildren either. I mean, Jenny and Gordy seem to be on the rocks. And Suzy told me she never wanted children.'

Rebecca looked amused. 'I know, Suzy's told everybody that. But she's changed. Since Hunter moved in, she's got much . . . softer. She's not even moaning about Jenny staying. Well, not much, anyway. And the other day she actually said she was looking forward to meeting his daughters.'

Katie beamed. A result at last. 'Really?'

'She's in love,' Rebecca sighed. 'It can happen.'

To her surprise, Katie felt a pinprick of envy. She didn't know why. She had a man of her own, didn't she? It was great if Suzy was happy too. It was just . . . everyone seemed to be changing. Even the happily single Rebecca had a zingy air to her. And although Katie loved to see that, she couldn't understand why she didn't feel so ecstatic herself. She was nervous, she supposed, waiting to see what the rest of the world made of the love trainer.

Jenny had left alternately hysterical, pleading, abject, haughty and – at Katie's suggestion – controlled messages on Gordon's mobile. He didn't reply, so she wrote him a letter pleading her case. He didn't answer.

Oh well, she comforted herself. At least she still had Paris to look forward to. On Thursday evening – having failed to make a date with any of her friends – she stayed in at Suzy's and packed. Her Eurostar left the following evening. It was her only reason for living.

She passed a happy half-hour selecting two tight T-shirts, a long floaty skirt and a denim jacket for chilly evenings. Suzy had gone down to Balham after work on Monday and returned with two mammoth suitcases full of Jenny's clothes. Gordon had packed all her nicest underwear – the stuff he had never appreciated. She wondered if Felix, her hairdresser, could squeeze her in tomorrow morning. It would be better than mooching around the house all day.

She realized she hadn't thought about Gordy for almost an hour. Maybe Katie was right. Maybe they were better off without each other. At least she could go to Paris now without lying or feeling guilty.

She'd just check that her passport and the ticket that had been the cause of all her problems were still inside her wallet. Then everything would be in order and she could go to sleep.

Her passport wasn't there.

Jenny's stomach backflipped. Where the hell was it? She remembered putting it away when she arrived at Heathrow on Sunday and she certainly hadn't got it out again. It must be in her handbag. She searched once, twice and – desperately – a third time. Gone.

When Suzy and Hunter came in laughing just before midnight, Jenny was curled up in a ball on the living-room sofa, her face red and streaky with tears.

'Oh, Jen, have you had another horrible night?'

'I can't find my passport. Have you seen it?'

Suzy ducked her head as she took off her jacket. Was it Jenny's imagination or was she avoiding eye contact?

'Why do you want your passport?'

'Have you seen it?'

'No, I haven't. But why do you need it?'

'I just do, that's all.' She couldn't tell Suzy about the Paris trip. She'd told her she was going to stay with her sister in Nottingham. 'For a form I'm filling in.'

Suzy looked concerned. 'Maybe it's still in Balham?'

'No! It can't be. I had it on Sunday night.'

'I'm sure it'll turn up,' Hunter said, patting her on the shoulder. 'But what's the rush? Surely your form can wait a couple of days?'

'Well . . .' Jenny couldn't think of an answer. 'I guess so.'

Suzy yawned. 'Well, don't worry about it then. Come on, darling, I'm pooped. See you in the morning, Jen.'

Jenny was left flabbergasted. She had a horrible suspicion Suzy had her passport. But short of bursting into her bedroom brandishing a search warrant, there was nothing she could do.

'See you in the morning,' she said, defeated.

Jenny lay awake most of that night panicking over the mystery of the missing passport. She had searched every corner of the flat. Perhaps she had dropped it somewhere between Heathrow and Suzy's. She doubted it. But she was always losing things – so how could she be sure?

At 3 a.m. she had a brainwave. The Passport Office in Victoria. She was almost certain that it issued passports on the spot. Gordon had gone there once when he realized on the morning they were leaving for Ibiza that his passport was out of date. She'd go in the morning.

Satisfied, she slept, then woke an hour later, assaulted by a new worry. What about Fabrice? In all the misery and drama of the past week she hadn't checked her emails once – she could only access them at work. He *did* know she was coming, didn't he?

She'd have to go in to work. She'd check her email and then ring the Passport Office. But the security guards didn't open up until 7.30. She'd have to rest for a few hours first. She set the alarm on her mobile and, soothed by her efficiency, immediately fell into a dreamless sleep.

By the time Suzy rose at seven, Jenny had long gone. Suzy only discovered this when she gently knocked on her friend's door to ask if she would like orange juice. Since Hunter had moved in, Suzy had had to start eating breakfast with him. To her surprise, it was a nice, relaxed time for both of them – often their only truly intimate moment of the day, since Hunter seemed to be going out so much more now. And the food part wasn't so bad: she only had a couple of slices of toast and Marmite and it did stop her stomach growling loudly in 10 a.m. ideas meetings.

The sight of Jenny's empty bed almost made her heart stop. Then she remembered the drama of the previous night.

'I guess she'll be on her way to the Passport Office,' Hunter said behind her. He was wearing his sharpest suit and looked gorgeous.

'They won't be able to help her, I've checked. They can issue a new passport in a couple of hours, but if your old one was lost or stolen, it takes a few days.'

Hunter snorted. 'And where is the passport?'

'In my drawer at work.'

He laughed and bending over, kissed her hard on the mouth. 'You are an evil woman, Suzanne Bell.'

'It wasn't my idea,' said Suzy. 'It was the love trainer's.' Then she stopped, surprised at herself again. Normally she took the credit for everything. What was wrong with her these days? And she hadn't touched drugs for more than a fortnight. Somehow, seeing Jo in daylight on Primrose Hill had put her off. Did she really want stuff up her nose that had been sifted by those grubby hands? Besides, she had had some lovely evenings with Hunter lately, drinking wine and enjoying leisurely dinners, when it just seemed like too much hassle to slip off to the ladies with all her paraphernalia. Hunter might have got suspicious (and he had scarily firm views on drugs) and anyway, she would have lost her appetite and got all twitchy and, quite frankly, the mellow mood would have been ruined.

She'd been supposed to be going to a fashion party tonight where the stuff would be flowing. The prospect seemed incredibly dull.

'What are your plans for tonight?' she said to Hunter, who was just pulling his phone out of his pocket.

'I was going to have a drink with some people,' he said, then glancing up saw her face. 'But I could meet you later.'

'That might be nice,' Suzy agreed. 'How about I cook for you?'

'Cook for me?' Hunter raised an eyebrow. 'Oh God, don't put yourself to any trouble.'

'No, no,' Suzy said, waving brusquely at her driver, who had just pulled up outside. 'It will be a pleasure. What time can I expect you back? About eight?'

Hunter looked troubled. 'Make it eight-thirty – or nine, to be safe, baby.'

'OK,' Suzy said, wondering why his vagueness bothered her so much. But she didn't want to lay down the law. No man likes a nag, she thought as she stepped out of the front door, and wondered what the love trainer would have to say on the subject.

42

At 7.30, the office was empty. Nervously, Jenny turned on her computer. Forty-seven emails. She scrolled hastily through all of them. Work, work, work, work, work. A couple of round-robin jokes. More work. Friends wanting to know if everything was all right.

Nothing from Fabrice.

She felt a dull thud in her chest. Quickly, she banished it. He'd probably tried to call her.

She checked her voicemail. Work, work, work, friend, work, friend, friend, work.

Oh well, it was only Friday morning. Perhaps he had been intending to get in touch today. She would just send him a quick email and all the confusion would be at an end. Even if he didn't get in touch, she was still bloody going to Paris. After all the gloom of the past few days Jenny needed cheering up.

Hi, Fabrice, she wrote. Keep it light and jolly. *Just a reminder I'll be in Paris from tonight, so hoping we can meet up. Give me a call on the mobile! Jenny.* She thought, then added an *X*.

Still, she wasn't satisfied. Suppose he wasn't in the office today? Or their computers were down?

She'd told him what time her Eurostar was getting in, maybe he was planning to meet her off it. But she needed to know for sure. How annoying that she didn't have his home or mobile number! But she could try him in the office. They were an hour ahead there. Even if he wasn't around, someone might be able to inform her of his plans.

She dialled a loft in the Marais. *Brrr, brrr,* the phone rang.

'*Bonjour.* Blue Custard Paris.'

'Er, *oui, bonjour,*' said Jenny. She had never really got the hang of other languages. 'Um. Fabrice, *s'il vous plaît.*'

'Just a minute, I'll put you through,' the woman replied in perfect English.

It was voicemail and it was all in French. Damn. Jenny couldn't understand a word. She was about to hang up when it switched into English: ''Allo, this eez Fabrice Dupeignier. You can leave a message or you can call me on my portable.' And there was a number in English.

Finally! Jenny scribbled it down and dialled it straight away. It rang so long, she was about to hang up.

''Allo?' It was a woman's voice. She sounded young and sprightly.

Damn. She must have dialled the wrong number. She wasn't going to explain that in French, so she hung up and dialled again.

''Allo?' This time the woman sounded a bit annoyed.

'Er, 'allo? Fabrice? His telephone?'

'Oh, yes. Who may I say is speaking?'

'Um, it's Jenny. From the London office.'

She heard her calling, 'Fabby! Fabby!' There was a muffled conversation that included the word Jenny. An exclamation of annoyance from him. A sharp enquiry from her. And Jenny knew.

''Allo, Jenny? How are you?' He had such a sexy voice. 'Why do you call?'

'Oh, Fabrice, I'm really sorry to bother you.'

'Ah, *non*, it's OK.' He sounded curt.

'It's just, you know, I'd emailed to say I was going to be in Paris this weekend. But now I'm not coming. You know, work and stuff. So . . . just thought I'd better let you know in case . . . well . . . you know.'

There was a pause. 'Oh yeah. I'd forgotten. And in fact, I am not in Paris. I am in Bordeaux. It is the 'olidays, you know.'

'Uh, yes, I know. But you know . . . worth a shot!' She laughed shrilly.

'Well, thanks. Goodbye.'

'Goodbye.'

So in the end Jenny never discovered that the Passport Office would have taken a week to replace her lost passport and she would never have made it to Paris anyway.

Her weekend was wretched. By Monday, she was desperate to get back to work just to take her mind off her nightmare. Suzy had been incredibly patient and sweet and shown no sign of wanting to get rid of her, but she must be dying to spend time alone with Hunter. Who really was extraordinarily nice. Jenny couldn't understand why Suzy had hidden him away for so long.

Everyone in the office knew about her and Gordy and they all gave her understanding looks. She held her head high and ignored them.

Then she turned on her computer and saw an email

lurking from F. Dupeignier. For a moment, she basked in a final sunbeam of hope.

Jenny, please I must ask you not to phone my portable again. It make my girlfriend very angry. I hope to see you next time I am in London. Fabrice.

Bastard! As if she had any intention of calling him again! God, men were swine. How could he treat his live-in girlfriend like that?

But her anger was offset by another feeling of deep, deep foolishness. Hadn't she always known that she and Fabrice was just a flirtation? He had fed a few crumbs to Jenny's eternally hungry ego and she had decided she wanted a whole meal. It was just a way of injecting a little fizz into her otherwise mundane life.

But Gordon did love her, loved her more than anyone ever would, he just wasn't great at showing it. Something Katie had said came into her mind. *Actions speak louder than words.* Maybe she hated it when Gordy belched loudly, but he didn't mind her dirty clothes all over the bedroom floor. He surprised her with weekends in Berlin. He was funny and kind and utterly honest. She'd been bloody lucky to have him.

Even if she had to break the door down, she would talk to him. She'd lost a bit of weight in the past week from not eating and – because everything else was at the dry cleaner's – she happened to be wearing her black dress, which he had always loved. She'd book herself a lunchtime blow-dry. When he saw her he wouldn't be able to resist.

She hung around late at work, reading her horoscope online. No point in arriving at the house first and having to wait on the doorstep like a refugee.

She left shortly after eight, to Zack, the security guard's, astonishment.

'First you come in early, then you leave late. Are you stealing company secrets, Jenny?'

'I bloody wish,' she said grimly.

Zack shook his head. She was behaving most eccentrically. Still, the poor girl was getting over her grandmother's death. Zack thought all the office jokes about how so far seven of Jenny's grandparents had died were unfair. She was a lovely girl and very friendly.

Jenny caught the Tube down to Balham. There was still the same grumpy Bangladeshi man selling *Evening Standard*s in the foyer and the same teenage beggar slumped outside in his sleeping bag. Jenny gave him a couple of pounds and set off on the familiar route through the rows of backstreets lined with cosy semis to her old house. Damn it, it was still her house. A quarter of her salary was going towards paying for it each month.

She stopped on a street corner and breathed deeply like Suzy had taught her.

It would be all right. One horoscope had said, *A good day for getting to the heart of the matter*. And Gordy's had said, *Romance is in the air tonight*. How much more promising could you get?

She walked on past the cornershop, the launderette, the blood stains on the pavement where there had been a stabbing. She paused at her old front gate. The lights were on. Good, he was home and not drinking himself to death in the pub. God, she had done a terrible thing to him. How would she ever make it up to him?

The curtains were open, so Jenny had a very good view

367

of the long living room at 27 Fraser Street, SW17. Of the walls she and Gordy had painted together. The prints and the Buddha statue they had bought together in Indonesia. Her books, his CDs stashed in the old dresser they found in Chapel Street Market.

And of Gordy, her Gordy, passionately kissing a small, brown-haired girl. She looked familiar. It took Jenny a second to remember where she had seen her before.

It was the bloody love trainer's cousin. It was Jessica.

43

That same day, Ally and Katie met for lunch at a wine bar in the City.

'How will you recognize me?' Ally had asked on the phone.

'Actually, we've met already. At Jenny's party. You won't remember me but I'll remember you.'

'Uh oh,' said Ally, humming a few bars from the *X-Files* theme. 'Creepy.'

But actually, when Ally saw Katie waiting at the tiny round table in the dark basement, she remembered her quite well. The waitress from the party who'd kept topping up her glass.

Katie, for her part, thought Ally looked even more strained than three weeks ago. Her skin was grey and streaks of Touche-Eclat were clearly visible under her puffy eyes.

They didn't have much time. Ally absolutely had to be back in the office in an hour for a New York conference call.

'Rebecca said that normally you'd spend a bit of time observing me and Jon,' she said, skipping all the normal pleasantries. 'But she also said you'd seen us together at Jenny's party and maybe that would do.'

'Maybe,' said Katie. She took a sip of her Perrier. Ally had offered her wine, but she was meeting journalists from the *Sunday Standard* and the *Correspondent* this afternoon. 'Tell me how you and Jon met.'

Ally started to talk. More than a year of keeping her problems to herself, of pretending she had got what she always wanted, and now, finally, she could tell the truth. She found she couldn't stop. Her plate of grilled salmon grew cold.

'I feel I'm going insane. He's so bad-tempered and he snaps at me if I ever disagree with him. But at the same time he's so clingy.' She told Katie how he had tracked her down in the pub, plus a few other stories.

'It's classic passive aggression,' Katie said. 'You see it in dogs all the time. They dominate their owners by claiming to be submissive. For example, they may scratch at their owner's legs and demand to be picked up. It's just a different way of showing they're in charge.'

'And what should I do about it?' Ally breathed.

'You need to withdraw all affection from the dog,' Katie recited from memory. 'If the dog wants to gain your attention, he has to do something for you. Ignore the dog until it stops making demands, then command it to sit and stroke it. The dog will quickly learn that you are in control.'

She looked at Ally, who seemed fascinated. 'The thing is, Jon had another owner before you and it sounds like she trained him really badly. Sometimes these things are irreversible. You may just have to put him down.'

'Murder Jon?' Ally had been expecting Katie to tell her to get her hair done or treat herself to a massage.

'No, not *murder* him. But maybe . . . dump him?' She knew she'd got it wrong with Jenny and Gordon, but this time was definitely different.

Ally shook her head. 'Oh no. I can't.'

'Why not?'

'Because I want to have a baby.'

'You want to have a baby with someone who's whiny and bad-tempered and monitors everything you do?'

'I know it sounds silly. But I'm nearly thirty-four and I'm running out of time.'

'If you're thirty-three, you've got loads of time to have a baby. Chérie Blair had one when she was forty-six.'

'Yes, but she was *lucky*! What if I have problems conceiving? So many women do, you know.'

'So many women don't. And there's always IVF.'

'But suppose I never meet anyone else to have IVF with? I'm thirty-three-and-a-half, I'm losing my looks.'

Oh please, *not* the old 'I'm almost fifty' routine. Why were all these women so hard on themselves?

'Ally, you're at the peak of your beauty,' Katie insisted. 'You will easily meet someone else.'

'So you're telling me to dump Jon?' Ally asked.

'The only reason to stay with someone is because you can't bear to live without them,' Katie said firmly. 'Could you bear to be without Jon?'

Ally shrugged.

'Would you be happier?'

She shrugged again.

'Well, look,' said Katie. 'You don't have to make any decisions now. Here's a list of dog-training rules. If you just give me a minute I'll underline the ones I think apply especially to you and Jon. Give them a go and see if you get anywhere.'

Ally waved for the bill while Katie highlighted the relevant rules.

'I'll have to hide these from Jenny,' Ally said, slipping the list in her bag. 'She thinks you're a homebreaker. But Rebecca will be thrilled. She's always hated Jon.'

'Oh, I don't think she really knows him,' Katie muttered tactfully.

Ally collected herself and stood up. 'Well, that was a lunch hour well spent. Much better than dashing round M&S looking for Jon's supper. Do you invoice me or what?'

'Oh, you don't need to pay me,' Katie said, blushing. 'This was hardly a tough one.'

'Of course I'll pay you!' Ally fumbled in her bag for a cheque-book. But Katie shook her head.

'Well, if you insist,' said Ally, looking pleased. 'I tell you what, I'll put the word round my office. I think Zara, who's the head of marketing, could do with a session with you. And my PA, Belinda, she's in a bit of a women-who-love-too-much situation. They'd all love to see you. And they'd pay top City rates.'

Ally was walking home from the Tube when her phone rang. She thought it would be Jon demanding to know where she was. She felt a twist in her stomach. As she pulled her mobile out of her pocket, she realized that every evening her journey home was overshadowed by apprehension at what sort of mood he would be in.

But the caller was Jenny.

'Oh, Al! It's awful! Gordy got off with the waitress from my party.'

What on earth was Jen talking about? 'Gordy and a waitress?'

'Yes,' Jenny wailed into her mobile. She was standing outside Balham Tube, undecided where to go. 'You see, Suzy and Rebecca planted her. She's the love trainer's cousin.'

Katie's cousin? Ally had no idea what she was talking about.

'Jenny, why don't you come round? And if you don't fancy going back to Suzy's you can stay.'

So Ally, who had been looking forward to curling up with Katie's rules, went home and divided an M&S ready-to-eat spaghetti vegetariana into three.

'Are you trying to bloody starve me?' Jon whined as he watched her.

Ally was suddenly reminded of her granddad's flea-ridden old mutt, Chester, and how he used to nuzzle against her legs at mealtimes, whimpering, until finally she gave in and fed him some scraps.

'Jenny's in a state, she needs to eat,' she said firmly. 'There's loads of fruit you can snack on.'

'You know I don't like fruit,' he growled. 'Why's she coming round? I want to be alone with you.'

'Me too, darling,' Ally said through gritted teeth. 'But you've got to be there for your friends.'

Jon looked put out. He didn't really have friends – well, perhaps Dave who lived two doors down whom he went fishing with and Rick whom he'd been in the band with all those years ago. But they were always messing him around: blowing out pub sessions, saying they had to babysit, or that they'd promised to take the wife out to dinner. People always let you down.

'But can't you talk at the weekend?' he tried.

Ally looked at him. 'No. Now go and watch telly or something. I'll talk to Jenny in the bedroom.'

They lay on Ally's big double bed and talked until eleven, when Jon popped his head around the door and announced huffily that he had an early start and more than five hours' sleep really would be appreciated.

'Sorry,' Ally said sweetly. 'Jen and I will finish off the conversation downstairs. And then Jenny can sleep on the futon.'

By quarter to twelve, Ally had finally grasped the situation.

'So Jess was one of the girls serving drinks at the party?'

'Yes, but she was only there because of Katie. And I'd never have got to know Katie if Rebecca and Suzy hadn't suggested it. They've ruined my life.'

They had been through this several times already. 'Jenny, there's no way Suzy and Rebecca could have known that Gordy would get off with the little slapper. He only did it because he's lonely and miserable and confused.'

'I can't believe it! Gordy. He's the last person in the world I ever thought would be unfaithful.'

'Well, strictly speaking he wasn't being unfaithful. I mean – you were separated, weren't you?'

'*He* may have thought so.' Jenny's lip wobbled.

'And you were planning to go off to Paris and see that French guy. What happened there by the way? Did you go?'

'Of *course* not! That would have been totally out of order. I'm engaged to Gordy.'

When Ally finally came upstairs at two, Jon was waiting.

'For fuck's sake, what is this? A psychiatric ward?'

Usually Ally would have apologized profusely and covered him in kisses.

Tonight, however, she merely pulled off her clothes, slid under the duvet and turned her back to him.

'Actually, a psychiatric ward is exactly how this house feels most of the time,' she said meditatively.

And then she said nothing. Jon lay there for a moment, waiting for her to recant, then he prodded her.

'Al?'

'What?' she yawned.

'Are you angry with me?'

'No,' she sighed. 'I'm just tired.' She rolled over and for the first time in weeks fell into a drug-free sleep.

The following morning, a rather frightened Jon brought her a cup of tea in bed.

44

Seduce! had scrabbled around to find a case study for Katie. Eventually they came up with Gemma's best friend's older sister, whose boyfriend didn't seem to have much time for her. Undeterred, she had started leaving makeup in the bathroom, then clothes in his wardrobe, finally – when her lease ran out – she moved in. But now she found herself constantly home alone, while he went out to parties she couldn't come to 'because it was work'. He seemed reluctant to let her get to know his friends, let alone introduce her to his family.

A female Hunter.

Katie gave her exactly the same advice she gave Hunter, then sent her away for a week. When she reported back, things were going much better. Now Katie had to write her column. She spent all Tuesday at the computer and, to her surprise, found she rather enjoyed it. At the end of the day she emailed it to Rebecca for approval. Then she got on the Tube to travel to Holborn where she was meeting Crispin for dinner in a little Lebanese he had discovered in a basement near his chambers.

They drank Lebanese rosé and feasted on trays of tabbouleh and falafel, raw vegetables, halloumi, hummus and spicy meatballs. They ate until they could eat no more.

'That was fantastic,' Katie breathed. She patted her belly in disgust. 'God, I might as well be pregnant.'

Crispin gave her a funny, shy smile. 'And would that be such a terrible thing?'

Katie looked at him suspiciously. What on earth was he talking about? It would be a disaster. 'Well, it wouldn't be ideal, would it?'

'Well, maybe not quite yet. But sooner rather than later.' He had that soppy look on his face that always made her slightly nervous.

'Er, yes, I suppose so,' she said, picking at the wax dripping from the candle. She didn't want to talk about this. Didn't want a row. Didn't want anything that could lead to pain. Her hand moved too close to the flame. 'Ow!'

She smiled at him. 'I think I'd rather have a dog.'

He wagged his finger. 'Now, Katie, you know what I think of dogs. They're not hygienic, for one thing, and they can be dangerous.'

Normally she would have argued. Now she shrugged. She was suddenly desperate to be out of there. Crispin paid the bill and they climbed up the metal staircase and out on to the pavement.

'So back to mine?' Crispin said eagerly.

Katie's mobile started to ring. She reached into her bag.

'Leave it, Kate!'

It was home calling. Probably Jess or Ronan wanting to know if she'd paid the gas bill or something. She switched it to divert.

Crispin looked smug. 'Thanks for that.'

Voicemail started calling. 'Just let me listen to the message,' Katie pleaded. 'It might be important.'

It was Ronan. 'Katie, have you heard about Jess? I'd rather tell you in person. When are you going to be home?'

Heard about Jess? What about her? Was she sick? Katie's heart started beating fast.

'Babe, something's happened to Jess. I've got to go home.'

Crispin's happy expression evaporated. 'Can't you just call her?'

'No, apparently I have to get home.' Guiltily, Katie knew that if it was *that* awful, Ronan would have said. Probably it was another pregnancy scare or something. Pregnancy: that was what Katie was afraid of. Crispin taking her home and wanting sex and refusing to wear a condom. She didn't want a baby, not now anyway, but the thought of breaking that to him filled her with dread. She wanted to be home, home with the people she loved.

But you love Crispin, don't you?

She tried to get rid of the thought, but it was like trying to cram a hot-air balloon into a washing machine.

Flustered, Katie kissed Crispin. 'I'm really sorry, babes. I'll make it up to you tomorrow. I'll come round after work, yeah?'

'Whatever,' Crispin said.

Before there could be any further argument, she had darted into the Tube, slipped her travelcard into the machine and was being carried down the escalator.

Once she was sitting on the Central Line, she wondered why the baby question had freaked her out so much. Of course she wanted a baby – just not yet. Her career was finally taking off and besides, none of her friends had one. Well, all right Clare did, but since little Peter's arrival Katie no longer truly considered her a friend – fussing as she did all day about nappy rash and organic mush. What was the rush? Why should she and Crispin change the easy pace of their relationship?

She thought of Ally putting up with grouchy Jon all so she could get impregnated. It made her feel slightly guilty. Maybe she should offer Crispin to Ally, she thought, smiling. Now *that* would be good service.

She changed at Bank and took the Northern Line down to Elephant. As soon as she got outside, her phone started ringing. 'Oh, shut the fuck up,' she snapped, reaching inside her bag to turn it off.

Normally the flat was full of cooking smells and loud music, but tonight it was strangely quiet.

'Hello?' she said, pushing open the living-room door.

Ronan and Jess were sitting there in semi-darkness. Jess had her defiant look on her face. Ronan looked grim.

'What's happening? Jess, sweetheart, are you OK?'

Jess wouldn't look at her. 'I'm fine.'

'It's her behaviour that's been bad,' Ronan said. Why did he look so annoyed? Jess was always behaving outrageously and they all laughed about it.

'Oh, what have you done now? Raided Ronan's chocolate stash again?'

'I slept with Gordon,' Jess said.

Gordon? It took Katie a moment to register. 'Gordon? As in Jenny's boyfriend?'

'Yeah, but he's not her boyfriend any more. They've split up.'

'I'm not quite sure Jenny sees it that way,' Ronan said.

How did Ronan know so much about it? But of course, he was Rebecca's cleaner now. 'I was at Rebecca's when she got the news,' he explained. 'She's pretty pissed off about it.'

I bet she is. 'Jess! How did it happen?'

'I went round to clean after the party. Gordon and I had a laugh. Jenny had to go out to meet you, so we had a couple of beers, listened to some music.' She caught Katie's eye. 'Nothing happened that night!'

'So when did it?'

'After he and Jenny split up. He called me and we went for some drinks. He needed someone to talk to.'

'How come he had your number?'

'I'd given it to him. He was going to put in a word for me with Ben. After all, *you* hadn't.'

'Ben? Oh. Ben!' Katie said dismissively. 'So what's the deal now?'

'Well, we slept together. Last night. And it was . . . nice.'

Slept together? Jess never used phrases like slept together. She said shagging or fucking, or perhaps in polite company, bonking.

'Jenny's distraught,' said know-it-all Ronan gloomily. 'She blames it all on you.'

'On me?' Katie was outraged. 'I'm not the one who can't keep my knickers on!'

'Oh, fuck off,' said Jess and haughtily left the room, head held high just like they had taught her in drama school.

The phone started ringing. 'I'll get it,' Ronan said wearily. 'Hi. Yeah, hi, Rebecca. Yeah, she's back now. I'll get her.'

He rolled his eyes as he handed Katie the phone.

'Katie!' Rebecca was using her headmistress voice. Katie

had almost forgotten how scary she could be. 'Why's your mobile switched off?'

Shit, she had forgotten about that. 'Oh, sorry, Rebecca. The battery's flat. Listen, I'm really, really sorry about Jess.'

'Why?' said Rebecca. 'It's not your fault.'

Katie was taken aback. 'Well, no . . . but, you know . . .'

'You know I don't like Jess,' said Rebecca. 'I don't know why you and Ronan hang out with her. But Gordy and Jenny had split up. He can do whatever he wants.'

'Uh. I guess so.'

'Jenny's furious with me, but it'll blow over. Always does. This is probably the shock she needed. After this she might value Gordy a bit more.'

'I hope so.' *If they ever get back together*, Katie thought.

'I gather you told Jenny she should leave Gordon. She thinks it's because you wanted your cousin to get in on the act. I think I've managed to convince her that's rubbish. But I wish you'd told me what your advice was. I don't understand where you were coming from.'

'Sorry, Rebecca. But I had my reasons. Jenny told me a lot of stuff I don't think she'd told anyone else.'

'Well, whatever. Suzy says the whole relationship was a lot shakier than I realized and something like this would have happened sooner or later. So I guess I can't blame you. I'm still a satisfied customer at any rate.'

'That's great,' Katie said a little nervously. She wasn't quite sure where this was going.

'Anyway, that's not why I'm calling. I've read your column, Katie, and I think it's great. If truth be told, it's far better than I expected. I forwarded it to Suzy and she loves it too. In fact, she's really excited. She wants to give you a big launch: plenty of publicity. You know, a couple of interviews with tabloids, maybe an appearance on *Breakfast Today*. So well done. I'm really pleased. It's all gone exactly according to plan.'

'Thanks, Rebecca,' said Katie. She wasn't really taking it all in.

'I was thinking a feature about you and Crispin could be nice. You know, "Behind every great woman, there's a gorgeous man". You'd get a nice set of pictures of the pair of you out of it.'

'I don't think so,' Katie said quickly.

'Well, whatever,' Rebecca said again. She didn't sound remotely bothered. 'Come into my office tomorrow and we'll talk about it more. Ten OK?'

'Fine.'

'Bye then. Oh, and say hi to Ronan. Tell him he did a great job in my bathroom.'

Katie passed on the message, but it made her feel surprisingly jealous. Rebecca had never praised *her* skills with the Mr Muscle.

45

Katie's life had become a whirl. Rebecca had fixed up interviews with *The Times*, the *Sunday Standard*, the *Daily Express* and the *Correspondent*, starting today at the Greenhall and Graham offices.

Katie thought she would be nervous, but as she clunked there on the Tube, her mind was on other things.

I must tell Crispin tonight, I must tell Crispin tonight. He would be very angry if he found out any other way, and rightly so. Relations were dodgy enough as it was.

She called him when she left the Tube. He sounded harassed.

'I was thinking of coming over tonight,' she said.

'God, Katie, it's not brilliant. I mean, I'd love to see you, but I don't think I'll be able to leave chambers before eleven.'

'No problem. Tomorrow then?'

'Tomorrow'll be the same. I'm sorry.'

'Well, what about the weekend?'

'Oh, didn't I tell you? The weekend's out. Mum and I are going to Spain.'

Crispin's mum – to whom he was naturally devoted – was a widow and slightly bitter about the cards life had dealt her. Crispin and his two brothers were trying to jolly her up by encouraging her to buy a flat in Spain, so she could sit out the long British winters and make a nice rental income in summer. Every month one of the sons would accompany her on an EasyJet flight to Malaga, where they would have a tense weekend criticizing properties and drinking Sangria. Katie always offered to accompany them, but Crispin told her it would be hell and to put the idea right out of her mind.

'Oh. Well, have a great time,' she said. 'When will you be back?'

'We're flying back Sunday evening. So assuming the flight's not too delayed, I'll definitely see you Sunday night.'

So she would tell him on Sunday night. Giving her the whole weekend to work out what to say.

The guy from the *Correspondent* was tall and skinny with bad skin. Katie disliked him on sight, but she pretended he was her oldest friend, just like Rebecca had told her to.

'I mean, what exactly is the point of a love trainer?' he sneered. There was something green stuck between his teeth. 'Aren't there enough agony aunts and shrinks and gurus in this world?'

'Well, the love trainer is something different,' Katie said, and went on to explain how she was in the business of quick, face-to-face, no-nonsense advice. 'What your best friend would love to tell you, but doesn't dare,' she said earnestly.

'And how can you possibly apply the principles of dog training to your love life?'

Katie waffled on about hunter-gatherers and he seemed satisfied. They talked a bit about her background ('So your degree's in history? How does that equip you for sorting out people's emotional lives?'), but he didn't really seem interested. He didn't ask if she had a boyfriend.

'I hope that was OK,' said Rebecca after she'd ushered him out, all smiles and charm. 'I was expecting another journalist who's a mate, but his kids are sick so they sent that guy in his place.'

After that, the *Sunday Standard* interview proved surprisingly painless. Dee, the journalist, was dark, toothy and matronly, quite unlike the power bitch Katie had imagined. She oohed and aahed at the cleaner story. 'Our readers'll love it!' she cried. 'Rags to riches.'

'Well, I'm not rich. And it was hardly rags before.'

Dee leaned forward and winked at her. 'So who is the special someone in the love trainer's life?' It took Katie a second to work out what she meant.

'There is someone,' she said, just as Rebecca had instructed her. 'But he's a very private person. I'd love to tell you all about him, but he's not having any of it.'

'Fair enough,' said Dee, completely unperturbed. 'So, Katie, any words of advice for our readers struggling with their love lives?'

'Well, Dee, every case is different, so I don't like to generalize. But the basis of love training is the same as in dog training. Make sure you are leader of the pack.'

'Too true, too true,' said Dee, chuckling and switching off her tape-recorder. 'Well, I'll send in the photographer now.' She leaned forward and kissed Katie on both cheeks. She smelt of Anaïs Anaïs. 'Bless! It's been lovely meeting you, Katie. Best of luck, sweetheart.'

'You see,' Rebecca chirped, after Katie's pictures had been taken. 'Nothing to this media star business.'

Katie found herself agreeing. Tara made them cups of tea and Katie told her about the lunch with Ally. Rebecca was delighted.

'You've talked sense into her at last. You are a *goddess*, Katie.'

She was looking stunning in a lacy shirt and leather trousers. Katie wondered if she'd been having plastic surgery. Or sex. But surely Rebecca would tell her about that.

Katie spent the rest of the week doing interviews for various local radio programmes as well as *Dogs Today*. By Friday night she was knocked out. She stayed in alone and watched TV.

On Saturday she rallied and spent the day shopping. That night she went round for supper at her old friend Barnaby's. She told him all about the love training and he squealed with excitement.

'You're gonna be a star, Katie! Oh, this is so exciting. I'll say I knew her way back when.'

'Oh, shut up.'

'I've got a love-training problem for you. I'm madly in love with this bloke I met in the gym called Guy.'

'Tell me, tell me,' she squawked, although Barnaby falling in love was hardly unusual.

'He's everything I want in a man,' he continued. 'You know, grey hair, deep-set blue eyes, domineering.'

'Is he a Tory MP?' Barnaby was the head of marketing for a major drinks brand, but his dream was to be an MP's 'wife' where his days would be spent hosting light lunches, his evenings making dinner-party small talk and his nights trussed up in a gimp suit, a love slave to some cold-hearted public schoolboy.

'No, he works for Lambeth Council. But that's not the problem. The problem is he's married.'

Katie sighed. Where had she heard this before? She trotted out all the usual if-he's-cheating-on-his-wife-he'll-cheat-on-you spiel.

'You're so right,' said Barnaby. 'Treat him like a dog,' he giggled. 'Maybe I should buy him a muzzle and a choke-chain.'

He clearly hadn't taken in a word she'd said.

It was a beautiful summer night lit up by a harvest moon. They sat talking in his little Kennington back garden until three. She got a minicab home. The house was deserted. Heaven knows where Ronan was, while Jess – she guessed – was at Gordy's. Katie hoped she would at least make an appearance in the morning, so she could consult her about the Crispin problem.

She watched a bit of telly and went to bed at four.

She woke at eleven. The telephone was ringing. She let it click on to answerphone and shut her eyes.

But immediately her mobile started.

She fumbled around in her half-darkened bedroom and retrieved it out of her bag.

Crispin.

He was probably calling to tell her the flight had been delayed. She almost switched it off. She'd been hoping to snooze for another hour. But maybe it was important.

'Hi, babe.'

She had never heard him so angry. 'Katie, what the fuck is going on?'

'Crispin, where are you?'

'I'm at Malaga airport. Katie, what is this about a love trainer?'

When in doubt, delay. 'A what?'

'A fucking love trainer! Katie, you heard me. It's all over the *Correspondent*. The chattering classes' latest guru. Katie Wallace.' He put on a silly girl's voice. '"Basically, it's very simple. There's nothing like the unconditional love you get from a dog. You just have to train men to behave the same way." Katie, what are you doing? Why didn't you tell me about this?'

'I was going to. Tonight.'

'Tonight? Katie, my mates have been calling me all morning, taking the piss, wanting to know what this is about. I had to drive to the airport to get a copy.'

'I don't know how it happened. The article wasn't meant to go in for a couple of weeks.'

'Oh, Katie, don't give me any of your excuses. You've been making them for months. All this shit about cleaning for Rebecca.' Suddenly his voice caught.

'Crispin, I'm sorry. I can explain . . .'

'I'm not sure you can.'

'I thought you'd think love training was stupid,' she said in a small voice.

'Well, it is stupid. But that's not what I care about. I care about you lying to me. I'll call you when I get to Luton.'

He hung up.

46

Katie pulled on a jumper over her pyjamas and rushed down the road to the corner shop. What on earth could they have said about her? She seized a copy of the *Correspondent* and wildly flicked through it. Politics, war, famine, ah! Here it was on page 17, a picture of Katie grinning coyly next to a fat sheepdog that belonged to the photographer.

Heart thumping, her head both hot and cold, she speed-read the article. Its tone was sneering. Katie, came the message loud and clear, was a con artist taking money from silly women who should know better. A box to the side contained a list of other 'must haves' for society girls. They included an astrologer, a colonic irrigator and a stylist.

It was so unfair. They had taken her words and twisted them into something quite different. Hundreds of thousands of people would have read them and there was nothing Katie could do about it. She was powerless.

She spent the rest of the day leaving messages everywhere for Rebecca. She didn't reply. Everyone else in Britain appeared to have read the *Correspondent* though and the phone rang non-stop.

Some of Katie's friends laughed at her, but, surprisingly, more were impressed that she had made it into the paper under any circumstances, however humiliating.

'God,' sniggered her old mate Fergus admiringly. 'I didn't know you were a sex trainer.'

'Not sex, Fergs. *Love*. I deal with people's love lives.'

'But you like to do it doggie-style?'

Thank God Mum and Dad were on a seven-day tour of Alaska and completely uncontactable.

Suzy's call came early in the afternoon.

'Well, all publicity is good publicity, I suppose.'

'I'm very sorry.'

'Katie, it's not your fault. Anyone could have been stitched up like that. If anyone's to blame it's Rebecca. I told her to let our in-house publicity people handle this, but she insisted.'

'Have you spoken to her?'

'No, I can't find her. You?'

'No.'

Suzy sucked at her teeth. 'Silly cow. She'd better surface soon. I've got some Dee woman from the *Sunday Standard* going mental. Apparently Rebecca promised her she could run the story first. But the *Correspondent* broke the embargo. I've told her it's not my problem and it's Greenhall and Graham she should be dealing with.'

'Does this mean the column can't go ahead?' Katie asked.

'Oh, Katie, of course it doesn't!' Suzy laughed. 'All these insecure women will read the article and say how silly and then sneak out and buy *Seduce!* to find out more about you. Dog owners will love it too.'

'Well, if you're sure.'

'Trust me.'

Suzy was being so nice, Katie almost started telling her

about her angry boyfriend flying back from Spain. She stopped herself. If Suzy knew the love trainer couldn't keep her man, she might be less sympathetic. For the rest of the afternoon she sat by the phone, feeling like Mary Queen of Scots in her dungeon.

At seven the call came from Crispin.

'I'll see you at eight,' he said, his voice icy.

She took the Tube to his place. Her limbs felt impossibly heavy, but at the same time as light as helium. There was a roaring in her ears.

He opened the door, his face blank. Katie leaned forward to kiss him but he ducked away. Turning his back, he walked into the living room. Katie followed.

'So now are you going to explain?' he asked.

Katie tried. Just as she'd promised herself, she told him the whole story, trying to leave nothing out. Crispin listened. Sometimes he looked sceptical, sometimes hurt, but most of the time his face showed absolutely nothing.

'So I didn't tell you because I knew you'd think it was silly, and I didn't think it would ever come to anything and I didn't see the point in us falling out for nothing.'

'But you're my girlfriend, Katie. I tell you everything. Why can't you do the same?'

'I just didn't want to upset you.'

'But don't you see? I can't trust you any more, Katie. What else have you been lying about?'

'Nothing, Crispin. I swear I've always been straight with you.'

Katie had a sudden flicker of *déjà vu*. Her and Paul talking on the phone late in the night all those years ago, when she had discovered he hadn't gone to Oxford. 'I've

391

always been straight with you,' he said. But Paul had lied to her about a lot of things.

Katie remembered something else. That lunch with Ally. Only three days ago. It seemed like years. *The only reason to stay with someone is because you can't bear to live without them.* That was what she had told Ally and she had really meant it. She had stayed with Paul despite the deception and the mind games, because she thought her life would be meaningless without him. Of course that had turned out to be crap, but at the time she sincerely believed it.

And why was she staying with Crispin? Because it was safe, because it was easy, because she never lay awake at night, her mind full of snakes, wondering why he hadn't called.

She had suspected it for a while, although every time the thought had popped up, she had tried to suppress it. But it just wouldn't stay down any more.

'So where do we go from here?' Crispin said.

She could stay with Crispin and never feel pain. But she would never feel real love or joy either. Not like she had felt with Paul. And even if Paul had broken her heart, for a while, just a short while, they had had a ball.

It was the last thing she'd expected to say. But now it just came out – like the time she had told Paul she loved him.

'Oh, Crispin. I don't want to be with you any more.'

He was ashen with shock.

'Katie, what are you talking about? We're just having a silly row. Of course you want to be with me.'

'No, Crispin, no, I don't. I haven't done for ages.' And Katie cried her way through two mansize packets of tissues and a whole roll of Crispin's loo paper. Then he wept too. They sat on his sofa, arms tight around each other, comforting each other through the sobs.

Eventually Katie disentangled herself. 'I have to go.'

'Stay,' he pleaded.

'I can't.'

He walked her to the door, and on the threshold they held each other for the longest time.

'I'll wait,' Crispin whispered.

And Katie felt like the most evil person in the world.

It was so weird, going home on the Tube as if nothing had changed. Other passengers read the paper or stared at the adverts, their faces calm and blank. Had nothing bad ever happened to them. Had they never done something so terrible to another person they wanted to die?

Katie let herself into the flat as quietly as she could, but Jess and Ronan were both sitting in front of the television.

'Heeey, the famous woman!' Jess yelped. 'Weren't they wankers in the *Correspondent*? But fuck, who cares? You're a superstar.'

She stopped as she took in Katie's expression.

'Katie? What is it? It wasn't *that* bad.'

So Katie told them about her and Crispin.

They didn't believe her.

'But you were the perfect couple,' Jess kept saying.

Katie sat on the sofa, clutching a double whisky her cousin had poured her. 'Oh, Jess, no we weren't! You just wanted to think that.'

'You'll get back together,' Ronan tried. 'It's only a blip.'

'No, Ro, it's over.'

'I really liked Crispin,' Ronan said mournfully. 'He was a good guy.'

'I liked him too,' Katie said, and she started to cry again.

Jess hesitated for a moment. Katie *never* cried. Then she put her arms around her and rocked her like a baby. 'There, there. It'll be all right.'

The phone rang. 'That's probably him now,' Jess said.

Ronan had already picked up. 'Hello? Oh hi, Rebecca. Yeah, I know. Look, there's been a bit of a crisis . . .'

Katie was making cut-throat gestures. The last thing she wanted was Rebecca discovering she had split up with Crispin.

'Well, I'm not sure she can come to the phone right now, she . . .'

Jess was never going to be able to handle this. Katie snatched the phone. 'Hello?' Her voice sounded remarkably normal. 'Yes, yes, I know . . . Well, I did try to get hold of you . . .'

'I know,' said Rebecca. 'I was busy, I forgot to turn my phone on. But now that bitch from the *Sunday Standard* is on my case. She's demanding to know what's happened to her exclusive. She says the only way we can make it up to them is by letting her interview you and Crispin.'

'Well, that's impossible.'

'Katie, in the circumstances, I think we have no choice.'

'But it's not up to us, it's up to Crispin. And I know he won't do it.'

'Well, can you just ask him?' Rebecca said pleasantly. 'He may be more understanding than you think. What did he say about the article?'

'He . . . uh . . . he didn't think it was very nice.'

'It wasn't. I should never have trusted that little weasel. But it's not a catastrophe. *If* we get Crispin to do the interview.'

'I'll ask him, but the answer will be no.'

'You do that,' said Rebecca sweetly. 'We'll speak in the morning.'

As soon as Katie put the phone down, she started to sob again.

'Kate, what is it now?' Jess pleaded.

'I'm a fucking awful love trainer. Every relationship I touch turns to shit. Look at my clients: Rebecca's single. Jenny's single. Ally's about to be single and now I'm single.'

'I'm not single,' Jess said smugly. 'Any more. I've been with Gordon all weekend.'

Ronan glared at her, then cleared his throat. 'Well, Katie, you are the one who always said it was better to be single than wasting your time with an arsehole.'

'Crispin isn't an arsehole,' Katie said. 'He just isn't the right man for me.'

Jess and Ronan exchanged worried looks. Katie had told them a million times that there was no such thing as the 'right' man. She must be suffering from shock.

'Katie,' Jess said gently, 'I think you should go to bed. We'll talk about this in the morning.'

'Did you see the *Correspondent*?' Jenny asked Gordon. They were lying in bed, limbs entwined.

'Mmmm,' he said, stroking her thigh. He'd forgotten how soft her skin was.

'I feel like such an idiot. Allowing myself to be conned by that charlatan.'

'Well, you always were a bit gullible,' he said fondly, running his hand through her curls.

'I know,' she said. 'But I've definitely learned my lesson now. Oh, Gordy, I love you so much.'

'I love you too.'

Jenny could hardly breathe with relief. Over the weekend she had gone for some long walks in Sherwood Forest with her sister, Fiona. Fi had told Jenny to keep grovelling. On the way back to London, she'd called Gordon, more out of habit than hope. But to her surprise, he had picked up the phone and suggested she come round.

They talked for two hours. Jenny apologized profusely for everything she had ever done wrong, told him repeatedly how wonderful he was and – with an astonishing effort of will – managed not to berate him over Jessica. After all, she had been planning to snog Fabrice. They were even now, and the knowledge that Gordy wasn't just a fluffy puppy but could bite would make her treat him far, far more carefully in future.

Eventually, she stroked his arm, he put his hand on her back, they exchanged smiles, then leaned into each other and kissed with tongues, like new lovers.

Five minutes later, they were in bed.

But afterwards, Jenny *had* to know. 'Gordy,' she said tentatively. 'It was never really serious with you and that Jessica, was it?'

Gordy thought how only this morning, Jessica had been lying where Jenny was now. Two women in one day! He'd never thought of himself as that kind of guy. It would be something to remember when he was an old man on Viagra, but he didn't think he would make a habit of it. Jess was very sexy and she was fun. She had helped him get a lot of the anger out of his system. But as soon as he saw Jenny standing on the doorstep looking scared, in her long denim coat, he knew that she was what he wanted.

'No, honey, it was just a silly fling. I was hurt, you know. Anyway, what about you and the French guy?'

'I already told you!' she said, nudging him fiercely. 'Nothing ever happened.'

She rolled on to her stomach and kissed his cheeks, his brow, his eyelids, his full lips.

'I love you, Gordon. I'd never cheat on you.'

She rolled out of bed and strolled towards the window. It was growing dark. Time to draw the curtains.

She caught Gordon staring at her naked arse.

'Do you think I've put on weight?' she panicked.

47

The following morning there were pieces about Katie in the *Daily Express* and *The Times*.

'They're really nice,' Ronan said, determined to cheer her up.

'They're not bad,' Katie agreed, although at the moment she absolutely couldn't have cared less. In fact, the *Express* piece was positively gushy – probably because Katie had given the thirty-something journalist some off-the-record advice about her going-nowhere relationship with a twenty-two-year-old member of a boyband. *The Times*'s tone was a bit more arch but still perfectly friendly and they had used a really nice photo of her and a Rhodesian Ridgeback.

A few minutes later Rebecca called. 'You see, it's not a disaster after all. My only problem is that heifer from the *Sunday Standard*. Did you ask Crispin?'

'Tell her he's away on a business trip,' said Katie.

'Did you ask him?'

'Yes, I did. And he said no. I'm really sorry, Rebecca, but there's no way he's going to change his mind.'

'They'll pay you.'

'He won't take their money. It's not going to work.'

'We'll see,' Rebecca had said.

A little later, after Ronan had gone out to the gym, she called back sounding much more friendly. 'Katie, we've had our first book offer. Unsolicited! Howard and Otter are really interested. I've said we'll go and meet them tomorrow. Isn't it fantastic?'

'Yes,' said Katie.

'Oh, and more good news. Jenny and Gordon are back together!'

'That's great,' said Katie, thanking the Lord that Jess had gone out and she'd have a few more hours before breaking the news.

A couple of hours later, Crispin rang. 'I don't understand this,' he said curtly. 'We were always so happy. We have to talk some more.'

Katie couldn't bear the thought of a painful meeting. But she had never forgotten Ian, her boyfriend after university, just turning up at her house late one night and announcing it was over. Katie hadn't been in love with Ian but she had liked him a lot, and she hadn't enjoyed being left forever in ignorance as to why he had gone off her.

But she still needed time to clarify her own thoughts. It would be so easy to rush back into things with Crispin, to pretend none of this had ever happened. And she couldn't do it.

'I think we should leave it a week,' she said. 'Then I'll come round and we'll talk.'

Crispin wasn't happy with this, but he didn't have a lot of choice.

'I still love you, you know,' he warned. 'I'm going to get you back.'

'We'll talk,' Katie said sadly and put the phone down. She was the biggest bitch in the world.

The phone continued to ring all day, more friends who

had seen the papers. Ronan's mum. Jess's mum, Auntie Gillian, calling from Belfast.

'A celebrity in the family! Gran's so excited. She's cutting everything out to put in her scrapbook. But why didn't you warn us?'

'I was going to,' said Katie, touched. 'But it all took off a bit quicker than I expected. Jess isn't here, Auntie G. Oh no! She's just come in.'

The door had slammed. Jess marched in. There was mascara all over her face.

'It's your mum, Jess!'

'I don't want to talk to her! Not now!' Jess marched into her bedroom and slammed the door.

She must have heard. 'Auntie G, she's got someone with her. Can she call you back?'

'Sure she can. And well done again, Katie. You were always such a kind girl. Thinking of others before yourself. I'm not at all surprised you've ended up doing something like this.'

Katie had tears in her eyes. If only Gillian knew how badly she'd messed everything up. But her aunt was such a sweetheart. And married thirty-five years. No need for a love trainer in that house.

'Jess,' she said timidly, knocking on her cousin's door. 'Jess?'

'He's back with that bitch!' Jess shouted through the door.

'Oh?' Katie tried to sound shocked. 'Oh, how awful. Poor Jess.' If Gordon was anything like all the others, Jess would have forgotten about him within the week, she thought.

'This isn't like the others, you know,' Jess shouted, as if she was telepathic. 'I really liked him.'

Katie opened the door. 'I know you did.'

'We had something special.'

'I know. Would you like a cup of tea?'

'What is this? Fucking *EastEnders*?'

'A whisky?'

'I should hope so.'

Katie was pouring two large ones. The phone rang again.

'Oh, who the fuck is it this time?' She grabbed the handset. 'Hello?'

'Is that Katie?' It was a man's voice. Posh. Amused. Katie recognized it, but she couldn't quite place it. Maybe one of the journalists she had met the previous week.

'Yes.'

'Thought so. Although these days you're so famous I'm surprised you haven't got someone to answer the phone for you.'

'Who is this?' But as she said it, she knew.

'Oh God, you've forgotten me. Katie, baby, it's Paul.'

48

'Paul? Where are you?' Katie squealed like a dodgy wheel.

'I'm in London,' he squeaked back, imitating her voice.

Her knees felt loose, as if they had lost a screw. 'When did you get here?'

'Oh, a couple of days ago. And there you were. All over the place.'

'From LA?' she interrupted.

'Yeah, LA, that's where I live. I'm here on business.'

'Oh.'

'Lovely to hear you, Paul,' he teased. 'What a nice surprise.'

'Yes, it is,' said Katie faintly. 'A lovely surprise.' She had fantasized about this conversation for years. How she would tell him she was busy and put the phone down. But in reality it *was* a nice surprise. Really nice.

'So how are you, famous girl?'

'Oh, I'm fine. You know . . .' Katie giggled, suddenly hysterical. 'A bit overwhelmed by it all.'

'I bet. But Katie, it's so cool. I had no idea you were going to do something like this. Though you always did like dogs.'

He still remembered. 'But how are you?'

'I'm good,' Paul said. 'Doing really well. But listen, I'd rather tell you in person. Can we meet?'

Katie had rehearsed this too. *No, I'm afraid not, I'm pretty busy at the moment.* It was what she would have told Rebecca or Jenny. It was love-trainer common sense.

'That could be nice.' She sounded far more enthusiastic than she intended. Her call waiting was bleeping. She ignored it.

'Cool. Cool.' He sounded pleased. 'Well, listen, I'm staying at the Charlotte Street Hotel. So maybe we could meet there? Tonight, if you're around.'

'Lovely. What time?'

'Oh, well I don't know.' Suddenly his tone switched to guarded. Paul had always hated making definite plans. 'I tell you what, I'll call you a bit later, when I know my schedule.'

'Do you have my mobile number?' Again she noticed that note of eagerness in her voice. *Why are you being so nice to him? He hasn't contacted you in years.* But it was OK. Paul wasn't a boyfriend, he was a friend. She was getting over Crispin and she was just pleased to see him after so long.

'No, I don't, give it to me.' She did. 'Well, listen, I've gotta run. But we'll speak later. *So* nice to hear your voice.'

'And yours.' But he was gone.

Katie stood very still. She felt dazed, as if she had walked into a door.

It's been a tough few days, she told herself. *You're stressed. A drink with Paul will cheer you up.* Shame she had just split up with her long-term boyfriend. She didn't want Paul to think she was a loser. But then she remembered that every paper she had been in had mentioned her 'mystery man'. Well, that was all Paul needed to know. She would show him her life was great now, without filling him in too precisely on any of the details.

The phone rang. 'Hello,' she said. She tried to sound nonchalant and amused.

'Katie, are you OK? You sound weird.' Rebecca again. 'So listen, here's the deal. There's a big party tonight for Gail Anderson.' Gail Anderson was, in Katie's opinion, a totally unfunny comedian from New York, legendary for her plastic surgery. 'We're going to go and I'm going to introduce you to the guys from Howard and Otter and then afterwards we're all going to go out for dinner. Much more fun than a boring meeting in an office.'

'Oh, I can't do that.'

'Why not?'

'An old friend's in town.'

'Well, cancel her,' Rebecca snapped. 'This is really important, Katie.'

'Well, so's this.'

'Look, we can't blow this. You can see your friend tomorrow night.'

'I'm not sure if – er – she's free tomorrow.'

'Well, call her and find out.'

'OK, OK,' Katie said miserably. She realized Paul hadn't left a mobile number.

'So the party's at the Sanderson,' Rebecca bubbled on. 'Totally A-list. Now, if I were you I'd go and get your hair done and buy a nice outfit.'

Who did Rebecca think she was? Ivana Trump? 'That's a good idea.'

When she hung up, she tried to work it out. She could call the Charlotte Street Hotel and leave Paul a message. That was what a love trainer should do. *Sorry, but we'll have to have a rain check, I'd forgotten I had a prior engagement. Gail*

Anderson's party, you know. Actually, that made her sound like a complete arsehole. But Paul would be impressed. He had always been in awe of celebrities.

But at the same time, she really didn't want to cancel. She had no idea how long Paul was in town, how busy he might be. Besides, it was rude to blow him out for a better offer.

'Are you all right?' said Jess curiously behind her.

'Never better!' Katie turned round and inspected her cousin's puffy face. 'How about you?'

'Oh, I'll survive.' Jess grinned. 'Men. They're all wankers. But we knew that, didn't we, Katie?'

'We sure did.' Katie was very tempted to confide in Jess about Paul. But it would be insanity. Jess had spent the past two years cursing the day Paul was born, inventing ingenious forms of torture for him.

Anyway, she was coming back to her senses. The more she thought about it, of course she was going to cancel. This was a big night for her career. There was no way Katie was throwing it all away for the man who had broken her heart.

By six, Katie had lifted the phone to dial the Charlotte Street Hotel three times, only to put it down again, undecided. Four times she picked up her mobile to check she hadn't missed a call. Nothing. Well, Paul was probably working.

Meanwhile, Rebecca was hassling her for an answer. So in the end, Katie made up her mind. She would go to the party and the dinner and afterwards – if he was still interested – she would meet Paul. Rebecca would be happy,

Paul would be impressed by her glittering social life, and the Sanderson, after all, was only five minutes' walk from Charlotte Street. She'd checked in the *A to Z*.

Eager for a distraction, Jess helped her with her makeup and blow-dried her hair. Katie put on her prettiest matching M&S underwear and her foxiest green dress from Karen Millen that made the very best of her curvy figure.

'That's the dress you wear to weddings,' Jess said.

'I know,' Katie said defensively. 'Gotta look my best for the publishers.'

'A head transplant might help.'

Katie sighed. 'I know, but my plastic surgeon's on holiday in Barbados.'

By 7.30 p.m. she still hadn't heard from Paul. He'd be in touch, she told herself, ignoring the knot in her stomach. She decided to treat herself and get a minicab into town.

On the way, she smiled at herself in the driver's mirror.

'Just checking my teeth for lipstick,' she explained, catching his eye.

'No need to make excuses,' he laughed. 'A girl like you should be arrested for being too pretty.'

Normally Katie would have snubbed such a sleazebag, but tonight she smiled graciously. She hoped he meant it.

Inside the party it was hot and very noisy. Her phone was tucked in her little red handbag. Katie realized it would be difficult to hear it ring. She would have to hold it in her hand, so she could feel it vibrate.

She spotted Rebecca straight away, talking to two men in suits.

'Katie!' she shrieked. 'Come and say hello!'

Rebecca introduced her to Jake and Stuart from Howard and Otter.

'So nice to meet you, Katie,' Jake said. 'We're so excited about this love-training concept.'

Katie automatically noted Stuart's wedding ring. So he would be no good for Rebecca. Jake might be all right though, but perhaps he was a little young.

The four of them chatted away, but Katie's mind was on her phone, tucked motionless in her hand. She had a glass of champagne in the other, which made her gestures slightly awkward.

Jake noticed. 'Expecting a call from your mystery man?'

Katie jumped slightly and caught Rebecca's eye. 'Yes, yes, I am. He's out of town at the moment.'

'Not very love-trainer to be hanging on the telephone,' Jake said.

'Well, after – what is it, Katie? – three years, you can relax a little bit,' Rebecca said, smiling.

Normally it would have been a great evening. The place was packed with stars – Katie spotted Ulrika Jonsson, some of the boys from Blue and Fergie – and the canapés were delicious. Rebecca introduced her to lots of people, who told her how wonderful the love-training idea was and how she should meet their friend, who was totally hung up over this useless womanizing bastard. They kept asking for business cards.

'We'll get you some done tomorrow,' Rebecca promised.

But Katie's phone didn't ring, even though it had a perfect signal and was fully charged.

The four of them left about nine. 'I thought we'd go to L'Etoile in Charlotte Street,' Stuart announced.

Katie's heart lurched. Charlotte Street. Where Paul's hotel was. Maybe they would bump into him in the street. He'd say, 'Katie, thank God, I'd lost your mobile number and I didn't know how to track you down.'

They strolled around the corner to Charlotte Street. The others were all laughing and joking, a little drunk. Despite all the champagne, Katie felt completely sober. Nor was she hungry.

At dinner, Jake and Stuart talked excitedly about the book.

'We've got to discuss figures with the rest of the team,' Stuart said as, two hours later after seemingly never-ending orders of liqueurs, they got up to leave. 'But I've got a feeling it's going to be good news.'

'Well, just remember that four other companies are sharking around,' Rebecca said firmly. 'I've spent all day putting them off.'

'I didn't know that!' Katie gasped.

Jake laughed. 'You didn't know because it's not true. Becky's just trying to create a buzz, aren't you, darling?'

'Oh, fuck off,' said Rebecca cheerfully.

They stood on the street, waiting for taxis. Katie could see the Charlotte Street Hotel on the other side of the road. She shivered. Autumn was coming. Normally it was her favourite season, time to throw away her razor and develop a new layer of fat, but now the thought of the summer ending made her unutterably sad.

'Where are you heading, Katie?' Jake asked.

'The Elephant,' Rebecca answered for her.

'Perfect, I'm in Camberwell. I'll drop you off.'

So Katie's plan of popping into the hotel and asking

408

them to call up to Paul's room was scuppered. She had no choice but to share a taxi with Jake, who belched loudly all the way to South London.

'Sorry,' he said. 'I've got terrible digestion problems. Drives my girlfriend mad.'

'What does she do?'

'She's a risk analyst for a German bank. Very high-powered. We have nothing in common.'

'Oh, I'm sure that's not true,' Katie said, bored.

He grinned and stroked her arm. 'You're very sweet.'

A wave of depression swept over her. Why were all men such shysters? The car stopped outside King Kebab.

'Is this where you live? Bloody handy when you fancy a doner.'

What an original remark. 'Good night, Jake.'

'Good night. Speak soon.' He blew her a kiss. She smiled grimly.

She felt such a fool, she thought, as she fumbled in the red bag for her keys. How could she have fallen for Paul's bullshit all over again?

If she'd seen him, she would have slept with him. She could admit that to herself now. Thank God he'd blown her out, so she could remember just what a prick he was.

49

Katie went straight to bed, but it was a while before she fell into a light sleep. Nine hours later, she was woken by Jess knocking on her door, holding the phone at arm's length, like a used nappy.

'It's for you,' she said. She wrinkled her nose and whispered loudly, 'It's that cunt, Paul!'

'Oh right,' said Katie, throwing off the duvet.

'Why's he calling?'

'He's in town. Now give that to me.'

Jess gave her a very hard look. 'Well, just remember he's a tosspot,' she hissed.

'I'm under no illusion there,' Katie snapped.

Jess slammed the door.

'Glad to see Jess is still as charming as ever,' Paul remarked.

'Hello, Paul.'

'Katie, sweetheart, I'm *so* sorry about last night. I was in a meeting until eight and then they insisted we went straight to dinner and we didn't leave until midnight and I thought it would be too late to call you.'

'You could have called me earlier.'

'I know, I know, I should have, but I kept thinking the meeting was going to end. And then at dinner I was jammed right in the middle of a booth. I couldn't get out.'

'You couldn't use your mobile phone at the table?'

'No, I couldn't.' Paul sounded hurt. 'It wasn't that sort of restaurant.'

Katie remembered herself. 'Well, don't worry, Paul. It's cool. I had a party and a dinner and I didn't get out until midnight either. It just wasn't meant to be. Never mind. Maybe we'll see each other next time you're in London.'

'Oh no, Katie, that's no good. I'm dying to see you. I've missed you so much, you know. Can't we reschedule for tonight?'

'I'm busy.'

'Don't be like that!' he laughed. 'I've travelled thousands of miles just to see you. Surely you can find a window?'

'Not really.'

'Just half an hour? For old times' sake. I'll buy you lots of strawberry daiquiris. They were always your favourite, weren't they?'

'Just half an hour,' Katie said. 'But then I have to go.'

'I'm sure I'll persuade you to stay.'

'No, Paul, you won't.'

'OK, Mrs Serious! What time suits you?'

'Six-thirty?' No one could end up in bed with someone at 6.30 in the evening. She'd be away by 7 p.m., home in time for *EastEnders*.

The day passed in a blur of phone calls, something Katie was getting used to. *Seduce!* were already on to her next case study. 'It's one of the work experience girls' best friend from school,' Gemma told her. 'She thinks her boyfriend might be gay.'

'I don't think you get gay dogs,' Katie said. This canine theme was becoming a bit of a burden. She felt as if she was on autopilot. With a start she realized she'd hardly given Crispin a thought all day. All that was on her mind was Paul. But only so she could show him how well she was doing, she told herself firmly.

As evening approached Katie dressed again. Her brown leather skirt (Crispin had given it to her for her birthday, she thought with a pang) and blue, silky top that did a lot for her tits. Her favourite slingbacks. Hair up, just a little makeup. She wasn't going to have sex with Paul, but she was still going to let him see what he was missing.

She thought she was prepared for the sight of him, but when she saw him her heart almost stopped. He was sitting at a corner table on a low armchair, a strawberry daiquiri and a beer in front of him. Still a bit chubby, still that cheeky schoolboy's face and curly hair. Her hands were clammy. It was like she was still back in the newsroom, fresh out of college and ripe to fall in love.

He saw her, grinned and stood up.

'You look gorgeous,' he breathed.

'Thanks.' It was as if someone else was saying her words. 'I see that all that sun and surf hasn't helped *you* shed the pounds.'

He shrugged. 'It's my hormones, I swear.'

'Bollocks,' she said, nodding at his glass. 'You just drink too much beer.'

'Possibly, possibly.' He gestured to the other chair. 'Anyway, Katie, sit down. How *are* you? I want to hear everything.'

'Really good.' Dazed as she was, at least she was remembering the script.

'So it seems. You've got to tell me all about it. Love

412

trainer.' He chuckled. 'Well, you always kept me in order.'

'That's not quite how I recall it,' Katie said drily.

'Anyway, plenty of time for all that.' He waved his hand expansively in the air. 'So much to catch up on! How's your old witch of a cousin? And your parents? Still globe-trotting?'

This, she remembered, was the difference between Paul and Crispin. Paul always wanted to know the gossip. Crispin thought idle chat was a waste of time. She'd missed it: lying in bed, assassinating their acquaintances, laughing at their work colleagues, analysing Jess's sluttiness.

'They're all fine,' she began. 'Mum and Dad are in Alaska and Jess has just had her heart broken . . .'

'That ball-breaker. Never!'

Katie drank her daiquiri and then another one. She glanced at her watch. An hour had passed already.

'Told you, you couldn't resist.'

'My next date's at eight-thirty,' she lied. 'So there's a bit of time. But if you're busy . . .'

He put his hand on her arm and she felt that old, familiar flutter between her legs.

'I'm doing nothing,' he said.

She decided she would have just one more daiquiri. Paul was on his fourth beer. She felt a little woozy now, but what the hell. She was catching up with an old friend, demonstrating that the murky past could be transformed into a sweet present.

She told him all about Rebecca and Jenny and Ally and the cleaning and he bawled with laughter and said it was the funniest story he'd ever heard.

'Rebecca's Australian, right?' he asked her. 'Where's she from?'

'Uh. Sydney, I think. But she's lived here for years.'

He went to the loo, returning with a fourth daiquiri.

'And what about this mystery man of yours?' he asked, raising an eyebrow suggestively. 'Are you going to tell me who he is?'

'No. Otherwise it wouldn't be a mystery.'

'Oh, come on, Katie.' He leaned in close. 'I need to know who my rival is.'

'Well, his name's Crispin. But . . . actually, we've split up.'

Paul choked back a laugh. 'Sorry, Katie. I am sorry. It's just not very love-trainer, is it?'

'I know,' she agreed. 'And don't be sorry, it just wasn't working out.'

'Crispin what? Do I know him?'

'McKeith,' she said absently. 'And no, you don't know him. Anyway, Paul. What about you? What's happening in your life? How's work?'

He was leaning forward as if he was tying his shoelace, but he straightened up. 'Work's really good. I'm freelance now, doing loads of stuff for all the US networks – TV as well as radio. And I'm writing for some of the papers as well.'

'That's great,' Katie said sincerely. She'd wanted to hate him, but she was genuinely pleased for him, as she always was for anyone with good news. Paul had always wanted to break into newspapers. 'And still living near the beach?'

'Still living near the beach.'

'So what exactly are you doing here?' Paul had been vague when she'd asked him earlier.

He blushed. 'Well, actually, I'm thinking of coming home. So I've been meeting up with some radio and newspaper people, seeing if there are any jobs available.'

Paul was coming home. 'So they booted you out for crimes against the body beautiful.'

'And for totally failing to learn to surf. Those waves are huge, Katie. They scare me.'

'You wussy,' Katie laughed.

'And I'm frightened of sharks,' he whispered, lowering his voice. 'You know? *Jaws*? Dah-dah, dah-dah.' He made a fin motion with his hand while rolling his eyes in exaggerated terror.

It wasn't that amusing, but Katie was a bit pissed. She started to laugh.

Paul leaned forward and gently touched her face. 'I've always had fun with you,' he said.

It just popped out. Just like the time she told him she loved him.

'I've really missed you.'

He smiled. 'I've really missed you too.'

And suddenly they were kissing in the corner of the bar of the Charlotte Street Hotel.

'No,' said Katie, pushing him away.

'Katie,' he said and his voice was strangled.

They started kissing again. And after a bit Paul said huskily, 'Come to my room.'

50

They kissed all the way up in the lift and stumbled down the corridor, lips glued together like molluscs. Paul fumbled in his pocket for his key card. Still holding on to each other, they staggered backwards into the room and fell on the bed, stroking, tasting, inhaling each other's almost forgotten bodies.

On top of her, his erection rubbing against her leg, Paul stopped for a moment and looked hard into her eyes. Suddenly, Katie was taken back to that night years ago in the Brewer's Motel, on the way back from Devon. That was the first time she'd told him she loved him. At the time she'd thought he'd been overcome with emotion. It was only later she realized the look in his eyes was guilt.

For a moment Katie panicked. *What the fuck was she doing here, with this man?* But then he started pushing slowly inside her. She yelped and then groaned.

I love you, Paul, I've always loved you, you're coming back, we'll be together again. She hadn't felt like this in so long.

'To use a dog metaphor,' he breathed, 'you, Katie Wallace, are a sexy bitch.'

When they had finished, he kissed her on the neck.

'Thank you,' he murmured. Then immediately he fell asleep. She pulled herself on to her side and stared at that chubby face. A million emotions wrestled inside her.

Suddenly she felt exhausted. Paul had always done this to her.

They both slept for about an hour.

'I'm starving,' said Katie, when they woke up.

'We'll get some room service,' Paul said.

He ordered two omelettes and a bottle of champagne,

'This is an expensive hotel,' said Katie, lazily flicking through the menu. 'You must be doing well to afford to stay here.'

Paul said nothing, just smiled vaguely.

It was midnight by the time they finished eating. They had sex again, this time more slowly, on the carpet. Katie would have burns in the morning, but she didn't care.

'Shall I stay?' she whispered afterwards, lying on her back and staring dreamily at the ceiling.

Paul looked pained. 'Well,' he said, 'I don't want to be rude, but perhaps you should go. I've got an early start, you see and . . .'

Katie felt a sudden warning stab. 'Well, I've got an early start too.'

'I know,' he said with a gurgly giggle. She'd forgotten how annoying his laugh was. Then he smiled. 'Of course you can stay, if you'd like.'

But Katie was already getting up and pulling on her clothes. 'No, I'll go. Stuff to do tomorrow . . .' She could feel her neck reddening with humiliation. She grabbed a hairbrush from her bag and dragged it through her curls.

Paul had pulled on his fluffy dressing-gown and was looking at her nervously. 'Are you pissed off?' he asked.

'No, no.' She was making every effort to keep her voice

steady. *It's been a one-night stand*, whispered the little voice at the back of her head.

It was like the feeling she got when the lights went up at the end of a really good movie and she realized that instead of sitting in some dream world, she was in a run-down cinema, with Coke stains all over the carpet and polystyrene food cartons everywhere.

Paul had had sex with her because she was there. He was alone in London, he was feeling horny, and he knew he could have her. He'd always been able to play her like a pair of maracas.

Paul didn't love her. He hadn't then, he didn't now. And Katie didn't love him either. But she had wasted years of her life waiting for him, living in an emotional void, hurting poor Crispin, unable to get on with her life.

She had never felt so stupid.

A survival instinct kicked in. She had to go out of there. And she had to get out of there with some dignity. Once she was outside, she could collapse, fall to pieces, lie on the pavement waving both legs in the air.

But she would *never* give that bastard Paul Grant the satisfaction of knowing what he'd done to her.

She kissed him briskly on the cheek. 'Well, it was good to see you,' she said and turned to the door.

'Wait a minute,' he said, placing himself between her and the door. Just then the phone started to ring.

'Oh shit!'

'Aren't you going to get that?'

'No, no, it's not important.'

The phone stopped, but immediately started again.

'Paul,' said Katie, realization dawning, 'who's trying to call you?'

'How should I know?' Suddenly his voice was sharp.

'Well, not many people call your room at midnight.'

'Katie, they'll be calling from LA. It's the afternoon there.'

'Whatever,' Katie said, 'you need to answer it.' She put her hand on the doorknob. 'Goodbye.'

'*Please!*'

'Answer the phone.'

He grabbed it. 'Hello? Oh, hi, hi.' He was trying to sound relaxed. 'No, sorry, I was in the shower. Just got in. Heavy day, here . . . No, it went well. Listen, darling, room service are knocking on the door. Can I call you back in just a minute? Yeah, you too. Bye.'

'Darling?' Katie said.

'Katie, come and sit down.' He patted the bed next to him.

'I don't think so.' She folded her arms about her protectively. 'What's your girlfriend's name, Paul?'

He looked at his feet. 'Actually, she's my fiancée.'

Katie felt a rush of pity for this unknown woman thousands of miles away, enduring the same maelstrom of emotions that had once attacked her.

'So what are you doing in bed with me?'

'I didn't mean to. It just happened.'

'You did mean to! You were plying me with drinks. You wanted to get me pissed and fuck me.'

'You just looked so gorgeous,' he said, touching her arm. 'And it was so good to see you again.'

'Why did you want to see me in the first place, Paul? Because I was famous?' She meant it as a cheap shot and was surprised to see him recoil slightly.

'I saw you in the paper,' he said in a small voice. 'And I remembered how great you were.'

Afterwards Katie could never work out how she spotted it. All she knew was her eyes were drawn to the floor where Paul's trousers lay, tangled with his shirt and belt. Sticking out of one pocket was a notebook. She walked across the room and picked it up.

There in large, loopy letters were Paul's notes. *Rebecca G – Sydney. Jenny – loopy. Ally – married man.* And then scribbled even more hastily: *Crispin McKeith – split.*

'What the fuck is this?' She was trying to keep her voice from trembling.

Paul put his head in his hands. The phone started to ring again. He snatched it. 'Hello? Babe, hi . . . Sorry . . . No, I'm just on the other line . . . Mum . . . Yes, it is late . . . she's an insomniac. Call you back in five, I promise.' He slammed it down.

'Katie, I'm sorry,' he said.

'You were making notes about my love training. You were going to write an article.'

Paul said nothing.

'You called me up because you're trying to make a name over here and you decided to write an article about me. Why didn't you tell me, Paul? Why did you go behind my back?'

Still silence.

Katie flicked through the notebook. On the inside cover, Paul had scribbled Harry Knox, Features, *Sunday Standard* and a phone number.

'You were going to write something for the *Sunday Standard*?'

He nodded sadly.

'Goodbye, Paul,' said Katie, slipping the notebook into her bag. 'I hope I never see you again.'

She shut the door and with leaden legs, walked down the hotel corridor to the lift.

Somehow she got a taxi home. The flat was in darkness and she crept quietly to her room. All night she lay on her bed twisted in a little ball. For the first couple of hours she howled, a duvet stuffed in her mouth, until her throat was raw and her eyes stung. Eventually the bawling subsided into gentle sobs.

She thought she had known pain last time she had been with Paul but this was on a different level. The only time she'd come close was when she'd dumped Crispin. Oh God, how must it have been for him? How had she ended up in this terrible mess?

Katie felt like a warped version of Sleeping Beauty in her castle. For the past few years in a coma. Refusing to feel pain. But then the evil prince had come and kissed her, and with that kiss the spell had lifted and she was wide awake again, to the world and all the evil that was in it.

She felt human again. And she wasn't sure she liked it at all.

Oh my God, how do people get through their lives? And all Katie had done was sleep with a nasty man. How come she was so weak that a few hours with Paul could do this to her? What would happen when she had to face something really terrible like illness or death?

She was a pathetic specimen, she berated herself, and she cried some more.

At dawn, Jess opened the door.

'Not a happy night?' she said gently.

Katie shook her head and started crying again. Between racking sobs, the whole story of last night emerged. Jess listened, horrified. At the end she cradled Katie in her arms. 'Paul is a monkey's anus,' she said quietly. 'He is not worthy to lick the soles of your shoes.'

'I feel such a tool,' Katie sobbed.

'No need. Everyone gets fooled now and then. It's like kidding yourself Guy and Madonna are happily married. You want them to be so much, you ignore the truth.'

Katie giggled, but it transformed itself into a sob. 'But I thought I could deal with it.'

'Hey. We've all been there. All thought that we could change things. That the rules didn't apply to us.' Jess stroked her hair. 'You're going to feel very sad for a while. But you will get over it.'

'I won't. Not ever. Call myself a love trainer, I promise.'

'It's always much easier to advise other people than yourself.'

Since when had Jess become so calm and wise? It was like they'd reversed roles. Katie didn't mind at all, in fact she felt quite peaceful lying there, listening to this soothing voice. But then she remembered herself last night, covering Paul's face and naked body in passionate kisses. She felt hollow with misery.

'You sleep now,' Jess crooned. 'Do you want a valium? I've still got some from my Thailand trip.'

Katie took one, but her dreams were still wild and angry.

51

Ally read all the articles about the love trainer. So did Jon, with much sneering about the vapid ways in which people wasted their money.

'They've earned it, they can do what they like with it,' Ally said once.

'They should be giving it to a fucking charity,' Jon replied. He patted the sofa. 'Come and sit here.'

But Ally had been reading Katie's rules. *Do not respond to requests for attention and affection from your dog. Leaders of the pack are only affectionate when they choose to be.*

'Oh, Al,' he whined. 'Let's get cosy.'

'No, I've got stuff to do,' she said and wandered out of the room.

She went up to her room and read for a couple of hours. When she came down, Jon was very polite.

'Shall we watch *Newsnight* or something else?' he asked. He'd never offered her a choice before.

'Oh, something else, I think,' she said and seizing the remote, started flicking through the channels.

'This is nice,' she said as they sat in front of a documentary about celebrity drug addicts. Normally, it was the kind of thing Jon loathed.

She remembered another rule. *When your dog is good, then is the time to be nice to him. Wait until he is quietly lying down, then go over to him and praise him.*

She leaned over and kissed him on the ear. 'You look nice,' she muttered.

'Oh?' He grinned. 'Thanks.' He turned to her. 'But this programme really is bollocks.'

She smiled back. 'I know. But it's the kind of bollocks I enjoy.'

'Fair enough,' he said. 'But I'm going to bed.'

The only flaw in this otherwise perfect evening was that by the time Ally joined him, Jon was fast asleep.

Still, Ally was very pleased with her advice from the love trainer. And very relieved that putting Jon down no longer figured as an option. Even though she knew Katie was right and there was still time to meet someone else, the thought of the search still made her guts freeze. No, better to creep through life as if she was on a crumbling canyon lip. No false steps, she might go flying into the abyss.

She would count her blessings: OK, Jon could be grumpy but he was her pal too, wasn't he? He listened to her download after work – even if he did growl a lot about filthy capitalism. He accompanied her to parties – even if he wanted to leave early. He was there waiting when she came in late – even if he did sometimes go out and drag her home. He was someone to go on holiday with – although they had never actually had a real holiday together, as any spare time he had was taken up visiting the girls.

He was someone to watch telly with, she thought, slightly cheered. Well, at least they had made such progress on that front tonight.

And then there was the most important thing of all, that one day soon he would give her a baby.

Jon would make a lovely dad. A great house husband. And hopefully now she was training him, his bark would be worse than his bite.

The rest of Katie's week passed in a kind of numbness. Apart from the odd vital trip to the shop, she stayed in, curled up on the bed, paralysed with misery. She felt as if she had been sucked dry by a vampire.

Rebecca was incredibly nice to her. 'Ronan says you're having a bad time,' she'd said in a message. 'So don't worry about anything.'

On Saturday, she and Jess snuggled on the sofa, enjoying an orgy of cheesy movies. Ronan was off – most uncharacteristically – on a lads' holiday in Spain.

'I hope he pulls,' Katie said.

'He hasn't had a woman since Suzy,' Jess sighed.

Katie grinned. 'I'm surprised that experience didn't make him join the priesthood.'

She went to bed feeling a bit better. On Sunday, she woke at eleven and wandered into the kitchen in her pyjamas.

Jess was sitting at the table, looking solemn.

There's more bad news,' she said.

She handed her the paper. It was the *Sunday Standard* opened at page nine. There was a black and white photo of a good-looking man opening the door of a building. He was glancing over his shoulder at the camera and he looked extremely annoyed.

'Oh God,' Katie gasped. 'It's Crispin.'

Beside it was a picture of Katie, looking peculiarly unattractive. The caption underneath said 'liar'.

She read the article. *Love Trainer in Love Disaster*, read the headline. The byline was Dee Padfield. Nice, cuddly Dee, who'd hugged her and said 'Bless.'

Love trainer, Katie Wallace, claims she owes her happiness to a mystery man. But the Sunday Standard *can exclusively reveal that Katie has never been more single.*

This is a picture of Katie's ex-boyfriend, Crispin McKeith, 32. In a heart-to-heart chat, he confided that they split up over a week ago and that the woman who claims to know exactly how to handle her man has been begging Crispin to take her back.

Yesterday, Crispin, a body builder and her lover of three years, said: 'It's all over between me and Katie. I don't know if I'll ever see her again.'

Standing on the doorstep of his luxury home in Islington, North London, the barrister added, 'She's lied to me so many times I don't know what to believe any more.'

Katie, 29, from Elephant and Castle, South London, has a column in Seduce! *magazine, telling readers how to 'get and keep their man'. She is believed to be on the verge of signing a £1 million book deal with publishers Howard and Otter. Last night a spokesman said: 'We will be reviewing the situation.'*

Miss Wallace was not available for comment.

Jess was watching her face as she read. 'I'm sorry,' she said.

'It's not your fault,' Katie said.

To their surprise Katie started to laugh hysterically. 'The bastard sold it to the *Sunday Standard*. Could my life get any worse?'

'The piss-bism,' said Jess, her nose scrunched up in

indignation. 'He will never be safe from me, you know. I'll hunt him down to the ends of the earth and chop his nuts off and feed them to the lions in the zoo.'

Katie's hands were shaking. 'But I took away his notebook. He must have just remembered it all. Has Rebecca called?' she asked, suddenly fearful.

Jess shook her head.

'Oh.'

Just then the phone rang shrilly. They jumped in fright. Then it rang again. Jess picked it up.

'Hello?' she said cautiously. 'Yes? Who may I say is calling, please?' She turned to Katie, whose eyes were open wide with alarm. '*Ben Graham*,' she mouthed.

Ben Graham? For a second, Katie had no idea who Jess was talking about. Then it came to her. Ben! Ben, who disapproved of her. Whose every suspicion about her had been correct.

She felt as if a bird was fluttering violently in her chest. She shook her head. '*Tell him I'm out*,' she whispered.

'I'm afraid she's gone out,' Jess said primly. 'All right. Thanks. I'll tell her. Goodbye.' She put the phone back in the cradle. 'He's going to try the mobile.' And just then Katie's mobile started to trill.

Katie stood and watched it vibrating on the table.

'I think you should get it, Kate,' Jess said gently.

'Do you?' Katie looked at her, terrified. Jess pushed past her, clicked it on and pushed the phone into Katie's hand.

'He . . . hello?'

'Katie!' It wasn't Ben at all. It was a woman. Fuck.

'Oh, hi, Suzy.'

'So I take it you've seen the *Sunday Standard*?'

'I'm afraid so.'

'And have you and Crispin split up?'

'Well. Yes. No. We're having . . . a blip. A temporary separation.'

'Oh,' said Suzy. Katie braced herself for a bollocking, but instead she heard, 'Well, I'm sorry to hear that.'

'Th . . . thank you.'

Suzy snorted with laughter. 'Well, I have to say, at least you're getting us a lot of publicity. When we get the report on how many times we've been mentioned in the national press this month, you'll have brought the average right up.'

'Oh.'

'And I think we could get a nice article out of this. "I trained people to love, but inside my heart was breaking." That kind of thing.'

Not in ten million years. 'Yes. That could be good.' Katie was distracted by the bleeping of her call-waiting.

'So has Rebecca called you?'

'Er, no. Not yet.'

'Well, that doesn't surprise me. She's in Mallorca.'

Is she? Katie hadn't known that. 'Oh yes, yes, so she is. But her phone works in Mallorca, doesn't it?'

'Yes, but she's at a spa, remember? So she probably turned it off. And if she's lucky she hasn't seen the papers yet.'

The call-waiting was still bleeping, meanwhile Jess was fending them off on the landline. 'No, Auntie Minette, she's gone out. You could try her mobile. Oh, it goes straight to voicemail? So how was Alaska? Did you really? Polar bears? No!'

'Well, we'll wait until I get into the office, Katie,' Suzy said. 'See how much damage has been done. In the meantime, don't take any calls from the media. Refer them all to our press office. Do you have a pen? I'll give you the number.'

Katie wrote it down. 'By the way, Katie,' Suzy said, suddenly sounding less sure. 'I meant to ask you something about dogs.'

'Yes?'

'Is it better to have a pedigree than a mongrel?'

Katie didn't understand why she was asking. But she knew the answer.

'Not necessarily. Pedigrees may look a little nicer – because they live up to a received standard of beauty. But they're often completely insane. All those years of inbreeding, you know. Mongrels usually have much nicer temperaments and they're not doolally and they live much longer. My granny had a lovely mongrel. Penny, her name was.'

'Did she indeed?' Suzy said archly. 'Well, thanks for that, Katie. Just . . . interested.'

Whatever, Katie thought as she hung up. Jess was standing in front of her, waving a list.

'So we've had calls from the *Sun*, the *Mirror*, the *Mail*, the *Express*, the *Daily Standard* . . . Oh, fuck off!' she bellowed as the phone rang again. 'And your mum. And my mum.'

Katie looked down at her phone. She had a text. A number she didn't know.

Better open it. With luck it would be some hot sexy Swedish bitch phoneline.

Sorry about your latest troubles. R away for week, I'm dealing with this. Need to talk. Ben Graham.

'I'd better call him,' Katie sighed. But then she remembered.

Crispin! He was the most important person in all of this! What on earth must he be thinking? Could she be a more horrible person? What was she going to do?

She texted him. *More sorry than I can say. Beg forgiveness, know I can't expect it. K x*

The reply came immediately. *Forgiveness possible. Can we meet tonight?*

Katie's eyes filled with tears again. She texted back, *Tonight fine.*

It took her an hour to summon up her courage, but then she called Ben.

He was very nice.

'These things happen,' he said. 'You should just have told Rebecca you'd split up with Crispin. The *Sunday Standard* decided to attack you because we kept fobbing them off with bullshit excuses why the pair of you couldn't give an interview. It's the way it works, unfortunately.'

'Ben, I'm so sorry. I completely screwed it up.'

'Katie, please don't worry.' He sounded as if he really meant it. 'It's our fault just as much as yours. We shouldn't have thrown you to the press like that.'

'No, it's my fault for trying to control everything,' Katie said.

Ben ignored this. 'Everyone's going crazy trying to find you. Tara's telling them you're out of the country. We should meet and decide what we're going to do.'

Katie, who had been pacing around her bedroom, immediately darted to the mirror to check her hair.

'How about tonight?' Ben said.

'Tonight! Oh, I can't! I have to meet Crispin. Apologize to him.'

There was a pause. 'I can understand that,' Ben said. 'But we do need to talk this through.'

'Tomorrow morning?'

'I'm busy in meetings all day tomorrow. We'll have to make it a drink after work. Come to the office and we'll go to the pub. About seven?'

'Fine,' said Katie, thanking the Lord she had an extra day to sort her hair out. 'And should I call Rebecca? I didn't know she'd gone on holiday,' she added plaintively.

Ben paused again. Then: 'No. No. I'll talk to Rebecca. She's having a break, we don't want to overload her.'

Well, at least that was one nightmare she'd been relieved of. 'OK, I'll see you tomorrow then.'

'See you tomorrow. And chin up, Katie. It's all fish and chip paper.'

Crispin was waiting for her in a pub near his flat. He looked thinner than he had done less than a week ago: paler and tauter. She noticed his hair was greying at the sides. They sat in a booth at the back of the bar. He was knocking back his pint. Katie guzzled her glass of red wine with equal enthusiasm.

'I'm so sorry about the *Sunday Standard*,' he told her. 'They just turned up on my doorstep when I was leaving for work on Friday morning. I hadn't got a clue what was going on. But I shouldn't have told them anything.'

'It's OK,' Katie said. 'It's my fault.'

'I don't know how they found me in the first place.'

'Rebecca says the press can get anything they want. They're evil.'

He nodded wryly, then looking up gave her his sweetest, fondest smile.

And Katie knew he was still hoping. That this would get them back together. She had to be straight with him.

She felt as if until now her heart had been held together by Velcro. Now it was being slowly ripped apart.

'Crispin,' she said with a big gulp. 'I did a terrible thing to you. I made you believe you were the perfect man for me for three years, when in my heart I knew we weren't right for each other.'

He stared at her in disbelief. 'But Katie, we were great together. I thought we'd be partners for life.'

Katie thought she had reached her nadir after the night with Paul. But this was much, much worse.

'I think you're a wonderful, kind, clever, handsome guy. I think there's a girl out there who's going to be very, very lucky to get you. I'll probably envy her. But it's not going to be me.'

'Oh God,' said Crispin. He looked dazed. 'I thought we were going to get back together.'

Katie shook her head. 'I wasted your time, Crispin,' she said truthfully. 'I was hung up on another man and I used you to try and take the pain away. You were handsome and clever and so kind to me, and I thought that was more than enough. But I was wrong. It isn't. I don't feel enough for you, Crispin, and I know I could feel that much for someone else. Staying with you wouldn't be fair on me or on you. Because you need someone who adores you.'

It sounded like bullshit, it always did. She deserved to be sent to prison for hurting such a lovely, decent man.

Crispin always kept his cool, it was one of the things she liked about him. But now he grabbed her hand and held it tight.

'Whatever I did wrong, I'll make it better.'

She smiled sadly. 'Crispin, you did nothing wrong.'

'You may change your mind,' he said, still hopeful.

'I won't,' she said in anguish.

'But we'll stay friends?' There was a look of such desolation on his face, she thought she couldn't bear it. The temptation to lie, to tell him it was all going to be fine was overwhelming. But she couldn't do that. He was going through so much hurt, why should she make herself feel better?

'Maybe one day we'll be friends. But not now. Not for a while. You need to be left alone to recover. Seeing me will give you false hope. Make it much more difficult.' She had totally failed as a love trainer, but at least she could remember the rules of breaking up.

Suddenly Crispin's air of defeat turned into anger. 'I don't believe this, Katie. You're making a terrible mistake. You're going to regret this for the rest of your life.'

I think you're going to realize this was the best thing for both of us. But she didn't say it. Instead, she sat there, staring at her hands.

'Goodbye, Katie,' he said.

'Goodbye, Crispin.' She watched him walking stiffly out

of the pub and she knew that she would never see him again.

'I'm sorry,' she whispered to herself. She wondered if there would ever come a time when she could stop apologizing. And then she started to cry, silent tears for poor Crispin who'd loved her and whom she'd never loved back. Guilt mingled with huge relief. She'd really done it now. It was really over. There'd not be another chance.

52

After a lot more tears, Katie woke early the following morning. She mulled over the events of the night before, then thought with dread of what the day held in store.

Ben. Ben who had always looked at her so sternly and disapprovingly, who had sounded so nice on the phone yesterday, but who obviously thought she was a complete idiot. And he was right. She was.

And what really bugged her was she still cared like crazy how she would look this evening.

Jess went out and bought all the papers. There were little stories about her and Crispin in the *Daily Mail* and the *Sun*, but nothing new from yesterday. Katie had passed on all the numbers of journalists who'd called to the *Seduce!* press office and they had obviously fobbed them off with some mind-numbingly dull answers. And today, the phones were almost unnervingly silent.

The time passed somehow: a long bath, a bit of daytime telly, some time reading a detective novel. She almost wished she could go and clean Rebecca's place. But this week Rebecca wasn't even around to clean up after – it turned out that was why Ronan was on holiday.

Finally it was 5 p.m. Time to leave. OK, it had never taken her two hours to get to Greenhall and Graham before, but given what trouble she was in she'd better bargain for public transport meltdown. A bubble of anticipation was blocking Katie's windpipe. She checked herself in the mirror.

'Don't be a prat,' she told her reflection. 'It's work. It's about how you fucked up by telling your dodgy ex all your secrets, which he then sold to a newspaper.'

Still, she did look rather nice tonight. Her curls fell perfectly and her cheeks glowed. She wore a red V-neck jumper and a black pencil skirt. As ever, nothing overtly sexy, but definitely body-hugging.

You're going to sleep with Ben, said her little voice. *No, I'm bloody not*, the other one retorted. *Right after Paul. Are you insane? I'm never having sex with any man again.*

OK, her other voice relented, *maybe not tonight. But one day you will. It's inevitable. It's fate.*

'There's no such thing as fate,' she exploded.

'Talking to yourself again,' said Jess, sticking her head round the door. 'First sign of senility.'

'Well, I've already got the incontinence pads, so what's the difference?'

Jess looked her up and down. 'Look at you!' she exclaimed with a wolf whistle. 'Where are you off to then?'

'To a business meeting,' Katie said. 'With Ben. I'm trying to save myself from a bollocking.'

Jess laughed. 'Well, you shouldn't have a problem there. You look fantastic. No man could resist you.'

Katie arrived way too early at Bond Street Tube and ended up having to window-shop in Oxford Street for an hour until dusk started closing in and it was almost seven.

Arriving at the offices, Katie was hit by an unpleasant wave of *déjà vu* as she remembered her first meeting there with Rebecca. She'd been nervous then, she was terrified now. With Rebecca on holiday, Ben was free to tell her to give up the whole love-training charade.

She should have taken that job with the pizza chain.

'Hi, Katie,' waved Tara as she walked nervously into the office. 'How's it going? We're all so proud of you.' She waved at the chocolate leather sofa in the corner. 'Ben's on the phone, but he'll be with you in five!'

Katie saw him through the glass wall. He was in a suit and tie and there was a serious expression on his face. Once or twice, he slammed his fist down on the desk. But then he looked up, saw Katie, and suddenly smiled.

'Five minutes,' he mouthed at her. She nodded back, smiling herself. He didn't look angry at all. It was like when an aspirin kicked in. Everything felt instantly better.

'Sorry, sorry,' he said, coming out of his office. Katie stood up. There was an awkward moment when he bent towards her as if to kiss her and she stepped back. They both stood and smiled at each other.

'I'm so busy with Rebecca away,' he explained.

'You must be.' *Katie, if you can't say anything interesting, then why don't you just keep your mouth shut?*

'Well. Shall we . . . go to the pub? Or would you like a bite to eat? I'm starving and there's a good Thai place around the corner and . . .' His voice trailed away. 'Maybe you've eaten already?'

'I haven't eaten,' Katie said. *I think he's nervous too*, she thought with a start, and power stirred inside her.

Awkwardly, they travelled down in the lift together, eyes not meeting. He walked briskly along the street, round the corner and into a pink-fronted restaurant. It was dark inside: candles glowed on the table and there was a particularly unpleasant smell of joss sticks.

'Is this OK?' Ben asked. Sweat glowed on his brow.

'It's great,' she said warmly.

They sat down. Ben ordered a bottle of red and a mountain of food.

'So you live at the Elephant, do you?' he said. 'How do you like it?'

'It's fine,' Katie said. 'Handy if you like kebabs. We've got a shop downstairs.'

'I'm in Camberwell,' Ben said.

'Oh really? That's where Jake from Howard and Otter lives.'

'Does he, the little shit? Well, that will have brought property prices right down.'

'Do you own your place, then?'

'I own. You?'

'Oh, I rent. I can't afford to get on the property ladder.' God, were there any two more boring people on God's earth? But then they were in a business meeting.

But as the wine took hold, they relaxed, nattering more stupidly about town versus country, Britain versus the rest of the world.

'I think I'd like to live here eventually,' Katie said. 'But I wouldn't mind doing a stint in another country. I've never really travelled. It's one of my secret regrets.'

'Not a secret now,' Ben smiled. 'But it's not too late, you know. You're hardly in a bathchair.'

He was telling her to go travelling. He thought she had no future elsewhere. 'But if the love training does work . . .'

she began. They might as well get it over with. But then her phone rang.

'Sorry,' she said, pulling it out of her bag. 'I'll get rid of this.' But then she looked at who was calling.

'Actually,' she said more snootily, 'this is business. I'd better take it.' She lowered her voice. 'Hello.'

'Just seeing how you are, baby,' Hunter said.

'I'm fine,' Katie said politely. 'You?'

It was a regular thing: he'd call her and talk a little flirtatiously until Suzy walked in, at which point he'd hang up abruptly. It kept her on her toes. The consequences of Suzy ever finding out were too dreadful to contemplate, but as long as Hunter destroyed his phone bills and paid her in cash, there seemed no reason for her ever to know.

'Couldn't be going better. I've put the offer in on a house in Hampstead and I think she's going to come with me.'

'Lucky Suzy.' Ben looked interested. 'Actually, Hunter, I've really got to go now. I'm with someone. But we'll talk later. Glad it's going well.' She was blushing slightly as she put away the phone.

'That was Suzy's Hunter?' Ben asked.

'Actually it was a private call,' Katie said, but she couldn't help smiling.

He smiled too. 'So you're training Suzy's man.'

'Don't ever tell her!'

'Of course not,' Ben said, still grinning. 'Suzy's man. How hilarious.' His voice suddenly grew stern. 'Don't ever tell the press about it!'

'Er, as if!' Their eyes locked. Katie felt her cheeks grow hot.

'Anyway!' she almost shouted. 'You were saying. I should go travelling.'

Ben looked surprised. 'Well, only if it's what you really want to do.'

'But what about love training?'

He smiled. 'Love training can wait.'

'But what about Greenhall and Graham's cut?' She sounded teasing but she *had* to know why she was there. Was he trying to get rid of her?

'Oh, fuck Greenhall and Graham,' Ben laughed. 'You've got to do what makes you happy.' He looked at the empty bottle and gestured to the waiter. 'Can we have another, please?'

'Do you think I should give up the love training?' she persisted, confused. 'Have I messed everything up?'

Ben looked stricken. 'Hey, Katie. Of course not. You've done a great job. You've got masses of press attention – perhaps a little unwittingly – and Howard and Otter are still foaming at the mouth for this book deal. I'm just saying you shouldn't pursue the love training if other things are going to make you happy.' He put his glass down. 'You've had a tough time recently, haven't you?'

Katie shrugged. Like she was going to tell *him*. 'You play with lions, you get bitten,' she tried. It sounded all wrong.

'Yeah, but . . . . a mauling in the papers. Breaking up with your long-term boyfriend. It can't have been easy.'

'The break-up was long overdue,' Katie said tightly.

'Maybe it was,' Ben said. 'But it's still not easy. I should know, I've bloody been there.'

'Have you?' Automatically, Katie felt her auntie side

switch on. She wanted to know more, to offer advice, to heal.

'Hasn't everyone?' Ben sighed. 'At least, by my bloody age they have. You're still very young, Katie. In fact, I'm amazed you can talk so wisely about misery and suffering.'

'Well, I've been there too,' Katie cried and was shocked when her eyes filled with tears.

Ben leaned over. His hand brushed comfortingly against hers.

'Hey,' he said softly, 'I'm sorry. Do you want to tell me about it?'

'I'm OK,' she said gruffly.

'Well, if you ever do need to talk, I'm here.'

She looked up and their eyes locked. Her body was tingling. Her lips were dry. She wondered what her breath smelt like. Perhaps she should slip to the loo and check her makeup. Or would that kill the moment?

'Katie . . .' he began, when his mobile rang.

'Shit,' he said. 'Excuse me.' He pulled it out of his pocket, then grinned when he saw who it was.

'Hi, babe . . . Yeah, actually I'm in a restaurant . . . with the love trainer. She's giving me some tips.' He grinned at Katie. 'It's Rebecca, she says hi.' He put the phone back to his ear again. 'Yeah, is he? . . . No, of course I won't . . . I won't! . . . Look, I haven't got the flight details on me, but I think I get in around six. I'll call you later . . . Well, have fun . . . Not too much though . . . Yeah, yeah . . . See ya.'

'Are you going to Mallorca too?' Katie asked. There was a horrible feeling in her stomach.

Ben looked shifty. 'Yes, I'm going tomorrow. Just for a couple of days.'

The glow which had been building inside her began to fade. Suddenly Katie felt chilly and very stupid. It all made sense. Ben and Rebecca. They were an item. Of course they were. Rebecca was a glamorous businesswoman from Australia, while Katie was a – well, she was a failure with frizzy hair – from Solihull.

No wonder Rebecca was always in such a great mood these days. Katie had done it again. Got it all wrong. Misread the signals. Failed to see what was happening right under her nose.

It was so embarrassing, she almost laughed. Thank *God*, Rebecca had called when she did. Otherwise, she might have behaved seriously stupidly in front of her boss's man. She swallowed hard.

'More curry?' Ben asked, holding out a dish. He was looking at her quizzically. Katie wanted to slap him.

'Oh, no,' she said, her voice thick. 'No, thanks.' She looked at her watch. 'Actually, I'd better go. Long day tomorrow.' She laughed falteringly. 'But it was a lovely meal.'

Ben stood up. 'Oh, come on, Katie. We've hardly got started. Don't be like this.'

'Like what? I'm just a bit tired. But thanks again. It was lovely.' *Stop using that freaking word.*

Ben's face was a jigsaw of annoyance and confusion. 'Look, it would be polite if you just stayed while I finish my main course.'

'OK,' Katie agreed unhappily, and she sat there while

he picked at his noodles and asked her questions about where she'd like to travel to.

Stop patronizing me. Katie gazed into her glass and answered him as monosyllabically as possible. She knew she was behaving like a baby, but she couldn't stop herself. She really liked this guy. It was the first time in years. She hadn't felt this way about Crispin even. But yet again she'd judged the situation completely wrong. She was an even worse love trainer than she thought.

She pulled herself together. None of this was Ben's fault. He'd tried to be friendly.

'Let's split this,' she said as he called for the bill.

'Don't be silly.' He smiled faintly. 'I'll get it. Anyway, it's tax deductible. Dinner with client.'

How romantic. 'Look,' she said. 'I'm sorry I have to go so early. I just . . . really don't feel very well.'

'You should have told me,' Ben replied. He didn't look remotely bothered. 'Do you want to call a cab?'

'No, no, I'll get the Tube.'

'Well, you go on ahead. I'll finish up here.'

'Do you mind?' He didn't. Katie pulled on her coat and hurried out into the night. Through the window she could see him chatting on his mobile. Probably telling Rebecca what a loser she was.

53

Three months passed. Christmas came, then New Year. Rebecca, who had returned from Mallorca with a perfect Clarins tan, kept Katie busy. She wrote a couple more *Seduce!* columns, which went down remarkably well.

Readers and viewers sent in hundreds of supportive emails and dozens of problems. Rebecca had negotiated a reasonably lucrative book deal with Howard and Otter and was in the process of landing Katie a fortnightly slot on *Breakfast Today.*

Other things were happening too. For a start, Orla – of all people in the world – had emailed Katie from Brazil to inform her she was getting married to her Tae Kwon Do teacher and to ask if Katie would be her bridesmaid in Sao Paolo at Easter.

Of course! Katie emailed back and then did a little dance. At long last she was going to get on a plane and fly far away somewhere. She started researching Brazil on the Internet and planning a two-week backpacking trip for straight after the wedding.

I'm going on holiday! she thought. And she looked back to all those times Crispin had been unable to get away because of work and so she too had stayed in London, following the same old routine, because the thought of going anywhere alone struck her as sad and Jess and Ronan could never take a fortnight off in case they were called in for an audition.

But since then things had changed in Katie's life. She was single. And she honestly didn't mind. She hadn't yet bought a cat, nor had she joined any evening classes. Occasionally she accompanied Jess out on the pull, although her heart wasn't really in it. But they had a lot of fun together. They always had, of course, but it was even better without the looming, nagging feeling that she should be with Crispin, that she wasn't being fair to him.

Orla's engagement had taught her a lesson. There was someone for everyone, however odd they might be. She realized that all the time she had been scoffing at girls who were too terrified to walk away from bad relationships, she'd been doing exactly the same thing – petrified that there was something wrong with her, that no one else would ever like her, that she'd been lucky to have her second chance with Crispin. And she'd pretended to be something she wasn't with him: the perfect girlfriend, who liked Bruce Springsteen because she was sure if she blew it that would be it.

Slowly, her way of dressing started to change. The neat little skirts and cardis and kitten heels she'd favoured because they were pretty and non-threatening lay untouched in a pile on the floor. She bought two new pairs of jeans, dug out her old trainers and tracksuit top, stopped incessantly brushing her hair and became obsessed with lipstick shopping.

Sometimes she saw Ben in the Greenhall and Graham office and her heart ballooned, but she popped it. Silly hormones. Gradually, her hopes faded. She just wished Rebecca would have the guts to come clean about their relationship, rather than mooning around all day looking smug. Sometimes Katie worried that she was turning into Rebecca. One day I'll meet someone nice and it won't just be about sex, she told herself. But then she remembered that that someone nice had been Crispin.

'Basically I used Crispin,' she said to her cousin one Saturday afternoon soon after New Year as they trailed round the Selfridges beauty department. 'He was like a shield, so I could get on with my life, while not worrying about finding a boyfriend.'

'Tell me something new,' Jess said, dousing herself in the latest number from Elizabeth Arden.

'But he's with someone else now,' Katie pointed out. She'd felt so much better when she heard this – she still had nightmares about the way she treated Crispin.

'Yeah, who is she again?'

'Another barrister from his chambers. Emily. I met her once. She seemed really nice.'

'And aren't you jealous?'

'Not at all. I wish I was. But he deserves it.'

'There's someone for everyone. Except you, me and Ronan,' Jess sighed, rubbing orange blusher over the back of her hand.

'Oh, don't! I'm so aware of that. I'm always terrified some newspaper will do an article on the love trainer and her sad, singleton friends.' Ever since the *Sunday Standard* experience, Katie had been a bit jumpy.

'But there's no shame in being single. That's what you tell people in the column and in phone-ins.'

'Yeah.' Whenever someone asked why Katie was single, she explained it was better to be alone than with the wrong person for the wrong reasons. 'But I'm ashamed at how when I was with Crispin I was forever banging on about all that. I couldn't see that the person I was lecturing was myself.'

'Couldn't you?' Jess smiled faintly.

'And I was always so keen to run other people's love lives and tell them how to do it, because it stopped me having to focus on my own. Which, frankly, was a disaster.'

'It wasn't a disaster. You had lots of good times. Concentrate on them.'

Katie's mobile rang.

'Rebecca!'

'How are you?' Rebecca, as usual these days, sounded abnormally cheerful. Katie knew why. She wondered when Rebecca was going to tell her.

'Fine, fine. Just shopping.'

'Good for you. Now, listen. What are you and Jess doing on Saturday night?'

'Me and . . . Jess?' At the sound of her name, Jess put down a tub of bronzing powder, fascinated.

'You heard me.'

'Well . . . I'm free. Jess, I don't know about. Why?' She ignored her cousin mouthing: 'What? What?'

'I want to invite you both to dinner. I've sold the flat. We're going to celebrate. Eight.'

'You've sold the flat?' Why didn't Ronan tell them anything? It occurred to Katie that Ronan must know about Ben and Rebecca too. He was still cleaning for Rebecca, but he never really talked about her and her piggish ways. 'Have you found somewhere else?' Katie asked.

'Yes, but I'll tell you when I see you. Can you come?'

'Yes, yes, it sounds lovely. But . . . why do you want Jess to come?'

'I don't,' Rebecca said bluntly. 'But Ronan refused to do the cooking unless she was invited.'

'So Ronan's going to be skivvying in the kitchen?'

'Of course. But I'm going to allow him to eat with us.'

'It sounds lovely,' Katie said, still astonished at her cousin's inclusion. 'I'll check Jess can make it and I'll call you back.'

'With any luck she's booked on a flight to Outer Mongolia,' Rebecca sighed.

'I'll let you know,' said Katie, glancing at her very excited cousin.

'Of course I'm going to go!' Jess yelled, but then she had a thought. 'Oh no, I can't.'

'Why not?'

'Jenny and Gordon will be there.'

'No they won't,' Katie reassured her. 'They're on honeymoon in Egypt.' She looked anxiously at Jess, but she seemed happy mixing lipstick shades on the back of her hand. Since Gordon there had been at least eight more men.

'I can't believe Ronan blagged me an invitation,' Jess said. 'Shows who my real friends are.'

'It *is* weird,' Katie agreed. 'Why does Rebecca pay any attention to what he thinks? We never do.'

'Will there be any agent types there?'

'Probably,' Katie said and flushed as she thought again of Ben.

On Saturday, Katie arrived at Rebecca's slightly after eight. Jess – who had spent the afternoon with Miranda – was waiting for her in the lobby, chatting to Johnny the porter. 'I wasn't going in there on my own,' she giggled.

They stepped into the lift. Up to the top floor and down the corridor to the red door. Rebecca opened it, smiling.

'Welcome, for the last time, to my humble home.'

The flat was immaculate. The floors gleamed, there were flowers everywhere. From the kitchen came enticing smells of roasting meat.

Jess ran her finger along the top of a picture frame. Not an atom of dust.

'You've done well, Rebecca. Ronan's the best cleaner in town. Unlike some we could mention.'

'He's not bad,' said Rebecca, smiling graciously. She clearly still disliked Jess, Katie thought, but equally clearly she was trying to get on with her. 'But of course, I'm moving on now. The flat's sold.'

'Where are you going?'

'I've put in an offer on a house in Archway. Four bedrooms and a lovely garden. You have to come and see it.'

'*Archway?*' Why on earth was Rebecca moving there? She always claimed leaving Zone One gave her jetlag. But rather than explain her bizarre decision, she just smiled serenely.

'Have a drink.' She poured them both some champagne. The doorbell rang.

'Hello?' Rebecca said into the intercom. 'Oh, Suzy! Come on up.'

Suzy swept in like a black widow, followed by Hunter. Jess and Katie exchanged concerned glances. Did Ronan know she was here?

'Hello, love trainer,' she said, kissing Katie brusquely on both cheeks. 'Our readers loved the last column. We've had fifty emails already.'

'Are you going to introduce me?' Hunter asked. He grabbed Katie's hand so hard it brought tears to her eyes. 'I'm Hunter, Suzy's . . . friend.'

'Nice to meet you,' Katie lied.

'And you.' He leaned forward. 'Though I'm scared of you. You've got a pretty harsh reputation. I'd better behave myself in front of you, or I'm going to be history quicker than I know.'

'Ha, ha,' said Katie. She was willing him not to, but he still winked at her. Suzy, talking to Jess, didn't notice.

Rebecca was busy, meeting and greeting at the door. Freddie had just arrived, splendid in his sheepskin jerkin.

'I'm so happy to meet you,' he said, kissing Katie's hand. 'You *have* to sort me out. I'm sick of the club scene and snogging eighteen-year-old boys. I think it's time I settled down. I'm looking for a wife.'

'We'll have a chat,' said Katie, thinking instantly of her friend Barnaby. OK, the only thing they had in common as far as she could see was they were both gay, but that was better than nothing, wasn't it?

Next to arrive was Ally. Jon stood behind her, glowering unpleasantly, even when Rebecca embraced him fulsomely on both cheeks.

Ally wouldn't catch Katie's eye.

'Well, we're just missing one person,' cried Rebecca. She was lying back on the sofa. Her skin was beautifully translucent. Katie remembered that night almost a year ago when she had watched her pacing around the flat, pale and drawn, waiting for horrible Tim to arrive. Tonight, she was utterly at ease.

At least I did some good work, she thought.

The doorbell rang. 'Oh, that must be him now! Hi, darling, come up.'

Two minutes later, Ben entered the apartment. His face was pink from the cold outside.

'Sorry I'm late, I just stopped off to buy these,' he said, handing Rebecca a huge bunch of red roses.

Rebecca squealed and hugged him tight. 'You are an angel!'

Despite herself, Katie felt a wave of sadness. She wanted so much to be happy for Rebecca. It was just such a bloody irony that the only man the love trainer had wanted in years had walked off with her best client.

At least no one would ever know how she felt.

'So now all my favourite people are here, we should have a toast,' Rebecca proclaimed. She yelled in the direction of the kitchen. 'Ronan, could you bring out the champagne?'

Ronan, whom they hadn't seen so far, emerged from the kitchen brandishing two bottles of Moët. Katie glanced at Suzy. She seemed fascinated by the pattern of the rug.

'Hello!' Freddie purred. Ally kicked him. 'Aagh! What was that for, Al?'

Ronan popped the corks and they all exclaimed as the fizz gushed out.

'Quick! Quick! Hold out your glasses,' Rebecca exclaimed. She smiled at Ronan. 'Just a droplet for me.'

They stood round in a circle. 'So!' cried Rebecca. 'A few things we need to toast tonight. First of all, here's to the love trainer. Not only is she going to be one of Greenhall and Graham's most successful clients in years, but, on a personal level, she's done wonders for me and my sad little life.'

'To the love trainer!' Everyone clinked glasses, except Jon, who had removed himself from the group and was studying Rebecca's book collection.

'I hadn't finished!' Rebecca cried. 'She did wonders for my life, she made me dump my useless boyfriend and I'm very glad she did, because . . .'

'What? What?' urged Freddie.

Katie knew what she was going to say: and now she had found love with the boy (in the office) next door. It had been there all along, she just hadn't known where to look for it.

Rebecca paused, then took a deep breath.

'I'm pregnant,' she said.

They all gasped in delight. 'Congratulations! Congratulations!' The glasses clinked again.

'Rebecca,' said Suzy. 'I know it's a very old-fashioned question. But who's the father?'

'I was wondering who'd be the first to ask. Well, he's standing right here.'

Ben, Katie almost blurted out, but just then Rebecca walked across the room and wrapped her arms around Ronan's neck.

'Oh my God!' Jess screamed. She put down her glass and embraced them both.

Everyone started talking and laughing. Rebecca cried a little. Katie did too. Suzy was beside herself with excitement. Ronan was puce with pride.

'I'd like to make a toast too,' he yelled over the din. 'To my beautiful girlfriend whom I love with all my heart.'

'To your beautiful girlfriend,' everyone except Jon exclaimed, and Rebecca turned pink and hid her face in her hand.

'How long gone are you?' Ally asked, swallowing slightly.

'Twelve weeks today,' Rebecca said. 'I had a scan yesterday and they told me it was fine to make it public.'

She got out the photo of the scan and they oohed some more.

'They all look the same, don't they?' Suzy asked, and it was her turn to be thumped by Ally.

'So you're going to leave us?' Jess said quietly to Ronan.

He nodded. 'I'm sorry. I was waiting for the right moment to tell you. It'll mean breaking up the flat.'

'Don't be a prat,' Jess said, planting a kiss on his cheek. 'We can't all stay together for ever. It just means Katie's going to have to learn how to cook.'

'In your dreams,' Katie laughed. But she felt a pang. Everyone had thought she would be the one to end their little threesome. But it was so much better this way.

'And you won't be cycling across Costa Rica,' she said to Rebecca. In fact, now she came to think about it, Rebecca had been very quiet on that front of late.

'My bike cost £860 and I only used it twice,' Rebecca

laughed. 'Ronan won't let me now. He says it's too dangerous.'

They sat down to eat. Ronan had made a Caesar salad to start with, with portions minus cheese, dressing and anchovies for those who were on a diet. Afterwards, they moved on to roast beef and all the trimmings, with a vegetable lasagne specially for Jon.

'I don't like broccoli,' he mumbled, fishing out the spears.

'This is the best meal I've eaten in ages,' Ben said. 'Rebecca's done well for herself, hasn't she?'

'I'm gonna get so fat,' Rebecca smiled cheerfully.

'You're eating for two, babe,' Freddie said. 'Enjoy it.' He pouted at Ronan. 'Are you sure you wouldn't rather marry me?' Ronan turned scarlet.

'So how did it all happen?' Jess asked.

'Well, Ronan was basically making my house so beautiful, and he was so gorgeous, and in the end I just had to ask him out for dinner,' Rebecca explained.

'You asked him out!' Jess shrieked. 'But that's so naughty. It's against all love-trainer rules.'

'It is,' said Katie, highly amused. 'Make the dog do all the running.'

'I know, I know.' Rebecca blushed slightly. 'I did think of consulting you, Katie. But I knew you'd be cross. I was breaking the rules and it was Ronan. I couldn't believe you and Jess didn't want him for yourselves.'

'Want Ronan!' Jess chortled. She had genuinely forgotten how she once felt about him. 'You're welcome to him.'

'Anyway, I'm really happy she did ask me out,' Ronan

said. His eyes fell lovingly on Rebecca. 'I didn't dare do anything, because Katie kept telling me that I always came on too strong.'

'Thank God none of you listened to me,' Katie said. She felt a bit embarrassed, but she was so overjoyed for Rebecca and Ronan, it didn't really matter. And as well as her happiness for them, there was the fact that someone else might be free now. He was sitting to her left. Katie glanced at him. Their eyes met and she felt that now familiar sizzle in her stomach. *If I was a dog, my tongue would be hanging out.*

He bent into her. 'So you really didn't see this coming, love trainer?' He spoke quietly and no one else heard him.

'I didn't have a clue,' Katie smiled. 'It's like you always said. I'm a fraud. I have no idea what I'm talking about.' She realized she was bit pissed.

'Actually,' she confessed, 'I thought Rebecca had got it together with you.'

Ben threw back his head and laughed. 'Me and Rebecca! You must be joking. I know everyone's been predicting something for years, but it would never happen. I love her dearly, but . . .' He stopped suddenly as if he had run into a wall.

'But?' urged Katie coyly.

'But the chemistry's not right,' he said, and their eyes locked together again.

'So, how's the love training?' he asked abruptly.

'It's good,' Katie said. 'Well, most of it is. I love helping people, but I find the attention a bit embarrassing. Someone like Jess would enjoy it so much more.' She nodded in the direction of her cousin, who was yabbering with Freddie about where to score the best Es.

'I'd forgotten about that,' Ben exclaimed. 'I promised Gordy I'd check her out.'

'I doubt he'd want you to do that any more.'

'Gordy has the brain of a pea. He'll never know,' Ben grinned.

After dinner, they lounged around on the sofas, talking and laughing. Everyone was very mellow, apart from Jon.

'How much are you selling this place for?' he asked Rebecca and when she told him, he snapped: 'That's obscene.'

'Rebecca's hardly responsible for the state of the London property market,' Ally retorted, and stood up to refill her glass, ignoring his look.

'So boy or girl?' Jess asked.

'We haven't found out,' Rebecca said. 'We want it to be a surprise.'

'Good idea,' said Suzy. 'If I know what my friends are having I lose interest right away. Best to keep something back for the big day.'

'Well, where was it conceived?' Jess persisted. 'That way, we'll be able to work out a name for it either way.'

Rebecca and Ronan looked at each other and giggled.

'Mallorca,' Rebecca confessed.

'Deia,' Ronan added. He looked at Rebecca. 'Actually, precious, Deia would be a lovely name for a girl.'

'It would, wouldn't it?' she agreed.

'Mallorca,' squawked Jess. 'So this was when you were on your so-called lads' holiday.'

'That's right,' Ronan said proudly. 'It was me and

Rebecca, although Ben came out and joined us for a couple of days.'

'Talk about a green and hairy,' Ben said. 'It was horrible.'

'Oh, Ben,' Rebecca said. 'We loved seeing you. And just think, you were in the next room when we . . .' She stopped as he raised a hand. 'OK, maybe you don't want to know.'

'Are you going to go back to work after the baby's born?' Suzy asked. She couldn't believe no one had asked this vital question.

'Not for the first three months,' Rebecca said. 'Mum's flying over to help out.'

'She's going to get on a plane?'

Rebecca nodded. 'She's going to try. I've booked her on a fear-of-flying course. She's beside herself with excitement.'

'And when the three months is up?'

'Ronan's going to take over.'

'I'm going to be a house husband,' Ronan said happily.

'You've really got him by the balls,' Jon said under his breath.

'Excuse me?' Ronan said sharply.

Jon turned to him. 'Well, you haven't done too badly either,' he snarled. 'Got yourself a sugar mummy.'

'Unlike *you*, I suppose,' Ally said.

Jon looked hurt. 'What are you talking about? There's just no money in the arts.'

Ally said nothing.

'So I'd like to make an announcement,' Hunter said, suddenly standing up.

They all turned to him expectantly. Suzy felt a rush of wild excitement combined with sickening terror. She'd been expecting this for weeks now, but he couldn't . . . surely . . . be going to do it in front of everyone else.

'Just to say: my decree nisi came through on Friday. So from next month I can base myself permanently in London. And I'm really looking forward to getting to know you all better.'

'Us too,' they muttered politely. Suzy smiled graciously, but there was a thud of disappointment in her solar plexus.

'Especially since I very much hope you'll all be guests at our wedding.'

Everyone – except Jon – shrieked. Another round of kissing, hugging, handshaking and congratulations ensued. And to everyone's amusement Suzy stood up and flung her arms around Hunter's neck.

'You're getting married!' Rebecca yelped. 'It's perfection. Perfection.'

'Bags me organize the hen night,' Ally said. 'Has anyone got the number for the Chippendales?'

'Hang on,' said Suzy, still red in the face. 'I haven't actually given my response yet.'

Hunter looked crushed. Suzy smiled lazily.

'I'll think about it,' she said.

'Suzy!' Rebecca protested. 'How could you?' Ally yelled, 'You hard bitch!' Freddie screamed. But none of them really believed her.

Katie bent down and kissed Suzy on the cheek. 'The love trainer is *so* proud. Make him sweat.'

'I will,' said Suzy, but then felt herself seized with panic. 'But not *too* long. He might change his mind.' Her eyes followed Hunter, who was standing on the other side of the room, laughing and talking with Ronan.

'He won't.' Katie straightened up. Ben was staring straight at her. She felt her cheeks glow too.

Jon glowered on the edge of the group. 'I notice nobody's mentioning the poor abandoned wife and children.'

Katie watched Ally carefully. As usual, her face revealed nothing as she turned to her boyfriend.

'I think they're doing OK, sweetie. Hunter's wife's madly in love with her horse trainer apparently. And the girls love Suzy. She gets them all this free makeup.'

Jon snorted. 'Like makeup can compensate for a father's love.'

Ally was digging her nails into her palms. 'If you say so,' she said sweetly. Her period was due in another week. She'd leave it until then to make up her mind.

Katie, meanwhile, sat down next to Rebecca.

'You know your bike?' she said. 'If you don't want it any more, perhaps you'd think about selling it to me.'

54

They drank lots more wine, they talked and laughed. Oddly, the first person to leave was Jess.

'I'm going on to a party,' she said in a high, slightly strained voice. 'It's at a lock-in in Brixton. You're all welcome to come.'

'Could be fun,' said Hunter eagerly. 'What's a lock-in?'

'Hunter!' Suzy sighed. 'I don't think so.'

Katie gave her a hug and a kiss goodbye. 'Are you sure you'll be safe getting there?' she asked, as was her custom.

'Oh yes,' Jess said. She smirked. 'Actually, I'm going with someone. He's waiting for me downstairs.'

'Downstairs? Jessie! *Who?*'

Jess smiled broadly. 'Johnny the porter,' she said in a stage whisper. 'I had a chat with him when I arrived. He's very sexy, Katie. I love his dreads.'

Johnny the porter! Katie chuckled appreciatively. 'Well, have a great time.'

'I will.'

Katie saw Jon nudge Ally hard.

'We'd better be on our way too,' she said reluctantly, getting to her feet. 'Early start and all that.'

She kissed everyone and thanked Rebecca and Ronan, while Jon stood a few paces behind her, looking at the carpet.

'I failed there,' Katie slurred as soon as the door shut. She was curled into a big cushion next to Rebecca.

'I don't know if you can say that,' Rebecca reproved her. 'I do think Jon's behaving a bit better, thanks to your advice. No more stomping into restaurants and demanding she comes home.'

'But he's still pretty horrible,' Suzy interrupted. 'He was at Jenny and Gordy's wedding looking like a wet weekend in Blackpool. Hunter asked him what was wrong and he said he hated weddings because they reminded him of his own failed marriage. He dragged Ally home at ten.' She stopped, seeing Katie's stricken face. 'Katie, don't take it personally. It's her choice. You told her to leave him. Some people just don't listen.'

'Maybe,' Katie shrugged. Time to change the subject. 'And how *was* Jenny and Gordon's wedding?'

'Lovely,' Rebecca gushed, while Suzy simultaneously said, 'But the food was terrible. And I'll have much nicer place settings.'

'Jenny looked gorgeous,' Rebecca said firmly. 'Although she didn't think so. She spent the whole wedding flapping because she had a minute spot under her nose. But I think Gordy calmed her down. And he gave the most hilarious speech.'

The rest of the party broke up around two.

'So I guess you're staying here,' Katie said to Ronan, kissing him goodnight.

He looked worried. 'Do you mind? If you're worried about going home alone, I could come with you.'

'Ronan, don't be ridiculous! I'll be absolutely fine.'

'Ben lives in Camberwell,' Rebecca said casually. 'He

and Katie could always share a cab. How about it, Benny? Katie's at the Elephant and Castle.'

'Sure,' said Ben, without any particular enthusiasm. 'Why not?'

Katie pulled her coat on, fingers shaking slightly as she did up the buttons. Ben sidled up to her. 'No point in calling a taxi, it'll take an age,' he said quietly. 'Let's go outside and find one.'

'Sounds like a good idea,' she agreed.

And so Katie and Ben found themselves standing on the threshold of Dartmouth Mansions.

'Actually,' Ben said, 'it's such a beautiful night. Would you mind if we had a bit of a walk first? Just to wind down.'

And the night *was* beautiful: oddly warm with a soft breeze and an almost full marmalade moon low on the horizon. They crossed the Bayswater Road and made towards Hyde Park.

'Shit,' said Ben, rattling the gates. 'They're bloody locked.'

They stood and looked at the vast padlock. 'We could climb over them,' Ben said doubtfully, looking at Katie's heels. Once, Katie would have agreed they could – anything to please – but now she just laughed and shook her head.

'Let's walk to Marble Arch,' she said.

So they walked back down the Bayswater Road. The Arch stood in the middle of a huge roundabout.

'Is it made of marble?' Ben wondered. 'I've never thought to ask about it.'

'Why don't we go and see?' Katie said.

So, wiggling through a gap in the fence, they ran – well, Katie tottered – across the deserted traffic lanes and into the little park that surrounded the Arch. Apart from a tramp snoozing on a bench, there was no one was in sight.

'It should be in ancient Rome, really,' said Ben, gazing up at the ugly white monument. 'Not surrounded by cinemas and McDonalds and traffic. And I'm certain it's not made of marble. Did you know this is the spot where they used to hang people?' He stopped suddenly. 'I'm gabbling, aren't I?'

'A bit,' Katie said, feeling indescribably happy. She sat down on a bench. He sat beside her.

'So who would have thought it?' Ben said. 'Rebecca Greenhall got to live happily ever after.'

'With the nicest man in the world,' said Katie, hugging herself against the cold. 'I can't tell you how happy I am for them.'

Ben glanced sideways at her. 'You really like to see other people happy, don't you?'

'Doesn't everyone?' Katie asked.

'Not like you do,' Ben said. 'I think it's great.'

Katie didn't know what to say, so she just bit her lip and watched a night bus whizzing around the roundabout. She could feel the warmth of Ben's body beside her, smell his aftershave, hear the rustle of his anorak as he turned round and looked at her.

Something scary began to thump inside her.

'So what now, love trainer?'

'Now?' Katie was overcome by confusion. 'Well, I guess I'll carry on love training, but I'm going to Brazil for my friend Orla's wedding and then I think I'm going to put my name down for the Costa Rica cycle ride. I've wanted to travel the world for so long and I'm not going to put it off any longer.' She stopped anxiously. 'But will you mind if I take a break from love training?'

Ben laughed. 'Katie, I've told you this already. I want you to do whatever makes you happy.'

He held up his cold hand and touched her face. A white-hot jolt ran through her. 'But I wasn't actually asking about your career. I meant: "What now?"'

'Oh,' she said. 'Oh?' And then: 'Oooh,' as Ben leaned forward and his mouth brushed against hers.

'Oh,' she said, quite a lot later.

'Love trainer, love trainer,' said Ben, 'I'm crazy about you.'

I'm crazy about you too. She wanted to say it so much, but she just smiled.

'I have been for ages. But you were always so frosty. So unimpressed. I didn't know how to get through to you.'

'I didn't want you to get through to me,' Katie confessed. 'I wanted to stay in my bubble. I didn't want anyone to come near me. I didn't want to fall in love.'

Shit! She'd bloody gone and said it. She was never drinking champagne again. Or anything else. 'I mean, I didn't want . . .' she began, but Ben held his finger to her lips.

'I have to kiss you again,' he said.

They kissed for so long that the sky turned from black to grey and the birds began to make little tweeting noises.

'The thing is . . .' said Katie, clinging to him while he nibbled each of her fingers. 'The thing is . . . I have to go away.'

'To Costa Rica,' he said calmly.

'To Costa Rica,' she agreed. 'And after that I don't know

where. I've spent my whole adult life in limbo. Not knowing what I wanted. Being in love with the wrong person and then being too frightened by the big wide world to leave a person I wasn't in love with. Everything I told Rebecca to do was stuff I wanted to do myself. Run guns into Afghanistan. Learn to belly dance. Have adventures.'

'I understand,' Ben said. 'I don't want you to go away. But I can see why you have to do it.'

'You can?'

'Go to Costa Rica,' he said. 'It's only a month. When you come back I'll be here. And if you want to go away again, then who knows? Maybe you'll let me come with you.'

'A love trainer should always be mysterious,' Katie said. 'But I daresay I might.' The first rays of the sun began to stroke Hyde Park. It was going to be a beautiful spring day.

Acknowledgements

With thanks to Lizzy Kremer for all her support. Harrie Evans, whose help has been incomparable and whom I will miss horribly, and Louise Moore for her love bombing. Fergus and Victoria Stoddart, Guy Gadney and Esther Bailey, thanks to whom most of this book was written within walking distance of Bondi Beach. For mutual love training, Victoria Macdonald, Frances Grey, Sarah Smith, Kate Townsend and Ruth Davis – I couldn't have written this without you. To Dr Bruce Fogle whose many books on dogs proved invaluable reference points. And thanks to James Watkins.